# LONG ROAD TO BAGHDAD

In the Middle East tension is escalating between the British and the Arabs. Misfit Lieutenant Harry Downe is sent to negotiate a treaty with a renegade Bedouin Sheikh, Ibn Shalan, whose tribe is attacking enemy patrols in Iraq and cutting oil pipelines. Greedy for arms, Shalan accepts British weapons but, in return, Harry must take his daughter Furja to be his bride. The secret marriage leads to a deep love, to the anger of Shalan and the disgust of Harry's fellow officers. But war is looming, and threatens to destroy Harry's newfound happiness, and change his life and that of his closest friends for ever.

# LONG ROAD TO BAGHDAD

*by*

Catrin Collier

**Magna Large Print Books**
Long Preston, North Yorkshire,
BD23 4ND, England.

British Library Cataloguing in Publication Data.

Collier, Catrin
    Long road to Baghdad.

    A catalogue record of this book is
    available from the British Library

    ISBN   978-0-7505-4104-6

First published in Great Britain in 2013 by Accent Press Ltd.

Copyright © Catrin Collier 2013

Cover illustration by arrangement with Accent Press Ltd.

The moral right of the author has been asserted

Published in Large Print 2015 by arrangement with
Accent Press Ltd.

Magna Large Print is an imprint of Library Magna Books Ltd.

Printed and bound in Great Britain by
T.J. (International) Ltd., Cornwall, PL28 8RW

Before the Great War, the campaign in Mesopotamia would have been considered a vast undertaking. In the immensity of a world struggle, it was a mere drop in the ocean – a 'side show'.

In spite of this; in spite of mistakes made by civilian and soldier alike; in spite of the horrors after Ctesiphon, the miseries of the wounded after Hanneh, the heat, the sickness, the desolation of the empty desert, and the 97,000 casualties that the campaign cost, the troops that fought in Mesopotamia can rest secure in the knowledge that they added imperishable glory to the record of the Imperial Army.

*A Brief Outline of the Campaign in Mesopotamia,*
*1926*
Major (Temp. Lt.-Col.) R. Evans, M.C., P.S.C.
Royal Horse Guards

This book is dedicated to the 97,000. And to Christopher Marley who came back and lived to tell me about it.

When Allah had made hell he found out it was not enough. So he made Iraq and then he added flies.

*Arab Proverb*

# Chapter One

*The desert North-east of Basra,*
*Saturday May 30th 1914*

Even if protocol had permitted Harry Downe to rise from the flat-footed, squatting position desert courtesy dictated, he doubted he'd be able to do so. Certainly, he wouldn't have been able to move with dignity, and to his host dignity was paramount. Sheikh Aziz Ibn Shalan, leader, as much as anyone could be, of the volatile tribal band of Bedouin who lived by grazing their flocks and raiding their neighbours along the valley of the Karun river bed, was judging the entire British tribe on Harry's performance. And he, Henry Robert Edward Anderson Downe, Second Lieutenant, Indian Army, by virtue of his father's influence, and seconded to service with the Frontier Commission in the Persian Gulf, for his many, and varied, sins, had cramp – mind-blinding, body-burning cramp.

Making a supreme effort, he continued to crouch immobile, facing Shalan's hooked nose and hooded eyes across the magnificent Persian rug. The staring match was not only painful. A year in Mesopotamia hadn't accustomed him to the heat the Arabs ignored so disdainfully. They might pay token homage to the climate – three sides of the Sheikh's tent had been rolled up to

11

catch the non-existent afternoon breeze – but he alone of the hundred or so men crowded beneath the canopy was visibly suffering as the moisture-laden desert air seared around them like scalding steam in a Turkish bath.

'You ask much of us, Ferenghi.' Shalan's softly spoken Arabic cut through the atmosphere like a whiplash, dispelling Harry's preoccupation with pain. Harry curled his lip: Ferenghi – foreigner.

The word stung his pride. He had learnt to respect both the Arabs and their lifestyle, long before he'd spent two weeks with Shalan's tribe. He would have liked to think that he, in his turn, had earned their respect.

'I ask for your friendship in the name of my King and the British Empire.' Harry spoke slowly, in painstakingly perfect Arabic. 'For myself, who is as the dust beneath Ibn Shalan's feet, the hospitality of this tent has been more than I dared hope for.'

'You speak like a son of the desert, yet you ask me and my people to stand against all, should they threaten your precious pipeline.'

'The pipeline is not mine, nor even my King's. It is, as its name, Anglo-Persian. It belongs to Arab and English alike.'

'The line is English,' Shalan agreed. 'Sheikh Muhammerah's and the Bakhtairi Khans perhaps also, but it is not mine, nor that of my people.' His dark eyes gazed unflinchingly into Harry's grey ones, but his dismissal of Harry's request hung between them like acrid dung-fire smoke on a windless day.

'The Anglo-Persian Oil Company will pay you. Gold, guns, whatever you wish.' Harry played his

12

last card.

'We are not mercenaries to be bought like goats in a bazaar,' Shalan railed, holding out his arms to the warriors silently encircling the divan. 'We are Bedouin – but Bedouin in bondage to our Turkish lords. Like you, Ferenghi, we are part of an empire.'

'Since when has Ibn Shalan or any man of his tribe bowed his head to a Turk?' Harry countered, allowing his pain to give rise to irritation.

Ibn Shalan's anger abated as swiftly as it had surfaced. He stroked his small, thin beard. 'You speak the truth, Ferenghi,' he murmured in softer tones. 'No man of this tribe bows his head to Turk, or – British.'

The silence shattered in one deafening, whooping instant. Shalan's warriors' agreement rang, a noisy foreboding of failure, in Harry's ears.

'We ask only for friendship,' Harry emphasised, shouting to make himself heard above the din.

'The British have asked for the friendship of others. Where it was freely given, more was taken. Your empire, like that of the Turks, is built on the lands of those you have "befriended".'

Lowering his eyes, Harry studied the blue and red abstract pattern on the rug that stretched between him and Shalan. It wasn't difficult for him or Shalan to predict the long-term policy of the British government towards Mesopotamia.

The Turkish Empire was foundering, its subject peoples straining to revolt, the Arabs with their secret 'Jihad' societies amongst them; but the great European powers were circling the Ottoman corpse like vultures. Thanks to Churchill, an

13

ambitious, speculative First Sea Lord at the Admiralty, the British Government had bought a controlling interest in the Anglo-Persian Oil Company, and with it, a foothold in Iraq. But the Arabs knew it wouldn't take many Indian regiments to turn the foothold into a seat of power if the Ottoman Empire collapsed. And then, instead of the free Arab State the Bedouin prayed for, Iraq would be dovetailed into a polished road that led overland from the Gulf to India. Given a few years of efficient British rule, the Gulf and the desert lands might well become no more than distant suburbs of Calcutta. Shalan had obviously considered the prospect, but Harry's CO's brief had been explicit.

'Our problem doesn't lie with Muhammerah and the Bakhtairi Khans, Downe,' he'd barked after a formal dinner in the officers' mess. 'Their share in the Anglo-Persian Oil Company ensures their loyalty to us. It's this Ibn Shalan chap. God knows what he'd do if he found one of our patrols pushed into a tight corner. Intelligence says he's as likely to slit our throats as those of the Turks. He travels in Muhammerah's territory but recognises no overlord. Not Muhammerah and certainly not the Turks.'

'I take it he's an independent customer, sir.' Harry's voice drawled back at him from the safe, comparatively comfortable world of the European compound at Basra. Despite the 'formal' aspect of the dinner, he'd succeeded in getting drunk and hadn't bothered to conceal his boredom with his colonel's warnings of possible catastrophe. Bloody-minded Arabs were legion in Mesopotamia.

'Independent isn't the word I'd choose,' Perry had interrupted testily. 'Three of Shalan's sons were hung by the Turks last year. They were embroiled in one of the pro-Arab, anti-Turkish groups. Shalan blamed a tribeless band of Bedouin for the betrayal. He attacked, slaughtered every male over 12, enslaved the women and children and turned his attention to the Turks. They've lost five patrols in his territory in the past six months. And when I say lost, I mean lost. Gone. Disappeared from the face of the desert. If the Arabs ever stop fighting among themselves long enough to get this Jihad of theirs off the ground, the Moslems in India could get infected with the fever, and our entire empire in the East jeopardised. Shalan's tribe will become the scavenging hyenas that pick the bones on all sides, including the Anglo-Persian Oil Company. If we sit back and allow that to happen, we will have failed in our duty as officers.' Perry had paused for breath long enough to allow the sepoy orderly to serve his brandy and cigars. 'One hundred and forty miles of pipeline runs through Shalan's territory and we haven't the resources to police a fraction of it. Someone has to go up into the Karun Valley, find Shalan, and persuade him to come down on our side.' He'd looked at Harry. It was a look Harry recognised. He was the only officer in the Basra Compound who'd taken the trouble to learn Arabic. 'You're free to offer whatever it takes, Downe. I'll get it through the budget.'

'Sir,' he'd muttered, mentally cursing the addiction to gambling that had prompted him to learn the language.

15

'We need Shalan. Without him, there won't be a pipeline or an Anglo-Persian Oil Company much longer. And that means no fuel for our navy. Disaster, Downe!'

Harry had looked across the mess to where his fellow officers were drinking around the piano. His closest friend in Basra, Peter Smythe, smiled sympathetically but didn't come near. Bored by Perry's pontificating, the others were well past the port stage and on to the brandy.

'Take that Arab orderly with you. What's his name?'

'Mitkhal, sir.'

'Damned fellow looks like a brigand. I don't trust him and I don't want him creeping around the barracks without you here to supervise him. I'll talk to you again before you leave. Brandy?'

He'd left Basra the following morning. The place wasn't wonderful, but it was the Piccadilly of the desert. A year of 'volunteering' for mapping patrols had given him a closer acquaintance with the baking mud flats than he'd desired and a greater respect for the town than it deserved. And here he was, one month later. The most expendable pawn in the Indian Army, about to be swept off the board by the Arab whom Perry, in his arrogance, had believed could be bought. But while Colonel Perry was safe in Basra, he faced Sheikh Aziz Ibn Shalan alone.

'You say nothing, Ferenghi.'

Harry raised his eyes. 'You believe the British want to govern your territory and your people.'

'You don't?'

'Not at this moment in time. For the future I

16

can't say.' He realised he was probably botching his mission, but he couldn't lie with those hooded eyes watching and evaluating everything he said. He glimpsed Mitkhal sitting at the edge of the divan, rolling his eyes heavenwards.

'Why not at this moment in time?' Shalan demanded.

'Because the British are concerned only for the safety of their pipeline; it is in danger just as everything here is in danger. The Ottoman Empire is crumbling and the jackals are loose. Skirmishes, feuds, attacks on peaceful travellers happen every day. The Turks cannot maintain order. And why should they? While Arab fights Arab, or the soldiers of the oil company, they cannot fight the Turks. And with the prospect of a jihad that will set the desert aflame...' Harry faltered when angry murmurs rose from the men. Honesty was one thing, recklessness another.

'Continue,' Shalan ordered.

'Britain needs oil. If the pipeline should be cut...'

'You lose money? Face?'

'Both,' Harry conceded.

'And should I ask my men to watch over your precious pipeline?'

'I'll be in your debt.'

'You?' Shalan stabbed a thin brown finger at Harry. 'You'll be in my debt, Ferenghi?'

'My CO has made the pipeline my responsibility, so the debt will be mine.'

'What manner of man are you?'

'An honest one, who pays what he owes.'

'If I should say otherwise. If I should call you infidel, unbeliever...'

17

Harry felt himself slipping out of his depth. The Bedouin rarely spoke of a man's religion, sensibly deeming the God he worshipped to be his own business. He couldn't imagine why Shalan was bending the inflexible rules of desert hospitality.

'I, like you, believe in the one true God,' he answered diplomatically.

'You believe Mohammed to be his prophet.'

'I believe Mohammed to be his prophet,' Harry reiterated, meeting Shalan's eye.

'As a true believer I can greet you as a friend. But...' A smile hovered at the corners of Shalan's mouth. He held out his hands in mock despair. 'It will take many guns to guard your pipeline. I am a poor man.'

'I will give you as many guns as you need.'

'Five hundred.'

'You will have them.'

'New, not old stock from your African and Indian wars. I'll take none with rusted mechanisms.'

'New, with as much ammunition as you can carry; and the promise of more when you need it.'

'Your pipeline is long. It lies in country that is hard on the hooves of camels and horses.'

'I will deliver 50 horses and 50 camels along with the weapons and ammunition.'

'Prime stock.'

'The best in our Basra compound.'

Just when Harry had expected the divan to end, it was beginning. Shalan was up to something. Something that involved him personally, but for the life of him he couldn't see beyond the demands. The Sheikh had decimated his offer of British friendship without looking at what had

18

been laid out on the bargaining table. Now he was retracing his steps. The sequence didn't make sense. But he had no choice other than to comply – and generously.

'Warriors need food. A herd of our goats are sick.'

'There are many herds of goats in Basra market. Choose one and I will pay the merchants their price.'

'You.' Again Shalan pointed his finger at Harry. 'You offer these things knowing my warriors could eat the goats, ride the horses, and turn the guns on the soldiers of the oil company. British soldiers,' he added, so there'd be no misunderstanding.

'I have lived in your tent. I know the Bedouin and Sheikh Ibn Shalan for the noble, honourable leader that he is. You will use the guns wisely, and in friendship.'

Shalan reached inside his black abba and pulled out his camel-skin tobacco pouch. It was a signal for relaxation. As a quiet hum of voices buzzed around the divan, Harry felt as though half time had been called in a punishing rugby match. Shalan withdrew a single paper and a pinch of tobacco from the pouch. Sprinkling a thin line of powdered tobacco along the edge of the crumpled paper, he began to roll the paper between the thumb and forefinger of his right hand.

'You are a strange man.' Shalan contemplated the finished cigarette. 'You are not Bedouin, yet you ride with us and live in our tents. You are Ferenghi, yet you speak our tongue and wear our dress. And, unlike every other Ferenghi I have met, you speak the truth.'

'You are gracious.'

'I accept your offer, my friend.' For the first time Shalan dropped 'Ferenghi'. 'Five hundred new rifles, ammunition, 50 of your best army horses, 50 camels, and a herd of goats.'

'They will be delivered as soon as I can arrange it.'

'You will seal this bargain between friends by marrying my daughter. Afterwards, my men will guard your pipeline as if it were our own.'

'Marry...'

'You are surprised, my friend. Gratified, I grant you that which I have refused so many others.'

'I am surprised.' Harry struggled to maintain his composure.

Shalan rose, signalling the end of the divan. 'It is agreed, my friend, your pipeline will be protected. We will talk later. Marriage is best discussed at night, after food. Dalhour?'

A black slave appeared from behind the wall of woven goat hair that separated Shalan's public quarters from those of his harem. With a practised flick of the wrist, the slave held back the cloth without revealing what lay beyond. Shalan salaamed to the assembly and disappeared into the closed world of his women.

Ignoring the glances and whispers fired in his direction, Harry remained where he was until the men began to disperse. He would have liked to join them but his legs were numb and, as he was bound to make an ass of himself when he moved, he preferred to do it before as small an audience as possible. Black-veiled women appeared and unleashed the ties that secured the tent walls.

20

One man, taller and darker than the rest, came and stood before him.

'So, the British lieutenant is to become the son-in-law of Ibn Shalan.'

'One wrong word from you, Mitkhal, and I'll kick you across the desert faster than a duck can fly,' Harry snarled, venting the frustration he'd been forced to keep in check all afternoon.

'That would be an interesting experience.' Mitkhal grinned, looking down on Harry from his six-and-a-half feet.

'First you help me up.' Harry extended his hand. 'Then you explain exactly what happened here just now.'

'If the honourable Ferenghi would care to walk to the outskirts of the camp, we can talk without an audience,' Mitkhal muttered in English as he heaved Harry to his feet.

Weakened by a rush of blood to his legs, Harry grasped Mitkhal's arm. Walking was impossible. Standing pure torture.

'You offered the Sheikh the one thing he could not refuse, Harry: guns. Whatever the future holds for the desert, it will involve bloodshed. The tribes with the greatest firepower stand the best chance of surviving.'

'That's it?' Harry gingerly lifted one foot and placed it in front of the other.

'The horses helped. Shalan's impressed with Dorset. Perhaps he's taken her as an indication of the quality of British stock.'

'And his daughter? Hasn't she a say in the matter?'

'Marriage among the Bedawi is often a matter

21

of compromise, just as it is among the Effendi. I overheard Colonel Perry tell Mrs Perry, when she took Miss Perry to India, that an officer with good connections and a private income would make the most suitable match for their daughter.'

'The Perrys' affairs are none of your concern.'

'But the Bedawi's are soon to become yours. And we all serve the interests of those who pay for our bread.'

'Save the philosophy for Shalan.' Harry tentatively moved forward. 'If you want to serve, you can begin by telling me why Shalan is prepared to accept an infidel as a son-in-law. I thought we were regarded as lower than desert sand.'

'Infidels are, but you have just proved yourself a true believer. I hope for your sake Shalan doesn't put your knowledge of the Koran to the test. But then–' Mitkhal shrugged his massive shoulders as they stepped into the dried-up wadi that served as a stockade for the tribe's riding mares '–any Sheikh would take the devil himself into his family for 500 guns.'

'And if the devil has no desire to marry an illiterate harem girl?'

'Ssh!' Mitkhal glanced around. Seeing no one, he continued in a whisper. 'The devil should think again. Shalan has offered his protection for the pipeline on the only terms possible. If he openly allied his tribe to the British, he would endanger his position with every independent tribe in the desert, including his own. He neither needs nor wants a British alliance, but he does need guns. In accepting them from you as his daughter's bride price, he compromises no one. His tribe will understand. After all, every man knows, or thinks he knows, something of young girls and love.'

'What do the Bedawi, with their bride-bartering and closed harems, know of love?'

'As much as, if not more than, the Effendi. Women see more than goats outside the harem. They often pick out the man they wish to marry, then it is up to their father, or brother, to contact the chosen one. Shalan is probably telling everyone who'll listen that, to his dismay, his daughter settled on you. As a Bedouin, he would like to oppose the match, but as a loving father, his daughter's happiness is paramount.'

When they reached the stubble of thorn bushes that provided sparse grazing for the horses Harry whistled. His grey mare Dorset cantered towards them; nuzzling into his abba, she searched for hidden food. Women's love wasn't even as straightforwardly selfish as that of an animal, he mused as he patted her neck.

He'd had enough of women's subterfuge to last him a lifetime. First, there had been darling cousin Lucy. It had taken a disastrous engagement to wake him up to the fact that her deep and abiding love was for his inheritance, not him. Then he'd met Alicia, a pretty but fortuneless Captain's niece who'd sworn undying affection until a 40-year-old major offered her a wedding ring. And Christina – despite the problems she'd caused him, he smiled. Elegant, beautiful, innocent-eyed Christina, the colonel's wife who generously made love to every lieutenant who joined the regiment; only to get caught in his bed.

Lucy – Alicia – Christina – scandal – Basra –

23

and now some damned Arab girl he hadn't even seen. He slid to the ground and rested his back against Dorset's legs. Wrenching his head coil and kafieh from his head, he ran his hands through his thick, fair hair.

'It's close to sunset but you could still get sunstroke.' Mitkhal crouched beside him.

'You think I should marry this girl?'

'Refuse the hand of Shalan's daughter and you will insult a great Sheikh. Shalan is not rich, but he is powerful, and even Colonel Perry would tell you it is not wise to offend a powerful Sheikh.'

'So, if I refuse to marry this girl, Shalan would lose face.'

'And you would probably lose your head, but there is a sunny side, as Lieutenant Smythe would say.'

'Really?'

'Really,' Mitkhal echoed. 'The Koran tells every man, beggar or Sheikh, he can have only four wives, no matter how he may lust for more, but the Koran also tells us how to divorce an unsatisfactory one. Alliances consolidated by marriage stand, provided the wife was treated well while the marriage lasted. And if the woman is returned to her family without a demand for the repayment of the bridal price, everyone is happy. The wife's family is richer, the wife free to find another husband, and the man has a vacancy which will enable him to make another alliance through the marriage bed.'

'Desert politics.'

'Common sense.'

'To an Arab.'

'What other kind of honourable man is there?'

Harry felt the sun burning his scalp and tossed his kafieh back on his head. 'Suppose I just go through the motions of marrying this girl?' He wound the Bedouin agal of black horsehair around his headcloth.

'If you leave her before you enter the bridal tent you would insult the bride and her family, and Shalan could be accused of retaining the bride price under false pretences. If you have a problem with women...' Mitkhal faltered, recalling Harry's lack of interest in the Bedouin gypsy girls he procured for the use of the British officers from time to time.

'The girl could be as ugly as sin.'

'She is rumoured to be beautiful. Shalan has received many offers for her. Sheikhs from the Muhasin, Bawi, Chaab, Sirdieh have asked for her, only to be turned away.'

'They may have asked, but for which daughter? Every Arab talks of his sons, but I've yet to meet one who's counted his daughters.'

'Shalan has only one daughter of marriageable age, Furja. Her mother, Aza, was very beautiful. Shalan loved her deeply.'

'Spare me the romance,' Harry pleaded, sensing the storyteller who was about to emerge.

'It is important you understand the relationship between this girl and Shalan. He loves her because she is all that remains of her mother's blood. Aza's family were Sirdieh, ordinary tribesmen, yet Shalan paid Aza's father a bride price fit for a princess. He married Aza because he loved her.'

'I take it he was fortunate enough to see her

before their wedding.'

'Shalan was 15 and Aza 13 when they married,' Mitkhal continued, ignoring Harry's interruption. 'During the 23 years that followed, he took no other wives. Aza bore him four children. His sons, Mahmoud, Faris, and Amir, and this one daughter, Furja. And his sons...'

'Were hanged by the Turks last year.' Harry recalled Perry's briefing.

'Aza and Furja were forced to watch. By the time Shalan returned, the Turks had left and the women had cut down the bodies and buried them. Shalan did not wait to eat or drink before riding out to avenge their deaths. That night, Aza left the tent and walked out into the desert. A week later, her body was found. When Shalan was told of Aza's death he was desolate. He had taken his vengeance but there was nothing left of his family except Furja. He married again, taking the four wives allowed by Allah's law; but has made it plain he loves none as he loved Aza. Now he has two sons and I think a daughter, but the eldest boy is a baby. He stands alone without the sons of his youth at his side. Only Furja remains. It is she, not his eldest wife, who rules the harem. Shalan has said he values her too highly to allow her to marry outside the tribe, which is why she lives in his tent although she is past the age of marriage.'

'How old is she?'

'Fifteen.'

Harry threw a stone at a lizard basking in the sun. He missed but the creature scuttled away. Fifteen! He remembered his twin, Georgina, at that age. Scrawny figure, grubby fingers, spotty

26

face, unkempt hair hanging greasily down her back, shrill, shrewish voice. A child of 15. His wife. Sharing his bed!

'Ibn Shalan wants Furja to stay in his tent, but apart from his love for her he is afraid that if he allows her to marry into one desert tribe, the others will see an alliance in the marriage. He already has a blood feud with the tribeless ones. The Turks have put a price on his head; Shalan may have no close allies, but at the moment, he has only two enemies.'

'But if I marry his daughter, won't the other tribes assume he has thrown in his lot with the British?'

'You haven't been listening,' Mitkhal answered impatiently. 'Shalan will present your marriage as a love match. If the bride price is mentioned, it will be dismissed as insignificant compared to Furja's happiness. Everyone will understand his wanting to please her after the tragedy of her mother and brothers, and then again, you are a truly tribeless one. The British have no tents, only houses in the towns and ships that cross the ocean. Where could you take Furja? To your bungalow alongside the barracks in Basra? I think Shalan will suggest you pitch your tent alongside his, and when the marriage fails and you divorce her, Furja will return to his harem. Precisely where he wants her.'

Harry shivered. The sun hung low on the horizon, a flaming ball that sank closer to the purple line that divided desert from sky with every passing minute. After the heat of the day, the air was cool, but it would soon become uncomfortably cold. That was the problem with this hellish

27

climate. Extremes. Always extremes.

He scrambled to his feet. 'You've discovered a great deal about Shalan.'

'People talk.'

'Apparently only within your earshot.' Harry hit Dorset on the flanks. She cantered off up the wadi.

'What are you going to do?'

Harry raised an eyebrow. 'Exactly what you expect me to.'

Mitkhal laid a restraining hand on Harry's arm. 'Be careful. You may secure the safety of the pipeline, but don't treat this marriage as one of your British jokes. Shalan is not a fool. He may be up to something I know nothing of.'

'I have you to protect my back.'

'With Ibn Shalan, you need Allah, not me, to protect your back.'

They retraced their steps along the stone-spattered wadi as twilight thickened. By the time they reached the closed circle of the camp, the tents were no more than shadows in the darkness. Only one side of Shalan's tent was rolled up, and that faced inward. The fat lamps were lit, hung high on the tent poles, their pungent, smoky flames ready to illuminate the evening meal. When Harry pushed his way through the throng of men, he detected the aroma of roasting goat flesh overlaying the odours of camel dung, coarse tobacco, and horse sweat.

Mitkhal sniffed. 'I'm ready to eat.'

'You're always ready to eat.' As Harry entered the confines of Shalan's tent, the curtain that

28

walled in the harem billowed. Was the girl alongside him, her body separated from his only by a layer of cloth? Was she studying him through a hole in the curtain, sizing him up the way dealers did stud camels? His masculine pride baulked at the notion. Then he remembered she'd been kept in seclusion. The only men who entered the harem were her father and his eunuch slaves; even her brothers would have moved out to the Mukhaad – the men's quarters – once they'd passed childhood. Hopefully seclusion meant inexperience and a brief 'marriage' to a naïve virgin couldn't be any worse than bedding one of the coarse, native whores in the Regimental Rag in India who took delight in discovering their customers' sexual foibles and even greater delight in broadcasting them to their fellow officers. But then neither would she be a Christina, he reflected regretfully. Christina had been kind, gentle, and quick to forgive his fumbling failings as she'd introduced him to an intense and erotic world.

'Shalan is waiting,' Mitkhal prompted.

Harry pushed his way through to the circle of favoured guests, leaving Mitkhal with the mass of Shalan's tribesmen. The Sheikh clasped his shoulder in an ostentatious show of friendship before leading the group outside. They crouched and scrubbed their hands in sand. Dalhour was waiting, brass jug in hand, when they returned. The slave poured a little water over the hands of each man, before passing around the towel slung over his shoulder. After the ritual cleansing, they squatted in a semi-circle under the open canopy of the tent.

Harry sat on Shalan's right and the Sheikh clapped his hands. Five men carried an enormous brass platter into the tent that held four goats' carcasses heaped on a bed of rice and gravy. Fold upon fold of soft, thin bread flaps rippled around the edge of the dish. On top of each carcass lay the bloodied, severed head of the goat, proof that the animals had been freshly slaughtered in honour of the divan.

The favoured circle moved in the moment the dish was set on the ground. Delving into a carcass, Shalan extracted a torn section of liver and offered it to Harry. Harry accepted graciously, swallowing it in one mouthful, gritting his teeth against the bitter taste he'd detested from childhood. Placing his left hand behind his back, he scooped a handful of rice into the palm of his right and tossed it over the dish, allowing the gravy to trickle through his fingers. Balancing the ball he'd made on his thumb and forefinger, he flicked it into his mouth. Noting the manoeuvre, his fellow guests nodded approval of his manners, followed his example and began to eat.

Mitkhal had expended a great deal of time teaching Harry desert etiquette. Bedouin customs and traditions were more steeped in ceremony than those of the average European Court. Thanks to Mitkhal, Harry knew better than to touch the dish with his left hand, or with fingers he'd licked or put into his mouth. As he continued to wade through the selection of morsels Shalan heaped before him, he wished the Sheikh would honour him with the burnt outside, rather than the undercooked entrails of the carcass. He was glad when the favoured few had eaten their fill and Shalan signalled to the slaves. When the dish was carried to the next group of warriors, Mitkhal among them, Harry rose and walked outside with Shalan. Together they scrubbed the grease from their hands. Harry pulled a pack of Golden Dawn from his abba; to his amazement, Shalan accepted one.

'How long will it take to deliver the bride price?'

'A week to travel to Basra, a week to assemble the livestock and guns, and a third for my companion and I to bring them to wherever you're camped.'

'A month in all.'

'Perhaps a few days less.'

'We will say one month; that will allow for the unexpected. It is not wise to count the days too closely when travelling across the desert.'

'So I've learnt.'

'Your friend will travel to Basra without you.'

'It is dangerous to travel the desert alone.'

'Twelve of my men will accompany him to assist with any difficulties he may encounter.'

'And what am I to do while he travels to Basra?'

'Marry my daughter. Tomorrow. She has waited long enough for her bridal night.'

'But the bridal price...'

'If your friend fails to deliver it within the month, I will take your head as payment.' Shalan stared at him from eye sockets that appeared disconcertingly empty in the moonlight.

'Anything can happen on the road between here and Basra.'

'My men will see it doesn't.' Shalan rubbed the

31

cigarette Harry had given him between his fingers, turning the tobacco to dust. 'But perhaps it is not the dangers of the desert that concern you. Perhaps you are worried your Commanding Officer will fail to supply the bridal price you have agreed to deliver.'

'The bridal price will be paid.' When Perry had said, "You're free to offer whatever it takes," Harry fervently hoped it had been the man and not the brandy talking.

'The marriage will take place before your companion leaves so he can tell your British friends of the union between our two great peoples.'

'And the bride?'

'Is delighted to be of service to her tribe. How delighted, you will see for yourself in the morning. Now you must excuse me. It is no small matter to arrange a daughter's wedding at short notice.'

After Shalan left, Harry went in search of Mitkhal. He found him gossiping to Dalhour at the back of the tent. Seeing him, the slave went off to seek the dish of food that was being passed down the descending ranks of Shalan's guests and retainers. It wouldn't be carried into the harem until every man had eaten his fill, and the slaves had to wait until after the women had finished.

'The wedding's set for the morning.'

'I heard.' Mitkhal reached for a cigarette.

'Shalan's only just told me.'

'Dalhour confided that the bride wasn't too thrilled at the prospect of marrying a Ferenghi. She said she'd as soon marry a donkey.'

'That makes two of us.'

'It's a good omen to agree on something so soon.'

'Save the jokes, Mitkhal.'

'Shalan is afraid if he postpones the wedding until the bride price is delivered he'll have no bride. Apparently, Furja can be headstrong and is quite capable of running off. There's no shortage of suitors who'd be delighted to run off with her.'

'That's just what a reluctant bridegroom needs to hear on the eve of his wedding.'

'There won't be a long ceremony. You and Shalan will sign an agreement in his tent. Afterwards, you mount your horse, lift the bride onto the saddle behind you, and ride around the camp until the whole tribe has been formally advised of your marriage. Then, you enter the bridal booth...'

He gave Harry a significant look.

'And?' Harry prompted.

'Begin married life.' Mitkhal pointed to a small tent being erected on the perimeter of the camp by the light of a thorn bush fire. 'You'll live there until I deliver the bridal price.'

'If I last that long.'

'With your leave coming up, you'll last. As I have some hard riding to do tomorrow, I'll get some sleep while I can.'

Harry dozed fitfully beneath the crowded canopy of Shalan's tent. He spent half the night watching the fleas that lived in great colonies among the mattresses and rugs hop huge distances from one sleeping figure to the next. Mitkhal was right: he had no option other than to fall in with Shalan's scheming and marry the girl, but he'd remain with her as short a time as possible. He'd use the excuse of pressing Ferenghi business. Shalan wouldn't be able to contest that. The moment the bride price was delivered, he'd offer the goods as compensation for his poor performance as bridegroom, and pray Shalan could accept the guns and livestock without losing the peculiar Arab notion of 'face'.

His cousin, John Mason, and friend, Charles Reid, were due to sail from India at the end of June. As soon as his business with Shalan was settled, he'd bolt back to Basra, pick up his ticket of leave, and meet their ship when it berthed in the Gulf. They'd travel home together, get drunk, play cards, talk trivia – God, how he missed the small things he'd taken for granted, like daily baths, clean clothes, and well-cooked food.

He'd spend a token week with his parents, then persuade John, or Charles, or both, to go climbing with him. North Wales possibly; Switzerland would be better. But before he went, he'd resign his commission. A year in India followed by 18 months in Mesopotamia had been enough to convince him that the poky little office his father had offered him in Allan and Downe's Bank was infinitely preferable to soldiering in the wastelands of the world. Anything had to be better, he decided, surveying the shadowy interior of Shalan's tent. Even a drawing room full of giggling Lucies.

Mitkhal woke him before dawn. Outside, they began the irritating practice of washing in sand. The sun rose as they finished. They had begun to dress when a veiled woman left the harem and extinguished the lamps that had burned throughout the night.

The sun was high before Mitkhal was satisfied with Harry's appearance. Harry was by no means as grand as Mitkhal would have liked, but his gumbaz and kafieh were clean. Made from white, finely woven linen, he'd been saving them for the return journey. The feel of fresh clothes against his skin was a luxury he'd almost forgotten and helped ease the anguish of his fleabites. His abba had been brushed and re-brushed by Mitkhal with an arm of thorn until he was convinced the cloth would tear. Round his waist, he wore his officer's sword. Mitkhal eyed it deprecatingly, as he commented on the lack of jewels in the hilt.

'Can you imagine the stir I'd create if I walked into the mess with a jewelled scimitar hanging from my belt?'

'I can imagine what Shalan's warriors are going to say about the absence of jewels. You need a token to give the bride. Gold, or at a push silver.'

'Shall we take a hundred-mile trip to the bazaar to pick up something suitable?'

'Give her some sovereigns. She can weave them into her necklaces.'

Harry felt for the purse he kept strung around his neck. He tipped the contents into his hand. 'There's twenty here.'

'They'll have to do.'

'Twelve will have to do.' Harry returned eight to his pouch.

'Bridegrooms don't have time to gamble.'

'Arab bridegrooms don't have time to gamble. I'm a Ferenghi.'

35

'The idea is to make everyone forget your faults.'

'It's time.' Dalhour materialised at Harry's side.

'I'll get Dorset.' Mitkhal pushed Harry forward.

'Come with me. I need a best man.'

'The Bedawi don't have best men,' Mitkhal replied in English as he left for the wadi.

The wedding, as Mitkhal had prophesied, was simple. Harry entered Shalan's tent and found himself facing a silent, red-veiled figure the same height as him. The Imam handed him a quill and he signed his name on a scroll beneath that of his new father-in-law. Free to look at his bride, he studied the only feature he could see above her veil: her eyes, dark, almond-shaped. Was it his imagination, or were they glittering with hostility?

At Shalan's prompting, they left the tent. The tribe had gathered to watch, Mitkhal in the forefront with Dorset. Harry lifted his surprisingly light bride onto the saddle before mounting. Mitkhal tugged on the rein and led them around the camp before halting outside the booth they'd watched Shalan's women erect the night before. A black-veiled matron opened the tent flap. Dismounting, Harry lifted his bride from Dorset's back. She preceded him into the tent. Mitkhal gave him a final look of encouragement and Harry followed her; the flap swung down behind them and the crowd roared approval.

'Hello, I'm Harry,' he ventured in Arabic.

His bride tore off her veil and threw it to the ground. 'You did not want to marry me, Ferenghi?'

'I am only a humble lieutenant in my King's

army. You are the daughter of a great Sheikh. I am unworthy of you.'

She stared at him frostily. 'Save the diplomacy and lies for the divan. I am your wife and this–' she waved her hand around the lavishly hung interior of the bridal booth '–is our home until I decide to leave you, or you decide to divorce me. Here I expect honesty.'

'Of course.' Despite his misgivings, he'd half hoped for the subservient slave girl of Arabian legend. Instead, he found himself confronting a slim, olive-skinned girl, whose unprepossessing looks were marred by a stern expression, not unlike Shalan's. He had an uncomfortable feeling that, given sufficient provocation, the daughter might prove even more dangerous and unpredictable than the father.

'Now, my husband...' She sank onto a pile of rugs and patted the ground beside her. 'You will sit here, and we will discuss this "marriage" of ours.'

## Chapter Two

*SS* Egra, *the Persian Gulf, Thursday 2nd July 1914*

'Don't they look as though they were made for one another?' Emily Perry whispered to Charles Reid when they walked out of the salon on to the first class section of the deck. Blinded by the gloom after the electric lights of the interior, Charles narrowed his eyes. He made out the tall, well-set-up figure of John Mason standing next to the slight, glittering figure of Maud Perry. Her gold lace evening dress was set with myriads of tiny amber beads that caught and reflected the light from the portholes, and her laughter, light and silvery, echoed through the warm air.

'If by that you mean they're oblivious to the existence of everyone else on board, I'll agree with you.'

'Charles, please,' Emily clung to his arm. 'Don't begrudge them their happiness.'

'I don't... It's – damn it, Emily, you know what I mean.' Leaning on the rail, he stared at the white-crested blue-black shadows swirling in the sea below.

'Isn't it enough I feel the same way as you?'

'Not when I have to leave you in Basra and go on to England alone.' He reached for her hand; the salon door opened and he dropped it. 'Leave him, Emily,' he pleaded when no one appeared. 'It's not as if you love him. We can sail on to England together.'

'My dear boy, I'm old.'

'Barely ten years older than me. What's ten years?'

'In four years you'll be a young man of 30, and I'll be 40.'

'It won't matter.'

'There'd be a scandal. Your career would be ruined.'

'I'll resign my commission.'

'And then what would you do?'

'Live off my father. Work? What does it matter as long as we're together?'

'You're a soldier, Charles. After living with the army for 20 years, I know what that means. You might cope with ostracism from society, but you couldn't bear the loss of the regiment. In time you'd hate me for taking you away from the life you love.'

'It's you I love. Without you I'm nothing.'

'Please, this is our last night together. Don't spoil it by arguing.' She started as the door opened again. Charles nodded to the ship's officers who left the salon.

'Bowditch, Grace,' he acknowledged.

'Mrs Perry, Captain Reid. Marvellous night, isn't it?' Lieutenant Grace stood on his heels and breathed in deeply.

'Marvellous,' Charles echoed.

'Time is creeping on, it's after 10.30.' The lights went out in the salon as Lieutenant Bowditch spoke. 'All unaccompanied ladies to their cabins and men to the smoking room. See you there, Reid?'

'If I'm not too tired.'

'It's time I said goodnight to Maud and John,' Emily murmured beside him. 'It's going to be a long day tomorrow.'

'Half an hour?' Charles mouthed silently. She inclined her head. He offered her his arm. Together, they walked along the deck.

'I wonder if I'd be swept up by Lieutenant Grace if I didn't have you to protect me.' Mischief glowed luminously in Maud's deep blue eyes as she smiled up at John.

'Alf Grace would be more likely to take my

39

place. You're beautiful in this light.' He stared, captivated by her pretty face and shining abundance of golden hair. Ever since he'd seen *Romeo and Juliet* on his 15th birthday he'd been longing to fall in love, but never in his wildest imaginings had he foreseen the advent of anyone like Maud sweeping into his life. She looked like an angel – the Pre-Raphaelite copies of the Botticelli angels that decorated the chapel at Clyneswood. Slender figure, perfectly formed red lips, cherubic cheeks, long, curling blonde hair, enormous, innocent eyes – but that's where the resemblance ended. Maud looked like an angel but frequently behaved like a devil, particularly when the strait-laced and pompous were around.

'Stop looking at me like that.' Maud pursed her lips, inviting a kiss.

'Have I told you that I love you?' he whispered huskily.

'Not for at least five minutes.'

'I love you.'

'You could kiss me. We're the only ones here.'

'You're shameless.'

'Only where you're concerned.'

Despite her assurance, John glanced over his shoulder. 'Your mother and Charles are walking towards us.'

'They don't count.'

'Why, you...'

'Lover's tiff?' Charles enquired sourly.

'Nothing I can't handle,' Maud replied with confidence.

'I dare say.' Charles lightened his tone in response to the pressure of Emily's hand on his arm. 'But look at the result of your handling. John hasn't got drunk, played cards, or visited the "men only" sections of this ship once since we sailed. He's your lap dog, Maud. How can I face Harry with a lap dog in tow?'

'I'll tell Harry it's my fault.'

'I keep forgetting you've met him.'

'Harry was the reason I was sent to India.'

'Maud!'

'It's true, Mother. I've told John all about it, not that there's much other than Father's imaginings, but given Harry's reputation...'

'Maud, that's enough. Don't keep her up, John. We've a long day tomorrow.' Emily kissed her daughter.

'I won't, Emily. Goodnight.'

'Think I'll go to bed too.' Charles yawned. 'Don't disturb me when you come in.'

'I won't,' John replied. 'Goodnight.'

Maud waited until her mother and Charles had disappeared through the door that led to the deck cabins. 'Now we're really alone.'

John checked. The deck was deserted. Wrapping his arms around her, he drew her close. Bending his head to hers, he finally kissed her.

'I adore you, Captain Mason.' Lifting her arms, she pulled his head to hers once more. The thin silk of her evening gown fluttered in the breeze and her bare arm brushed against his cheek.

'You're cold. Here–' He arranged her shawl around her shoulders. 'And I'm not Captain Mason any longer. Just plain John Mason, civilian.'

'Doctor John Mason.'

'A very undistinguished doctor with no ambitions beyond marrying you.'

'And living happily ever after?'

'I'm not a prince.'

'Then you must be a knight. A knight who's rescued me from a fate worse than death.'

'Harry?'

'Most certainly not Harry. He's fun. You've rescued me from life in Basra. You've no idea how bad it can be. Heat, flies – ugh, you can't even begin to imagine the flies.'

'Now I've rescued you, you can forget Basra and the flies. I intend to carry you off to the depths of the English countryside and find a sleepy little village...'

'What will we do in a sleepy little village?' she broke in.

'Be happy. I'll cure the natives of their mumps and measles, and you, my beautiful wife, will make a home for us. We'll fill it full of lovely things. Furniture, books, friends, and children. Dozens of children.'

Maud held him at arm's length. 'Dozens of children are not a part of any "happily ever after" I've read about.'

'Don't you want children?' he asked seriously.

'In moderation.'

'Then I'll amend our future to include children in moderation.'

'There's someone behind us.'

John glanced over his shoulder and saw an Indian steward peering around the door. 'We're holding up the workers. They need to clean the decks for tomorrow.'

'Can't we keep them waiting a little longer?'

'It wouldn't be fair. They have to get up horribly early; besides, I promised your mother we wouldn't be late.'

'But I want to stay with you,' she protested petulantly.

'There's nowhere for us to go, my darling. The lounge is closed. I can hardly take you into the men's smoking room. If you so much as stood outside the door you'd create a sensation.'

'I could live with a sensation if you could.'

'I like the quiet life. How about I walk you to your cabin?'

'Whatever my lord and master decrees.'

'I won't be that legally for a few more days, and knowing you, my love, I doubt you'll take notice of anything I decree.'

'You could teach me subservience.'

'God help the man who tried.' He pulled her into an alcove, then, after glancing up and down to make sure they weren't in view of the small army of hands swarming over the deck, cleaning, and straightening chairs and cushions, he kissed her. On the forehead.

'Is that all I get?'

'On account. Full payment comes on our wedding night.'

'If you came to my cabin we could forget about accounts.'

'What would people say if we were seen? Your reputation – your mother.' Taken aback by her suggestion, John failed to notice the effort it had cost her to make it.

'Mother wouldn't be able to say anything considering Charles has spent every night in her cabin since we sailed.'

'Maud!'

'There's no use pretending you're shocked. You must know, seeing as how you and Charles are supposed to be sharing a cabin.'

'I didn't realise you knew.' The secret was Charles and Emily's. John would rather not have been a party to it but, as Maud reminded him, he and Charles were supposed to be sharing a cabin and that made him a conspirator, albeit an unwilling one.

'I found out the morning after we left India. Our maid slept late; hardly surprising if a tenth of what I heard really went on in the third-class lounge the night before. Anyway, I went to see Mother early; I'd lost a button from my grey silk, and hoped she'd have a replacement. When I opened my door I saw Charles sneak out of her cabin.'

'Did you tell your mother?'

'Don't be ridiculous.'

'You don't intend to?'

'No.' Encircling his waist with her arms, she laid her head against his chest. 'I'm pleased for them. If I hadn't seen Charles leaving, I might not have realised that he and Mother were actually – but I would have to be blind not to notice the difference in her. All she talked about in India was love. How the right man could make a woman happy. It wasn't only her maternal interest in us. She smiled more when Charles was around and although she tried using our happiness as an excuse, it fell flat when you were on duty and Charles visited us alone. They managed to make me feel like a middle-aged chaperone. Wouldn't it be marvellous if they ran off together?'

'They'd become social lepers.'

'Nothing would matter if they had one another. You wouldn't mind if they lived together, would you?'

'Your mother will always be welcome in our house, when we get one. But I don't think either your mother or Charles would be happy. Charles would have to resign his commission, and outside of us, no one would receive your mother.'

'Surely, once everyone saw how well-suited they are...'

'Whatever we think is irrelevant,' he interrupted. 'It's none of our business.'

'It is mine. You haven't met my father. Don't misunderstand me,' she qualified. 'He's a good father and husband in the provider sense. Mother and I have always had most of the things we've wanted: clothes, jewellery, things for the house. But he's so – wooden. Grade one British Army, officer material for the use of – wooden.'

'What would he do if he found out about your mother and Charles?'

'The honourable thing, whatever that might be. Shoot Charles, throw out my mother. He's not going to find out, is he, John?'

'Not from me. And that's enough for one night. It's time you were in your cabin.'

Sensing John's disapproval of Charles and her mother's affair, Maud was in emotional turmoil as she led the way to her cabin. She'd lived all her life in army quarters among healthy young men. According to her father, the proximity had led to the development of a coarse, unfeminine streak. If Emily's health had been stronger, he would have sent her to a girls' school in England to be inculcated with mannerisms befitting a colonel's daughter. He'd frequently warned her she'd overhear things no lady should if she persisted in wandering around the barracks. She had.

Even before her 16th birthday she knew what 'Rag' meant, and she'd caught sight of enough whores sidling in and out of the men's quarters to realise sex was a saleable and, for men at least, enjoyable commodity, but she'd never considered any of her illicit discoveries relevant to her, until she'd met Captain John Mason.

From the first moment she'd caught sight of him at the ladies' dinner given in the officers' mess in honour of her mother's arrival, she was conscious of his dark good looks. It didn't take her long to discover that he was as unaware of them as he was of the effect he had on his fellow officers' wives. She discovered she liked being alone with him, teasing and, later, kissing him. And, during the whole of their courtship, hovering in the background, whispered, rarely openly spoken of, were the sexual mysteries, embellished and passed on at the claustrophobic, sweltering, all-female tea parties.

Knowing winks and nods exchanged between the older matrons. Congratulations accompanied by blatantly envious looks from the younger wives. Major Harrap's wife had unbent enough to follow her routine good wishes with the confidence that John had attended her during the long and difficult birth of her first child and throughout the whole undignified, painful, ordeal he had been a pillar of strength, gentleness, and comfort.

'My dear.' Marjorie had laid a damp, pale hand on her arm. 'You can have no idea how kind your fiancé was. He brought my son out with considerably less pain and embarrassment than Major Harrap inflicted putting him in. You, my dear, Maud, have not only caught yourself the best-looking officer in the regiment but also the most considerate.'

'Penny for them?'

Maud realised they were outside her cabin door. 'I was thinking of you.' She gave him her key; he turned it in the lock. She grasped his hand. 'Come in. Just for a little while.'

Seeing no one in the corridor, he followed her. Closing the door behind him, he locked it.

'I gave Harriet the evening off.' Maud turned her back to him so he wouldn't see the nervousness in her eyes. 'Would you unhook my dress for me?'

'That's him. The tall, fair one speaking to the waiter,' the steward whispered.

The sepoy pressed closer to the porthole.

'In the name of Allah, get back. If you're seen, we'll both be done for. You know the rule about sticking to your own deck.'

The Indian moved away from the porthole and slid into the shadows. 'You're sure that's Captain Reid?'

'I serve early morning tea to him and Captain Mason.'

'He's leaving the ship at Basra?'

'I heard them talking. Captain Mason's getting

married there.'

Chatta Ram pressed a few rupees into the steward's hand. He closed his eyes, pictured the man he'd seen. Yes, he'd know him again. 'You go first. I'll find my own way.'

The man needed no second bidding. He'd risked his job by taking the sepoy to the first-class deck. Chatta Ram took one last look. Captain Charles Reid, long legs crossed in front of him, whisky glass in hand, was laughing. Chatta wondered if he'd laugh as loud in the Spartan Indian section of the ship. There were no upholstered chairs, thick carpets, crystal glasses, or whisky there. Only thin sleeping pallets, canvas buckets and rough wooden stools. One day–

Chatta Ram left the porthole and crept along the deck towards the stern.

*Basra, Friday early hours of Friday 3rd July 1914*

Harry woke to see the moon shining, a huge golden ball segmented by the carved stonework of the trellis windows. Turning on his side, he watched the shadows play across Furja's cheek. Their first night together under a roof. Already he was regretting the ease with which he'd acceded to Shalan's demands.

'I know the Ferenghis, Hasan.' It hadn't taken Shalan long to Arabicise his name. 'I know their ways. Their contempt.' Shalan had spat into the dust. 'You will not take my daughter among your people.'

And he'd agreed. How readily he'd agreed, but

48

that had been before he'd known Furja. The first three days after their wedding had resembled Tottenham Court Road at pub closing. Furja had fought like fury, taking respite only during the night when she'd retreated in high dudgeon to the side of the tiny booth she designated as "hers", leaving him a single rug.

He'd actually looked forward to the times when he could leave the booth for the dubious pleasures of the all-male coffee circle and evening meal. On the third evening after their wedding, Shalan had informed him it was past the time for proof of the consummation of their marriage to be displayed. Fuming, he'd returned to the bridal booth, and while Furja'd watched, cut his arm with his sword, staining the white cloth tradition decreed should be flown above their tent with his own blood. But before he had time to do anything with it, Furja had snatched the rag from his hands and torn it to shreds.

'I will not permit any member of my tribe to believe this "marriage" holds any importance outside of the bride price you paid my father.'

Weary of argument, he said nothing.

The following morning, he left the tent while she slept. Taking Dorset, he rode into the desert. Before he'd travelled a mile, she'd caught up with him on one of Shalan's black mares. Having nothing better to do, he'd followed her. When the sun reached the climax of its scorching heights, they'd halted at a well. He'd unsaddled and watered both horses. After tethering them in the shade of the only clump of palms that grew at the lonely spot, he'd stripped to his cotton trousers

49

to wash the dust and sweat from his skin. Revelling in the feel of the first water to touch his body for nearly a month, he'd almost forgotten Furja.

When he'd finished, he slipped on his abba without drying himself. She'd made a tiny, makeshift tent of her outer robe, pitching it in the minuscule shade of a large boulder. She'd beckoned and he'd walked warily towards her, expecting another outburst, but she'd held out her hands. In them were some dried dates and a gourd. He'd taken a date and eaten it while he filled the gourd at the well. The water was brackish, and contained some peculiar debris, but she strained it through her robe into his hands. After weeks of sour camel's milk, it tasted like wine. She invited him to sit alongside her. Glad to get out of the sun's unrelenting glare he'd accepted, but he was careful to leave as many inches between them as the covering allowed. Emotionally and physically drained, he'd wrapped himself in his abba, leant against Dorset's saddle, and closed his eyes.

He'd woken to the absolute silence of the desert. Furja was lying beside him, her head on his arm. He moved. She opened her eyes. He'd looked around and realised that for the first time they were truly alone. No one could see, or hear them. Perhaps the same thought had occurred to her, because she kissed him. A drawn-out, sensual kiss that marked the end of animosity and the beginning of a sensual sexual relationship that consigned his memories of Christina to oblivion.

Furja was a virgin, but her knowledge spanned centuries. That moment of passion-filled, urgent action marked his initiation into the erotic secrets that had been passed from mother to daughter in the harems of the black tents. When they'd ridden away from the well at sunset, his eyes had been opened to a magnificent and breath-taking new world.

The two weeks it took Mitkhal to reach Shalan's camp after that day passed in a frenzy of lovemaking that left little time for meals, or sleep. Much to Shalan's chagrin, Harry ceased attending the coffee circle and evening meal. Furja's aunt, Gutne, brought them what little they needed, including their food.

Mitkhal rode in with a baggage train that carried the bridal price in full, along with a note from Perry extolling Harry as 'a good chap', the ultimate Perry accolade. He'd also brought fresh clothes for Harry, a flask of brandy small enough to hide from Shalan, a strict Moslem in all matters pertaining to alcohol, and a razor to replace the one Harry had blunted by trying to shave without soap or water.

Five minutes' conversation with Mitkhal made Harry realise how weary he was of fencing words with Shalan, all-male coffee circles, Islamic formality, Bedouin lies or truths, depending on which way you viewed them, grit, heat, washing in sand, fleas, flies, discomfort and, above all, the uncompromising harshness of the desert. He wanted to eat at a table, bathe in a bath, sleep in a bed – alongside his wife – and live with something more substantial than a strip of cloth between him and his neighbours.

In short, he wanted to return to civilisation, or failing that, Basra, and he intended to take Furja with him because her absence would annoy Shalan – or so he snarled at Mitkhal when the Arab dared to comment on the success of his marriage.

He left Mitkhal and returned to the booth to try out a new role on Furja, that of masterful husband. He informed her he wanted to follow the Ferenghi tradition of a honeymoon, one on which they could be truly alone, and ordered her to pack for his quarters in Basra. She said little in reply and he left the tent congratulating himself on his victory, but, within the hour, Shalan had reminded him forcefully of their agreement: no infidels near his daughter, and no infidel house in Basra. It had been left to Furja to settle the argument. Alternating between playing dutiful wife and dutiful daughter, she agreed to accompany her husband on a Ferenghi honeymoon. That, she told her father, infringed no Islamic rules, but as a devout daughter and a devout Moslem she refused to live among Ferenghi. Which was why they'd arrived at Shalan's town house in Basra with Mitkhal, four of her male cousins, an aunt, and six of her women in tow.

That, she informed him, was as alone as a Sheikh's daughter could get.

He'd surrendered with good grace and not entirely empty-handed, he mused, staring at the sleeping figure stretched out alongside him. Rolling on his back, he studied the ornate plasterwork on the ceiling. It was no use; he couldn't sleep. Stealing from the bed, he pulled on his native cotton trousers, found a cigarette, lit it, and padded barefoot into the tiled courtyard. A fountain played in the centre of cultivated flower-beds. The mixed perfumes of pomegranate, orange and almond blossoms hung in the still night air. He had to hand it to Shalan; the house was cooler, and more comfortable, than his bungalow next to the barracks. He wondered why the Sheikh spent his time travelling the desert in a never-ending search for fodder for his flocks, when he could live in style. The masters lived out a harsh life with their herds, while the slaves lived a life of ease, caring for town houses that were rarely visited. The situation was ridiculous.

'You couldn't sleep, Harry?' Furja stood beside him, struggling to put on her robe.

'I didn't mean to disturb you.' As he pulled the silk over her shoulder, his hand lingered on the curve of her naked breast. He couldn't help contrasting her smile and the warmth of the embrace that followed with the reaction of another woman to whom he'd once done the same thing.

It had happened during the ball his parents had given to celebrate his engagement to his cousin, Lucy Mason. He'd inveigled her into the depths of the conservatory, but when he'd plunged his hand down the neck of her low-cut evening gown, she'd closed her eyes and stiffened like a board. Rather than pursue the matter, he'd walked away. Shortly afterwards, he'd ended the engagement.

'You're thinking about tomorrow when the friends of your childhood arrive.'

'John and Charles? Yes, they'll be here in a few hours. It will be good to see them again.' He sat on the tiled slab that edged the fountain and pulled her onto his lap. She locked her fingers around his neck and kissed his bare chest. 'Furja?'

'Yes, my husband,' she whispered, preoccupied with her kisses.

'Sail to England with me?'

'No.' She sat upright and glared at him.

'You're my wife.'

'I'm also Bedouin.'

'And I'm Ferenghi,' he replied cryptically, 'but that didn't stop your father from forcing us to marry.'

'Our marriage was necessary. My travelling to England is not.'

'Forget I mentioned it.' He retreated in the face of her temper.

'I will.' Her fingers moved skilfully, massaging the nape of his neck.

'Have you ever loved anyone?'

'The Bedawi teach that love follows marriage. It must be true. When I first saw you, I couldn't bear for you to touch me, and now, I have learnt to like it.'

'I didn't ask for a lecture on the ways of the Bedawi,' he replied abruptly. 'I wanted to know if you've ever been in love.'

She studied him gravely for a moment. 'Once, I watched a prince ride into my father's camp, but I only watched. We never spoke.'

'You fell in love with him?'

'I thought so at the time.' She felt the muscles stiffen in his spine. 'You're jealous?'

'Of course not,' he snapped.

'He was tall, and very handsome. With a little moustache.' She ran her finger over Harry's bare upper lip. 'He was a Sherif. Descended from the house of the prophet.'

'I do know what a Sherif is.'

'There was gold thread in his agal, and at his belt he wore the gold-sheathed Sherifan dagger,' she continued, seemingly oblivious to his mood. 'He was a true son of the desert.'

'If you felt that way about him, why didn't you marry him?' he demanded.

'Because he had four wives, and a waiting list of 20 to fill the vacancies when he divorced them. My father's tribe is a poor one. My position on that list would have been very low. I would have had to wait many years, perhaps until I was old and shrivelled.'

'I doubt he'd have kept you waiting that long.' Despite the jealousy that gathered destructively inside him, he smiled at the notion of her wracked in spinsterish old age.

'But–' she kissed the frown on his forehead '–none of that matters now. I am your wife until you divorce me, or I decide to leave you. Then you can marry a Ferenghi. Is it true Ferenghis have only one wife?'

'Yes, and if marriage to you is anything to go by, one is enough.'

'Then I am glad I am not Ferenghi, because marriage would be too much work. I would have to run the household alone, and bear all the children. I would grow old and ugly before my time.'

'Most Ferenghi women cope. My mother bore all of my father's children, and she is neither old nor ugly. At least she wasn't the last time I saw her.'

'Then your father cannot have many children.'

'Not as many as yours.' He opened her robe and teased her nipple with his tongue.

'Do you think we'll be married for any length of time?'

'I hope so.'

'Because if we are, I think you should take another wife. I would have an equal to talk to when you are away, someone to share the responsibilities of the household.'

'Are you serious?' He stopped what he was doing, and looked hard at her.

'My Aunt Gutne is unmarried. She is lonely.'

'She can remain lonely. The answer is no. No other wives. Absolutely categorically.'

Without warning, she entwined her fingers in his hair, twisting his head until his mouth was close to hers. 'There are advantages in having two wives; perhaps we should show you what they are.'

'The answer is no,' he warned sternly, wincing in pain.

'I'm sorry I asked,' she said in an unapologetic tone. She slid her hands down his chest to his waist. He grabbed them before they could travel any further.

'I can't think straight when you do that.'

He found it difficult to cope with her mood changes. Often while she purred loving nothings into his ears, he seethed with an anger she had stirred only moments before. Yet she could claw and bite him one minute and kiss him the next.

'You wouldn't need to think,' she replied, speaking to him in English as she slid from his lap, knelt before him, and lowered her head between his thighs. 'Not if we returned to our bed.'

# Chapter Three

*Basra, Friday 3rd July 1914*

Harry left the gardens of Shalan's house as dawn crept over the muddied, sepia waters of the Shatt-el-Arab. He was bone-weary, already looking forward to the heat of the afternoon when he could return to bed. If he was going to survive until his leave, he'd either have to sleep apart from Furja, or forget going to the barracks this early in the morning. He stretched and breathed in deeply, shuddering when the cool morning air hit his lungs. He called to Farik, the slave on gate duty, to close the iron bolts behind him, slipped through the high wooden gates, and moved off, walking quickly, head low, voluminous native robes flapping at his heels, no different from any other native leaving the residential quarter for the business sector of the town.

No one gave him a second glance as he made his way through the labyrinth of fetid lanes. Alleyways opened and closed behind him, each indistinguishable from the last. How could he ever have considered this place civilised? He only had to breathe the stench that was as much a part of the town as the sun-baked mud bricks that walled the inward-facing houses. It was enough to make a camel retch. Excrement, Turkish coffee, stagnant pools of liquid refuse, spices, and overriding all else, even at this unearthly hour, the acrid odour of human sweat.

He reached a square that fronted a wharf on the Shatt. The stalls in the bazaar were shuttered, but a group of turbaned waiters stood outside a coffee house, cups in hand, watching fishermen offload their nets. He looked at the fish, picked out half a dozen, and offered to buy them; the boatman argued the price. He repeated his first offer. When it wasn't taken, he walked away. A fisherman ran after him and Harry beat the price down even further. He handed over a few coins and told the man to deliver the fish to Shalan's house. The fisherman bowed effusively at the mention of his father-in-law's name. Bored by the proceedings, Harry turned up the comparatively broad street that led to the palm-fringed European quarter that housed the barracks and consulate.

The sentry jack-knifed to attention when he reached the gates. 'Lieutenant Downe, sir. Lieutenant Smythe left orders that he be informed the minute you came in, sir.'

Peter Smythe wandered out of the duty office when he heard the sentry, an orange in one hand, a cup of coffee in the other. His vivid red-gold hair was standing on end despite the vigorous brushing he'd subjected it to that morning.

'Harry.' He shook his head at the sight of his fellow subaltern in native dress. 'The old man's been shouting for you for over a week. Where the hell have you been?'

'Here and there.'

'Gambling in the bazaar?' Peter grinned. 'Lose a lot this time?'

'Don't I always?'

'No. You'd better get up to your bungalow and change. Can't visit the old man looking like that. And watch out for Crabface. He's on duty. You know his views on Arab skirts. He'd shoot the natives for wearing them, let alone British military personnel.'

'Dress uniform wasn't the order of the day in the social circle I've just left.'

'Dare say, but you can't get the locals to respect you unless you stick to your own traditions, and that means your own, decent clothes. Understood?' Peter barked in a fair parody of Crabbe.

'What's the flap about?'

'Mrs and Miss Perry are returning today and the colonel's ordered a ladies' dinner to be served in the mess tonight. He's invited the usual outsiders, and told the chaplain to prepare for a wedding.'

'Maud's?'

'Can't think of anyone else who'd be getting married, can you?'

'Who's the lucky man?' Harry asked.

'No one knows.'

'Thank heavens it's not you.' Stephen Amey, the youngest subaltern on the post, stuck his head around the door.

'What's that supposed to mean?' Peter bristled.

'That frightful colonial you persist in mooning over.' Stephen rolled his eyes.

'Americans are not colonials.'

'They're worse. Rebellious colonials who didn't know how to behave, and as if her country's not enough, she's a missionary to boot. Smythe, where's your taste?'

'My taste is none of your concern. And Angela – Miss Wallace,' Peter corrected swiftly, 'is not a missionary.'

'She lives with missionaries. That amounts to the same thing. Can you imagine what will happen if you do marry her? She'll want to socialise with other missionaries. The colonel's lady will call to take tea and your bungalow will be full of Bible-carrying Presbyterians.'

'I find their company preferable to yours.'

'Then you should ask for a transfer. I suggest a remote outpost on the North-west Frontier. No decent European society to speak of, so she won't disgrace you. Plus an abundance of hostile natives for her to convert.'

Peter smashed his fist into Stephen's jaw.

Harry pushed past the gaping sentry and pulled the two men apart. 'In the office,' he hissed. 'Before Crabface gets wind of this and you're both put on report.'

'I didn't say anything that wouldn't be said in the mess in India.' Stephen rubbed his jaw after Harry closed the door behind them. 'That time Johnny Leigh was engaged to a tradesman's daughter from Liverpool, the whole mess told him he couldn't marry the girl.'

'If I remember rightly, they told him every day for six months and he didn't marry her,' Harry agreed. 'What's your point?'

'Someone has to do the same for Smythe. Everyone falls for an unsuitable female at some time but no one in their right mind marries them. Look at Leigh: he married Captain Bull's daughter and he's a happy man.'

60

'Is he? I always thought Ida Bull...'

'You know the rules, Smythe,' Harry warned. 'No talking about a brother officer's wife.'

'Amey has insulted a girl I admire.'

'For which he's going to apologise, aren't you, Amey?'

Peter and Stephen glared at one another.

'If you want to dine in the mess tonight, bury your differences. You know what a nose Crabface has for sniffing out trouble. There aren't so many ladies' dinners you can afford to miss one.'

'Sorry, old man.' Stephen extended his hand. 'Spoke out of turn.'

'Accepted, on condition you give your word not to mention Miss Wallace again.' Peter massaged his aching knuckles and waited for a nod before taking Stephen's hand.

Stephen stroked his jaw. 'If you gentlemen will excuse me, I'll put an ice pack on this.'

'Thank you, Harry.' Peter shook Harry's hand after Stephen left.

'You pair of idiots. You make me feel 80 years old. Eighteen months of seniority has turned me into a father figure.'

'Not quite.' Peter fingered Harry's Arab robes.

'Pay a visit to the office,' Harry suggested. 'There'll be invitations for the Reverend and Mrs Butler and the Wallaces. If you volunteer to deliver them, you might see your lady love.'

'Don't you start on me.' Peter threw an orange at Harry.

Harry ducked and it squelched against the wall. 'Temper. If you want to survive in this man's army you must learn forbearance.'

'And how to take insults?' Peter countered.

'Part of an officer's training, like drinking. God bless Maud's fiancé, whoever he is, for giving us an excuse tonight.'

'As if you've ever needed one.' Peter picked up another orange as Harry vanished through the door.

Attired to his bearer's satisfaction, Harry presented himself at the door of Colonel Perry's large, whitewashed office 15 minutes later.

'About time,' Perry barked as Harry was ushered in. 'Where've you been, Downe?'

'On honeymoon, sir.'

'You being facetious?' The colonel glared at him over the paper he was reading.

'Don't think so, sir.'

'You just got into Basra?'

'No, sir.'

'You weren't in your bungalow last night.'

'No, sir, my wife and I...'

'Your what?'

'My wife and I, sir. We've moved into Sheikh Aziz Ibn Shalan's house in the Arab quarter, sir.'

Dropping his paper, the colonel pushed his chair away from his desk. 'Don't misunderstand what I'm about to say.'

'I won't, sir,' Harry interrupted.

'We're all exceedingly grateful to you.' Perry stared at him through pink-rimmed, beady brown eyes. 'Your tame Arab mentioned Shalan, cunning bastard that he is, forced you to marry his daughter. I realise it couldn't have been easy. Going native out here is worse than India. The women haven't the saving graces of the Hindus. Put camel piss on their hair from what I've heard. And the country's not like India. The desert's a hostile place.'

'I noticed, sir.' The remark was one too many.

Perry thumped his desk. 'I know you had to stay with this woman, this...'

'Furja bin Shalan, sir.'

'As I said, "this woman". But Shalan has his weapons; you've completed your mission. It's time to leave her. That's an order, Lieutenant Downe.'

Harry stared at Perry obstinately, and in silence.

'Damn it all, man, there isn't an officer in the Indian Army who hasn't enjoyed a fling with a native woman. Only natural and healthy in this bloody climate. Regrettably, you were forced to go one step further and marry this one, but I shouldn't need to remind that you it is a native marriage. It doesn't mean a damn thing to the church, or–' he gave Harry another telling look '–the British Government. Now we've paid Shalan to do our dirty work, finish the thing off. No sense in hanging about. Do it tonight. You don't want any loose ends dangling with your leave coming up.'

'Sir,' Harry murmured.

'Glad we understand one another. Just one more thing before we close the subject. There's no need to mention this "marriage" to anyone. On the base or back home. Don't want word to get out that a British chap was forced to tie himself to a heathen. Might be misunderstood. High Command can be touchy about that kind of thing. Not your father, he's a good chap. Served under him in Bengal. He'd understand why it had to be done, but I doubt your mother would. Ladies can be finicky. Know my wife would.'

'Sir.'

'Well, now that's over with, we'll move on. Ah, just what the doctor ordered. Breakfast.' He turned to the orderly who wheeled in a trolley laden with silverware. 'Brought two servings?'

'Yes, Colonel Perry, sir. Bacon, eggs, fish, toast, butter, marmalade and tea, as ordered, sir.'

'We'll serve ourselves. Close the door on the way out.'

Harry prepared to follow the orderly, but Perry forestalled him.

'Join me, Downe. We can talk more informally here than at the mess. Well, sit down, man,' he added when Harry hesitated.

'Yes, sir.' Bewildered by the privilege, Harry sat uneasily in the chair the colonel indicated. Perry pushed the trolley between them and handed him a napkin.

'Fact is, wanted to talk to you about a personal matter. Well, come on, man, don't be shy,' the colonel shouted, in a noisy attempt at camaraderie. 'Help yourself.'

Harry lifted the lid on the dish closest to him and saw eggs. Pungent Mesopotamian eggs, he realised with distaste. He ladled the smallest possible portion onto his plate.

'Had a wire from my wife. She's arriving with Miss Perry today. Appears the girl has got herself engaged to a chap you know. My wife's given her approval. Nothing I could do, I was here, she was there, and the fellow's a captain, so he can't be a bad sort. Name of Mason, John Mason.'

Harry almost choked on his eggs. 'He's my cousin.'

'Your cousin!' Perry's disapproval was evident. 'This is informal, sir? Off the record?'

'I said so, didn't I?'

'He's all right, sir. Never been any scandal about John. Not like me.'

'Hmm. Sandhurst-trained?'

'Sir?'

'Your cousin. Is he Sandhurst-trained?'

'No, he's a doctor with the Indian Medical Service.'

The colonel's face fell. 'Not a professional, then.'

'Not a professional soldier, no,' Harry confirmed. 'He studied medicine at Guy's.'

'His father a professional?'

Harry helped himself to toast. He was beginning to enjoy his breakfast. He wondered why Perry didn't come out with the questions he really wanted answered; questions about the financial and social status of the Mason family.

'My uncle, John's father, was never in the army but he is a physician of some standing. He's been consulted by the royal family.'

'Is he Sir John Mason?' Perry asked with sudden interest.

'He was honoured with a life peerage a few years ago.'

'I had no idea his son was in India.' The colonel managed a smile. Evidently a peer's son, even that of a life peer, was the next best thing to a professional soldier when it came to prospective sons-in-law. 'What's the relationship between your father and Sir John Mason?'

Harry continued to butter his toast. 'My father and John's mother are brother and sister.'

'Your mother's American, isn't she?'

Harry knew that, to the colonel, American was synonymous with 'native'. 'Yes. John's parents introduced my father to my mother. Uncle John bought Stouthall; it's a sizeable property not far from my father's place at Clyneswood. When Father returned from India, Mother was staying with Aunt Elizabeth...'

'How big is this place of your uncle's?' the colonel interrupted, unable to contain his curiosity.

'The house is quite large.'

'How large?'

'Forty or so bedrooms, and there's farm tenancies amounting to some 2000 acres. There's also a sanatorium two miles from the house, but my uncle's main interest lies in his London practice. He also sits on the boards of several hospitals.' Harry pushed aside his eggs and helped himself to bacon.

'Glad to see the prospect of a modest inheritance didn't stop your cousin from making a career for himself in the Indian Medical Service.'

'John's resigned his commission.' Harry regretted the words the instant they left his mouth.

'Why would the fool do that?' Perry thundered.

'My uncle's over 70,' Harry mumbled through a mouthful of toast. 'And he always hoped John would take over his practice.'

'How old is this cousin of yours?'

'Twenty-five; we're the same age. Grew up together, John, Charles Reid, and myself. Took our commissions the same year and sailed out to India on the same boat.'

'Charles Reid. General Reid's boy?'

'Yes.'

'Tragic about his mother,' the colonel mused, lost in a past of which Harry knew nothing. 'Upset the entire regiment at the time. The general behaved impeccably. I remember him packing the boy off to England. Good of your father to see to his education.'

'Charles lived with us until his father retired and returned to England,' Harry volunteered, glad of an opportunity to steer the conversation away from John's civilian life.

'Is Captain Mason Sir John's only child?'

'No, but he is the eldest,' Harry reassured him. 'He has a younger brother, Thomas, who is a final year medical student at Guy's. And John's sister, Lucy, is 20. She came out three years ago.'

'I hoped my daughter would become an army wife. The life has so much to offer.'

Harry remained tactfully silent.

'I trust Maud's thought the matter through. Personally, I can't help wondering at the credentials of a man who embarks on a military career knowing it's going to be curtailed to suit family requirements.'

'Perhaps John thought a short military career better than none. He wanted to make a study of tropical fevers and diseases. India is the best place.'

'Quite.' The colonel refused to be mollified. 'No doubt he'll take Miss Perry back to England after the wedding. She'll find it difficult to adjust. She's lived all her life in the East, you know.'

'Sir.' Harry crumpled his napkin and threw it over the debris on his plate. He'd done what he could. The rest was up to John, and he'd rather wait out his arrival in the more congenial atmosphere of the mess.

'Steam launch is due in at the jetty in two hours, fifteen minutes.'

'I'll be there, sir.' Harry felt he hadn't done John justice, but the news of Maud's engagement had destroyed what little humour the colonel possessed.

'One more thing, Downe.'

'Sir?' He left his chair and stood to attention.

'As you're acquainted with Captains Mason and Reid, see to their quarters.'

Harry left the office and bumped into Crabbe. He saluted the thickset, bullet-headed major and walked on. Crabbe was a 'ranker'. Feared by the men and distrusted by his fellow officers, especially Harry, who figured in Crabbe's reports as the epitome of the slovenly, undisciplined junior officer.

Back in the shrouded mists of time, Crabbe had left a slum family of dubious, if not downright criminal, tendencies to join the regiment as a private. Hard work and immaculate soldiering gained him rapid promotion. As Regimental Sergeant-Major, he'd led a charge at the battle of Paardeberg in the Boer War. His men had gained glory, the regiment honours, and he the doubtful privilege of promotion to second lieutenant. At the time, he'd wondered who in command hated him enough to recommend he be commissioned. RSMs received good pay and had their uniform and mess bills found for them. Newly created second lieutenants had to pay their own tailors' and mess bills, and his first year in the officers' mess would have been his last if he hadn't been a reasonable card player. He survived, and continued to survive during subsequent promotions, proving to the delight of the War Office recruiting department and the popular press that the British Army was truly democratic in its selection of officers.

'Ah, Crabbe.' Perry greeted Crabbe with the bluff enthusiasm he used to conceal his dislike of the man.

'Sir.' Crabbe snapped to attention. 'Duty officer's report, sir.'

Perry flicked through the pages. 'What's this about Downe?' he asked, seeing Harry's name on a charge sheet.

'Lieutenant Downe was seen crossing the parade ground in native dress this morning, sir.'

'I gave Lieutenant Downe permission to wear native dress, Major. He was returning from a secret mission.'

'If you had seen fit to inform me of your dispensation, sir, I would not have put Lieutenant Downe's name on the sheet.'

'Secret missions have to be kept secret, Crabbe, that's the point of them.'

'May I remind the colonel that only last March, Lieutenant Downe was confined to barracks for wearing a gumbaz and abba on duty?'

'Crabbe.' Perry swallowed his annoyance and

tried the friendly approach. 'Can we talk about this off the record?'

'Sir.' Crabbe remained rigidly at attention.

'Basra isn't India, and sometimes these Johnnies who dress up and go native succeed in dealing with the locals on a more – shall we say productive level, than those of us in uniform.'

'Sir, Captain Shakespear has had more success than any other British officer in treating with the natives, and he has met them man to man on his own terms, without relinquishing his uniform.'

'I sympathise with your opinion, Crabbe,' Perry interrupted, 'but Shakespear's efforts amongst the tribes who inhabit the empty quarter, commendable as they are, can hardly be held as an example for us to follow here in the Gulf. Sometimes we, in command, find it necessary to bend a few rules.'

'Sir, none of this alters the fact that Lieutenant Downe spends more time cavorting in the bazaars dressed like a native...'

'I know Lieutenant Downe better than you, Major. I know his people.' He glared at Crabbe to ensure the major comprehended the social distinction he was drawing. 'I'm fully aware what he does with his free time. But he's young and bored. I would have found this posting tedious myself at his age. No action, no social life worth speaking of. It's hardly surprising he finds amusement where he can. It's up to us older, more experienced officers to guide him. Utilise his abilities as a man and an officer, and that's precisely what I'm doing. Lieutenant Downe mixes well with the locals. He's learnt their lingo, something no other officer on this post has seen fit to do, and he keeps me informed of local rumour. Perhaps you'd like to take that as an example, Major?' Leaving his desk, Perry strode to the window, turned his back on Crabbe, and stared out over the Shatt-el-Arab.

Flotillas of low-slung native barges scudded downstream to the Gulf, but the colonel remained oblivious to any beauty the scene might have held. Crabbe infuriated him. The insufferable base-born nobody had dared criticise a Downe. Whatever Harry's failings, he was of sound family. The fifth generation Downe to hold a commission in the regiment. Damn High Command and their notions of promoting dregs from the ranks.

'Our work here is on a different level to Shakespear's,' he continued. 'We're not dealing with would-be kings, like Saud, but petty tribal chieftains. Dozens of them. Each more vicious than the last. And Downe, speaking Arabic, and wearing native dress, negotiated a treaty where adherence to the book would have failed. I don't think you realise, Crabbe, the Bedouin can be the devil to deal with.'

'As we're speaking off the record, Colonel,' Crabbe interceded, 'in my opinion there's only one way to deal with lying, murderous natives. Arab or...'

'We haven't the men to cover the territory of the oil company, much less curb the natives. Downe persuaded Ibn Shalan to not only leave our pipeline alone, but safeguard it from sabotage by other tribes.'

'And you believe Ibn Shalan will honour such an agreement, sir? Sheikh Muhammerah admitted at the last conference that he has as much control over the snakes in the desert as Shalan, and of the two, the snakes are more predictable.'

'I have the treaty bearing Shalan's signature. It clearly delineates the responsibilities he's assumed for the security of the pipeline.'

'May I ask what it is costing us, sir?'

'The usual: horses, livestock, guns.'

'You gave that bandit guns knowing he could use them against us?'

'You're out of order, Major!'

'I assumed we were talking off the record, sir.'

'Our off the record conversation pertained only to Downe, and that remark suggests you're questioning my competency. As your CO, I find your attitude insubordinate and offensive.'

'I apologise, sir. No slur was intended on your judgement or competency as CO.' Crabbe paled. For the first time in his career, he'd spoken first and thought afterwards.

'I gave Ibn Shalan guns so he could defend the oil pipeline. If he should use them to any private ends, you can rest assured they'll be compatible with British interests. He knows we can halt his supply of ammunition whenever we choose.'

'Sir.' Crabbe had never made a friend among the officers in the regiment, but he'd managed to avoid invoking open animosity. His only hope was that Perry wouldn't bear a grudge for long.

'Take this–' Perry threw the report at him '–and remove Downe's name from the charge sheet. Then perhaps we can begin to run this post the way it should be run.'

'Sir.'

'And when you've finished, clean up this base. If I've told the sepoy sergeant once, I've told him a thousand times that the wood that cannot be housed in my woodshed should be stacked in the general stores, not outside my veranda.'

'I'll see to it immediately, sir.'

'Make sure you do, Crabbe. Dismissed.'

Tucking the report under his arm, Crabbe turned and marched out of the office.

Perry watched the door close behind Crabbe, then returned to the window. Crabbe was an ill-bred idiot. It showed in his blundering, graceless ways. The man wasn't a gentleman, let alone officer material. He gazed out over the river and tried to forget the minor irritations of the morning: Maud, and her engagement to what amounted to a civilian; Downe's various misdemeanours; the foul eggs at breakfast. Why did every trifling annoyance in this place blow up to twice the size it would have elsewhere? He watched a steam barge chug its way down river towards the Gulf. Perhaps it was going as far as India.

If Shalan kept his side of the bargain, he might be able to manipulate Downe's triumph and use it as a lever to prise his way back to a post at Regimental HQ. India was hot, but never as downright unbearable as this. He glanced at the thermometer fixed to the window. One hundred and twelve and it was only just after nine. Pulling his handkerchief from his pocket, he mopped his brow, but it proved useless. The moisture came as much from the atmosphere as his body. Even the ceiling fans were more decorative than functional. They only swirled the same hot, damp air around the office. It was like living in a steam bath. Difficult to breathe, to dress, to live; everything rotting around you, even the clothes on your back.

India could be hot, humid, and uncomfortable – he held no illusions about the place in the physical sense – but it had so much more to offer. The companionship of like-minded chaps, polo matches with teams fielding a full complement of officers, plus an ample number of good men in reserve, not scratch sides like this place. In the evening, there was always a dinner party that offered a variety of interesting people, instead of the same tired old faces. And servants – he hadn't realised how much he and Emily relied on them until they came here and found the locals downright uncivilised and untrainable. When they returned to India he'd take up polo seriously again, buy some more ponies. After work, he'd drink in the club without worrying about having to go home to Emily. She'd have other wives to talk to. They wouldn't have to see too much of one another as they'd been forced to here. It was damned unhealthy spending all your time with a woman and, with Maud gone, Emily would need friends around her. India had suited her; she'd been happy there, relieved of domestic duties, busy doing womanly things, leaving him free to relax. Visit the Rag once or twice a week.

He missed the Rag; the Bedouin gypsy girls Mitkhal procured were no compensation for the loss of that pretty little Hindu. She'd looked innocent, but by God, the tricks she knew...

He turned on his heel and returned to his desk,

anger forgotten. He was already drafting the report that would get him back to India. He'd have to give Downe some credit, but he'd stress the whole thing had been his idea. The objective had been achieved, the pipeline secured, and his name was inscribed on the treaty alongside Shalan's. Downe had merely co-signed as the envoy who'd carried the terms he'd drawn up. A communication like that should convince HQ that a chap capable of such a diplomatic victory would be better deployed running the show from base, not put out to grass in a desolate backwater like Mesopotamia.

He'd have to be a bit subtle, but he was a past master at subtlety. Subtlety had gained him a full colonelcy five years before his time. And while he was about it, he'd put in a word about Crabbe; nothing too obvious, just a casual mention that Major Warren Crabbe lacked finesse – polish – and the right kind of experience. That he needed more time in his present post with its small officers' mess, where social blunders were easier to contain. He'd mention that a strong CO with the time and patience to instruct Crabbe in correct and acceptable behaviour would be an advantage. There was always a troublesome Johnny, someone's darling son, the Brass was looking to shelve sideways; an awkward chap guaranteed to make Crabbe's life hell. All he had to do was make some discreet enquiries, finger the right man, and Crabbe would become a fixture in this Arab-lined latrine. Possibly even permanently.

# Chapter Four

*The Shatt-el-Arab, Basra, Friday 3rd July 1914*

The steam launch seemed to have been hovering towards the quay for an eternity and still its engines spluttered with asthmatic wheezes that fixed, rather than propelled, the hull out of the central stream towards the shore.

'May I, sir?' Harry enquired of Perry, who'd refused to leave his carriage. Perry nodded, jerking greasy rivulets of perspiration from beneath his topee. Harry gauged the distance between quay and deck before running and jumping in a single movement that sent him sprawling to the paint-blistered door of the launch's cabin.

'I might have known it would be you.' Maud, dressed in a long-sleeved blue silk shift and wide-brimmed, feather-trimmed, cream straw hat, looked down at him.

'Maud, how marvellous to see you looking so well, and–' he arched his eyebrows as he rose and dusted himself off '–beautiful.'

'My fiancé might hear you. He's bigger than you, and terribly jealous.' Maud batted her eyelashes and twirled her parasol coquettishly.

'In that case, I'll take advantage of his absence and kiss the bride while I have the opportunity.' Harry planted a kiss on her left cheek.

'I saw that, Harry. If you want to kiss and

cuddle a girl, find your own.'

Releasing Maud, Harry turned to his cousin. 'Good God, you've grown a foot across the shoulders and acquired two stone of muscle since I last saw you.'

John fingered the ends of his dark moustache and looked down at Harry's slight figure. 'And you've shrunk.'

'It's the heat,' Harry warned. 'It could happen to you and Maud. Not that it will matter much in your case, but there'll be nothing left of Maud.'

'Well?' Hooking her arm into John's, Maud nestled close to him. 'Do you approve of my choice of husband, Harry?'

'Wholeheartedly, but as for me looking for a girl of my own, there's no point, John. My heart is broken. You've scooped the only catch worth taking this side of London Bridge.'

'I see you haven't forgotten how to flatter, Harry.' Emily bustled towards them, her hat pulled low over her eyes. Harry kissed her cheek, then noticed Charles glowering in the background.

'Basra isn't that bad, Charles.'

'I don't believe you.' Charles smiled. Harry was just the person he needed to see him through the hours ahead that he'd be forced to spend in the company of Emily – and her husband.

'Where's George?' Emily enquired fractiously.

'On the quay. I couldn't wait to see these two reprobates.' Harry laid one hand on John's enormous shoulder, the other on Charles's fractionally shorter, slimmer figure. 'Out tonight? We'll have to make it special. It's John's last night of freedom.'

'Father's arranged the wedding?' Maud queried.

'So rumour has it.' Harry winked at John. 'Barely time enough to say your prayers, let alone change your mind.'

'Harry Downe...' Maud began.

'Are we going to stay on this boat all day?' Emily was at breaking point. Before dawn, Charles had created the most awful scene in her cabin and now she was faced with an ordeal of introductions that promised to be even worse torture.

'Do forgive me, Mrs Perry. I've been incredibly selfish, keeping you waiting while I talk.' Harry offered her his arm. 'If the gangplank is down I'll escort you to your carriage. There's no need to concern yourself with your luggage. I've told my bearer to take care of it.'

They left the cabin for the blinding, asphyxiating heat on deck.

'Dear God!'

'Beautiful, isn't it, Charles?' Harry looked out at the palm-fringed mud banks, and low, flat-roofed buildings.

'I'm used to India. Wharves in the middle of town and all that.'

'This is the middle of town. The centre of all social and industrial life for miles, but it's not at its best. We take longer midday breaks here than India. When it's cooler the town will wake up and there'll be a few people around.'

'Will that make a difference?' Charles enquired.

'I'm glad you haven't enlightened him,' Harry whispered to Emily. 'It's going to be fun showing him the sights.'

78

'Emily.' The colonel unbent sufficiently to step outside his carriage and kiss his wife's forehead. 'Good trip?'

'Yes, George.'

'Maud.' He greeted his daughter in like fashion. 'And this is...?'

'Captain John Mason, Father.' Maud pulled John forward. 'The most wonderful man in the world.'

'I'm pleased to meet you, sir.' John offered the colonel his hand.

'Likewise.' The colonel shook John's hand vigorously.

Maud smiled. Her father didn't appear to be displeased with her fiancé. Now all she had to do was persuade John to keep wearing the uniform she'd bullied him into donning for this crucial initial meeting.

'Colonel Perry, may I present my good friend, Captain Charles Reid.' John effected the introduction Emily had been dreading.

'Glad to meet you,' the colonel barked. 'Knew your father. Good man. Good soldier.'

'Kind of you say so, sir,' Charles managed.

'Well, can't hang about here in this heat. We'll go up in separate carriages, but lunch together. One sharp, my bungalow. All invited. You too, Downe.'

Emily sat beside the colonel, John shut the carriage door, the sepoy whipped the horses, and Maud waved, blowing kisses as the carriage turned the corner. Harry waited until John joined them, then whistled. Mitkhal hauled a second carriage close to where they were standing.

'A landau!' Charles exclaimed. 'Old, but in superb condition. Where did you find a turnout like this, Harry?'

'It belonged to a sheikh who hit a run of bad luck. John, there's no need to look hangdog. It's a ten-minute ride to the European quarter; if appearances are anything to go by, Maud will wait for you.'

'I wasn't looking hangdog,' John protested in the face of his friends' combined laughter.

Harry climbed into the carriage, pulled out his cigarette case, and offered it around. 'After the wedding, Charles, you'll be bunking with one of the lieutenants. Peter Smythe. Don't worry, he's the right sort.'

'If that means he's a close friend of yours, pity help me.'

'You're a close friend.'

'I had no choice in the matter.'

'I'll give you a suitable reply to that when I've had time to think of one.' Harry lit his cigarette and tossed Charles his lighter. 'You're welcome to my bungalow for as long as it suits, John. There are two bedrooms so we can all sleep there tonight, but I thought you'd prefer to honeymoon in my place rather than impose on your in-laws. Mrs Perry's an angel, but your father-in-law – let's say he's not the person I'd choose to take along on my bridal trip.'

'Given your record of loving and leaving girls, Harry, I'm amazed you've taken your thoughts as far as a honeymoon,' Charles commented.

'It's good of you to offer,' John interrupted, before the conversation turned to the topic of

Harry's escapades. He hadn't forgotten his cousin's brief engagement to his sister. 'But where are you going to sleep after tonight?'

'I'll find somewhere.'

Charles removed his helmet and wiped the sweat from his brow. 'Who is she, another Christina?'

'I've learnt my lesson. No more married women – at least not those married to other men,' Harry amended. Strange how quickly he'd come to think of Furja as his wife.

'Harry, I've a problem with my best man,' John broke in, covering Charles's embarrassment at the mention of married women.

'You've decided to break with convention and have two.'

'No, Charles...'

'Is leaving before dawn tomorrow,' Charles interrupted.

'You can't.' Harry protested. 'The wedding's not until 11, and then there's the reception in the mess. Not to mention the fun I've lined up for us once John's sobering influence is out of the way.'

'No can stay.' Charles forced a laugh. 'It would mean spending at least a week here, and from what I've seen' – he peered beneath the landau's fringed shade at the fly-spattered, broiling street – 'this isn't the place to revive a weary soldier after a spell in India. Not when he has the option of visiting the West End.'

'What are you babbling on about? You can't leave until the ship you came in on sails out. That won't be for three or four days.'

'The *Egra's* going out on the first tide tomorrow.'

'But the liners always berth in the Gulf for at least three days,' Harry insisted.

'Not this time.' Charles extinguished his cigarette in the brass ashtray sunk into the leather upholstery. 'The captain called us into the salon this morning. Some Archduke or other has been assassinated in the Balkans...'

'They're always assassinating archdukes in the Balkans,' Harry broke in.

'Not Austrian ones,' Charles said. 'There's talk of war.'

'There's been talk of war for months, years if you're referring to the Balkans,' Harry said dismissively.

'I wholeheartedly agree with you.' Charles had enough problems without adding to them by arguing the intricacies of Balkan politics with Harry. 'But the good old Peninsula and Oriental Shipping Line, God bless her gilded lounges, has got the wind up. The captain's been ordered to proceed forthwith for home, and forthwith means the minute she's loaded, which will be first tide tomorrow. If this assassination does stir things up, there's no telling when the next boat will arrive, and I'm not prepared to take the chance on one turning up soon. Unlike John, I have no beautiful Maud to amuse me while I wait.'

'This is John's wedding you'll be missing,' Harry said. 'He won't be having another one.'

'I sincerely hope not,' John commented.

'I grant you this place looks bloody awful,' Harry coaxed, refusing to be placated by John's good humour, 'but it's not that bad, and you'll have me as your guide. Come on, Charles, the fleshpots of London can wait; we'll sail home together. Get drunk every night on the boat.'

Charles made a great show of settling his helmet on his head. He wanted to tell Harry the real reason that lay behind his flight, but not in an open carriage travelling through a public street.

'Six months' home leave will soon fly, Harry,' John defended Charles.

'You're only talking about a week...'

'If there's trouble in the Med, who knows how long we could be stuck here,' John pointed out. 'I always hoped one of you would be around to be my best man when the time came but it's a lot to ask either of you right now. So, if you want to sail with Charles, I'll understand. I'm sure to find someone here who'll be prepared to fill in.'

'What do you say, Harry?' Charles demanded. 'England on the *Egra* with me, or best man here?'

'I'm staying.'

'But you could lose a lot more than a week's leave.' Charles suddenly realised he faced a long, lonely voyage home.

'Oh what the hell, I may as well tell you. I'm thinking of resigning my commission. The army and me – well, we aren't exactly cut out for one another.'

'Have you discussed this with your CO?' John asked.

'Perry? Not bloody likely.'

'Is this one of your spur of the moment things, Harry?'

'It's been at the back of my mind for a while. But seeing you two made me realise I haven't been too happy here.'

83

'I'm not surprised,' Charles observed.

'Harry, you're 25, hardly a young man on the threshold of life,' John reminded. 'What will you do with yourself?'

'Go into Father's bank. He's always wanted me there.'

'But you hated the idea.'

'The army changed my mind.'

'Harry.' John adopted the paternalistic approach he'd developed to deal with recalcitrant patients. 'Are you sure you're doing the right thing?'

'No. But whatever else, you can't accuse me of not trying to find my niche. A year in medical school. Two in Sandhurst. India. Here.'

'And, if you and the bank don't work out–' John ventured.

'I'll dig a canal somewhere, or breed chickens on one of my father's farms. Write poetry; sing comic songs in the music halls. I'll think of something. I always have.'

'That's your problem, Harry,' Charles interposed. 'You think of everything, but stick at nothing. You can't carry on drifting, doing whatever the mood dictates.'

'That's a bit strong, Charles,' John admonished him.

'Look at it this way.' Harry exhaled a thin stream of smoke. Despite the movement of the carriage, the grey fug hovered in the air between them. 'You two were lucky. You hit on the right thing straight away. You couldn't have possibly been anything other than a doctor, John – and you, Charles, just look at that uniform. I couldn't get mine to look like that if I had a battalion of bearers pressing and polishing in my quarters.'

'I agree, you would have made a poor doctor,' John concurred. 'But a bank clerk, sitting in an office all day, simply isn't you.'

'We won't know whether it's me or not until I try. But that's enough about me. Tell me about Maud and yourself. Where did you meet?'

Knowing better than to try to get any sense out of Harry when he was in one of his evasive moods, John looked to Charles for support. When Charles turned aside, he answered Harry's question. There wasn't anything else he could do.


*Basra, Friday 3rd July 1914*

Reed shutters had been pulled over the unglazed, stone lattice windows, dulling the glare of the mid-afternoon sun to sepia shadows that were kind to the faded hangings and simple furnishings. Harry and Furja lay side by side, naked beneath the gauze mosquito net that tented their couch, but neither slept. The only movement was that of Harry's right arm as he lifted a cigarette to his mouth. He smoked mechanically, without enjoyment, while mulling over his conversation with John and Charles.

'You are worrying of something, my husband.'

'Thinking, not worrying.' He rolled from his back on to his stomach. Keeping his cigarette clenched between his teeth, he pushed his palms against the roughcast wall at the head of the bed, tightening the aching muscles in his shoulders.

Furj a watched him for a moment before rolling

85

beside him. They lay there in silence, broiling in the oppressive heat.

'What is it that you are thinking of?'

'My leave.'

'It is time for you to go back to your country.' She ran her fingers from the base of his spine, finally burying them in the thick curls at the nape of his neck.

'I'm not going back to England.' Reaching down the side of the bed, he extinguished his cigarette on a clay tablet. 'Not immediately, and possibly not for some time.'

'I don't understand.' Furja moved closer, wrapping her arms and legs around his body. 'You said after our wedding that you'd be leaving soon.'

He pulled away from her and rummaged in the folds of the abba he'd flung to the floor when he'd undressed. Extracting his cigarette case, he rolled on his side and stared at her. Long, slim, olive-brown body; thick black hair streaming over the tarnished gold silk of the pillows. Rounded, and considering the rest of her, surprisingly full breasts, crowned with coffee-coloured nipples. The inward curve of her stomach leading to the henna-dyed triangle between her thighs. And her eyes: enormous, liquid pools, watching him, accepting his admiration without any false modesty, or puritanical shame. So beautiful, and his – for the moment.

He kissed her lips. She responded, pushing her knee between his legs and stroking his back with quick, sensuous movements.

He wanted to tell her he was staying because of her. It was the truth, but the knowledge that she loved a tall Sherif with a black moustache, not him, silenced him. She'd married him because her father had forced her to; it was simply his bad luck that he'd grown fond of her.

'You don't mind if I stay on for a while?' Releasing her, he opened his cigarette case.

'No, I don't mind. Do you want me to return to my father, or remain here?'

He dropped the cigarette he'd extracted. 'Don't you want to stay with me?' His mouth was dry at the thought of her disappearing from his life, possibly for ever.

'You are my husband. It is for you to tell me what I must do. I thought our marriage would have ended by now. My father...'

'To hell with your father. Do you want it to be over?'

'You will never, never, say that again!' Her temper flared. 'My father...'

Catching her hands, he pinned her to the bed. 'Your father was only interested in his precious guns. He didn't give a damn about you. I was the idiot who supplied them. You the price he paid. The price I had to take, whether I wanted it or not.'

'You gave my father the guns to guard your beloved pipeline. He paid the debt with my body because that was all he had to give. You've used it. If you no longer want it, divorce me and the affair will be forgotten except for the men of my tribe who will die wielding your guns, guarding your property. But their deaths won't matter to you, will they, Harry? What's one more dead Arab to a Ferenghi?'

'They matter to me. You matter. Damn it all, woman, I'm asking you to stay with me. I want to spend my leave with you. But you won't tell me what you feel. What you think. To hell with it, Furja, what do you want from me?'

'Nothing. I married you because I had no choice. Now I am your wife, I am yours to do with as you wish. You own me, so it is for you to make the decisions. For both of us.' She stared at him, wide-eyed, defiant.

He looked into her face, searching for something. When he didn't find it, he released her. Retrieving his cigarette, he lit it, lay on his back, and studied the pattern of stick shadows the shades were making on the ceiling, while waiting for the fury she'd kindled in him to cool.

She'd reinforced Charles's observations. He had never made a conscious decision in his life. He'd drifted, consistently taking the easiest, most attractive options as they presented themselves. If anything threatened his comfort, he simply ignored it. He'd refused to heed the warnings John and his tutors had given him in medical college because knuckling down to work would have interfered with his social life. As a result, he'd been asked to leave at the end of the first year. He couldn't even be proud of passing out of Sandhurst. He'd succeeded only because he was his father's son and General Reid's godson. And, after Sandhurst, he hadn't worked. Not like Charles. The polo- and mess-centred life at Regimental Headquarters had swallowed him whole, barely allowing him time to make the odd sortie into native low life. He'd listened politely enough

88

to the high-minded lectures the senior officers had given on work, duty, and setting an example to the men, but he'd gone his own sweet way once the pep talks were finished.

And it had been a sweet way until the Christina incident had broken the delightful, thoughtless thread of his social life (he'd had no life other than social in India). Even after he'd been exiled to Basra he'd disregarded Perry's advice to seek career redemption through hard work. Instead, he'd flung himself wholeheartedly, and profitably, into gambling with the natives in the bazaars. He'd done nothing worthwhile, nothing he could be proud of. And now where was he going – back to England as he'd told Charles and John? To a boring office in a bank he didn't give a damn for and a claustrophobic, tightly governed social life, which meant an endless, tedious circle of balls and house parties. And all the while, he would be searching for a soulmate – a more sympathetic, less frigid version of Lucy, or another Christina who slept with any and every man who winked at her.

Was that really what he wanted, when he had Furja?

He felt her fingers massaging his thighs. Her hand crept upwards, slipping between his legs, cupping his testicles. Moving quickly, he caught it.

'You are tired?' she enquired innocently.

'No, you little devil, I'm not tired. I want a straight answer from you. Do you want me to stay, here, in this house, married to you?'

She looked at him without answering.

'Well?' he demanded hotly.

'You have to learn, Harry, the Bedawi have more ways of answering a question than with words.' Closing her mouth over his she kissed him, deeply, thoroughly, her tongue probing between his lips, her hands fluttering confidently, assuredly over his skin. He plunged headlong into the private world of eroticism she'd created, and could now conjure at will. Thoughts, problems, worries, slid – so much superfluous baggage – from his mind.

Later – he'd sort out his future later. When the present didn't demand all of his attention.

*American Mission, Basra, Friday 3rd July 1914*

Angela Wallace had no illusions about her looks. She deplored her lack of height (she was barely four foot ten), her figure tended to a plumpness she only managed to keep in check by abstaining from the cake and biscuits she adored, and her features, although regular, were undeniably plain. She lifted the candle and peered in the mirror, hoping to see more. But the same oval face, brown eyes, medium-sized nose, medium-sized mouth, and fair skin spattered with a dash of freckles stared back at her as they'd done that morning. Only her hair had any pretensions to beauty, and she spent a wicked amount of time styling it into the fashionable coiffures she copied from the illustrated magazines Mrs Butler's sister sent out every month from New York.

Dressed in her underclothes and a coarse linen wrap that covered her from throat to ankle, she sat at the dressing table in the cramped box room that served as her bedroom and pinned one shimmering chestnut wave after another on to the crown of her head.

Lieutenant Smythe had called that morning. She'd glimpsed his uniformed figure from the window of the classroom where she taught the native Christian, Jewish, and Persian children who attended the mission school. Tonight she would see, talk to, and, she hoped, dance with Peter Smythe. She spent far more time thinking about him than she should. The sketches she used to illustrate her drawing class bore more than a passing resemblance to his lean, raw-boned figure. Whenever she drew a face, his high forehead, wide eyes, and full mouth smiled up at her from her pad.

She glanced at the invitation he'd brought. It was a pity she had nothing grander to wear than her white cotton afternoon dress. She suppressed an unchristian pang of envy for Maud Perry's wardrobe. She should count her blessings, not covet Maud's good fortune. She'd had loving parents and an idyllic childhood in the small town of Fairfield in Connecticut. There'd never been much money, but somehow that hadn't mattered. Her father's parish had encompassed a scattered but tightly knit farming community and although silk dresses and mahogany furniture had been in short supply, food, books, and necessities had not. She hadn't seen real poverty until she was 15, when her father had left Connecticut to found a Presbyterian mission in Kuwait.

The only tears she'd shed on leaving America had been for her brother, Theo, who'd stayed to finish his medical studies at Harvard. For two years, she'd worked alongside her parents. They'd set up a school and a children's clinic; all had progressed well until an outbreak of cholera had decimated the mission. The natives who worked for them succumbed first, then, three months before her 17th birthday, her parents died within 24 hours of one another.

Sick, tired, alone for the first time in her life, she'd wanted to die with them. Not even knowing how to withdraw money from her father's slender bank account, she had thrown herself on the mercy of a bachelor German merchant in the town. He'd telegraphed Theodore in America, the Reverend Butler in Basra, and, mindful of her reputation, found her a room in the house of one his married subordinates.

The Reverend Butler reached her first. He closed the mission, withdrew the money from her father's account, packed her few belongings, and bundled her on to a ship bound for Basra where Mrs Butler had welcomed her into their home as if she'd been their own child. They'd offered her a teaching post and when Theo arrived, six months later, persuaded Doctor Picard to take him on as his assistant in the Lansing Memorial Hospital, which the Church also financed.

She and Theo missed their parents, but they had one another, and although they might wish the bank account the Reverend Butler had opened for them were larger, they were content. Theo was a good doctor. In a year or two, when they both had more experience and enough savings to finance the setting up of a practice for Theo, they intended to return to America and pick up the threads of their life in Connecticut.

She jabbed a hairpin into the palm of her hand. Usually she liked daydreaming about Connecticut, its green, sunlit summers and crisp, snow-filled winters, but with the invitation lying next to her elbow all she could think of was Lieutenant Smythe. If she returned to America, she would never see him again...

'Angela, can I come in?'

'Of course, Theo.' She faced her brother with her mouth full of hairgrips.

'Mrs Butler helped me to pick this out for your birthday. I know it's not for ten days, but the chances are we won't be invited to another party for months, so I thought you'd like to wear it tonight.' He opened a large, flat box and pulled out an ostrich feather fan and a green silk gown, beaded at the hem and bodice.

'Oh, Theo!' She released the wave she'd been securing, and pulled the grips from her mouth. Her hair cascaded halfway down her back as she rushed across the room to hug him. 'It's the most beautiful dress I've ever seen. You shouldn't have. It must have cost a fortune.'

'It didn't.' He flicked his dark hair out of his eyes. 'Mrs Butler bought the silk at the bazaar and asked the Jewish tailor to copy that brown dress of hers you've always admired.'

'But the size...'

'We stole one of your work dresses from the laundry.'

Holding up the dress, she pranced before the mirror, dancing backwards and forwards, trying to view as much of herself as possible in such a

93

small glass. She saw him laughing at her, stopped dancing, and kissed his cheek.

'You'd better get dressed, or we'll be late.'

She laid the dress gently on the bed and retrieved her hairpins.

He hovered in the doorway. 'Sis, about tonight. I know how you feel about Peter Smythe – don't look at me like that.' He parried her mute glare of reproach. 'Everyone's noticed how you blush and stammer whenever he's around.'

'I don't...'

'Sis, I like him.'

'But?' she demanded defensively.

'There's no future for you with him. You do know that?'

'If it's money you're worried about, Theo, he knows I have none.'

'Peter Smythe has talked to you about money?'

'No, but we talk about books. He loves art, particularly the Italian masters, and we have the same taste in poetry. Peter admires the English Romantics, Shelley and Keats and–' She fell silent, realising she'd said too much.

'Reverend Butler told me that Peter has no private means either, sis, and before you say anything, we weren't talking behind your back. We're concerned for you.'

'I don't mind how long it takes. If he asks...'

'He won't, sis. He's a British officer, and like marries like. When the time comes he'll marry the daughter or sister of a fellow officer.'

'Is that what he told you?' she challenged.

'It's common sense. This party tonight is for Maud Perry. She's marrying a captain in the

Indian Army. When he's ready, Peter Smythe will look around the British posts as this fellow has, not the American Missions.'

'Maud's engaged. How wonderful.' Determinedly, Angela ignored Theo's final comment. The smile was prompted more by relief than by happiness for Maud. She would have sooner died than admit it, but she'd been worried by Maud Perry's golden-curled, cherry-lipped beauty and elegant wardrobe. She couldn't see how any man could fail to fall in love with Maud. And with Maud and Peter Smythe living in such close proximity...

'Sis?'

'Sorry, I was miles away.'

'About as far as the Basra mess?' Conceding defeat, Theo stepped outside. 'I hate to see you disappointed, Angela, but if you set your sights on marrying Peter Smythe, you will be.'

'With this to wear?' She picked up the dress. 'I couldn't possibly be disappointed with a single thing, Theo. Thank you.'

## Chapter Five

*Basra, Friday 3rd July 1914*

Half a dozen bottles of beer procured Peter a seat next to Angela at dinner but, intimidated by the presence of his fellow officers, the intimacy nurtured during discussions on art and literature at 'mission socials' rapidly dissipated in a welter of self-conscious embarrassment. It was as much as Peter could do to reply to Angela's gentle enquiries after his health in inarticulate monosyllables.

It wasn't only the disapproving glances Amey and the colonel sent his way; Angela herself was strangely altered. Dazzling, in a magnificent evening dress and complicated coiffure, she shone like royalty, beautiful and just as unattainable. Despondent, scarcely daring to raise his eyes to hers, he sank deeper into depression as the evening progressed.

Angela was as overwhelmed as Peter, but more skilled at concealing her feelings. She smiled at him and the room in general, while ignoring the condescending glances bestowed on herself and the other Americans. John sat across the table from Theo, and the food grew cold on their plates as they discussed the merits of irrigating kidneys as a treatment for cholera, a topic that disgusted Maud.

There weren't enough ladies to 'go round', and the talk at the far end of the table where the bachelors were seated, Harry and Charles among them, was centred on the probability of war. Resolutely ignoring them, the ladies exchanged opinions on the competence, or otherwise, of the few tailors in Basra brave enough to try their hand at European fashions.

While dessert was being served, Major Crabbe hit the table to emphasise a point, sending the crockery and cutlery rattling. Amused by Crabbe's gaffe, Harry glanced at Charles and saw him watching Emily. He turned aside. Charles was playing a dangerous game. He knew exactly how dangerous. He had once looked at another man's wife the way Charles was gazing at Emily and had paid for his infatuation with his career prospects. A price he suspected Charles would find too rich.

The meal ended, the ladies retired to the small lounge for coffee. The chamber pots were passed around, then the brandy and cigars. The orderlies cleared the table, the ladies returned, and the padre's wife obliged those who wanted to dance by playing waltzes on the mess piano.

Harry and Charles burst out laughing when Peter fell over his own feet in his eagerness to reach Angela, only to lose out to Theo.

'Better luck next time,' Harry commiserated.

'If there is a next time,' Peter muttered. 'She doesn't know I exist.'

'She does,' Harry teased. 'You dribbled gravy over her dress at dinner.'

'I didn't, did I? Oh God...'

'Before you shoot yourself, I was joking. My God, Smythe, I've seen some hopeless cases, but you're terminally afflicted.' Opening the veranda windows, Harry stepped outside. The night air was no fresher and only marginally cooler than inside, and the mosquitoes were biting. Closing the windows behind him, he lit a cigar to keep the insects at bay, offering one to Peter when he joined him.

'If I could be sure of my captaincy I'd ask Angela to marry me tonight,' Peter confided. 'But even if by some miracle she should say yes, I can't keep myself, much less a wife on a lieutenant's pay. Unlike you, I've no private means. My father was killed on active service in Africa when I was three, and my mother only has her widow's pension. My father's name got me a commission, but the vicar back home had to get up a subscription to pay for my uniform.'

'Joking aside, Angela's not used to our way of life. She might not be happy stuck on an Indian Army outpost miles from anywhere.' Striking a match on the window frame, Harry lit Peter's cigar.

'She survived living in a mission in Kuwait.'

'Then I stand corrected.' Harry mused on the irony of him, of all the men, daring to advise Peter on a woman's suitability as a wife. 'If you can't live without her, then don't. You could ask her to get engaged on the understanding you'll marry when you get your captaincy.'

'That could take years.'

'Not if there's a war.'

'You really think there will be one?'

'It's a possibility.'

The padre's wife played the final notes of the waltz.

Peter opened the window to the sound of polite applause. 'Thanks for the chat, Harry, must dash.' Tossing his half-smoked cigar over the rail, he charged in, hoping to waylay Angela before the next dance.

Harry stared down at the lights in the Arab quarter. Was Furja awake? He'd told her he wouldn't be back before tomorrow afternoon, but he was tempted to go to her now. Steal through the narrow streets, knock up Farik, slip into the bedroom they shared…

'I take it you're hiding from the nauseating sight of young love that abounds in this mess.' Charles joined him.

'Just wanted some peace and quiet.' Harry offered his cigar box.

'Smythe almost knocked me over. Does he always behave like an ass?'

'Only when Americans are around. Or, to be more accurate, one American in particular.'

'Just like John with Maud.'

'Do I detect a note of jealousy?'

'Probably,' Charles conceded.

'There are dozens of Mauds in England.'

'It's not a Maud I want.'

'What do you want, Charles?' Harry asked.

'That night out you promised.' Charles helped himself to a cigar. 'Anywhere will do as long as Perry isn't in the vicinity.'

'He did come on a bit strong. "Got your promotion at Christmas, what?"' Harry's rendition of Perry's voice was uncannily accurate.

'And what the devil was all that nonsense about medical men getting promotion every time they dangle their stethoscope in front of a general?' Charles demanded. 'When I tried to tell him John was given his captaincy a full six months before me, the man wouldn't even listen.'

'Quiet!' Harry pulled Charles along the veranda. Perry stood, swaying in a doorway six feet away from them. 'It's time we went to bed,' Harry shouted in Perry's direction before leading the way to his quarters. 'I think Perry would have preferred you for a son-in-law,' he revealed when they were safely within doors. 'Your father's a general. You're a professional and therefore unlikely to do anything as iniquitous as return to civilian life. He wanted Maud to be an army wife.'

'John has better prospects and a larger inheritance than me.' Charles threw himself down on a rattan sofa.

'Not in the regiment, and the regiment is the only thing that matters to Perry.' Harry turned up the lamp. 'All the comforts of home apart from my bearer. I've given him the night off. Brandy or whisky?'

'Whisky, please.' Charles pushed a cushion beneath his head.

Harry poured two generous measures of whisky and handed one to Charles. 'Do me a favour: as you're determined to go home tomorrow, take some letters for me.'

'Is there any point when you'll be home yourself soon?'

Harry stretched out on the second sofa. Swinging his feet on to one arm, his head on the other, he rested his glass on his chest. 'I don't know when I'll be back.'

'I'm sorry I got het up this morning, exaggerating the problems and all that, but I don't want to stay here...'

'Whatever's going on between you and Emily Perry, is your own affair – business,' Harry corrected.

'John told you.'

'He didn't have to. I saw you looking at her. I've had some experience. Christina...'

'Emily's not Christina!' Charles exclaimed and,

swinging his feet to the floor, he sat up. 'We're not having a sordid little affair. I love her and she loves me.'

'Then God help the pair of you.'

'I didn't want it to happen.' Charles reached for his whisky. 'Not like this, not with another man's wife.'

'The problem is it never happens the way you imagined it would.'

'What?' John walked through the door.

'Love, but then you wouldn't know anything about love, would you?' Charles taunted. 'The party's still going on and you've deserted the ladies.'

'Maud's having an early night.' Sensing the atmosphere, John trod carefully.

'Grab a chair and a glass and we'll celebrate your last night of freedom,' Harry offered.

'The man can't wait to fasten the ball and chain.' Charles finished his whisky.

'Who wouldn't with a gaoler like Maud?' John poured himself a small measure.

'Bridegroom's taking it easy.' Charles winked at Harry as he took the bottle from John.

'I don't intend to crawl through tomorrow with a colossal hangover.'

'Hangovers in this heat are no fun.' Harry drained his glass. 'Well, where do you want to go?'

'No Rags, no native brothels, and no low-life bars,' John said firmly. 'I've seen what your sense of humour can do to a bachelor night. Johnny Leigh...'

'Behaved like an ass,' Charles snapped.

'I'm not disputing that, Charles. But I remember the identity of the donkeys who led him to the whisky-filled trough.'

'Don't look at me, it was Harry's doing,' Charles protested.

'I don't mind taking the blame.' Harry set his glass on a side table. 'But that doesn't solve the problem of tonight.'

'A quiet little bar with a belly dancer for John.'

'I don't want a belly dancer,' John demurred.

'Basra isn't India. You can drink in the mess or the Basra club; neither has dancing girls. For those, you have to visit the coffee shops, and the devout Moslems who own them won't sell you alcohol for love or money, and the bars that are run by the non-devout Moslems or Armenians are rough, even for me.'

'Are you saying you haven't found a native bar worth visiting in Basra?' Charles was incredulous.

'I drink in the mess.'

'I don't believe it. John, did you hear? Harry's trying to tell us he leads the quiet life of your average officer.'

'I gamble occasionally in the bazaar.'

'But you don't visit bars.'

'I've just spent the last five minutes telling you there are none.' Harry clamped his hand over his glass to stop Charles refilling it.

'My God, you're serious.' Charles stared at him.

'About the non-existent bars, yes.'

'It's not just the bars. There was a time when you would have been on your second bottle by now.'

'Looks like this posting's done you good, Harry,' John commented. 'No bars, moderate drinking, and now you're going into your father's bank.'

'I've decided against going into the bank.'

'But this morning you said...'

'I hadn't thought it through this morning. I've decided to hang on to my commission. Stay here for a while.'

'That's great news,' John congratulated him. 'With that attitude you could even get posted back to HQ.'

'I don't want to. When I say, "stay here", I mean it.'

Charles frowned. 'You like this fly-ridden hole enough to spend your leave here?'

'Yes.'

'Who is she, Harry?' Charles demanded. 'And don't insult us with that innocent look. We grew up with you. You disappeared this afternoon, went out before we slept, and didn't reappear until after we woke up. And during that time, you decided to forget about home leave and your father's bank. Come on, out with it. Who is she?'

Perry's warnings about keeping his marriage secret were to the forefront of Harry's mind, but there was no way he could remain in Basra without telling John, Charles, and his family the reason why he wanted to stay. He faced Charles. 'My wife.'

*The Perrys' bungalow, Friday 3rd July 1914*

Emily sat before her dressing table, unpinning her hair. Strand after strand floated to her waist as the collection of hairpins on the Doulton tray

103

grew thicker. After she removed the last pin, she ran her fingers over her scalp to make sure there were none left before she brushed out the heavy waves, counting the strokes as her Nanny had taught her in childhood.

She was dreading George joining her. On their return from the mess, he'd slumped into a chair in the drawing room, and leered, 'You go ahead, Emily, I won't be long.'

Bitter experience had taught her what that remark inevitably preceded.

A knock at the door startled her. Her hand jerked and she banged the ivory hairbrush against her head. She cried out as the brush fell to the floor.

'You all right?'

She looked in the mirror. George was behind her, eyes glazed, brandy fumes heavy on his rancid breath. 'Quite all right, thank you.'

'Pity about that Mason chap, leaving the army.' George fell on the bed and fiddled with his boots. 'I hoped Maud would marry a serving soldier.'

'I didn't.'

'Whyever not?' He looked at her, hurt, bewildered.

'Because John will give her a settled home in England with friends and relatives within easy reach. She won't have to put up with this heat, the filth, the rotting damp...' Tears coursed down her cheeks.

'Damn it all, Emily. Don't you ever think of anyone other than yourself? You've been away for the best part of six months.'

She struggled to regain her composure. 'I'm

tired. It's probably the journey. Would you mind sleeping in your dressing room, just for tonight?'

'Of course I bloody mind. Blast it, Emily; it's not healthy for a man to live like a monk.'

'Please, George, just give me a little time.'

'I'll give you as long as it takes Harriet to undress you, not one minute longer.' He stormed out of the room.

Emily stared into her glass. Only that morning she'd told Charles she wanted to resume her married life. To continue playing the part of the colonel's wife. How could she have forgotten George's piggy eyes, his fat, dimpled hands, his slack, wet lips...?

'I'm sorry, Miss Emily.' Harriet, the Cockney girl who'd travelled out to India with Emily when she was a bride and remained to nurse her through the trials of her married life, bustled in. 'I shouldn't have stayed so long with Miss Maud. The colonel's in a right tizz with me. But I told him straight, it's Miss Maud. She's that excited.' Harriet unfastened the hooks at the back of Emily's dress. 'I don't believe she'll get a wink of sleep, but then–' Harriet stared dreamily into space '–I wouldn't if I were her. Captain Mason's so handsome and kind. It's not many that think of others, but he does. Why, when Mrs Major Cleck-Heaton's ayah was doubled up with stomach pains, I told her straight, "Go to Captain Mason, he'll see you right." And he did. He might be a gentleman, but he's not too much of a gentleman to forget there are others beneath him, even heathens.'

Harriet spread a sheet on the floor and guided Emily on the centre of it before sliding the gown

105

over her shoulders and onto the sheet. 'If you'll step out, Miss Emily, I'll hang it away.' She lifted the mass of silk into her arms, running her fingers lightly over the silver- and pearl-beaded bodice to make sure none of the holding threads had worked loose. 'This is a beautiful dress,' she prattled, unperturbed by her mistress's silence. 'Not as stunning as Miss Maud's wedding dress, of course. That really is something. I told Miss Maud, you'll be a beautiful bride but your mother – well, I don't think anyone could hold a candle to you, Miss Emily. Not on the day you married the colonel.'

Emily placed the dress on a hanger, and folded a muslin cover over it before stowing it in the camphor wood wardrobe. 'But what a bride Miss Maud will make for the captain tomorrow. It's kind of you to ask me to the church. I'll be that proud.'

Emily slipped her corset's straps from her shoulders and grasped the bedpost.

'You're going to have to breathe in more than that, Miss Emily; there, I've got it started. It'll be downhill all the way now, as Captain Reid says. Lord, miss, this is soaking. Shall I wash it?'

'Please, Harriet.' Emily massaged her waist, cramped and aching from the pressure of the steel and whalebone stays. Harriet took a starched, white nightgown from inside the wardrobe and handed it to her mistress. Emily pulled it over her head, and allowed the empty sleeves and loose, un-waisted skirt to fall full length. Removing her chemise under cover of the gown, she kicked it aside. 'You can wash that too, Harriet.'

Perry barged in, the smell of brandy intensified

106

by fresh stains on his shirtfront.

'That'll be all, Harriet.'

'Very good, Miss Emily. Sir.' Harriet bobbed a curtsy.

'You give that girl too much latitude, Emily,' he slurred as Harriet closed the door. 'She takes advantage. We'd be better off with natives.'

'Harriet has been with me for 19 years, George. I have no intention of giving her notice now.'

'You'll have it your own way, I suppose. You always do.'

Turning her back, she rested her foot on a stool, reached beneath her nightgown and unfastened her velvet-grip stocking supporter. 'Another thing, George, don't ever walk in here again when Harriet's undressing me. Not without knocking.'

'You had enough time.'

'If I'd had enough time would I still be taking my stockings off?' She glared at him, intending to freeze his temper, until she saw the light of brandy-spawned madness in his eyes. The last time he'd been like this was when the Rag in India had closed during a typhoid scare. She shouldn't have argued back. Not without ascertaining his mood. Charles had spoiled her, led her to expect the same level of intelligence and humanity from every man.

'You've forgotten your wifely duties.' The slur disappeared with the advent of anger.

Frozen by guilt, she wondered if she or Charles had done something to arouse George's suspicions.

'Lost your tongue?' he goaded in his parade-ground voice.

107

She rolled the silk stockings from her legs with unsteady hands. When he went into his dressing room, she pulled down her drawers, and folded them onto a stool. She heard him fumbling in his wardrobe and wondered what he was doing. His bearer usually saw to his uniform in the morning. Wrapping her arms around herself, she closed her eyes. Perhaps if she tried to pretend he was Charles...

'Lie down.' He stood beside the bed, his hairy stomach bulging above his spindly legs. She slid between the crisp, linen sheets, holding the hem of her nightdress down with her toes, clinging to the forlorn hope that he'd fall into a brandy-induced stupor the moment his head touched the pillow. The bedsprings groaned as he sat beside her; there was an ominous plop when he shifted his weight and tossed his drawers to the floor.

Clenching her fists, she tensed herself. It would soon be over. Not long and he'd sleep. Leaving her alone in the darkness. Alone with her thoughts of Charles – no, she had to forget Charles. Forget he was close, that if she cried out he would hear her.

George's fingers, wet, fumbling, pawed at the lace collar of her nightgown. She lifted her hands, but too impatient to wait, he wrenched it open, snapping the lace and sending pearl buttons flying. One landed on her neck, bruising her. She cried out, and he thrust his hand against her mouth.

'No noise, old girl. You know I hate noise.'

She nodded dumbly, gagging at the salt taste of his sweat on her lips.

'Your nightdress.'

'Can we have the light out?' she begged.

'Down, not out. Have to see what we're doing.' He reached for the oil lamp on the side table. The light dimmed as he lowered the wick. 'Your nightdress,' he repeated.

She sat up; he pulled it over her head and threw it on to the bedpost before pressing her on her back. She complied. It was her duty. Her mother had stressed that on the eve of her wedding. The wife submitted to the husband. It was what was expected of her, the natural result of feminine weakness. In return, the wife was cared for in every sense of the word. Until India, and Charles, she'd not only believed it, she'd lived by it. But now it was so very, very hard.

George heaved himself on top of her. She gasped as his weight pressed the breath from her lungs. He pinched her nipples before his fingers travelled downwards, prodding and poking at her tense body. She tried to divorce herself from what was happening by closing her eyes and concentrating on Charles – India – rides in the brittle, sun-bleached countryside. Dances in perfumed, humid ballrooms. Dinner parties held in sweltering heat. The images barely formed before fading until only the memory of their love remained. She'd been fortunate. Some women went through their entire lives without experiencing what she'd shared with Charles.

'Have to show the ranks who's in command.'

She opened her eyes. George's face bulged above her own, his skin purple, the whites of his eyes yellowed, veined with red. Saliva drooled from his lips onto her breasts. Relief coursed

109

through her aching limbs when he rolled off her. He'd finished using her. She could go to the bathroom. Wash away the sweat and smell...

He swung alarmingly back into her line of vision. Her eyes widened in terror when she saw what he was holding. She moved quickly, but not quickly enough. Catching the back of her neck, he forced her face down into the bed. The feather bolster cloyed around her eyes, nose, and mouth. She tried to scream but, muffled by the pillows, the sound faded to a whimper. The first of the pains came, its edge dulled a little by pre-knowledge.

Tears started in her eyes and she struggled, but George was sitting astride her, his bulk pinning her to the mattress. There was nothing she could do but grit her teeth and bear it. She could bear it! Just until morning.

The heat had driven George insane. No one would blame her for leaving an insane husband. Charles would take her back to England. To cool, calm sanity. Green fields – damp autumns – gloomy grey stone churches... She didn't have money for the fare. George held her inheritance; he paid her accounts. Even in India, she'd only handled enough cash to tip the stewards. George would never buy her a ticket home. Charles would have to support her. Would he? He'd told her he wanted to live with her

A searing stroke on broken skin drove all thoughts from her mind. Closing her teeth into the pillow, she bit down hard. Charles – blond, wavy hair; clear, tanned skin. She imagined touching him, running the tips of her fingers along his cheekbone. His eyes, deep blue, crinkling at the corners as he smiled... His image receded faster than she could conjure. She was thrust deeper into a red-tinged world of brutality and pain that offered no respite. No escape.

*Harry's bungalow, Basra, Friday 3rd July 1914*

'Charles packs quite a punch.' Harry rubbed his jaw.

'You shouldn't have taken a swing at him,' John reproached him.

'He shouldn't have laughed when I told him about my wife.'

'This is the craziest thing you've done, Harry. A Bedouin girl...'

Harry picked up the whisky bottle, refilled his glass, and offered it to John who shook his head. 'I admit I was forced to marry the girl, but I like her. We get on, and I intend to stay with her. For the present.'

'Have you considered the consequences of this latest lunacy? Charles...'

'Still want that night out?'

'No.' John gave up. As a child, Harry had been stubborn. As a young man, impossible, and Charles's antagonism had only served to entrench his attitude. 'It might be as well if the groom and best man have an early night.'

Harry looked towards the Arab quarter. 'I'm happy for you. Maud is a nice girl.'

'I think so,' John agreed.

'Sure you won't have a nightcap?'

'I'm sure.'

'Sleep well, and don't worry about waking Charles.' Harry nodded towards the bedroom where Charles had retreated in umbrage. 'I'll call him at four.'

'It might be better if I do that.'

'He'll be in such a foul mood at that hour it won't make any difference if the Queen of Sheba or I wake him.'

John hesitated, decided there was nothing more to be said, and left the room.

Harry went to the table and opened the mahogany and hide portable desk that had been a parting gift from his mother. 'Wishful thinking,' Georgiana had said at the time. She'd been wrong. He'd written some letters. Not many, but some. He took out two envelopes and addressed them in his distinctive, upright hand.

*Colonel and Mrs H Downe, Clyneswood, Dorset.*
*Georgiana and Michael Downe, Clyneswood Dorset.*

Propping them against the brass base of the oil lamp, he took a clean white sheet of paper. Dipping his pen into the inkwell he began to write.

*Dear Mother and Father,*

*I've decided not to come home this leave because I've married an Arab girl and I'd like to spend some time with her. I'll see you both on my next leave. I hope you are well. I am well.*

*Your loving son, Harry.*

Resting his pen on the stand, he blotted and read what he'd written. It looked ridiculous. He pushed the note to the edge of the table and took another sheet.

*Dearest Georgie and Dear Michael,*

He held his pen poised over the paper until a blob of ink fell from the nib. He wouldn't have believed it could be so difficult to write to two people he was so close to. He stared at an empty chair. Imagined Georgie sitting in it, her mousy hair scraped in a bun, her face fixed in the stern expression she habitually wore in the ridiculous belief it made her look older. Her rimless glasses would be perched on the end of her nose, and she'd be dressed like a Sunday school teacher in a plain, high-necked, linen blouse and grey serge skirt. What would hardworking, intellectual Georgiana make of a sister-in-law as exotic and lively as Furja?

Perhaps the new socialism Georgiana had recently adopted and written at length to him about would enable her to accept his wife. But then there was Michael. Dear, self-effacing Michael, the younger brother who'd hero-worshipped him all his life, even after he'd repeatedly told him he simply wasn't worth admiring, let alone emulating.

This letter would put an end to Michael's adulation, he realised with a pang of remorse. He'd hurt his family often enough in the past to predict their reaction to the news of his marriage. His mother, American roots forgotten, now more English than the English, would have hysterics. His father's fury would turn to sullen anger. Georgiana alone would try to defend him; just as she'd done through all his scrapes, from the time he'd hidden frogs in the cook's flour bins, to his expulsion from medical college. Michael would try to join forces with her but, unable to withstand

113

parental pressure, he would ultimately toe the line dictated by their mother. Georgiana never would.

With Georgiana's exception, his family's attitude would be the same as Charles. Any Englishman crazy enough to wed a native and take the heathen marriage seriously deserved to be ostracised. Until the day he divorced Furja, he would be *persona non grata* in the Downe household. He looked at the ink-stained sheet of paper, and threw it to the floor. Taking another, he began to write quickly, without giving too much thought as to what he was putting down.

*Dear Twinnie and Mikey,*

*This is not the easiest letter I've ever had to write, and I'm writing it in a hurry, which doesn't help. It's after midnight and I want to finish it so Charles can take it when he leaves at four to catch the morning tide. I won't be home because I'm married and spending my leave with my wife, Furja. She's Bedouin. I didn't want to marry her, I didn't even see her before the ceremony, but all things considered, it's worked out fairly well between us.*

He chewed the end of his pen and stared at the ceiling. How could he begin to tell them about his wife: her laugh – her dark eyes? The way she made him feel – when they weren't quarrelling

*That's enough about me. I'm going to congratulate you now, Twinnie, on passing your finals and becoming a doctor. I know you'll do it. No one deserves success more than you. You've always had better staying power than me, and you'll make a good doctor, but must you work in the East End? I read your last letter and I agree they need someone to help them, but I'm sure you'd be more comfortable working*

114

*with Uncle John in Dorset. There's no law that says
you have to work in miserable conditions. I'm glad
there'll be a Dr Downe for Papa and Mama's sake,
perhaps it will make up for their disappointment in
me. Hope you're happy in the bank, Mikey. I might
not be coming home, but I think of you, all the time...*

Leaving the table, he went to the window. He'd
hardly thought of his family since he'd sailed for
India. For the first time, he realised why. He
missed their presence with a physical intensity
akin to pain. He imagined himself in Clyneswood.
Hiding in the smoking room with Michael,
listening as the skinnier, curlier-headed version of
himself recounted the grim story of a tedious day
in the bank. He saw himself teasing Georgiana at
dinner, affecting loud, innocent conversation as he
tweaked the hair out of the ludicrous bun at the
nape of her neck.

To his surprise, he realised he missed his father
too. The colonel's exasperation with him had never
entirely reached the level of complete despair.
That had been left to his mother, who'd been
exasperated, despairing and disapproving of him
since the day he'd been born. From her point of
view, it was probably just as well he'd decided to
forgo his home leave. Or had he?

He took out the pocket watch that had been his
parents' gift on his coming of age, and flicked the
case open. There was still time to change his
mind. It wouldn't take long to pack. All he had to
do was notify Perry he was leaving. He could
send his goodbyes to Furja via Mitkhal. Furja -
her guttural whisper echoed huskily,

'You have to learn, Harry, the Bedawi have more

ways of answering questions than with words.'

It took all his powers of concentration to remember she loved another.

# Chapter Six

*Basra, Saturday 4th July 1914*

Emily crawled out from beneath the snoring, jellied mass of her husband. His snoring became a snuffle. He moved. She froze.

Heart pounding, her lips mouthed a silent prayer that he wouldn't wake. He rolled on his back. The snuffle deepened. After an eternity, it steadied back to a snore. She was safe – for the moment.

She stole cautiously along the bed. The lamp had flickered to an end hours ago. The only illumination came from the moon, its waxy light muted by the lace at the windows. The familiar outlines of the furniture loomed, acquiring new and terrifying shapes. She waited for her eyes to become accustomed to the gloom. Her nightdress gleamed, a splash of white at the foot of the bed.

She stooped to retrieve it; thrusting her hand into her mouth to stifle the pain the movement cost her. Holding the gown close, she staggered into the bathroom. Closing the door, she turned the key. She was secure. George couldn't get to her without battering down the door and he would never risk waking the servants.

She fumbled with the candle and box of safety

matches that were kept on a rattan shelf below the mirror. At the third attempt, she managed to light it. The jugs on the washstand were full, ready for the morning baths. She strained to lift the enormous pitchers, tipping their contents into the slipper bath. When she laid her nightdress on the linen basket, she saw the gown was stained with great streaks of crimson. Glancing down, she stifled a cry at the damage George had inflicted. Bloody weals curved around from her back, ending in gaping, jagged wounds that bordered her breasts and abdomen. She glanced in the mirror. Her face was white; her lips swollen where she'd sunk her teeth into them.

The wreckage of her body triggered emotions George had failed to whip into being. Sinking on the side of the bath, she sobbed uncontrollably. For years, she'd fought against debilitating heat and hostile climate to retain the remnants of her beauty. Now she was scarred, repulsive. How could she go to Charles and ask him to help her looking like this?

She heard the distant boots of sentries marching. She had no idea how long it would be before dawn broke, but she couldn't stay locked in the bathroom. She had to leave before George woke. She looked into the bath. Rivulets of blood had coursed into the water while she'd sat, clouding the surface like flowers opening into bloom. She had to wash, cover her wounds, get away.

Stepping gingerly into the tepid water, she reached for the soap and loofah. Gritting her teeth, she scrubbed at her raw skin, trying to cleanse herself of the foul taint of George. Why hadn't she listened to Charles? If they'd remained on the *Egra* this would never have happened.

Misery and humiliation rose on an acrid tide of bile. She leant over the side of the bath and vomited her disgust on the floor. The one thing she was certain of was that she couldn't stay with George. She never wanted to see him again. But would Charles help her? Would he still want her, looking the way she did? She had to reach him to find out. Without waiting to bind her wounds or dry herself, she slipped on the bloodstained nightgown. Unlocking the bathroom door, she crept out.

George was still snoring. Emily inched past the door into the drawing room. Heart pounding, mouth dry, she fought with the bolts on the French windows. Two of her nails broke, splitting to the quick. When the rusted catch gave way, she stumbled on to the veranda. There was a light burning in Harry's bungalow. Someone was up – Charles?

She fell down the steps onto the ground. Pain pierced her foot, one more unpleasant sensation among many. She staggered over the warm, compacted earth. A black fog wavered between her and Harry's window. Thinking only of Charles, she walked into it. The sound of buzzing insects filled her ears. She reached for the rail that enclosed Harry's veranda. Her hands closed on air. She fell – screamed 'Charles', but no sound issued from her lips.

She crawled forward, the hem of her gown entangling her feet. Grasping the foot of a wooden rail, she heaved herself up to her knees. One more effort, a few more steps, and she'd be in Charles's arms.

*Basra, Saturday July 4th 1914*

Harry whistled the chorus from *The Sunshine Girl*, the big hit of 1912, and the last musical he'd seen at the Gaiety before sailing for India. He and Charles had reconciled their differences on the drive to the wharf and the warmth of his friend's parting handshake said what neither of them put into words.

They would remain friends, no matter what. He could breakfast with John with a clear conscience, and after the wedding, he'd leave John and Maud to their happiness and see to his own. Book his leave, effective from that day. Pack a couple of cases of brandy and take them to Shalan's house for six uninterrupted months of Furja and the pleasures of marriage.

Abandoning his whistling, he sang a resounding refrain of *Come into the Garden, Maud*. He turned the corner that led to the officers' bungalows. If John wasn't awake, he soon would be.

He stopped singing when he saw the flies. A teeming layer of metallic greenish-black blanketing a mass slumped below his veranda. He didn't see the white gown until he crouched down. He shouted to John, pulled the topee from his head, and waved it over the seething, parasitic swarm. As fast as he knocked the flies away, others crawled in to take their place. John's bare feet slapped across the wooden boards.

119

'Who is it?'

'I can't see. The flies...' The stench of rotting blood assailed his nostrils. He managed to turn his head aside before he heaved up his morning coffee.

John vaulted the rail and did what Harry had baulked at. Pushing his hands through the crawling mass, he uncovered a head. Harry watched John's fingers – black, swollen with flies – lift a strand of ash-blonde hair. Ash-blonde, not light.

'Emily,' Harry breathed.

'Help me get her inside.' John assumed command. 'There's a weak pulse at her neck. She's alive.'

Maud woke to the sound of weeping. She stretched, revelling in the feel of cool sheets against her skin. The sobbing continued; an even drone. Typical of Harriet's sentimentality. She hoped the maid wasn't going to cry all day. A few tears at a wedding were permissible, but not a dam burst. It was John she was marrying, not an ogre. She smiled, recalling the time they'd spent together in her cabin. Marjorie Harrap had been right. John was gentle, and very, very loving. The temptation to savour the moment was too great. Keeping her eyes closed, she slipped further beneath the bedclothes.

'Maud?'

She opened her eyes and wondered if she were dreaming. John sat beside her bed in full uniform, a serious look hardening his handsome features.

'Don't you know it's unlucky for the groom to see the bride before the wedding?' she murmured.

He reached for her hand. 'It's your mother. Darling, I'm so very sorry.'

She stared at him dazed, uncomprehending.

'She died early this morning. Harry found her after he'd taken Charles to the wharf.' He closed his mind to the ghoulish image of Harry's Arab servant hacking the blood-soaked, maggot-infested earth from the ground in front of Harry's bungalow. He and Harry had discussed the situation. Harry had agreed there was no point in precipitating a scandal. No one's interests would be served by publicising the gruesome details of the Perrys' married life. Aside from Emily and Maud, there was Charles. If it should get out that Emily had died running from her husband, Charles would be the centre of a furore that would shake Indian military society. A few white lies were necessary. He'd impressed that on Harry, and white lies were what he was going to tell Maud.

'Your mother left her bedroom last night – perhaps she couldn't sleep, perhaps she wanted some air. She walked out onto your veranda and trod on a scorpion, a small yellow one. We discovered its body beneath hers. Darling, even if we'd found her right away, she would have died. There was nothing I or any doctor could have done.'

'No!' The scream was bestial in its intensity. 'Not Mother. Not my mother.' Maud rose to her knees and beat her fists against John's chest. 'No.' The scream dulled and thickened to a sob.

John folded his arms around her as she shuddered in paroxysms that cut deeper than grief. Fighting his own tears, he prayed she'd never discover the truth. That Harry had found Emily torn,

121

bleeding, but alive. That she'd continued to live through 20 agonising minutes, despite the morphine he'd poured into her. He'd never witnessed a death so ugly or lacking in dignity. Emily had deserved better than he'd been able to give her.

'I'm sorry, Maud.'

She lifted her tear-stained face to his. Read the truth in his eyes. John held her against his chest until her sobs grew weaker, less violent, then he fed her a glass of laudanum and wine. When the drug took effect, he laid her back into the bed and opened the door. Harriet was slumped outside on the hall sofa, Angela Wallace next to her.

'My sincerest condolences, Captain Mason,' Angela sympathised. 'Mrs Butler and I came as soon as we heard. She's with the padre but she'll be along shortly. Is there anything I can do?'

'I'd appreciate it if you would sit with Maud.'

'Poor, poor Miss Maud, and on her wedding day,' Harriet sobbed.

'Come along, Harriet.' Angela patted the maid's work-roughened hand. 'You have to be brave for Miss Maud. She needs you, and you'll be no use if you carry on like this.'

John was amazed by the young girl's strength and practical attitude. 'I've given Maud something to make her sleep,' he said when Angela ushered Harriet into Maud's bedroom. 'If there's any change you'll let me know.'

'At once, Captain Mason.' Smoothing her grey linen dress, Angela sat on the chair he'd vacated while Harriet hovered in front of the dresser. 'Miss Maud will need mourning clothes, Harriet,' Angela prompted. 'She will be grateful if you lay them out.'

'Miss Wallace.' John removed the glass from beside Maud's bed. 'Thank you for coming.'

'Please, call me Angela; I'm not used to Miss Wallace.' She spoke without any of the primping or flirting he'd come to expect from Indian Army ladies.

'Thank you, Angela, we appreciate your help.'

'I wanted to stop living when my parents died, Captain Mason, so I know exactly how desolate Maud feels. Strangers showed me the solace God can give to the bereaved. I pray I'll be given the privilege of doing as much for Maud.'

John wasn't a religious man. If he thought of God at all, it was the God of church parade who existed only on Sundays. Angela's matter-of-fact referral to the deity made him feel faintly uneasy. He left the room. Harry's servant was in the hall.

'Everything is cleared outside, sir.' The 'sir' sounded like an afterthought.

'Mitkhal, isn't it?' John asked.

'Yes.' No 'sir' this time, John noted.

'Could you find someone to clean this bungalow? Particularly the bathroom and carpets.' John indicated the heap of bloodstained rugs he and Harry had taken up from the hall and drawing room floors.

'Harry didn't think it wise to ask the bearers. They talk. He sent into town for a man he trusts. He'll be here soon.'

John was taken aback by the familiarity with which Mitkhai treated Harry. His cousin had always been hopeless with servants, making friends of everyone from the stable boy to the

123

butler. But this man was a native. John glanced warily at Mitkhal. The Arab stared coolly back.

'I'll see if the coffin's ready.' Mitkhai left John with the feeling he was the one being dismissed.

John knocked on Colonel Perry's bedroom door. Harry opened it. The smell almost sent John reeling back into the hall. A fetid, animal-lair stench of blood and sweat. The windows were closed, the blinds pulled, shading the light to the yellowy brown of old-fashioned staged photographs. The scene added to his impression of a tableau. He even thought of a title for it. *Remorse*, or *the Morning After*. It wouldn't have looked out of place in a gallery.

Perry, in breeches and collarless shirt sat hunched on the bare mattress, his face buried in his hands. Harry stood opposite, a bundle of sheets at his feet.

'How's Maud?' Harry asked.

'Sleeping. I gave her a sedative.' John struggled with the foul air. 'Miss Wallace is with her, she said she'd call if there's any change.'

'She will. She's a capable young lady.'

'I noticed.'

'The colonel has ordered a grave to be dug in the European cemetery.' Harry gave Perry credit for his own initiative. 'He would like the funeral to be held as soon as possible.'

John tripped over something protruding from beneath the bed. He picked up a bullwhip. Streaks of bloodstained, dried flesh clung to its plaited thongs. He hadn't lied when he'd told Maud he could do nothing to save her mother.

The sting of the yellow scorpion was invariably fatal, or so Mitkhal had assured him, but the thrashing Emily had received before her death hadn't helped. He assumed Perry had found out about Emily and Charles. But what kind of a man would flay the skin off his wife's back for falling in love with another man?

Harry saw the whip and paled. His reaction gave John the impetus he needed to pull himself together. Tossing the whip aside, John gripped his cousin's arm and walked him to the door.

'If you'll excuse us, Colonel Perry, we'll check the padre has everything in hand.' Pushing Harry into the hall, John closed the door. 'Emily's dead. We agreed; there's nothing we can do to alter that.'

'Damn it...'

'What's done is done,' John interrupted. 'Perry didn't kill her, the scorpion did.'

'You saw that whip.'

'The beating didn't cause Emily's death. What happens between a man and his wife is private.'

'And Charles?' Harry asked.

'Is best out of it.'

'You know as well as I do Emily was trying to reach him.'

'We can't be sure of that.'

'I am,' Harry countered. 'If Emily had lived she would have left this morning with Charles.'

'No, she wouldn't have, because she reached the bungalow after Charles left.'

'She could have followed him.'

'And that would have given Perry cause to go after them and shoot them both. As it is, he only managed to lay his hands on Emily. Her death was an accident, Harry. Charles will have to get over it as best he can. Consider Maud,' John begged. 'Don't do anything to jeopardise the chances of our wedding going ahead. She's under age; I need Perry's consent.'

'You can't possibly marry Maud today!' Harry was horror-struck at the thought.

'I have to get her away from here and I can only do that if we're married. If I can't get berths for England out of the Gulf in the next couple of days, we'll return to India, and sail home from there. You haven't said anything to Perry, have you?' John questioned urgently.

'Only what we agreed. That I found Emily and she died of a scorpion bite. When I pointed out that the sheets on the bed were blood-stained, he left the bed and helped me strip the mattress.'

'I doubt he remembers much about last night. He downed a bucketful of brandy in the mess.'

'And that excuses what he did?' Harry retorted.

'No. But who knows what a man who whipped his wife to shreds would do to his daughter if she stayed with him and he started drinking again. Do me a favour, Harry, find the padre and tell him I want the wedding to go ahead this evening?'

'I'll see if he's in the mess.' Harry looked at his cousin. 'You always were the one to think things out and weigh up the consequences.'

'Perhaps it's as well someone in the family does.'

The shaft hit home. Harry picked up his topee and left.

John returned to the bedroom.

'Did Harry explain that Mrs Perry died of a

scorpion bite? One of the Arabs thought it might have been carried in with the wood. There was a pile of cut thorn against your veranda.'

Perry lifted his head and dropped his hands. He stared at John out of bloodshot, expressionless eyes.

'There was nothing I could do.' John was gentle with Perry in spite of his revulsion.

'I ordered Crabbe to clear the wood yesterday.' Perry's voice was high-pitched, remote. Suddenly it snapped to life. 'I'll kill the bastard. Kill him for disobeying orders. Mark my words, captain. I'll kill him.'

John had studied shock; he knew about guilt transference and the illogical, misdirected anger it could give rise to, but this wasn't a textbook case. He'd loved Emily for her own, Maud, and Charles's sake, and the sight of this arrogant, dishevelled officer railing against some hapless minion for causing Emily's death disgusted him. He fought to keep his emotions in check because, as he'd told Harry, he had Maud's welfare to consider. He interrupted the colonel's flow of invectives against Crabbe.

'We have to bury Mrs Perry.'

Perry stared blankly at him.

'As soon as possible. You know army regulations on burying the dead in this climate.'

'Army regulations,' Perry repeated. 'I'm a colonel. Of course I bloody know army regulations...'

'Afterwards, I'll go ahead with the wedding. It will be a quiet one: Maud, myself, and two witnesses. It won't be necessary for you to give her

127

away.' John deliberately left the question of Perry's attendance open. Of preference, he never wanted to see the wretched man again.

'You can't rush Maud into this. Her mother's not in her grave...'

'The sooner I marry Maud and get her away from here, the better. Maud was close to Emily. She loved her, and after...' He faltered at the sight of the bloodied whip on the bare mattress. The colonel saw what he was looking at.

'I understand, Mason. You've decided to marry Maud come hell or high water. Well, if she's content to let a bloody civilian make her decisions for her, then go ahead. Marry and be damned.'

At that moment, John hated the colonel more than he'd ever hated anyone in his life. It took all his powers of self-control to recall the advice he'd given Harry. Maud had told him her father was wooden. 'Grade one British Army Officer material, for the use of.' She was wrong. Her father wasn't wooden. He was petty-minded and vicious, with the meanness that blighted the small-brained who remained in India too long. Poor Emily; little wonder she'd fallen in love with Charles.

John left the room. A great deal remained unsaid but a quarrel between him and Perry would only hurt Maud. A few weeks from now, he and Maud would be half a world away, building a new life in England. His only consolation lay in Perry's devotion to the army. The colonel would stay in India with the regiment until he retired. And if he had a single shred of humanity or consideration for Maud, he'd stay on after that.

Perry picked up the whip and cringed at the sight of the strips of dried skin caught in the thongs. He couldn't bear to think of Emily, but he could think of Mason. The pompous young ass who wasn't even army any more. Who the hell did Mason think he was, threatening him? And he'd got his own way. Telling him that he was marrying Maud on the day of her mother's death without so much as a 'by your leave'.

He threw the whip into the wastebasket, went to the window, and pulled up the blind. Mason was on the veranda with his back turned towards him. He was close, so close, that if it hadn't been for the glass he could have touched him; or – his mouth curled maliciously at the thought – pushed a knife between the captain's ribs.

As his anger escalated, he failed to realise that it wasn't John but the memory of the night he wanted to expunge. Emily was dead. John lived. He despised the man for knowing too much. It was a situation he abhorred and didn't want to live with.

*European Cemetery, Basra, Saturday 4th July 1914*

'Man that is born of woman hath but a short time to live...' Padre Powell's voice droned into the suffocating, sun-blinded atmosphere. Harry heard the voice, but the words resounded like the cadence of an alien ritual. Bored, miserable, he looked past the padre and encountered the disapproving glare of Crabbe. He obviously wasn't behaving in the manner proscribed for a military funeral bearer. Ignoring Crabbe, he turned to Perry. The colonel was swaying on his feet at the head of the open grave, his eyes bloodshot and his breath brandy-stale as it wafted towards the mourners.

Harry saw a few matrons exchange tight-lipped, knowing nods beneath their wide-brimmed, black hats. The gossip generated by Emily's sudden death would keep the post going for months and the news had yet to break that Maud's wedding had only been postponed until evening. It was as well he'd found time to write out the formal notification of his leave and place it on Perry's desk. If he stayed, he'd be hunted by every gossip-monger in the quarter as a source of titivating tales.

The padre deepened his voice to heighten dramatic effect. John moved his arm protectively around Maud's shoulders and closed his free hand over her black-gloved fingers. She remained upright, silent and dry-eyed, as she had since the beginning of the service. She and John stood together at the head of the grave, separated from Perry by the robed figure of the padre; but for all her stoicism, Maud looked pathetic.

Her small figure was swamped by the volum-inous folds of the old-fashioned black silk dress Harriet had unearthed from the recesses of Emily's wardrobe. Her eyes were clouded, life-less, and the unnatural pallor of her face was visible through the chequered mesh of her black veil. Harry wondered how much laudanum John had fed her – and Harriet. The maid who stood

130

at Maud's elbow was as remote and leaden as her new mistress.

'Ashes to ashes...' The padre poignantly flung his hands over the gaping hole.

Harry lowered his eyes to the coffin, covered by a profusion of flowers Mitkhal had scavenged from God only knew what green corners of the town.

'Dust to dust...' Bending his knees, the padre scooped a handful of dry soil.

Concerned for Maud, Harry tried to catch John's eye, but his cousin was already trying to lead Maud away.

Freeing herself from John's supporting hold, Maud took one last look at her mother's coffin before throwing the single white flower she'd clutched throughout the service into the grave.

The padre emptied his hand. Harry braced himself for the rattle of dry earth spattering on dead wood. He'd been to enough funerals both there and in India to come to dread the hollow, finite sound of parched earth falling on polished coffins.

He saw Perry stare at the retreating figure of his daughter. Without warning, the colonel swung round and stepped forward. Harry moved quickly. Perry's sway had become a stagger; one slip and he'd be on top of his wife, but before Harry could reach him, Perry lurched drunkenly and vomited into the grave.

An angry murmur arose from the mourners. Harry could neither do nor take any more. He fell out and followed John and Maud back to his bungalow.

# Chapter Seven

*Basra, Saturday 4th July 1914*

Dressed in the black gown she'd worn to her mother's funeral, Maud became Mrs John Mason in the barrack chapel at sunset. Harry doubled as best man and witness. Peter Smythe, Harriet, and Padre Powell were the only others present and, for the first time in his career, the padre cut a ceremony. The marriage lasted a scant, humane ten minutes.

After the funeral, the padre had tackled John on the propriety of marrying Maud on the day of her mother's death. John replied that someone had to take care of Maud. He didn't have to say any more. Perry had locked himself into his bungalow; rumour had it with yet another bottle.

Harry forced open the French windows of the drawing room so he and John could carry out Maud and Harriet's trunks, but, despite the noise they'd made, the colonel didn't appear. John was relieved. The last thing he wanted was another ugly scene and, when Perry failed to show at the chapel, he presumed the colonel was sleeping it off.

The moment John and Maud were declared man and wife, John shook hands with the padre and Peter and hustled Maud and Harriet out of the chapel. Harry had helped him make plans that afternoon. His, Maud's, and Harriet's trunks were already on a dhow berthed at Basra wharf. Less than half an hour after the ceremony, they joined them, leaving Mitkhal to drive Harry's carriage back to the compound stable.

Darkness had fallen, black and gleaming over the Shatt. A full moon attended by a bevy of stars shone down from the clear sky as the boatman steered past the palm groves and walls of the old city. John settled Maud and Harriet on a plank nailed across the stern, before heading for the prow where Harry and the native were holding a whispered conversation.

'How long will it take to get there?'

'Not long.' Harry's eyes shone in the moonlight. 'There are native robes under Maud's seat. Slip them over your clothes.'

'Is that necessary?'

'Ferenghis attract attention in the native quarter. I promised my father-in-law I wouldn't bring any infidels into his home.' Harry pulled his own abba out of a carpetbag.

'Harry, if we're going to make trouble for you...'

'Just do it and keep your voice down. Sound travels over water.'

After helping Maud and Harriet into their robes, John struggled into an abba. He felt like an undergraduate at a fancy dress ball. The hem flapped halfway up his calves, and the arms fell short of his uniform sleeves by several inches. He flung the head cloth over his head, it slipped over one ear. Harry tied it for him.

'That should stay on, but remind me to ask Mitkhal to give you one of his outfits.'

'When will I need to wear anything like this again?'

'When you leave.'

The boatman called softly and Harry returned to the prow. He crouched low, elbows on knees, features obscured by his head cloth, his attention focused on the shadows. The only sounds were the ones made by the boat as it cut through the Shatt, and the muffled dialogue between Harry and the native. Maud rested her head against John's chest. Despite all his efforts to stay awake, John's eyelids grew heavy. He woke with a start when the boat veered dangerously close to the bank. Maud clutched his arm as an inlet scarcely a few inches wider than the dhow opened before them. Harry peered over the side, and called back sharply. The boatman slowed. Harry struck a match and lit a nickel oil lamp that hung from the prow.

An overpowering stench wafted from the water as they continued to glide down channel. It intensified when palm groves gave way to mud-brick walls. They passed oil lamps set high in niches scraped in the walls. The channel ended as suddenly as it had begun. They floated out into a small lagoon busy with the flitting, fairy-like lights of other craft. A bewildering array of lamp-illuminated waterways opened around them. Harry guided the boat forward, directing the boatman through the maze. After a confusing 15 minutes, they halted before an iron grid gate set in a thick, high wall. Harry banged on the gate with the boat hook. A woman's voice hailed them. John looked, but saw no one. The boatman pointed upwards. A black-garbed woman stood on the wall.

'Gutne, my wife's aunt,' Harry explained. The gate winched noisily upwards on a rusted mechanism. They floated into a small pool ringed by fruit-bearing trees. John wondered if he'd done the right thing. Who knew what primitive accommodation waited behind the trees? Maud was shocked and tired. She'd put up with so much...

'Harry!' A figure in red hurtled towards them. It wasn't until Harry leapt out and caught it that John realised it was a girl. She flung herself on Harry, smothering his face with kisses.

'She's a native,' Maud gasped.

John was as shocked by the reality of Furja as Maud, and he'd been forewarned. Harry's wife was no cream-skinned beauty out of the *Arabian Nights*. She was dark, with sharp, hawk-like Arab features. But, oblivious to the shortcomings of his wife's complexion, Harry returned her kisses.

John realised that all Harry's offhand comments along the lines of 'we get on' and 'I'd rather spend my leave here than waste time travelling' had merely been excuses.

'He loves her.' John was taken aback.

'So it would seem,' Maud snapped. 'I hope for his sake this unfortunate entanglement ends before anyone else finds about it.'

*Basra, Saturday 4th July 1914*

The hasty, candlelit wedding ceremony had unsettled Peter. Missing Harry, and with no other sympathetic soul to confide in, he paced around the compound, checking his father's old pocket watch every five minutes only to be amazed that time was standing still. Dinner wouldn't be served in the mess for another hour and a half. What could he do until then?

He thought of Angela; her calm dignity during poor Mrs Perry's awful funeral, how beautiful she'd looked at last night's ladies' dinner, and what an utter ass he made of himself whenever he went near her. He glanced at his watch again. If he asked the stable sepoy to saddle his horse, he could be at the mission in ten minutes.

Fifteen minutes later, he arrived at the front entrance. He could see Angela through the window. She was sitting at the high teacher's desk in her classroom, marking a daunting tower of exercise books. He dismounted and tapped the window. She looked up, and ran round to open the door for him.

'Lieutenant Smythe, how kind of you to call. It's been a dreadful day. I know you must have a lot of duties to fulfil.'

'Not really.' Peter followed her into the classroom. 'Captain Mason married Miss Perry an hour ago. Harry drove them to the wharf, the compound is deserted, and dinner tonight in the mess is going to be hell...' He reddened. 'I'm sorry.'

'After the day you've had, you're entitled to swear.'

'Do you always work this late?' He sat on one of the low children's desks in front of hers.

'Not usually.' She took the pile of books she'd marked and carried them to a cupboard. 'But I took a few hours off today to attend the funeral.

136

Poor Maud, it must have been dreadful. Marrying on the same day her mother died.'

'Captain Mason wanted to take her away as quickly as possible, and he couldn't have done that if they hadn't been married.'

'A wedding day is important to a woman. Maud's memories will be very different from those of most brides.' She set the books on a shelf. 'I'm sorry, lieutenant, I'm forgetting my manners. Can I get you anything? Tea, perhaps?'

'Nothing, thank you.' He left the desk and paced uneasily to the window. 'I'm glad I found you alone, Miss Wallace. There's something I've been meaning to ask you but I haven't had the opportunity or–' he hesitated '–the courage.' His face was scarlet.

'The courage? Do you find me intimidating, Lieutenant Smythe?'

'No, Miss Wallace...'

'You have called me Angela before.'

'No, Angela, I don't find you intimidating; in fact, quite the reverse.' Steeling himself for rejection, he faced her. 'You must realise how much I admire you. I would like to ask you to marry me.'

'Is this a proposal, Lieutenant Smythe?'

'I only wish it were. If I had sufficient money I'd marry you tomorrow, but I haven't, so all I can ask is that you'll wait for me. A lieutenant's pay isn't enough to support a wife, but one day I'll get my captaincy. I wonder if you'd consider getting engaged to me now and marrying me when that happens.'

'Then you are proposing, Lieutenant Smythe?'

'I don't want to mislead you. Promotion can be

137

a long time coming in peacetime. We could be engaged for five or six years. Perhaps I shouldn't have spoken but I had to tell you how I felt. I wish I had more to offer you. I have no private means and I'm no one's heir. We'll only ever have my pay, but–' he reached for her hand '–I love you. And I promise to do everything in my power to make you happy.'

'And I love you, Lieutenant Peter Smythe.' Her eyes shone as she returned the pressure of his fingers. 'I'll wait for you. For ever if necessary.'

A lump rose in his throat. He dared to wrap his arms around her. She felt soft, fragile, like a fledgling bird. 'Are you sure?'

'Very sure, Lieutenant. Now you've asked, you're stuck with me.'

'You'll be an army wife. It will mean living in India, and India can be rough for a woman.'

'Like here?'

'Perhaps not quite as rough as here,' he conceded. 'The climate can be better, but it will be lonely.'

'With no fellow Americans to keep me company.'

'I could be posted to the frontier. You might not be able to come with me.'

'In that case we'd better have a few children to keep me busy while you're away.'

His colour heightened at the suggestion. 'I'll get you a ring. What sort would you like?'

'Anything as long as it's from you.'

'I must speak to your brother.'

'He's in the hospital, but, I warn you, he won't be happy with the idea of our engagement.' She

138

stood in front of him, hoping he'd kiss her, but he didn't. 'You'll come back after you've seen him.'

'If he invites me.' He smiled at her with more confidence than he felt.

*Hospital, Basra, Saturday 4th July 1914*

Theo was at his desk, sorting through order forms. 'Lieutenant Smythe, this is a surprise. Take a seat.'

'I don't want to interrupt anything.'

'I'll be glad to leave it. There are a couple of beers on ice in the storeroom. Would you care to join me?'

'Please.'

Theo disappeared into the marble-lined cupboard, emerging with two green bottles and a couple of glasses. 'We were all very sorry to hear about Mrs Perry.'

'Miss Perry and Captain Mason appreciated the presence of everyone from the mission at the funeral.' Peter avoided mentioning the colonel.

'It was the least we could do.'

'Miss Wallace was wonderful. Captain Mason said he couldn't have managed without her.'

'It was kind of him to say so.' Theo poured the beers and raised his glass. 'Your good health.'

'And yours.' Peter shuffled his feet. 'About Angela, I mean Miss Wallace. I rather hoped we could get engaged,' he blurted out.

'Are you asking my permission?'

'Yes. She's under age, and I know how close she is to you. Your blessing would make her – us – very happy.'

'Would it?' Theo's voice was strained. Despite what he'd said to Angela, he'd been half-expecting Peter to ask for her. But not so soon.

'I can't offer her anything other than a ring at present. But it will be different when I get my captaincy.'

'I don't know much about the Indian Army, Lieutenant Smythe, but I do know that promotion can take years.'

'I've explained that to Miss Wallace.'

'Do you think you're being quite fair to her?'

'No.' Peter stared into his beer. 'She's worth ten of me. I can't offer her anything now. And there'll only be my captain's pay in the future. I've no private means...'

'Neither has Angela.'

'I didn't hope for any. If it means anything, Dr Wallace, Angela will be rich in love, if not material possessions.'

'If you'll pardon my frankness, you're allowing your heart to rule your head.' Theo was only 27, but at that moment he felt more like Angela's father than her brother. 'I presume you've spoken to Angela.'

Peter nodded.

'You've pushed me into a corner, Lieutenant. If I withhold my blessing, Angela will hate me for it, and if I agree, I'll go against everything my parents and I wanted for my sister. It's nothing personal. I like you more than any of the other stuffed shirts in the compound, with the exception of Harry.'

'Everyone likes Harry.'

'It would be impossible to dislike the man. But we're not talking about Harry. I like you, Lieutenant Smythe, but I hate your way of life. The British Empire and the Indian Army are dependent on a class structure I loathe and detest. I believe in the American way of democracy and equality. I want Angela to be happy, and frankly, I doubt she will be if she marries you.' Theo held up his hand as though to stave off Peter's protests. 'I've noticed the way your fellow officers look at us. They don't like Americans. That's fine by me; they don't have to. But if you and Angela marry, it won't be fine. I've talked to American missionaries who've worked in India. They were ostracised by British military personnel. I won't stop you and my sister getting engaged, Lieutenant, but I will hope and pray that your relationship will end before you get your captaincy. You and Angela are from different worlds. In my opinion, they can't be bridged.'

'I have no skills other than soldiering, but if it came to a choice between my career and Angela, I'd give up my commission.'

'If you're serious about her, you may have to,' Theo warned. 'And how long will she have to wait then for you to support her?'

'I can only repeat that I love her,' Peter reiterated.

'It may not be enough.' Theo threw his empty beer bottle into the wastebasket. 'You may go to her and tell her I'll arrange an engagement party.'

'There's no need...'

'I only have one sister, Lieutenant Smythe. I do it for her.'

'In that case, thank you, Dr Wallace.'

'Under the circumstances I think you'd better call me Theo. Just one more thing, Peter. How-

141

ever long the engagement, and whether it ends in marriage or not, I will expect you to behave like a gentleman at all times.'

Peter's cheeks burned crimson. 'You have my word as an officer.'

Theo nodded. 'That will suffice.'

*Shalan's house, Basra, Saturday 4th July 1914*

John sat alone in the moonlit garden, smoking a cigar Harry had given him when they'd left the chapel. His surroundings were beautiful, but as he mused over the day's events he saw none of their shadowy attractions. The perfume of flower blossoms filled the air, but all he could smell was Emily's blood, sweet and putrid as it clotted beneath her fly-covered body. Had he done the right thing? Should he have told someone what Perry had done? The padre? The Reverend Butler? The Consul?

He examined every decision he'd made that day. Had he really been thinking of Maud, as he'd told Harry, or had he been driven by his need for her? Would he have behaved any differently if she hadn't invited him into her cabin that last night on the *Egra?*

She'd undressed down to her drawers then shyly, timidly, she'd turned to him. He'd caressed her breasts before helping her on with her nightdress. Fully dressed, he had lain beside her on her narrow bunk, but he'd done no more than kiss and caress her through the thin silk of her gown. Every footstep outside the door, every creaking board

142

had made him nervous. He'd worried about Emily, half-expecting her to walk in on them although he'd locked the door.

It had been a ludicrous situation. He was lying with the woman who was soon to be his wife and Charles and Emily were committing adultery in the next cabin. Yet he was the one who felt guilty.

He wanted his relationship with Maud to be perfect. He'd listened to the emotional outpourings of so many miserable wives in consulting rooms. Women who'd been led to their bridal beds in a state of stupefying ignorance, only to be shocked rigid by their first glimpse of a naked man. What followed that initial confrontation was usually confided in muted whisperings sandwiched between anguished sobs, detailing pain, discomfort, and the horrors of unwanted pregnancies and their husbands' excessive 'demands'.

He wanted to make Maud's introduction to sex as pleasurable as his had been. He'd had an excellent tutor. After Harry had abandoned his medical studies, he'd moved from the rooms they'd shared into a house that accommodated several people who worked at the hospital, including that rarity – a woman doctor. Helen had been 15 years older than him but the age difference was irrelevant. They'd never lived openly together – that would have been more than the hospital authorities could have borne – but they'd lodged on the same floor, which made it easy for them to slip in and out of one another's rooms.

During the four years they'd been together, Helen had taught him that lovemaking didn't have to be sordid or confined to a whore's bedroom, and the spectre of pregnancy didn't have to come into the equation. She'd shown him that sex could, and should, be enjoyable, even without what poets called 'love'. He'd been comfortable with Helen, he'd admired her and been fond of her, but he'd never loved her, not in the way he cared for Maud. Instead, they'd shared what Helen had christened 'a friendly intimacy'.

Helen had been an advocate of free love, birth control, and feminism, and she'd found an earnest disciple when Harry's twin, Georgiana, had joined the ranks of medical students a year after Harry left. Like most of his male contemporaries, he'd had little sympathy for Helen's views at first, but her forthright manner and common sense had won him over.

His one regret on qualifying was parting from her; but she'd brushed aside his tentative offers of marriage, knowing perhaps better than him how little he'd meant them. He'd spent his final hours in England with her, drinking champagne and sitting on the bed they'd shared for four years, studying an array of pamphlets and birth-control devices she'd assembled for his benefit.

She'd insisted it was his duty to spread the word that women didn't have to be slaves to their bodies. That they had the right to control the size of their families and, above all, that he should preach the message that lovemaking should be a carefree and pleasant occupation for both sexes. He'd packed the devices and pamphlets and taken them to India. And his subtle, probing questioning of some of the hysterical officers' wives who frequented his surgery had led him to

144

dispense Helen's offerings with gratifying results.

Incidents of miscarriages, maternal deaths, and unwanted pregnancies dropped sharply after his arrival at regimental headquarters. Although his superiors raised their eyebrows at the additions he made to their requisition lists when he needed to replenish the stock he'd brought to India, they didn't block his orders. Possibly because their own wives had been among the beneficiaries of his revolutionary prescriptions.

He intended to apply the knowledge Helen had taught him to his own marriage. He wanted children, but not at the expense of Maud's health and not until they were settled in England. Before then he would show her the contents of his valise and explain their uses. But not tonight. He walked over to the fountain and watched the water trickling down into the small pond. Tonight he'd lie beside her and wait patiently while she slept off the effects of the laudanum.

A movement on the roof caught his attention. He glanced up, glimpsing Harry and Furja behind a stone trellis. In silhouette, they resembled an illustration from a Hindu sexual manual. He stared, mesmerised, as they slowly explored one another's bodies with hands, lips, tongues...

'Captain Mason?' Harriet emerged from the suite he and Maud had been allocated. He rose to meet her. Ashamed of his voyeurism, he glanced up again, hoping Harry and Furja hadn't realised he'd been watching them. The new angle of the stonework trellis closed off the roof as solidly as if it had been a wall.

'Miss Maud is in bed, sir. If you don't want me

145

for anything else, I'll go to my own room.' Harriet pointed to a door set further back than theirs beneath the veranda. 'You only have to shout, sir, and I'll be with Miss Maud in a trice.'

'Thank you, but I don't think Miss Maud will need you again tonight. Is your room comfortable?'

'Very, sir. Not as nice as yours and Miss Maud's,' she said, wary of giving offence. 'But Lieutenant Downe's done me proud. What time would you like your breakfast in the morning, sir?'

'Sleep in, Harriet. We could all do with a rest.'

'Begging your pardon, sir, but how long will we be here? Not that it's not a nice house, and the people – they're lovely. Ever so kind, but I can't understand a word they're saying, and they're all heathens.'

John tried not to smile at Harriet's summation of their situation. 'We'll leave as soon as I can get passage out of the Gulf for all of us, Harriet. Goodnight, sleep well.'

'You too, sir.' A blushing consciousness came to her that it was his wedding night.

Thrusting his cold cigar into his pocket, John entered his bedroom. Emily's death had cast a long shadow. He consoled himself with the thought that this time next year he'd be climbing the stairs to the bedroom of his house in England.

An oil lamp shed a subdued yellow light over a divan bed, the only item of furniture in the room. Their trunks stood open but unpacked in the corner. Someone, probably Harriet, had found one of the nightshirts his mother had insisted he take to India although he'd slept naked since

146

adolescence, and laid it over his valise.

Maud was awake beneath an embroidered black silk coverlet.

He smiled. 'The lace on your gown is very pretty.'

'Mother picked it out. Where have you been?'

'Smoking in the garden. I thought you'd like some time alone with Harriet.'

'She asked if she could become my maid now.'

'Would you like that?'

'I don't know.' Tears trickled down her cheeks.

'I'm sorry, darling.' Leaning over, he kissed her gently. 'This isn't the honeymoon I planned for us.'

She flung her arms around his neck and sobbed. He held her until his arms grew numb. Stepping behind the bed, he undressed. For Maud's sake, he put on the nightshirt. Sliding into bed, he moved beside her. He pulled her head down onto his chest, wrapped his arm around her, and waited for sleep.

He was worried at the thought of making love to her for the first time. Something Helen had said came to mind.

'The first time is vital to a woman. Treat your virginal bride gently. Kiss and caress her until she is as aroused as you. If you can, hold back and see to her pleasure before your own; she'll be passionately grateful to you for the rest of your married life.'

He even remembered his response. 'There'll be no virgin brides for me.'

'Oh yes there will, John. You're the type.'

He ran his fingers over Maud's arm, to her lace-

147

clad breast. Her nipple hardened beneath his touch. She clutched him fiercely, digging her nails into his back through the thin cambric of his shirt as she kissed him wildly, inexpertly. He moved away. Opening her eyes, she looked at him and he stared silently back. He'd found it easy to talk to Helen, even about sensitive subjects. Now he had to build the same relationship with Maud.

'How much did your mother tell you?' he asked.

'Only what I told you on the *Egra*. That love between a man and a woman can be wonderful.'

'I want it to be that way between us, Maud.'

'Now,' she demanded.

'Now might not be the best time. We're both tired...'

'Now,' she repeated, moving closer to him.

He no longer had the self-control to resist her. Flinging back the bedclothes, he kissed her face, her throat. Unbuttoning her bodice, he exposed her breasts. His body burned for her, but Helen's warning rang through his mind. He pulled at the hem of her nightdress. 'Do you mind, darling?'

Maud shook her head, conscious that, unlike in the cabin, this time she'd removed her drawers. Lifting her in his arms, he pulled the gown over her head. She gasped as he slid his hand between her legs. She tensed, expecting him to withdraw, but instead he began to stroke her, first with his fingers then with his lips and tongue. She was horrified, shocked, and embarrassed at what he was doing to her, yet a strange excitement coursed through her veins.

Taking her hand, he pushed aside his nightshirt and pressed it between his thighs. 'What did your

148

mother tell you about this?' His voice was hoarse with passion.

'Nothing.' She opened her legs wider, not wanting him to stop.

He felt with his free hand in his valise and pulled out one of the pessaries he'd packed. 'I'm going to put something inside you; it won't hurt. Tomorrow we'll discuss having a family.' He slipped the pessary between her legs. She was moist. It should have slid in easily, but her hymen was intact. Using every technique Helen had taught him, he brought her to a climax, thrusting his fingers and the pessary into her at the final moment. She moaned, but her cry was short-lived. 'I'm sorry, darling; I didn't mean to hurt you.'

He continued to tease her, waiting until she responded to his touch once more. Gradually, taking his time, he replaced his hand with his penis. Her moans grew louder, only this time they were cries of pleasure, not pain.

Harriet heard Maud cry out. Then she heard whispers and a woman's laughter somewhere above her. She wrapped her arms around her thin, dry, spinster's body and turned her face to the wall. Clutching a cushion to her breasts, she failed to block out her loneliness. She had never felt so isolated or unwanted. The house was positively reverberating with love.

Lieutenant Downe and that shameless native girl who'd wrapped herself around him, kissing him, not caring who was there to see it. Miss Maud and Captain Mason sharing a bed the other side of the wall. For all that they were married, it didn't seem right. Not on the day of her mother's death.

And her – she hadn't shared a bed with anyone since the day she'd left home and her younger sisters. Her 35 years lay heavy on her. Life had passed her by and she hadn't even noticed.

## Chapter Eight

*Basra, Saturday 8th August 1914*

Maud burrowed beneath the coverlet as John slid sideways out of the bed. He watched her fumble for him in her sleep before relaxing back into unconsciousness. Only then did he reach for the uniform that had been folded away for so many weeks. The khaki felt rough against his skin. The coat constricted his arms, the leather belt bit into his waist. Just when he thought he could leave the army behind him, Germany had declared war on half of Europe, leaving Britain no alternative but to pitch in with her allies, call up the reservists, and ruin the plans he'd made for himself and Maud. The minute they'd become used to living with one another he had to leave her to join a shooting match on the fields of Belgium.

He had no idea how long the war would last, but he knew army red tape. Lack of transport could keep him in Europe and Maud in India for a lot longer than it would take governments to sign peace treaties. Why had he ever taken a commission? He could have taken his pick of the posts in the London hospitals. If he had, he'd be home now working with his father, well out of it.

Anger smouldering, he walked out, under the shade of the veranda into the walled garden. Turning his back on the pile of trunks heaped close to the river entrance, he went to the fountain. He'd come to love this small part of Mesopotamia. He'd whiled away many happy hours here with Harry and Furja or Maud.

He took the tiny cup of Turkish coffee a slave handed him and stared despondently at the goldfish swimming beneath the water lilies in the pool.

'Good morning, cousin.' Furja joined him, smiling and, as usual indoors, unveiled.

'Good morning, Furja.'

'Harry left for the barracks. He hoped to hear news from Europe but he will return before it's time for you and Maud to take the steamer.'

'I will be sorry to leave.' John sat next to Furja on the edge of the fountain. He'd grown fond of Harry's wife, admired her vitality, sense of humour, and occasionally brutal honesty, and was grateful for the happiness she'd brought Harry.

'It's kind of you to say so. I hope you will now tell your countrymen that we Bedouin are not entirely ignorant of the more gracious arts of living.'

'Of course.' He was embarrassed by what he took to be a reference to Maud's coolness towards all things Islamic. The idyll of the past few weeks had been marred by her attitude. Unlike him, Maud found it difficult to converse with the Arabs, or come to terms with Harry's marriage. He'd made excuses for her; the only natives she'd met had been servants. No allowances had been made in her upbringing for the introduction of a highborn social hybrid like Furja. But his excuses couldn't compensate for Maud's lack of warmth towards the Bedouin girl and, despite his and Harry's best efforts; the atmosphere between the women had remained frosty, strained, and polite. Always polite. Excruciatingly so.

'I'm sorry. I've made you unhappy on your last morning in my father's house.'

'We British tend to think we have a monopoly on good manners and culture,' he conceded.

'As do we Bedouin. I will forgive your race their failings, if you will forgive mine.'

'Done.'

They sat in companionable silence while he fixed the scene in his mind, sensing it was a memory he might be glad to conjure during the times ahead. 'Sometimes it feels as though we only arrived here last night, and at other times it seems as though we have been here for ever. A happy for ever. You made it possible for Maud and I to have a honeymoon, Furja.'

'You are kind.'

'It is you who is kind. Harry told me you took us in against your father's wishes.'

'My father's commands referred to Ferenghis. In your heart you are no more Ferenghi than Harry.'

'Would to God none of us were. If we weren't, we wouldn't have to go to war.'

'You don't want to fight?' she asked.

'Like every other sane, normal man I want to stay with my wife.'

'Harry doesn't.'

'Harry doesn't want to leave you any more than I want to leave Maud,' he protested.

'Oh, if Harry could be sure of not missing anything by staying with me he would. But when Mitkhal returned from the compound last night and told him the British soldiers expect to be sent to India, and from there to the war in Europe, he started jumping like a goat on a sun-baked rock.'

'You're wrong, Harry...'

'Needs excitement and likes playing the warrior.' She shrugged. 'I accept him as he is. What else can a wife do?'

'You misunderstand Harry's position. He holds the King's commission. He has no choice. He has to go.'

'It is you who misunderstand Harry. He is not like you, John. There is much of the little boy in him.'

'On that we agree.' He smiled.

'In time you will agree with everything I've said.'

'In my country we say women are always right.'

'Here too.' She laughed.

'What will you do when Harry leaves?'

'Return to the desert and my father's tent.'

'Should you decide to go to England...?'

'No. Thank you, cousin, but no. I will return to my tribe; it is where I belong.'

'When two people love one another as much as you and Harry they belong with one another.' He was thinking of himself and Maud as much as Harry and Furja.

'Our marriage was not made for love, but politics. When it has served its purpose, we will divorce.'

John stared at her incredulously. 'You don't love Harry?'

'No more than he loves me.'

'I thought you were happy.'

'We are,' her smile broadened, 'but we are too busy living life to worry about details.'

'Details?' he questioned in bewilderment.

'The relationship between a man and a woman should be simple. If it is good on the mattress, there is no need for useless talk. Now I have shocked you. I forgot that Fer ... the British don't like mentioning the active side of love.'

'I'll never understand the Bedouin.' John turned his red face to the pool.

'We are a simple people. We act rather than speak about important things. The unimportant things we talk to death in the coffee circle. You can talk about something until you kill it, you know.' She started at the sound of bolts being drawn in the outside door. Her face lit up. 'Harry.'

'I wonder if he knows whether travelling orders have been issued to the Indian regiments. They're bound to send us to the Western Front.'

'So Harry tells me. Soon you will be gone, and I have said none of the things I intended, or given you this.' She thrust a package wrapped in a scrap of blue silk at him. 'It is an amulet, containing the sacred words of the prophet. We believe it affords the wearer protection from all evils, including bullets. You will wear it, John. For me?'

'I will treasure it, but the protection will be wasted. A doctor sees little of the fighting, only the results.'

'This war might be different, even for doctors.'

'Perhaps.' He buttoned the package into his top pocket.

'John?'

'Yes.' He jumped up as Harry walked through the door, Mitkhal close on his heels, their robes billowing around their feet.

'Send Maud to your mother. When you are away she will need the wisdom of an older woman to guide and protect her.'

'I'll try.'

John greeted Harry, wanting to hear the latest news from the barracks. But even as they spoke of the possible transfer of troops from India to the European Front, and Harry's frustration at being left behind with the detachment detailed to protect the Basra consulate and the Anglo-Persian Oil Company, he filed Furja's words at the back of his mind.

He didn't think about what she'd said. Not then. Not until much later, when long, lonely months separated him from Maud. And Furja and the garden were no more than a beautiful memory to be cherished in the darkness of a world gone mad.


## Chapter Nine

*The Persian Gulf Monday 19th October 1914*

Harry left his desk when the first rays of the sun touched the eastern horizon. He stood at the window and watched the sky turn from silver to gold above the silhouette of the oil refinery's storage tanks.

'Day's broken, sir,' the duty sergeant commented.

'So I see.' Harry turned from the window that had been let into the wall of the shack that served as both company and duty office. 'Give the order for the changing of the guard.'

'Sir.' The sergeant's boots thundered over the planking. The door, followed by the insect screen, banged behind him.

Peter Smythe strolled in, the top button of his shirt undone, a yawn contorting his boyish features. 'Anything?' he asked.

'Nothing.' Flinging himself into his chair, Harry propped his heels on a mess of paperwork on the desk. 'Bloody nothing.'

'We're all fed up, Harry, but you're wound like a clockwork toy about to spring. For Christ's sake, calm down, before you have the rest of us as crazy as you.'

'War breaks out. The Turks and Germans decide to hold hands. Turkish emissaries go to India to promote "holy war against the Imperialist British" among the Muslims. And what do we do?' Harry demanded before answering his own question. 'Retreat to Abadan, leaving Basra and the Shatt to the mercy of the bloody Ottomans. While Turkish troops mass around us, we sit like ducks in a coop waiting. Waiting for bloody what – that's what I'd like to know.'

'Orders?'

'And if Johnny Turk attacks tomorrow? Do we wait for the Indian Office to give us the all clear to shoot back? It could be months before the damned politicians remember we're here, and by

156

then we could all be dead and, if I know anything about the Turks, not even buried.'

'The *Espiegle*...'

'Oh yes, let's not forget HMS *Espiegle*,' Harry mocked. 'The sole representative of His Majesty's shipping in the Gulf, holed up and surrounded at the mouth of the Karun. The poor blighters on board received the message of "Please you leave the Shatt before 24 hours" when we marched out of Basra 12 days ago. And what orders did they get from the powers above? Wait! The ship is in a worse pigging mess than we are. The Turks could have wiped out the whole bloody countryside for all they or we know by now.'

'The Turks wouldn't dare attack Europeans or Americans. They'd risk bringing down...'

'The whole of this magnificent Frontier Force on their heads?' Harry jeered. 'All 15 officers, and 200 native troops of us.' He lit a cigarette. 'I bet the 10,000 Turkish troops in Basra are shaking in their boots at the threat we pose.'

'But the Americans...'

'Are neutral, God bless their democratic socks. Your Angela will be safe, which is more than can be said for most of the women in Basra.'

Peter knew nothing of Harry's native marriage and wondered which one of the European women Harry was concerned about.

Lost in calculations as to how long Shalan with his 500 rifles could hold out against the Turks, Harry remained oblivious to Peter's train of thought.

Peter thrust a flask at Harry. 'Brandy? You've been up too long to see straight, so you may as well get drunk.'

'Thanks.' Harry left his chair. 'Wake me if anything comes up.' He crossed the derrick-spattered, oil-puddled compound, walked past the sepoys' barracks, and entered the six by six shed he and Peter shared. Exhausted, he sank down on his camp bed and unlaced his boots. Kicking them off, he stretched on top of the blanket and took a generous swig of brandy, before feeling in his top pocket for the last letter he'd received. The only letter that had reached him since Charles had arrived at Clyneswood and, with the Turkish blockade in place, the only mail he was likely to get for some time.

*Clyneswood, Sunday 9th August 1914*
*Dearest Harry,*
  *Charles has delivered your letter. Congratulations on your marriage.*

He'd spent hours trying work out whether that comment was sarcastic or not.

  *As you prophesied, I've qualified. You can now address me as Dr Downe, ma'am, instead of "dear Twinnie", which you know I hate. See what you could have accomplished if you'd studied, instead of played. You can also forget the lectures about the East End. This war has messed up my plans, along with millions of others. People are behaving quite idiotically about the whole affair, especially Charles, who's desperately trying to get himself assigned to a regiment under orders for France. He says he doesn't want to "miss out on the fun".*

  *I don't know what fun he's going to get acting as a target for German bullets. Personally, I won't be sorry to see him go; he's been like a bear with six sore heads*

158

since he returned. What happened out there to change him into a boor? If you come back in the same foul mood, I promise not to speak to you. Michael wants to join up but Lucy won't let him. I suppose he has some excuse for wanting to go. Life in the bank must be dreadfully tedious. He and Lucy are getting married next week, much to the delight of Papa, Mama, Uncle John, and Aunt Margaret. I blame myself for not being here to stop it. I've tried to talk sense into him. I even asked him if he's determined to copy every stupid mistake you've ever made, but the fool just went bright red and mumbled something about "Lucy wanting to marry quickly, before the war's over". Though what that has to do with anything escapes me.

I wish you were here. You could always handle Michael. Of course, he's heading for disaster. I don't have to tell you what Lucy's like, or how Michael's jumping through hoops to try to please the silly girl.

Papa, Uncle Reid, and Uncle John are frightfully busy touring the county trying to recruit "volunteers" for Kitchener's New Army. I had the most fearful row with Papa when he threatened to sack any man on the estate who didn't volunteer. He hasn't done it yet, but it's only a matter of time. Both Papa and Uncle Reid are carrying their roles of gallant ex-officers to the extreme. They've offered their services to the War Office, though what the War Office is supposed to do with a couple of garrulous geriatrics I don't know. Mama, Aunt Margaret, and, of course, darling Lucy have put the war charities, and "collections for gallant little Belgium" at the top of their list of priorities. What are the "Sisters of the Abyss" and "Clothes for Naked African Savages" going to do without their patronage? You're best off out of it, Harry. I'll be glad when I *leave Clyneswood next week for Charing Cross. I'm trying to go before the wedding, but I doubt Papa will let me. The only good thing about this war is the shortage of doctors it's created. I've been appointed to the surgical staff. Me! A mere woman. That should tell you how desperate things are. The post was Tom's, but the idiot's already in the New Army, and as they're unlikely to allow John to resign, that makes two Dr Masons out of the civilian medical circuit.*

*Thank God you're safe in Mesopotamia. That's one less thing for me to worry about. Is Mesopotamia as biblical as it sounds? Give my regards to your wife, dear brother; she must be an exceptional woman to put up with you. Tell her, should she ever decide to visit Clyneswood; I for one (probably the only one) will be at the door to greet her. Take care, Harry.*

*Your ever-loving sister Dr Downe (ma'am)*

*P.S. Do write and tell me what John's wife is like. All we can get out of Charles is that she's pretty.*

Refolding the letter, Harry replaced it in his pocket. Georgiana's caustic humour shone through every line. She was right, of course, especially about Michael being a fool. What on earth had possessed him to ask Lucy to marry him? Or had the prompting come from Lucy? If she'd heard about Furja from Charles, she'd probably decided that the younger brother was better than no brother at all. And, if she was more politically astute than Georgiana, who'd never given a toss about anything global, she might be nurturing hopes that he'd die here in the desert, leaving her to assume the role of mistress apparent of Clyneswood. Something she'd been after since she'd left her dolls and short frocks behind in the nursery.

160

And Charles? Was his boorishness due to the news of Emily's death, or was that bombshell still in the post, waiting to be delivered? Harry turned restlessly on the cot. If only he knew whether Furja was safe. Mitkhal had promised to guard her with his life, but what could he do against a battalion of Turks. And to think he'd left her for this interminable, useless bloody waiting.

*Military convoy at sea out of India,*
*Monday 19th October 1914*

'Mason!' Billy Miles burst into the sick bay where John was lancing a boil on a rating's backside. Billy stared at the pus-covered lesion and turned puce.

'Not a pretty sight when you're recovering from seasickness.' John reached for an enamel bowl of swabs.

'No...'

'If you're going to vomit, vomit in the slop bucket, there's a good chap.' John mopped up the blood-streaked pool of matter. 'You wanted me, Miles?'

'The old man's just opened the sealed orders.' Billy slid into a chair.

'I didn't know there were any.'

'Where've you been? Everyone knew about them; they were marked *"not to be opened until three days out from port"*. Guess what?'

'Suppose you tell me.' John irrigated the site of the boil with salt water.

'We're not going to France.'

'Then where are we going?'

161

'East, as I suspected from the supplies that were loaded. Some ghastly hole called Bahrain. According to the ship's captain, it's an island, 300 miles from the mouth of the Shatt-el-Arab. The whole of Force D has been ordered there. Force A, lucky sods, really are sailing to France, and to think you got transferred at the last minute.'

'What are we going to do in the Gulf?'

'That's the best part. We're going to "wait for further orders".'

'Can I go, sir?' the rating asked John.

'When I've covered this.' John slapped a plaster over the bloody hole where the boil had been. The man pulled up his trousers, buttoned his fly, slipped his braces over his shoulders, and ran out.

'You've started a nice rumour there.' John tossed the contents of the swab bowl into the bucket.

'It's all over the ship. You're probably the last to know.' Billy took out a packet of cigarettes.

'No smoking in here.'

'And no mademoiselles to look forward to.' Billy thrust the cigarettes back into his pocket. 'No Cognac, no chateaux, no French wine, and no home leave. Why did I have to be posted to this tail end of the King's Army?'

'When I heard all the officers on the reserve list were being recalled, I thought the quickest way home would be via India.' John dumped his instruments into the sink and poured antiseptic over them.

'Don't blame yourself for making a bad move. The logical thing for the brass to have done was move the professionals out of India to the Western Front and ferry Kitchener's amateurs to India for garrison duty. But the brass never do the logical thing. Tell me, what sense is there in dumping a division of crack troops in the middle of the Gulf?'

'Maud and I could have been in England now,' John murmured.

'Look at it this way, old man.' Billy Miles left his chair and slapped John across the back. 'We're chums together in our hour of boredom.'

'I told my wife to take the first transport out of India bound for England. I thought she could live in my father's London house and I'd see her when I got home leave. Belgium's just across the Channel...'

'If she does get there, she'll be all right. You've been to this part of the world, haven't you? Are the locals accommodating? Can they compare with, say, the Hindu girls in the Rag?'

John didn't hear him. All he could think of was Maud. And the irony of a fate that had driven them further apart than ever.

*India, Monday 19th October 1914*

'You're Mason's wife, aren't you?' Johnny Leigh leered at Maud.

'Yes.' Maud tried to be polite.

'Old boy did well for himself.'

Maud looked over Leigh's shoulder, hoping to signal for help. There was none forthcoming, so she stuck her elbow into his ribs. 'So sorry, must see Marjorie.' She pushed past him.

'I'll come with you.'

She gave him her frostiest glare, only to be

163

greeted by an inane, loose-lipped grin. She hadn't wanted to come to this party, but Marjorie had insisted. She was hating every minute. It wasn't just Leigh's drunken attentions. Although she knew most of the people in the drawing room, she felt lonelier than she had done in her bungalow. A surplus of elegantly gowned and perfumed chattering women flitted about, every one valiantly trying to pretend they were having a marvellous time, and not missing their husbands.

She reached the group around Marjorie and began to breathe a little easier. Then the broad back of a khaki-clad figure in front of her reminded her of John – his breadth, his strength, the overt masculinity of his physical presence. Her limbs grew liquid with longing. She closed her eyes as an erotic image filled her mind. She and John were lying on the silk-covered divan in Furja's house. John was kissing the inside of her thigh, and she was holding his pulsating erection...

'May I apologise for Lieutenant Leigh?' The cavalry officer whose back she had been studying pushed Leigh aside. 'I couldn't help overhearing what he said to you.'

Maud looked blank. 'I had no idea he'd said anything.'

'Which only proves what a forgiving lady you are.' The officer lifted two glasses of iced wine from an Indian waiter's tray and handed her one. 'Lieutenant Leigh's been overdoing the celebrating. His wife – she's...' He turned scarlet.

'Presented him with a son.' Amused by his embarrassment, Maud smiled. 'I heard. Thank you.' Taking the glass, she drained it.

'Another.' He offered the drink he'd taken for himself. She was about to refuse, but there was something about his mouth that reminded her of John.

She glanced at him over the rim of her glass as she sipped the second glass of wine. He appeared to be a pleasant young man. Tall, not as tall as John, or on inspection, as broad, straight brown hair, combed into a centre parting, deep brown eyes. Fair skin – too fair for him to have been in India long.

He introduced himself. 'Geoffrey Brooke, Second Lieutenant 33rd Cavalry, at your service, ma'am. As the new boy I've been left to mind the shop while the rest of the regiment's away enjoying the war.'

'Someone has to protect us ladies,' Maud flirted mildly. This clean young man was a pleasant contrast to Johnny Leigh with his foul innuendos and even fouler breath.

'That's the first kind word that's been said to me since I arrived. Your husband's with the Indian Medical Service, isn't he?'

'Yes.'

'Good chap. He was at school with my brother.'

'How nice.' Maud had heard too many schoolboy reminiscences to find them entertaining.

'To be honest it wasn't. Reggie, that's my brother, said John used to hang round with this awful bounder, Harry Downe.'

'I know Harry.'

'You do.' His blush returned in all its vermilion glory.

'How old are you?' Maud asked with all the

confidence of her married status.

'Nineteen.'

'You look younger,' she replied with unintentional cruelty.

'I try not to.'

Maud looked to the door. She'd spent enough time making small talk in the hot, overcrowded room; she wanted to let down her hair and take off her damp gown. She needed to be alone, to take time to remember and think of John. She missed him so much. She'd become accustomed to his strength, his lovemaking...

'You're not going,' the lieutenant remonstrated when she retrieved her shawl.

'It's late and I'm tired.'

'Leaving us already, Maud?' Marjorie Harrap appeared; a pale, spiritual vision in purple silk, two attentive sub lieutenants in tow.

'Yes, thank you for a lovely evening, Marjorie.'

'Thank you for coming, darling. I won't keep you because I know you want to go and mope for John. Don't forget you're lunching at the club with me tomorrow.'

'I won't forget. And thank you again for the party.'

'You're going to walk Mrs Mason home, Lieutenant Brooke,' Marjorie prompted.

'My bungalow's only next door.'

'Anything could happen between here and next door. If you'd seen the way some of the natives look at European women. Particularly blondes...'

Geoffrey's blush returned. 'Don't worry, I'll see Mrs Mason safely inside her bungalow.'

'Goodbye, Marjorie.' Maud put an abrupt end

to Marjorie's dire warnings by leading the way out of the house.

'It's a lovely evening.' Geoffrey stared up at the star-studded, navy sky.

'It generally is in India at this time of year.'

'I'm sorry if I've upset you. I've the most awful habit of offending ladies. Truth is I'm not used to being around girls. School, Sandhurst; you know how it is.'

'No, I don't.' Maud's irritation melted in the face of his honesty. She stopped at a gate set in the side fence of Marjorie's garden. 'You see, it really wasn't necessary for you to accompany me. That's my bungalow, or rather my temporary quarters until I can get a berth for England.'

Geoffrey peered at the white wooden walls and shutters only just visible through a circle of mature banyan trees. 'There's no light. Surely you don't live alone.'

'I have a maid, but she's dining in the sergeants' mess tonight with a sergeant from the Signals Corps.'

'I don't want to impose, Mrs Mason, but I'd be happier if you'd let me look around. What Mrs Harrap said about natives is not all bunkum. I've heard...'

'Haven't we all.' She tossed him her keys. He caught them and opened the gate. They walked up the path and onto the veranda. He unlocked the front door.

'Electric light switch to the left.'

He found it. 'Everything appears to be in order.' He looked around the sparsely furnished hall before opening the door to the drawing room.

Pieces of the same good quality utility furniture as the hall were dotted around the spacious, high-ceilinged room. The bungalow had the makeshift atmosphere he was beginning to associate with army quarters, married as well as single.

'As you see, it's not much of a home. Most of our–' Maud stressed 'our' '–belongings are crated. Waiting for England.'

'Would you like me to check the other rooms?'

'You may as well, as you're here,' she replied ungraciously.

'Only if you want me to.'

His humility stung her conscience. It was hardly his fault that John was half an ocean away. 'Hang your topee on the stand. John's left some whisky if you'd like a drink.'

'I'd love one.' He disappeared to the back of the bungalow.

Maud went to the cocktail tray. She poured Geoffrey a whisky, and took an apricot from the fruit bowl for herself.

'All sound and secure.' Geoffrey rubbed his hands nervously as he joined her.

'I'm glad to hear it. Your drink is there. Sit down.' It sounded like an order and he obeyed.

'I suppose your husband's been posted to the Western Front.'

'As far as I can make out. You know how difficult it is to be sure of anything in the army.'

'He's lucky. I'd give my right arm to be on the front line. The whole thing's going to be over by Christmas and I'm stuck here, out of it.' When she didn't reply, he finished his whisky. 'Thanks most awfully for the drink. Most kind of you to

168

ask me in.'

'You're going.' It was a statement, not a plea for him to remain. She followed him into the hall. 'Don't forget your topee.' They reached for it at the same moment and their fingers brushed. Maud thrust her hands behind her back. The scene was terrifyingly familiar. His touch warm, unsettling. She found herself staring at the hard, masculine figure sheathed in uniform. Somehow, the personality, the features, didn't matter. Only the male presence. An image of John's body, naked, filled her mind.

'Well, thanks again, for everything.'

The image dispersed. She glanced into Geoffrey's eyes. They shifted uneasily under her gaze. She stared guiltily at the floor. Had he read her thoughts?

'Thank you for escorting me home.' What was happening to her? Was she going mad? All she could think of was making love. First John. Now this boy.

'I'll be off then.' He stepped outside.

'Goodnight.' She slammed the door. Her limbs were trembling. She was liquid with longing, not for John, but for a man. Any man.

Since they'd returned to India and she'd been welcomed into the inner circle of officers' wives she'd been a party to enough whispered revelations to discover that when it came to the intimate side of married life she was different from other women. Most of them looked forward to the nights when their husbands visited the Rag.

'Better them than us,' Marjorie Harrap had sighed. She'd been the only woman present not to nod agreement. The implication was clear. Whores liked the disgusting things men did, ladies didn't. Did that make her a whore? Was she no better than the women who were passed down the lines of privates' beds in the barracks on pay nights?

Even John, who never baulked at discussing any subject with her, had been no help when she'd raised the matter. All he'd said was, 'I guess we're luckier than most, darling. Let's just count our blessings.'

Our blessings! She switched on the light. The empty bedroom gaped at her. She walked over to the cheval mirror and began to undress. First, the pale pink silk dress. She tossed it in a heap over the chair. Harriet could sort it later. Her petticoats, stockings, their supports, drawers, and last of all, her bust shaper and chemise. She wore no corsets. John had taken one look at the angry red marks where the steel and whalebone stays had constricted her flesh and forbidden her to wear them. He'd told her she didn't need a corset. That her body was perfect the way it was. But what was the use of having a perfect body when there was no one to admire it?

She pulled the tortoise-shell pins from her hair. Her blonde curls tumbled to her waist. She closed her eyes and massaged her throbbing flesh, desperately trying to imagine it was John who was caressing her, but the more she tried to concentrate on his face, the more elusive his features became. His uniformed body was easy to recall; it was the same as Geoffrey's – as any officer. But his face remained shrouded in a mist that refused to clear. She couldn't remember what he looked like.

Three days. Only three days since he'd left and she couldn't remember what he looked like.

Maud didn't realise she'd forgotten to draw her bedroom curtains until the moon shifted and shone through her window, rousing her from a blissful dream of lovemaking. Cursing her thoughtlessness, she rose and closed the drapes, unaware that at that moment Geoffrey Brooke was lying awake in his own bed, gazing at that same moon and blessing her neglect.

Maud's naked image, the first he had seen of a woman outside of a picture postcard, was one he would treasure for the rest of his life.

## Chapter Ten

*Sahil, Wednesday 18th November 1914*

'It was a brilliant affair. Quite brilliant.' Crabbe's voice, high-pitched, excited, carried down the rows of camp beds to where John was crouched over a lieutenant's head wound. 'The Turks were here.' Crabbe creased the sheet in the centre of his cot. 'General Delamain's brigade here.' Purloining a pair of forceps from an orderly's tray, he plonked it below the line. 'The brigade turned in on the Turks' left.' He pushed the forceps across the sheet. 'The Dorsets were here.' Snatching a bandage, he laid it next to the forceps. 'Johnny Turk threw all the hardware he had

171

at us. You wouldn't believe the strength of that fusillade. It was hailing shot and bullets.' His eyes shone like those of a slum child who'd been shown Christmas. 'Then slap bang in the middle of the bloodiest, hottest part of the day, Johnny Turk cut and ran. To a man, they crawled out of their trenches and swarmed back over the desert. We tried to go after them, but between the heavy ground and the mirage...'

'And the bullets.' John lifted Crabbe's shoulder dressing and peered at his wound.

'We got them on the run. And took two of their guns. Fine mountain guns. They'll be missing those.'

'And your company's going to be missing you for a while, Major.' John signalled to the orderly. Singh scooped the forceps from Crabbe's bed.

'Brilliant, I tell you. Quite brilliant.' Crabbe turned to the subaltern in the next cot. 'You were lucky to be part of it, Amey. I've been in the army 30 years...'

Lucky! John looked down the rows of cots. And this was only one tent. The 125th Field Ambulance had set up another for officers and six more for other ranks, and those were just to house the British wounded. The Indians were crammed into nine tents of their own. 'Lucky!'

He couldn't forget the pile of shrouded corpses, including what was left of Billy Miles, that had been lowered into pits dug below the new British stronghold of Sahil the same time a message had been sent out on the radio transmitter,

*Abadan oil fields secured. Oil company staff safe and well. Saniyeh and Sahil objectives achieved.*

*Casualties light. Moving on to Basra at dawn.*

'Mason?' Colonel Hale, his CO in Force D Field Hospital, stuck his head around the tent flap.

'Sir.' John hadn't realised how exhausted he was until he tried to move.

'What in hell are you doing, boy?' Hale demanded when John left the tent. 'Three hours after you complete an 18-hour operating stint I find you on the ward.'

'Knight discovered two cases of gas gangrene, sir. I'm checking this ward for signs.'

Hale frowned. 'Knight's certain?'

'I saw them myself, sir. Knight and I amputated one leg and an arm an hour ago.'

'British or Indian tent?'

'British ranks, sir.'

'Have you checked the Indians?'

'Knight's doing it now, sir.'

'All we need is an outbreak of gangrene with Delamain and Fry hell-bent on taking Basra in the morning. We've got off lightly so far.' He shook his bald head. 'But it's my guess Johnny Turk's going to hit back hard in the next offensive. And with this number of casualties... How's the supply situation?'

'Holding up, sir.'

'Total casualties?'

'Ten officers seriously wounded, twenty lightly. Sixty ranks, fifteen seriously, and two hundred and fifteen Indians, including officers.' John's face was ashen in the light of the lantern.

'You've finished checking your quota.'

'Yes, sir.'

'Get some rest. I doubt any of us will be able to

173

do much of that tomorrow.'

John saluted and made his way to his tent. He was lucky to be working under Hale. The colonel's first consideration was the welfare of his patients, the next, his staff; a long way after that came the army, and last of all himself.

He breathed in the night air, fresh and free from the tainted odours of the hospital stations. As far as he could see, campfires blazed between the shadowy outlines of tents. Soldiers' laughter, accompanied by the clang of billycans and the clinking of knives, echoed. From his right came the whinny of animals and the curses of the Indian muleteers who were shifting supplies closer to the front. A shadow leapt out in front of him.

'Damn you, Harry. You scared the living day-lights out of me.'

'Sorry.' Harry held out a hip flask. 'I thought you'd appreciate some brandy.'

John took the flask. The liquor slid easily down his throat. His legs weakened as his head lightened. 'I'm bone weary.' He ducked into his tent, leaving the flap open for Harry. 'Take Knight's bed. He's on duty until morning.' Striking a match, John lit the lamp. 'You're wounded.'

'More dirty than hurt.' Harry fingered the bandage above his right eye.

John shook his head at Harry's torn and muddy uniform. 'I suppose you were in the front line.'

'I was seconded as adjutant to the 18th, Fry's Brigade. I tried to keep my head down.' Harry grinned, and John recalled his conversation with Furja. She was right. Harry was enjoying every minute of the mess and upheaval, treating the war as an adventure.

'I heard you've volunteered for every skirmish since we rescued you.'

Harry retrieved his flask. 'We were doing all right until you disembarked.'

'You're the first Frontier Force officer I've heard complain about Force D's help.'

'Old Gulf hands are too generous to begrudge a fellow soldier a share of the fun.' Harry up-ended the flask in his mouth.

'You've volunteered for the show tomorrow.'

Harry swallowed a mouthful of brandy before returning the flask to John. 'The *Espiegle*, the *Odin*, and a couple of armed launches are going up river to take a look at the Turks. They asked for Arabic-speaking officers.'

'You put up your hand?'

'I was looking for a chance to take a look around on my own account. Maybe even as far as the Karun Valley.'

'You've no need to worry about Furja. The Turks are too busy trying to kill us to bother the natives.'

'I wish I had your faith.' Harry unlaced his boots and kicked his feet up on the cot.

John followed Harry's example. The thin pallet on the camp bed felt miraculously soft and comforting. He closed his eyes.

'The Turks hanged Furja's brothers...' Harry looked across. John was already asleep; he rescued the flask as it slid from John's fingers and took one last mouthful. He was tired and incredibly filthy. He spent a moment debating whether to wash, or sleep. He simply didn't have the energy to search for water and soap. Tomorrow

*The Shatt-el-Arab, Saturday*
*November 21st 1914 5.00 p.m.*

'Downe, you know Basra. What's burning?' Captain Bullock pointed to smoke spiralling from the bank.

Harry squinted at the horizon. 'Looks like the Customs House and warehouses, sir.'

'The European quarter?'

'If it was burning, we'd see it, sir. It appears the Turks fired the public buildings before retreating.' Leaning over the rail, he stared at the flat roofs of the Arab quarter. If Ibn Shalan had returned to Basra Furja could be in the hands of the retreating Turks. Imprisoned – tortured – dead...

'What say you, Langdon?' Bullock asked his second in command.

'I agree with Downe, sir. The Turks have pulled out. It would explain why we've met no opposition since Sahil. There are no launches on the river and although there's activity close to the fire, no one's wearing uniform.'

Bullock lifted his field glasses. 'Looters?'

'Could be,' Langdon agreed. 'Want us to ram a couple of shots into them from the bow guns?'

'No!' Harry protested in alarm. 'The fact they're still in Basra and not retreating means they're friendly natives, sir.'

'If they're well disposed towards us, Lieutenant Downe, why aren't they out in their dhows greeting us as liberators?'

'Possibly because the Turks fired their boats

176

along with the warehouses, sir,' Harry suggested.

A rating appeared at the top of ladder that led to the lower deck. 'Message from the *Odin, sir*. There are native looters on the bank. The *Odin* has them in their gun sights. They're asking what action you wish to take.'

'Our Arab advisor thinks we should keep our shot to ourselves in case they're allies.'

'We have few, if any, allies among the natives, sir,' Langdon said.

'We have few, if any, who are downright hostile to us,' Harry broke in. 'If the tribes remain neutral we stand a chance. There's little love lost between Turk and Arab. We haven't seen any Arabs fighting on the Turkish side.'

'Or ours,' Bullock commented.

'If we shoot them, they'll never join our forces.'

'Very well, Downe. You're the expert on Arab affairs; we'll try it your way,' Bullock conceded. 'Pass on the order, Langdon, to the *Odin* as well as our chaps. They shoot at the first sign of hostility. From Turk or Arab. If we have to fight the entire population of this damned country to secure our oilfields, so be it.'

'Sir.'

'As the expert, Downe, you can lead the shore party. Leaving in ten minutes.'

Harry left the bridge. So much for his idea of sneaking off and reconnoitring the Arab quarter. Officialdom had dug its claws in. It could be days before he had a free moment to find out if Furja was in Basra. Let alone alive.

Peter Smythe picked his way through the mass of soldiers, boxes of supplies, and half-erected tents only to be faced with a crowd of subalterns and officers awaiting orders in the corridor outside what had been Perry's office.

'Where are you going, Lieutenant?' Major Harrap demanded from behind a desk. A bundle of forms lay in front of him, his revolver was at his elbow.

'Reporting for duty, sir.' Peter saluted.

'All subalterns are detailed to camp duties.'

'I'm surplus to requirements, sir,' Peter lied. 'As I'm familiar with the town, the duty officer thought I'd be better employed on curfew duty.'

'You were with the Frontier Force?' he asked.

'Yes, sir.' Peter confirmed.

'Take ten sepoys and check out the area to the...' Harrap peered indecisively at the map of Basra pinned to the wall behind him.

'There's an American mission south-east of the European quarter, sir.'

'Check it out and patrol every street as thoroughly and frequently as time and manpower allow. You'll be relieved at dawn.' Harrap scribbled a note and handed it to Peter.

Peter walked away elated. The town was quiet; the advent of British gunboats in the Shatt and the sight of British and Indian troops marching through the streets had dispersed the looters. Thrusting the order into his pocket, he pushed his way out of the building. Less than an hour ago, Harry had assured him the American

178

mission and its staff had survived the Turkish withdrawal unscathed. But he wouldn't rest until he'd seen Angela for himself.

Angela sat in her schoolroom ostensibly preparing lessons, but she was unable to concentrate. The street was silent. Last night, Theo, Doctor Picard, Reverend Butler, and the mission's native servants had barricaded the doors and windows of the school and staff quarters and taken it in turns to man the doors. They'd expected marauding Arabs to attack. But, much to everyone's relief, the looting had remained confined to the wharf.

No pupils had arrived for school that morning so she and the other teachers had volunteered to help in the hospital. Doctor Picard and Theo had worked round the clock for three days and nights and were exhausted. The Turks hadn't set up medical facilities and the wards were carpeted with Turkish wounded. She'd spent the day washing and dressing gunshot wounds, and ladling water into the mouths of feverish and dying men.

The minute news filtered through that a British Force had landed, Theo left to beg medical supplies. He'd seen Harry and Harry had assured him Peter Smythe was fine, but when she discovered Harry was part of an advance party and the bulk of the troops were still travelling upriver from Sahil she began to worry. What if Harry had seen Peter before the fighting, not afterwards? Anything could have happened in a few hours. It was rumoured the Turks had left snipers...

The silence closed in. She heard the creak of floorboards, the tick of the clock. But silence, even this uneasy silence, was preferable to the nightmarish cries the wind had carried from the banks of the Shatt for two days and nights before the Turks withdrew. Furious at her own impotence, she dropped her pencil and went to the window forgetting that the Reverend had boarded it up. Had she really heard horses' hooves?

Picking up the lamp, she ran to the front of the building. She reached the door but her brother's cautionary warnings stayed her hand.

'Angela.'

It was a voice she knew. Heaving back the bolts, she wrenched open the wooden door. Peter stood bathed in the glow from her lamp.

'You're hurt!'

'This.' Lifting his hand to his face, he laughed. 'It's nothing. I tripped over a rope on one of the boats and fell against the side.'

Tears welled in her eyes as he stepped inside and closed the door. Taking the lamp, he set it on the hall table before gathering her in his arms. She buried her face in his tunic and wept before remembering practicalities.

'Are you hungry?'

'Yes,' Peter admitted, without relinquishing his hold on her. 'But I can't stay. I'm in charge of the curfew patrol for this sector. If I don't turn up in 20 minutes my men will send out search parties.'

'Twenty minutes...'

He stroked her hair. 'The last three months have been the longest in my life.'

'I've missed you too.'

'The good thing about war is the chance of promotion.' He closed his mind to the bodies they'd left in Sahil. Strange how he'd never associated promotions in war with the dead.

'I'll see to that—' she touched his cut cheek '—then get you something to eat.' He followed her into the school's first aid room. 'Are you in the same bungalow?'

'I'm sharing a tent on the parade ground with Amey. The bungalows have been requisitioned by senior officers.'

'But they were yours.'

'That's the army for you.'

'Was it very dreadful?' She tipped antiseptic into a basin.

'What?' Peter asked absently, unable to stop looking at her. She seemed so beautiful, so neat, so clean after the madness of Sahil.

'The fighting.' Tearing a ball of cotton wool, she dipped it into the basin before dabbing at his face. More dirt than blood came off on the swab. 'You're filthy.'

'Fighting isn't a clean occupation.' It was the first time he'd called her that. She looked into his eyes as he locked his arms around her waist.

'I've been out of my mind with worry about you.'

'Why? You knew I'd be fine here. We're...'

'Americans and neutral. Harry kept reminding me.'

He seemed older, harder, and there was a peculiar excitement in his eyes. She wondered if that was what war and killing did to men. He kissed her. Her first kiss, but she was aware only of his smell – cordite and sharp, acrid, male sweat.

'You found your way back to us, Lieutenant

181

Smythe.' Theo appeared in the doorway.

Angela threw the swab she was holding into the bowl. 'I was just bathing Peter's cut.'

'I only called for a few minutes to make sure Angela was all right.' Rising from the chair, Peter offered his hand to Theo. 'My men are patrolling this sector.'

'I'll get you some food, Peter.' Feeling like a coward, Angela retreated to the kitchens.

'You were going to behave like a gentleman,' Theo admonished him.

'I have and will. Angela is my fiancée, and kissing a fiancée is not only permitted, but expected of a gentleman.'

'Really?'

'I will marry your sister,' Peter warned. 'Just as soon as I get my captaincy, and in wartime that's likely to come sooner rather than later.'

Theo stared at Peter. The confident young officer facing him bore little resemblance to the shy, stammering boy who'd asked for Angela's hand a few short months before. 'Will the Expeditionary Force remain in Basra?' Theo enquired.

'Our brief is to secure the oilfields. To do that we need to secure the Basra Wilyat. We're here to stay.' Peter smiled at Angela, who reappeared with a packet of bread and chicken legs. The way they looked at one another made Theo feel old and superfluous. For the first time he realised just how much his sister was in love with Peter Smythe. He'd been a fool to underestimate the strength of that love. On both sides.

*Basra, Monday 23rd November 1914*

'Read it again, Lieutenant Downe,' Lieutenant-Colonel Cox ordered.

Harry mentally cursed the Arabs as he breathed in the wintry air. The doors, windows, and furniture had been looted from every Government building during the 48 hours that had elapsed between the Turkish withdrawal and the British arrival in Basra. As a result, he was freezing.

'Proclamation,' Harry rasped. *'Let it not be hidden from you that the Great British Government has to its great regret been forced into a state of war by the persistent and unprovoked hostility of the Turkish Government instigated by Germany for her own ends. The British Government has therefore been obliged to send a force to the Shatt-el-Arab to protect her commerce and her friends...'*

'Good point that,' Perry broke in. 'Get home to Sheikh Muhammerah just how important he is to us.'

'Carry on, lieutenant.' The lieutenant-colonel glared at Perry.

*'And expel the hostile Turkish troops. But let it be known to all, the British Government has no quarrel with the Arab inhabitants on the riverbank; and so long as they show themselves to be friendly and do not harbour Turkish troops, or go about armed they have nothing to fear, and neither they nor their property will be molested. They are clearly warned, however, that they must not carry arms; for it will not be possible to distinguish an armed man from an enemy, and thus any person going armed will be liable to be shot. Dated the 5th November and signed P.Z. Cox.*

183

*Resident...* Sir,' Harry ventured, 'does this proclamation apply to the desert tribes?'

'I am aware of the implications, Downe. Copies in Arabic, English, and Turkish to be posted in every public building and street throughout the town, and–' the lieutenant-colonel studied the faces of the assembled officers '–I trust every one of you gentlemen will see that the proclamation's terms will be discussed – and obeyed by your junior officers. Any outrages against the local population will be severely dealt with. Any questions?' The silence was punctuated by a few coughs and one sneeze – Harry's. 'Thank you for your time and attention. Colonel Perry, Lieutenant Downe, if you'd wait.'

Harry shivered while the room emptied. Perry ignored him.

'Colonel Perry tells me you are married to the daughter of a local Sheikh, Lieutenant Downe.' Lieutenant-Colonel Cox flipped through the papers on his desk until he found the relevant memo. 'Sheikh Aziz Ibn Shalan, who has influence and holdings in the Karun Valley.'

'Yes, sir.' Harry glanced uneasily from the lieutenant-colonel to Perry.

'Are you happily married, Lieutenant Downe?'

'The marriage was a regrettable necessity,' Perry interrupted before Harry could answer. 'I negotiated a treaty with Ibn Shalan whereby he agreed to police the pipeline of the Anglo-Persian Oil Company, saving us considerable resources and manpower, in return for arms and livestock. We could hardly hand the goods over openly. The Turks were in control at the time, so Downe paid

184

out the goods in the form of a bride price for Shalan's daughter. But one of the implicit terms agreed between Shalan and myself was the speedy termination of the marriage.' Perry strayed into the realms of fantasy. 'I gave Lieutenant Downe orders to divorce his wife months ago. Under local law such a divorce would have been instant.'

'It was a marriage of necessity only.' Cox looked directly at Harry.

'Yes, sir,' Perry answered swiftly.

'Have you divorced the lady, Lieutenant Downe?'

'No, sir.'

'May I enquire why you chose to ignore a direct order from a superior officer?'

'I felt it was a personal not military matter, sir, and neither myself nor my wife wished to divorce.' Harry met Cox's gaze head on.

'Have you lived with the lady?'

'Yes. In her father's camp in the Karun Valley and in Basra.'

'In the European compound?' Cox enquired.

'No, sir, in Ibn Shalan's house in the Arab sector. My wife will not live in British quarters, sir.'

'Are Ibn Shalan's men aware you are a British officer?'

'Yes, sir.'

'They treat you as such.'

'As far as I can tell they treated me the same as every other man in Shalan's camp. When I was with them I wore native dress, ate their food, and lived as they did.'

Perry reddened. 'I never gave Lieutenant Downe permission to...'

185

The lieutenant-colonel held up his hand. 'And in Basra, your neighbours know you are British.'

'Not that I'm aware of, sir. I've always worn Arab dress when travelling to and from my wife's home.'

'And into barracks, or so I see from this report.' Cox raised an eyebrow. Harry said nothing. 'So you have on occasion passed as an Arab?'

'Yes, sir,' Harry replied quickly, reading the political officer's train of thought.

'One of the problems we face is the gathering of accurate intelligence from the local tribes. We have no aeroplanes, but should they arrive tomorrow, aerial reconnaissance will only detail Turkish troop movements and the position of the various tribal camps. It will tell us nothing about the loyalty of the natives. It would be naïve to suppose they are all well-disposed towards us. The Turks have controlled the Gulf for centuries. I'm convinced they have many allies living under our flag. We need to identify them. You have demonstrated that you read and speak excellent Arabic. On your own admission, you have lived with the natives as a native. A person with those qualities could prove invaluable to my department.'

Harry could scarcely believe his luck. Cox was offering him a legitimate excuse to leave the irksome side of soldiering and work on his own, possibly even steal enough time to see Furja. 'I would regard it as an honour to work for your department, sir.'

'Colonel Perry, would you be prepared to release Lieutenant Downe from the Frontier Force?'

'We have been declared an integral part of the Expeditionary Force, sir,' Perry demurred.

186

'I'll see to your immediate transfer, Lieutenant Downe. You can begin right away. I need to ascertain the mood of the natives in the town. In a day or two you'll leave for the desert to try to gauge what we can expect from the tribes in this area.' He sketched a rough outline on the map. 'At the same time you will make them aware of the details contained in the proclamation. Particularly the sections on carrying arms.'

'I'll discuss the matter with them, sir, but the desert tribes have carried arms for centuries. They value their freedom.'

'It is your job to convince them that we alone can guarantee that freedom. Pay particular attention to the Bakhtairi Khans. Intelligence suggests they're pro-German and Turkish. I believe they'd be massing with the Turks north of here at this moment if it weren't for their interest in our oil-field. Financial concerns dictate loyalties more often than men's principles, Lieutenant Downe.' He returned to the papers on his desk. 'I'll leave the matter of dress to your discretion. Report back to me tonight.'

Harry saluted Cox and Perry, walked through the gap that had recently been a door, and headed for the European compound. Staff officers had requisitioned his bungalow, but he found a sepoy and sent him to the *Espiegle* to pick up his kit and deliver it to Abdul's coffee shop on the quay. He'd rent a room there. It wouldn't take long for the officers to find out about Abdul's dancing girls, or the extras they were prepared to offer. In a day or two, no one would notice one lieutenant amongst many walking out

187

of the place, or an Arab going in to drink coffee with his fellows. He'd arrange it with Abdul, set up his base, change, and visit Shalan's house. If he were lucky, Furja would be there, and then...

## Chapter Eleven

*India, Sunday November 22nd 1914*

'Would you like more tea?' Maud waited for the inevitable blush to colour Lieutenant Brooke's cheek.

'Yes, please. It's a terrific tea party. You ladies put us to shame, you work so hard for the war effort, and we...'

'Maud,' Marjorie interrupted, 'be an angel, go into the conservatory and track down the flower basket I made for Mrs Hale. I'd ask the Khitmagar but he can't read and he's bound to bring out the more elaborate arrangement I made for the general's wife.'

'I'll go, Mrs Harrap.' Geoffrey rushed to the door.

Marjorie pursed her lips. 'You really must do something to put that wretched boy out of his misery, Maud.'

'He's getting to be a nuisance. I can't move an inch without him dogging my heels.'

'Be gentle with him. He's a sweet child,' Marjorie advised.

'Who should be in the nursery.'

188

'Unfortunately, all we're left with are infants and bath-chair cases.' Marjorie sighed as an elderly major smirked at her. 'Count yourself lucky for attracting a child, darling. I'm surrounded by grandfathers.'

'I say.' Geoffrey came blundering back. 'There are hundreds of baskets, and they all seem to have cards to colonels' wives.'

'I'll get it.' Maud left her chair.

'It's the one with the blue irises, darling. Mrs Hale adores them. Oh dear, she's making her way towards me. That means she wants to get away early.'

Maud entered the enormous greenhouse Marjorie inaccurately referred to as her 'conservatory'.

'I'll carry the basket for you, Mrs Mason.' Geoffrey was at her shoulder.

'First, we must find the right basket.'

'Most of the ones with cards to colonels' wives were over here.' Geoffrey led the way to the far end of the greenhouse. Maud followed, searching the green-filtered gloom for a splash of blue.

'I think that's the basket intended for Mrs Hale.' She pointed to an arrangement on a table close to the door but, instead of retracing his steps, Geoffrey grabbed her, and kissed her full and clumsily on the lips.

'I shouldn't have done that but I'm not sorry,' he said defiantly. 'I love you, Mrs Mason. I've loved you from the first moment I saw you, you're...' His eloquence dissipated along with his courage.

Maud looked at him. His face was misty in the humidity of the greenhouse but she felt his body,

189

unyielding, pressed against hers. The rough, khaki cloth of his uniform scratched her skin. She could smell the metal polish on his buttons, the linseed oil on his leather belt. The same scents as John... Standing on tiptoe, she returned Geoffrey's kiss.

His nervousness vanished as passion overcame the inhibitions that had been drilled into him since childhood. His hands caressed her breasts; his tongue probed her mouth.

Feelings Maud'd fought to suppress since John had left rose to the surface. What she was doing was wrong, but John was hundreds of miles away; it could be years before she saw him again. She'd be old and ugly – perhaps even dead. Geoffrey loved her, would stay with her. And John wouldn't return to India. She wouldn't see him again until they were both in England. He'd never find out – her mother had been happy with Charles...

A door slammed shut somewhere in the house. She pushed Geoffrey away. 'Not here. Later. You'll have to find somewhere.'

*Basra, Tuesday November 24th 1914*

Harry's sandals flapped, soles rebounding off the compacted dirt road. His robes fluttered in the gale that whipped through the town. Clutching his abba, he wondered how women coped with their skirts in a wind. He made a mental note to ask Furja, or Georgiana in his next letter. Despite the cold that heralded the onset of winter, the commercial quarter was teeming. Believing a strong British presence to be the best way of introducing the town's population to their new governing body, General Fry had ordered all available troops be given a day's leave.

Soldiers mingled with Arabic, Armenian, and Jewish locals, the officers fingering the fine Persian carpets and brass bowls on sale, the ranks ogling the Druse Christian and Jewish girls whose families were either destitute or greedy enough to allow them to work in the shops.

There was a great deal of sign language and good-natured laughter, but traces of the looting remained, and not just in the desecrated public buildings. The Turkish-owned booths had been smashed, their battered brass ornaments and sweetmeats trodden into the dirt, their owners absent, presumably fleeing with the retreating Turkish Army.

Harry bought a handful of dates from a Bedouin who'd set up his basket in front of one of the broken booths, but no information came with the purchase. The old man fixed his toothless mouth into a grin, kept his eyes on the British soldiers and repeated, 'Business is good. Business is very good.'

Harry went on his way, peeling dates, wondering at the resilience of commerce. A week ago, the bazaar must have been witness to the same scenes, the only difference being the uniform of the soldiers.

Leaving the shops, he walked along the wharf. The ashes of the Custom House were scattered on the quayside. A few small boats plied their nets in the shallows of the Shatt, a row of swollen sacks by the remains of a warehouse representative of their catch. Black-veiled women huddled in wailing groups, their heads strewn with ashes from the wreckage. Sepoys, working under the direction of a thick-necked, bullet-headed British sergeant, were slitting the sacks open. Rock weights and water-distended limbs burst out. The stench of death hung in the cold air despite the high wind.

Harry recalled the tales of atrocities he'd heard in Abdul's. Evidently they weren't all propaganda. The Turkish governor, Fakhri Pasha, had sewn the prisoners he'd taken during his reign in Basra into sacks before retreating from the town; judging from the claw marks in the hessian, most had been alive when they'd been thrown into the river.

A spray of dark hair plastered into weed-like tendrils spilt out of the sack closest to him. He saw a woman's face and his blood ran cold. Ibn Shalan had taken British guns. One malcontent's whisper to the Turks could...

He clenched his fists against an image of Furja pleading, begging for her life as they dragged her from Shalan's house. Her screams as they tied her into the sack, her fight against the dead weight of the stones as they carried her down to the river-bed.

Pushing aside a sepoy, he widened the slit. The body was too short, too old to be Furja.

'Someone you know, Abdul? Someone you put there?' the sergeant taunted.

Harry shook his head.

'You sure?' The sergeant flashed a broad-bladed knife. 'You use something like this to cut off this poor bitch's ears, Abdul?' Grabbing Harry's shoulder, he pushed him down close to a mutilated

192

stump, all that was left of the woman's right ear. 'Take a good look at your handiwork, Abdul.'

Lifting his head, Harry wiped his mouth with the back of his hand. He crawled away from the corpse and stared at the sergeant. The sergeant lashed out with his boot.

'Wog bastard.' He sent Harry sprawling. 'You're all the bloody same. Murdering, sodding...'

Harry grabbed the sergeant's foot, sending him crashing. Red-faced, fighting for breath, the sergeant called out to the sepoys. All Harry could do was lie helplessly as the quayside, the bodies, the sergeant whirled in a kaleidoscope of fragmented images and high-pitched sounds. Harry saw the sergeant laugh as the sepoys' hobnail boots smashed into his ribcage. Perry was on the quay, smiling. Why in God's name was the man smiling?

'Perry,' he croaked. A foot obscured his vision. He curled into a ball in an attempt to shield his head. The sepoys chanted in their exaggerated Welsh accents.

'Kill Abdul. Kill Abdul. Kill Abdul...'

'What's going on here, Sergeant?' Peter Smythe stood over him, topee pushed back at a rakish angle exposing his red hair, a swagger stick under his arm.

'We caught one of the natives responsible for this, sir.' The sergeant indicated the corpses.

'You have proof of this man's guilt, Sergeant?'

Harry tried to move. A pain shot through his chest, crippling him. He saw Peter pale when he recognised him, heard him murmur his name. Then he plunged into darkness.

*India, Friday November 27th 1914*

Geoffrey Brooke rode along the main thorough-
fare. Swerving past Indian drays and European
carriages, he arrived at The Star of the East, an
Anglo-Indian hotel with a dubious reputation.
Tossing the reins to the stable boy, he vaulted off
the saddle, and ran into the faded red plush and
gilt reception hall.

'Sahib Brooke.' The obsequious Indian who
owned the place bowed. 'Madam is here. We have
given her all comforts. Shall I send up champagne, Sahib?'

'A bottle of the best, Joseph. Chilled – and with
better glasses than last time.' Geoffrey exercised
the confidence that came with his first sexual
conquest.

'My apologies. It was a bad servant. He is gone.
It will not happen again.'

'Tell the waiter to knock and leave it outside the
door.'

'Of course, Sahib, we...'

Geoffrey didn't wait. Taking the stairs two at a
time, he halted outside a door on the first floor
and knocked three times in quick succession.
When the key turned, he walked in. The curtains
had been drawn, closing out the glow of the sunset. A woman in an enveloping, shapeless dress
and veiled hat stood before him. He locked the
door behind him before lifting her veil and kissing
her.

'Maud. Darling, darling, little Maud.'

'You, darling Geoffrey, are late,' she com-

194

plained. Extricating herself from his embrace, she removed her hat and veil.

'I'll explain why in a moment, sweetheart. That will be the champagne,' he announced at a knock on the door.

'You think of everything.' She moved behind the dressing screen.

He unlocked the door and carried in the tray. Pulling a table close to the bed, he set the champagne and glasses on it, then re-locked the door.

'Help me with this dress.'

Joining her behind the screen, he fumbled with the fastenings.

'Why do men have such clumsy fingers?'

'Because we weren't meant for delicate work like lady's maiding. There, that's the last.'

She slid the dress over her shoulders. It fell to the floor.

'Maud!'

'I thought it would save time.' She enjoyed the shock on his face.

'But if someone should see...'

'You have. Isn't it time you did something about it?' Her hands roamed over his body, unbuttoning his uniform at speed. He began to tremble as he always did at the onset of their lovemaking. Her confidence, her demands, but most of all her hunger, terrified him. She expected so much and until the moment actually arrived, he was never certain he'd be able to satisfy her.

'Was that all right?' he whispered as she moved away from him in the bed.

'It was a start.' She poured two glasses of

champagne. 'Now, before we continue, what was it you wanted to tell me?'

He sat up and put his arm around her, taking the champagne with his free hand. 'I'm leaving for the Gulf tomorrow.' He blanched at the look on her face. 'I'm sorry, darling; I thought you'd be happy. We've taken Basra.'

'I know. John writes to me. He's there, remember.'

'That's what so marvellous. I shall be going in with the Indian police force Mr Gregson's recruiting to oversee law and order in the Gulf. I'll be settled in Basra. I can look up your husband, tell him about us and ask him to divorce you. I know it won't be easy for us at first, darling. People can be awkward about these things but once I explain and he realises how much we love one another, it will be fine. He can't blame us for falling in love. You were only married for a few short months...' Oblivious to her silence, he rattled on. 'I'll arrange passage for you to Basra as soon as I reach there and find us somewhere to live. It's perfectly safe now the Turks have been pushed back. We'll live quietly until the divorce is settled, then marry. It won't be a grand affair, but that won't matter. The minute this war is over, I'll resign my commission and we'll go wherever you want. Don't you see, darling, we'll be together. We won't have to meet like this – Maud?' He called after her as she left the bed.

'I forbid you to say a single word to John about us or anything else.'

Abandoning his drawers, he heaved on his trousers and followed her behind the screen. 'I thought you'd want me to tell him. You can hardly face him on your own.'

'John's working in a field hospital.' She tried to recall letters she'd barely scanned since she'd begun sleeping with Geoffrey. 'If he found out about us when he's in the thick of it, and something happened to him...'

'Darling.' He wrapped his arms around her. 'The Turks are on the run; the war's practically over.'

'The war's not over. If it was, they'd be sending John home.'

'We're simply consolidating the positions we've taken. It can't last much longer.'

'I don't want him to find out. If – if – I couldn't live with myself.'

He led her back to the bed, and cursed himself for being insensitive. Maud was a delicate, considerate woman. She couldn't ride roughshod over anyone's feelings, not even those of the husband she no longer loved. 'We'll wait, if that's what you want, darling. It will only be for a little while. The minute the peace treaty's signed we'll face–' he forced himself to say the name '–John Mason together.'

Maud didn't hear a word. All she could think of was that tomorrow she'd be alone again. Without a man to hold, comfort, and love her through her blackest moments.


*Base Hospital, Basra, Sunday November 29th 1914*

John walked down the avenue of convalescent beds into the curtained cubicle that had been

197

Harry's home for five humiliating, painful days. His cousin was sitting on the edge of his cot, his teeth clenched as he struggled to push his arms through the sleeves of his uniform shirt.

'Need help?' John offered.

'If I was proud, I'd say no,' Harry grimaced. 'But I'm too damned sore to be proud.'

'Five days isn't long enough to heal six cracked ribs, massive bruising and a fairly serious concussion. I'd be happier if you stayed.'

Harry winced as John lifted the shirt over his shoulder. 'Duty calls.'

'Duty, my eye. You're going to look for Furja.'

'I hope I find her.'

'You will, and when you do, I guarantee she'll be in better shape than you.' John watched Harry button his shirt over his bandages. 'I don't suppose there's any point in asking you to apply for a transfer out of your crazy job.'

'The brass wouldn't be amused if I did.'

'Damn the brass. You would have been killed by that sadistic maniac if Smythe hadn't happened along that quay.'

'And Perry wouldn't have lifted a finger.'

'Harry, we've been through that.'

'I wasn't hallucinating,' Harry insisted. 'He just stood by and watched me being hammered. Mark my words, you'll be next.'

'If you won't think of yourself, consider the people who care for you.'

'I am. I'm thinking of Furja. And working as a political officer and dressed as an Arab, I have a legitimate excuse to go into the desert. Journeys take weeks out there; occasionally I'll be able to steal time out of the war and no one will be any the wiser. So, as usual, I'm looking after number one. I'll be taking my ease with my wife, while you–' he grinned at John 'work yourself to a skeleton here.'

'And if you meet the Turks? Or another mad sergeant?'

'I'll be more careful next time.'

'You won't survive a next time, Harry.'

'If Maud was up the road and you were offered a post that gave you the opportunity to visit her now and again, what would you do?'

'Your ribs are wrecked, your lungs damaged, and don't ask about your head.' John avoided Harry's question.

'According to my nearest, if not dearest, my head was never right.'

'Rumour has it we're advancing soon; that means another show. I know you and shows. You'll be in the thick of it. I'm warning you, Harry, one more blow to your chest and it'll be me who has to look for Furja. I don't want to have to do that.'

'You will, if you have to.' Harry struggled to his feet.

'If I have to,' John reiterated.

*Evening, Saturday November 28th 1914*

Robed, leaning on a stick, Harry hobbled through the lattice of lanes that pierced the Arab quarter. He frequently stopped to rest while the pains in his chest subsided, and, while he waited, he looked around. The change of government had altered nothing. The usual odours of roasting meat, bak-

199

ing bread, spices, and effluent assailed his nostrils as he limped along, trying not to think of what he would find at journey's end. He'd dreamed so constantly of his reunion with Furja he was beginning to feel as though he'd already lived it.

She'd be spinning wool or weaving a rug in the garden. She'd look up, smile – he'd take half a dozen steps across the room...

Lost in musings, he walked past the familiar studded door. Turning back, he knocked, quietly at first, then louder. His bangs echoed with an ominous hollow sound before a bolt grated. A grill opened at face level. Dark eyes and a smooth, round face peered at him.

'Ubbatan.' Farik gasped the Arabic for captain. 'Allah be praised.'

The door creaked wide on protesting hinges. Harry stepped inside, and while Farik refastened the bolts, he looked around. Where he remembered flowers, shrivelled heads swayed in the cold wind that rattled even in this enclosed space.

'My wife?'

'Is in the desert, Ubbatan.'

'What has happened here?'

'Nothing.' The slave answered. 'The Turks have gone, the British come. We remained within the house and no one bothered us.'

'Have you received news from the desert?'

'None.'

'Is there anyone here beside you?'

'Mansour and three women. Are you well? You are trembling, Ubbatan.' Farik looked at Harry's stick.

'I am well now.'

'Would you like coffee, food? Will you be staying here, Ubbatan?'

Frustrated by a blanketing sense of anti-climax, Harry sank down on the edge of the fountain. The water trickled sluggishly behind him. He'd deluded himself. Nothing was the same. Nothing. He felt sick to the pit of his stomach.

'Yes, please, Farik, coffee, strong and black.' Setting his back to the shuttered room he'd shared with Furja, he cleared his mind. He could glean all the information Lieutenant-Colonel Cox wanted, albeit late after his hospitalisation, at Abdul's. If any of the desert Sheikhs were here in Basra, they would be gambling in the back rooms. Abdul would give him an introduction to the game. He'd enough sovereigns to buy his own stake, but it might be as well to ask the brass to finance future ventures.

If he satisfied Cox, and the advance John had spoken about wasn't imminent, he'd be able to leave for the desert tomorrow. He'd ride Dorset. She was so well schooled she'd carry him no matter what state he was in. The sooner he discovered exactly how, and where, Furja was, the sooner he could stop running from his own nightmares.

*The Mission, Basra, evening,*
*Saturday November 28th 1914*

Angela faced Peter. 'Did you volunteer for this?'

'I'm a soldier. Soldiers obey orders, and I've been ordered up river to Qurna. I have no choice.'

'But you want to go,' Angela complained.

'That's what I find difficult to understand. You can't wait to leave.'

'If I don't go I'll be court-martialled for desertion.' The wind gusted outside, hammering needles of rain on the windows. The classroom stove had burned out hours before and the temperature was close to freezing. 'The stable boy will have brought my horse around by now.' He picked up his overcoat.

She flung her arms around him. 'You will take care of yourself?'

He smiled, and her anger abated. 'The Turks didn't give me any trouble when we took Sahil and Basra. I'll return from Qurna in one piece.'

'I couldn't bear it if anything happened to you.'

'I'll be back, if I'm lucky with my captaincy.' He picked her up and sat her on a desk. 'Then, Miss Wallace, I'll make you Mrs Peter Smythe so fast your head will spin.' Shrugging his arms into his overcoat, he kissed her and left.

She went to the window and watched him walk down the garden. The stable boy was waiting. Peter mounted, turned, and took a last look at her through the window. She forced a smile; hoping the raindrops on the glass would camouflage her tears. Digging his heels into his horse's flanks, Peter rode away. She held her hand to the window, ready to wave, but he didn't look back.

# Chapter Twelve

*Qurna, Thursday December 10th 1914*

A freezing gale whipped Harry's greatcoat against his shins as he stood at the side of a shell-spattered street watching Turkish POWs march past. Both the Turks and the British troops who shepherded them along at gunpoint were blue with cold, but the Turks looked infinitely more miserable.

Smythe fell out, standing alongside him. 'I thought you'd still be in sick bay.'

'Someone has to keep an eye on you.'

'You're incorrigible, indestructible, and blessed by God or the Devil. I'm not sure which.'

'Which is responsible for that?' Harry pointed at the column.

'Your guess is as good as mine. Johnny Turk lost over 2,000 dead, and wounded besides. Not a bad catch for 1,000 British and 4,000 Indian troops.'

'Looks like you caught too many for the quartermaster's liking. Where are they going?'

'India. Our supply situation's not too clever.'

'We advancing?' Harry pulled out his cigarettes and offered Peter one.

'Consolidating.'

'We've reached our objective?' Harry fished.

'The brass don't know or aren't saying, at least not to underlings. See you tonight. There's a bar with...'

'Smythe!'

'See you around, Harry.' With that, Peter rejoined the column.

'Not tonight, and when you do, it'll be your round,' Harry called after him. Dodging through a break in the line, he headed for the town hall. A Red Cross flag whirled crazily on the roof, proclaiming its new status as hospital. Inside was chaos. Stepping over stretchers of wounded waiting to be carried downstream, he dodged orderlies dispensing water and bedpans. Judging by the cries of their patients, nowhere near quickly enough.

'Captain Mason.' Harry buttonholed an orderly, shouting to make himself heard above the prayers of the Indian casualties.

The sepoy pointed to a door. The smell of raw blood, unwashed bodies, and stale urine intensified when Harry ventured deeper into the building.

'Medical school never prepared us for this,' he observed when he finally found John.

'It did, but only after the first year, and by then you'd cut and run.' John didn't look up from the soldier's arm he was examining. 'Corporal, I'm sorry, but this hand has to come off.'

'Please, Captain...'

'If we leave it you're going to lose your arm. Orderly?'

Harry looked at the soldier. A raw-boned, fair-skinned, farmhand type from the Dorsets. He'd seen him before, here – or India?

'Could be worse.' He tried to sound cheerful. 'You'll be going home with one hand still

204

attached to your body.'

'Will I really, sir?' the boy asked eagerly. 'Be going home, I mean?'

'I guarantee it.' John handed the boy over to an orderly. 'Now, Harry, let's look at you.' Ignoring the men around him, John unbuttoned Harry's shirt and probed beneath the bandages that sheathed his chest. 'Any difficulty breathing?'

'No, and if I'd realised a doctor's licence would turn you into an officious bully, I would have sabotaged your medical career along with my own.'

'Have you seen Furja?'

'No. I didn't come here to be examined. I came to give you this.' Harry handed John a package before fastening his tunic. 'It's your wedding present. I thought you could send it to Maud. Give her something to think about, besides you. And before you ask, I won it, gambling. The letters are to be sent home. I can't find a clerk to see to them.'

'That's hardly surprising, we've just fought...'

'I was with Frazer on the *Espiegle*.'

'You promised to take it easy,' John reproached.

'I tried, but someone decided to take another slice of this miserable country.'

'No one's indispensable, Harry. The rest of us can run this war without you.'

'You're going to have to. I'm leaving before some idiot decides *Baghdad Captured by Dorsets* would make a good headline for civilians to read over their breakfasts in London.'

'There's no point in taking Baghdad,' John said.

'There was no point in taking Qurna. The oilfields were the objective, then Basra. Now it's this forsaken hole. Where next?'

'This is it. Our frontline buffer to Basra.'

'I hope you're right.' Harry buttoned his great-coat.

'Dare I ask where you're going?'

Harry tapped his nose.

'Try to stay out of trouble,' John cautioned. 'There won't always be someone around to bail you out.'

'I'll be fine. You take care. I'd hate to see you returned to Maud in fragments. A woman like that deserves a man in one piece.'

'So does Furja.' John offered Harry his hand.

An orderly clamped the arm of the boy who was waiting to have his hand amputated. He screamed. Glad to leave the building, Harry left the building and headed for the river. British gunboats surrounded by armed launches blocked the Tigris from bank to bank. Passing landing stages filled with British and Indian wounded, Harry went to a small pier. A native dhow was waiting, canvas stretched over hoops looped across its bows.

'Downriver, Farik.' Harry disappeared beneath the canvas, changed into Bedouin robes, sat on his haunches, and waited.

'No one in sight, Ubbatan.'

Harry crawled into the open. Both banks stretched flat, barren and deserted either side. The river itself was void of shipping.

'Everyone's at Qurna, Ubbatan.'

'Get some sleep, Farik, I'll steer.'

Wrapping himself in his robes, Farik lay on the boards beneath the canvas. Harry crouched next to the tiller, arm outstretched, holding a down-stream course. He mulled over the identity that

206

had been concocted for him by the Political Office. He was Hasan Mahmoud, a stock dealer of Druse origin, who'd been bankrupted by the war. Hopefully the story and his appearance would stand scrutiny. Many Arabs had grey eyes and fair skin, but he needed to concentrate on his accent. His attention drifted from Hasan to Furja – was she thinking of him as he was of her? Was she well? Happy without him? Alive–

*North of Basra, Friday December 11th 1914*

Mansour met them at dawn. He'd brought the horses Harry had asked for to a palm grove a few miles upstream from Basra. They were hardly magnificent beasts but they were dependable and, Harry hoped, too unattractive to attract the interest of any wandering Bedouin. Harry sent the slave, Farik, and the bundle containing his uniform and identity discs downstream to Shalan's house. He'd hated making use of Shalan's slaves but he couldn't think of any other way of disappearing from Qurna without his superiors knowing which way he was headed.

He stood on the bank, watching the red and black sail on the dhow grow smaller as the sun rose. When it was no more than a speck he mounted his horse, picked up the rein of the packhorse, and turned east, towards the Karun.

Days and nights merged as Harry rode from one group of black tents to another. Bedouin and Bakhtairi Khan greeted him with polite, occasionally cold deference as they granted him the traditional hospitality of the desert – a share of the evening meal, and a sleeping place next to the fire. He accepted the comforts graciously and restricted his conversation to an innocuous minimum, except when it was necessary to praise Allah or his host.

If pressed, he repeated the story invented by the Political Office. He, Hasan Mahmoud, had prospered in Basra until the day the retreating Turkish army (Allah curse their souls!) had taken his entire stock of horses. Disheartened and bankrupt, he was travelling to Ahwaz to beg charity in his brother's house.

The story appeared to satisfy the curiosity of those ill-mannered enough to breach the desert law that a man's business was his own affair. It was plausible. The desert was full of refugees and renegades, men who had lost everything, and those who had never owned anything and were looking to make their fortunes at the expense of the warring armies.

The first thing he discovered was the fate of the British and Turkish Empires held little interest for the natives. He picked up rumours, hints of gold being paid out by the Turks, the Germans, the British – it didn't matter who was paying because the money had always been handed over to a distant tribe. One related to a friend's cousin's cousin – the rumours were invariably fourth- or fifth-hand. The Sheikhs were engrossed in more practical and mercurial matters. The war had brought bounty; uniforms, rations, rifles and handguns that the more enterprising warriors scavenged from stragglers or the battlefields the minute the bullets stopped flying.

He concluded the tribes were solely and selfishly concerned with the state of their armouries, the comfort of themselves and their families, and, longer term, the question of self-government of their lands. The only problem he foresaw was High Command might not accept his report to that effect. As one of the Sheikhs of the Bakhtairi Khans announced before retiring for the night,

'British or Turk, both are interlopers. The land is ours and, in the end, Allah will call upon us to fight for it.'

Harry travelled out early the next morning, but only after pushing the gold he carried a little deeper into the belt concealed beneath his shirt. It was just as well. He was stopped twice that day by groups of bandits who took a cursory look at his rusty rifle and thin saddlebags before sending him on his way. Blessing Mitkhal's advice that 'the safest man in the desert is a poor one', he huddled into his robes, fought the cold, and rode steadily northeast.

Lost in thoughts of Furja, he failed to notice the sudden onset of night. The darkness that took him unawares found him in a part of the Karun Valley he'd never visited before. On his left, the fringe of the vast wastes of the desert loomed, an enormous black shadow, ostensibly as solid and tangible as a high wall. On his right, the yellow, muddied waters of the Karun had been transformed into a glittering ribbon that reflected the stars and a cold sliver of new moon. He urged his horses on, hoping to glimpse the glow of a campfire, but after two hours blindly fumbling in the wasteland, he resigned himself to the prospect of a freezing and solitary night.

Dismounting close to the river, he fed each of his horses a handful of grain before leading them to the water. Once they'd drunk their fill, he tethered them in the shelter of a thorn copse. Lighting a small fire, he crouched before the pathetic flame and ate half his ration of dates and bread flaps. Another of Mitkhal's maxims: 'Never gorge yourself on all your food. Only Allah knows when the next meal will appear'.

He took stock of what remained when he re-wrapped his rations in palm leaves. Four dried dates and one shrivelled bread flap. His first priority was to find another group of black tents. He drank the last of the sour camel's milk from his bag, squeezing the hairy leather in an effort to drain the dregs. If he didn't reach humanity soon he'd have to boil river water in a skin. He played with the idea. Boiled or not, Karun water wasn't an appetising prospect, but perhaps it wouldn't come to that. He could ride around the next bend and find Furja curled on a rug in a corner of her father's tent, looking up and laughing when she saw him.

He shivered and looked around. No Furja, only freezing darkness. The flame died to an ember of skeletal thorn. Tearing another branch from the bush, he heaped twigs on the smouldering ashes, tucked his robes around his body, and rested his head on his saddlebags. The final image he saw was the vast sky. Stars dotted like pinpricks in decaying velvet that was being held to the light.

Where had he seen that? Clyneswood, when the housekeeper had taken down the worn old blue-black curtains in the library. Deep, bone-penetrating iciness ached through his limbs and battered ribs, then a warm, tantalizing image of Furja, before dreamless oblivion.

Harry woke with a start when he felt the ground reverberate beneath him. Opening his eyes, he tensed his muscles. He was surrounded by a forest of brown boots that blossomed into the plumped-out bottoms of khaki breeches. A kick brought excruciating pain that drove the breath from his lungs.

'Bedawi!' He was hauled to his feet.

'I speak no Turkish,' he pleaded in Arabic, opening his arms to show he carried no weapons. A second kick aimed at his shins felled him to his knees. 'I am alone, a poor horse dealer from Basra...'

A man sporting an officer's insignia looked down at him. Dark eyes peered suspiciously into his. 'Basra?'

Harry nodded, praying the officer wouldn't see further than his Bedouin robes. He'd scraped his chin every day with the knife strapped to his saddle but the blade had lost its edge, and without soap or mirror, the exercise had become little more than a useless morning ritual. He sensed the officer staring at his stubble. His beard was so damned fair. If it were only his grey eyes he might stand a chance. Perhaps if he told them his mother was a Druse...

The cold barrel of a rifle pressed into his back and fear superseded panic. This was it! The end.

211

He'd wasted time living for a tomorrow that would never come. He'd done nothing worthwhile ... made no mark that would live beyond him.

He gazed into the face of the short, thickset Turk. Saw the bushy eyebrows beetling together, the syphilitic pockmark on the greasy chin. Watched the cavernous mouth open, displaying brown, broken teeth. Unintelligible orders were being shouted somewhere outside his paralysed consciousness. Grinning, the soldier raised a gun until the barrel glinted hollowly into his right eye. Harry held his breath and waited. Someone said you never heard the bullet that hit you.

Furja! She'd never know what had happened to him.

His hands were heaved behind his back and secured with a leather thong that ripped the skin from his wrists. He was thrown across a horse. The collision with saddle leather stung his chest; his face crashed into a metal stirrup. He'd been a fool. He knew the limits of the British line yet he'd ridden up the Karun Valley like a lovesick calf. And now he was going to be killed. Or tortured, or both.

How long would it be before he started screaming in English, not Arabic? He recalled the bodies on the banks of the Shaft. The claw marks in the sacks. Not long. Not long at all.

*A Turkish outpost on the Karun,*
*Saturday December 26th 1914*

Heaved from his horse, Harry was dragged into a

wooden shack and kicked to his knees. A hand locked into his hair, pulling his head upwards until he faced a man who sat behind a desk. A soldier dumped his saddlebags on the desk. The officer fired a question – in Turkish. Harry answered in Arabic.

'I am a poor horse dealer...'

The grip on his hair tightened. He screamed when a clump was torn free. The soldier behind him stepped forward and waved it in front of the officer.

Scalp smarting, Harry stared at the bloodied roots of strands that had been bleached by the summers he'd spent in the East. He could never remember his hair being that fair before, not even as a child. It was as blond as that of Georgiana's German governess. The governess he and Mikey had christened the Hun – Hun!

The Germans were allies of the Turks

He cleared his throat. *'Ich heiße Manfred Untern.'* His voice was cracked. He wished he'd paid more attention to the German lessons his parents had insisted he take. *'Untern aus Berlin.'*

The Turkish officer called to the man who was holding him. Harry felt a tugging on the bonds on his wrists, then a marvellous sense of relief as his hands fell free to his sides.

# Chapter Thirteen

*A Turkish camp, Karun Valley,*
*Tuesday December 29th 1914*

'Why do you ask the obvious, Commander?' Ibn Shalan gazed at the officer. 'You can see where my own and my companion's–' he gestured to Mitkhal, who stood behind him '–guns have come from.'

'They are British.'

Ibn Shalan turned his hands out, palm uppermost. 'We poor, desert tribesmen scavenge where we can. Our guns may have had the misfortune to belong to the Ferenghi, but they have no memories. We, who now wield them, have no more love for the invaders of this land than you.'

'Our prison compound is full of Arabs who scream their loyalty to the Ottoman Empire but whose actions tell a different story.'

'If I could but take one look into that compound, Effendi.'

'We are holding many dangerous criminals.' The officer focused on Shalan while spitting on the floor. 'If you went in, you would not come out alive.'

'Yet you placed my kinsman who is innocent of any crime among them.'

The commander left his canvas chair and walked to the small square of mesh that had been let into the wall of the shack. 'How can you be sure your kinsman is in our prison compound?'

'Ten days ago, one of my tribe saw him ride into this camp escorted by your soldiers.'

'Many soldiers ride in and out of this camp.' The commander narrowed his eyes. 'Do your tribesmen sit by our gate watching all our comings and goings?'

'No,' Shalan replied. If the commander suspected the extent of Bedouin surveillance neither he nor Mitkhal, let alone Harry, would leave the camp alive.

'If your kinsman was here, and I'm not saying he was, he could have left. He could be in your tent now, while you waste your time and mine.'

Shalan knew when to retreat. He salaamed. Before he reached the door, the commander called him back.

'Your name?' He picked up a pencil.

'Aziz Ibn Mohammed.' In the eyes of Allah, Shalan told no lie. Was not every one of the faithful a spiritual descendant of the prophet?

'And you.' The commander pointed his pencil at Mitkhal.

'Faris Ibn Mohammed.' Unlike Shalan, Mitkhal had no compunction about lying to a Turk.

'Should you forget where your loyalty lies, Sheikh, you will see our prison compound from the inside.'

Shalan thought of Furja. Her reaction when she'd listened to the report of Harry's capture, five days after it had occurred. Her pleading, when she'd begged him to save her husband. How could he return to her bereft of hope?

215

Mitkhal opened the door. Shalan glanced at him and read his thoughts. They had tried to get Harry out through the front gate and failed. Mitkhal was already plotting to enter the camp under cover of darkness. Two thousand Turks guarding one open wire compound. It was suicidal lunacy, but that wouldn't stop him from trying.

A sentry marched past Mitkhal. He snapped to attention. 'Herr Untern, commander.' His tongue stumbled over the alien name.

'Usher him in, man.'

A slim, fair man of middle height picked his way across the planks in the muddy compound. He held a battered umbrella over his head and leant on a stick. His face was in shadow but Shalan saw his Turkish dress uniform was cleaner than the commander's.

Herr Untern entered the office and looked at Shalan.

'Have we met, Sheikh...?'

'Aziz.' Shalan replied. 'I scarcely recognised you in your present dress.'

'You are dismissed, Sheikh Aziz,' the commander interrupted.

'Commander, this is one of the desert contacts I spoke to you about. He has done sterling work for both our Empires. May I enquire why you are here, Sheikh Aziz?'

'He came to look for a relative in our prison compound,' the commander answered.

'In that case we must do all we can to help.' Herr Untern pulled a notebook from his pocket. 'If you give me the name of your relative, Sheikh Aziz, I will endeavour to find him.'

216

'It is a trifling matter. Nothing to concern someone of your importance.'

'Nevertheless I will ensure all the prisoners are questioned. If one should prove to be your kinsman, I will oversee his return to your tent.'

'The commander believes the man I am looking for has left.'

'In that case, he could be lost in the desert, Sheikh Aziz. Have you looked for him there?'

'He is unused to desert life. Perhaps I'd be better employed preparing his wife for widowhood.'

'I wouldn't do that until we have searched the compound.'

'I will wait a few days, no more. His wife is sick with worry. In such a case bad news is preferable to no news.'

'Please, assure the man's wife that all that can be done to find her husband will be.'

Shalan bowed and left the office with Mitkhal.

'You wanted to see me, Herr Untern?' The commander asked in the same Arab dialect he had used when speaking to the Sheikh.

'I wanted to thank you for all your hospitality, commander. My stay here has been a pleasant interlude, but duty calls. I must leave for my embassy in Baghdad.'

'I understand, Herr Untern, but you will need supplies. While my men prepare for your journey you will have time to share a meal with me.'

'While we eat we could look over the maps one last time?' Herr Untern suggested.

'The more conversant we are with one another's plans, the greater our chances of bringing this war to a quick and righteous conclusion.'

217

The Turk repeated the argument the German had used when he had asked to look over the Turkish battle plans.

'I see I am going to have to take your name to high places, commander.'

'An officer tries to do his duty.' The commander unlocked a case that stood on his desk. 'Shall we begin?'

*The desert, December 1914*

No crimson-streaked desert sunset ushered in the darkness that night. The pewter skies grew gradually colder and heavier until the man standing on the ground could no longer make out the outline of his feet. Even the river could only be distinguished by the sound of rain falling on water.

Mitkhal retreated beneath his single-poled tent and pulled his sodden robes closer to his body. He'd been waiting for five hours, his senses stretched to their utmost; but it was too dark for anyone to come now. Resting his head on the flank of the camel that lay alongside him, he closed his eyes. The warmth of the beast went some way to dispelling the chill from his body. He would sleep, and tomorrow...

Out of the torrential streaming came the sound he'd been waiting for. The squelch of camel hoofs in mud. Pushing his hand out from under the goat hair blanket, he stroked the muzzle of his camel to steady her.

'Kush!' shouted a familiar voice. 'Kush, you cursed creature.'

218

Mitkhal peered into the gloom. 'Herr Untern.'

'Mitkhal.'

'You alone?'

'Yes,' Mitkhal confirmed.

'Where are you? I can't see a blessed thing and this wretched animal won't move in the direction I want to take.'

'You should have let me teach you to ride a camel months ago.'

'Months ago I hoped I'd never need to climb on the back of one.'

'I warned you if you ever had to travel the desert during the rains you'd have to. Stay where you are. I'll find you.' Mitkhal advanced and crashed into Harry's camel. The beast moved backwards; Mitkhal caught its neck, heaving it to a halt.

'This is a stroke of luck, finding you here.' Harry prepared to slide off the camel's back.

'Make it kneel, Harry. Hit it with your stick. That's it, sharp, on the neck. Luck has nothing to do with it. We heard you'd travelled up river since you left Bakhtairi Khan country. I guessed you'd continue on that route. I've been waiting for hours.'

'Thank you. Is Furja safe and well?'

'Safe, yes. Shalan would never allow her to be otherwise.'

'Shalan said she'd been worrying about me. Is his camp far? I'd like to move on.'

'It's an hour's ride. We'd never make it in the dark.'

'Then we'll...'

'Move out at first light.' Mitkhal noticed Harry winced at his touch as he helped him on to firm ground. 'Furja will be asleep. You'll see her in the morning. Shift this animal next to mine.'

'They told me horses would get bogged down in the mud.' Harry tugged at his camel's rein. 'So I took this stinking, insubordinate beast...'

'From the Turks.'

'I have some explaining to do.'

'To Furja, and Shalan, not me. Who am I to question you, if you chose to join forces with the Turks?' Mitkhal forced Harry's camel to lie alongside his own. After they crawled into the makeshift tent, he offered Harry dates and bread flaps. Harry shook his head.

'All I've done this past week is eat. Turkish food lies heavy on the stomach.'

'I'll take your word for it.'

'Is Shalan angry with me?'

'He wasn't pleased to see you in Turkish uniform,' Mitkhal confirmed. 'Furja begged him to rescue you. He risked his life walking into that camp. If the Turks had recognised him...'

'It doesn't bear thinking about.'

'Only to see you strutting about as if you owned the place. We heard you'd been taken into the compound trussed like a goat for the slaughter.'

'They were suspicious of my fair beard and skin, so they took me to their camp. When they started questioning me, I had a brilliant idea. If I had to be European, why not German? I spouted a few words I'd learnt as a child. Fortunately, their German was even worse than mine. If it hadn't been, I wouldn't be here.'

'They didn't hurt you?'

'Apart from pulling a chunk of my hair out, no.'

Harry rubbed his head. 'I hope it grows back. I told the commander I was an agent sent to encourage native tribes to attack the British Expeditionary Force. I explained I'd been forced to adopt Arab dress for my own safety as the demarcation line between British and Turkish territory was so uncertain. I implied it was the fault of the Turkish Army and if they didn't take the offensive soon, we Germans would have no option but to send in Imperial troops to take command of an Ottoman shambles.'

'It's a wonder he didn't shoot you.'

'By then I'd convinced him I was somewhat higher than a general and only a fraction lower than the Kaiser.'

'Why stay after you convinced them you were a German spy?'

'Because chance had given me an opportunity to shape Turkish policy on the Karun. Before dawn tomorrow, the commander is sending half his garrison to attack a British column he believes is advancing on the Karun from Qurna.'

'Over the desert?' Mitkhal asked.

'Over the desert. They swallowed my story of an impending British attack, hook, line and sinker. What a glorious catch. One thousand Turkish troops riding directly into Bakhtairi Khan territory. I travelled up through that country. The Sheikhs are armed and spoiling for a fight.'

'You sent lambs to the slaughter, Harry. Have you thought what will happen when the Turks discover the identity of Herr Untern?'

Harry rested his back against the steaming side of Mitkhal's camel. 'They'll put a price on my head,' he murmured, thoughts drifting over the desert to Furja.

'A high one. I hope your success is worth it.'

*India, 1 a.m., Thursday December 30th 1914*

The orchestra of native musicians played the Strauss waltz softly lest they disturb the conversation of the guests lingering around the supper buffet. Maud rinsed her fingers in the brass chillumchee a liveried footman held out for her. The moment she withdrew her hands, another footman handed her a damasked napkin.

'Madam Sahib would like grapes?' the Khitmagar enquired, seeing her glance at the fruit bowl.

'Yes,' Maud replied in the brusque tone she reserved for servants. He snipped at the stem of a bunch of purple grapes with silver scissors, easing his selection onto a Meissen plate.

'A wise choice after so heavy a meal, Mrs Mason.'

She glanced at the man who'd addressed her. From his sleekly brushed black hair, to his patent dancing pumps, he gleamed as though he'd been polished. Tall, around Geoffrey's height (she'd ceased to use John as a yardstick when comparing men), slender, in contrast to most British officers who tended to be thickset and muscular when young, and corpulent in middle age. Darkly handsome with the black eyes, long face, and pale skin that could mean the same Portuguese ancestry as her host or – she bristled as she

222

recalled the gossip she'd heard about the D'Arbez household – a touch of native blood.

He waved away a waiter who pivoted a tiered silver cake stand loaded with cream-filled layers of sugared pastries.

'I will join Madam in her choice of grapes. Forgive me for being so forward as to introduce myself, Mrs Mason. Unfortunately, I was detained by business, so I missed your and the other guests' arrival. I am Miguel D'Arbez, Carlos's elder brother.'

'I'm pleased to meet you.' She recovered her composure. Harriet's lectures on what a lady should or shouldn't do, and, what was infinitely worse, what Miss Emily would or wouldn't have done, had upset her more than she'd realised. After all, she was here with Marjorie, and Marjorie would never allow her to be placed in a socially compromising position.

'Marjorie has spoken about you so often I feel you are an intimate friend.'

'Exactly what did Marjorie tell you about me?'

'A little of this, a little of that. May I say that now I have met you, I am glad she persuaded you to celebrate New Year in our rural backwater.' He flicked his fingers at the elaborate decor of the largest and grandest reception room in the palatial plantation mansion. 'As you see, we Portuguese may not be British, but we are civilised.'

She laughed, attracting the attention of their hostess, Louisa D'Arbez.

'My sister-in-law adores entertaining her British compatriots. We Portuguese can be a trial to her. But Marjorie has been a loyal friend to both

223

Louisa and my brother. We owe what little social standing we have in your circles to her.' Miguel took two glasses of champagne from a waiter's tray and presented her with one. 'Marjorie has visited Louisa every week since she married my brother, and where Marjorie goes, others follow.'

'There aren't enough peer's daughters in India to make it otherwise,' Maud commented.

'Did you know Louisa's fiancé?'

'No, I was living in Mesopotamia when Louisa arrived here.'

'Very inconsiderate of the fellow to die before Louisa set foot in India.' He duplicated the regimental accent so accurately Maud choked on her champagne.

'You sound exactly like Colonel Hartley.'

He handed his empty plate to a servant. 'English as spoken by British officers is easy to acquire. Portuguese, on the other hand, is difficult to master. However, when you are ready to learn my tongue, I will be happy to teach you.'

'I'm no linguist.'

'You should make the effort. It will be invaluable after the war.'

'Are you suggesting Portugal will control India at the end of the war?' Maud's voice rose in indignation.

'No, dear lady. But when this war finally ends, most of Europe will be flattened and the majority of young men dead. Portugal will be one of the few havens of civilisation left.'

'The Allies are going to win,' she countered fiercely.

'I don't doubt it. My only question is at what

cost. I apologise.'

'For what?' she enquired.

'Talking about the war. I only meant to tell you how much Louisa values your visit. My sister-in-law is very dear to me.'

Maud found it difficult to imagine how any woman as plump, plain, and middle-aged as Louisa could be dear to a man as exotic as Miguel.

'Would you care to dance?'

She nodded assent. Miguel led her on to the floor. Marjorie glided past in the arms of an ancient colonel.

'Your thoughts are with your husband?' Miguel asked when they circled the room a second time.

'No,' she blurted out thoughtlessly.

'I am pleased to hear it. It is refreshing to dance with a beautiful woman whose thoughts remain her own. Your husband is in France?'

'Mesopotamia.'

The waltz ended. Couples applauded the orchestra. Maud left the reception room. She began to climb the stairs, intending to hide herself in her room, but Miguel caught up with her. Blocking her path, he rested his hand on the wall above her head.

'Tell me, *Senhora* Mason,' he enquired in bland, conversational tones, 'are you very bored with my brother's party? Or is it the war you're bored with?'

'The war.'

'On that point we agree. The war is boring and distasteful. Unfortunately, it exists. But it's not reason enough for civilised people to abandon the pleasures of life. May I suggest that as we cannot help the men at the front, we owe it to ourselves to forget them? Our misery will not make them more comfortable and beautiful women have a duty to enjoy life. Didn't one of your English poets write "we walk this way but once"? So, instead of hiding in your room, why don't you accompany me to my library where you can view the more interesting exhibits in my collections and sample my brandy?'

Maud hesitated.

'We will, of course, leave the door open to settle any question of impropriety.'

The doors to the reception room opened. A swell of music drifted towards them. A waiter scurried past with a tray of empty glasses. The music was lighter, more melodious than it had been earlier. Miguel D'Arbez was right, Maud decided as she ascended the staircase with her hand resting on his arm. Life was for living. There was little point in allowing the war to spoil what could so easily become good times.

## Chapter Fourteen

*The Karun Valley, Thursday December 30th 1914*

Harry slept fitfully; his dreams interspersed with bouts of pain and elusive images of Furja.

Furja sick with worry, her face thin and pale beneath her red bridal headdress. Furja pleading with him to come to her, but no matter how he struggled, she remained just out of reach. He summoned the last of his strength, made one final effort...

Cold, shivering, he started into consciousness. The waterlogged atmosphere had lightened to a shade that meant dawn was breaking somewhere above the leaden clouds and unrelenting rain. Crawling out of Mitkhal's makeshift tent, he stepped in a puddle of freezing mud that engulfed him to his waist.

'Why in hell didn't you warn me?' he demanded of Mitkhal, who peered sleepily at him from the cover of the tent.

'It was obvious we were sleeping on a rock.' Taking Harry's hand, Mitkhal hauled him out of the mess. 'I keep telling you. If you want to live in the desert you must learn the ways of the Bedawi.'

'If that means I have to sleep in disgusting filth...'

'The winter rains last only a few months. Soon the cold, dry weather will be here, and after that the summer. Then you can complain about the heat and the flies again.' Taking down the pole, Mitkhal gathered the folds of sodden blanket together.

'I remember last summer, and the tail-end of the summer before that. And not just the heat and flies – the dust...'

'You prefer mud?' Mitkhal surveyed Harry's plastered robe and boots. 'Don't worry; the rain will wash you clean before your wife will see you.' He reached into his saddlebag. 'Date? Bread flap?'

'No,' Harry growled.

'Then we ride.'

Mitkhal secured the blanket and pole to his pack. They saddled their camels, mounted them, and wound the folds of their kafiehs around their faces. Setting his face against the driving rain, Harry followed Mitkhal's lead.

After an hour's hard riding, he spotted a figure on the horizon. He wondered if the rain had blurred his vision but the figure remained, hazy, but definitely there. Mitkhal lifted his arm. The watchman returned the gesture. They'd reached journey's end, but the plain stretched unbroken around them. Turning, Mitkhal led his camel down a path that wound into a steep-sided wadi, invisible until you stood on the brink. When Harry guided his camel forward he realised he could have wandered the Karun Valley for months without stumbling on the narrow cleft.

A torrent of water hurtled over the riverbed far beneath them. Halfway down, the track widened into a shelf that had been carved out centuries before, during another wet winter. The shelf broadened, cut back under the cliff wall, and there, beneath an overhanging rock, Harry saw black tents. He looked for Furja, but the hands that took his camel guided him to Shalan.

The Sheikh sat within the public area of his tent and listened while Harry outlined his reasons for wearing Turkish uniform in a Turkish camp. When he mentioned he'd persuaded the Turks to send an expedition into Bakhtairi Khan country, to meet a non-existent British force, Shalan silenced him and summoned his warriors. The Arabs held an urgent whispered conversation. Hands on swords, rifles slung across their shoulders, two dozen tribesmen left the tent.

'Why place your men at risk when the Bakhtairi Khans can do your killing for you?' Harry asked.

'Because the Turkish soldiers are carrying arms.'

'I promised to supply all the arms you need.'

'You sold us British arms at a high British price. We pay for them in blood every time we ride out to guard your pipeline. The Turkish guns will cost only the blood spilled in one fight.'

'The British army will soon secure the land around the pipeline and when they do, your debt will be cancelled,' Harry promised. 'The Turks will lose this war and then there will be no need for the Bedawi to fight. If you want more weapons to see you through until that time, you have only to ask.'

'The last consignment cost more than I bargained for; the next will be offered at a price I cannot afford.'

Silence reigned thick and uncomfortable in the close, damp atmosphere. Harry rubbed the stubble on his chin. He felt as impotent as he had done during the divan when Shalan had informed him he was to marry Furja.

At length, Shalan spoke softly. 'The British have taken Basra. They are moving up country.' It wasn't a question.

'When I left three weeks ago we were in control of the Tigris as far as Qurna.'

'And your Indian soldiers were hammering notices on our palm trees.' Shalan lifted a scroll from the ottoman next to him and flung it at Harry. Harry didn't need to unroll it. He recognised the cheap yellow paper and coarse printing.

229

'*The natives must not carry arms,*' Shalan quoted, '*for it will not be possible to distinguish an armed man from an enemy, and thus any person going armed will be liable to be shot.* And you worry about my men being killed by Turks.'

'I have been looking for you since the day that proclamation was posted.'

'The Arabic is good.'

'It's mine.'

'I know.'

Harry braced himself to return Shalan's gaze. Was there nothing the man didn't know? 'The Arabic is mine, but the words are none of my doing.'

'You are a British soldier. You made your loyalties clear the day you left Furja with Mitkhal and rode off to guard the Ferenghi oil wells.'

'I am an officer in my King's Army. We're at war.'

'We also, with those who invade our land.'

'We had to come here,' Harry insisted. 'The Turks have allied themselves to the Germans – our enemies. We have to protect our oil wells.'

'Which are on Arab land. And you will protect them at the expense of Arab lives. When I saw you dressed in Turkish clothes in the Turkish fort, I knew you'd made your choice, Hasan.' Rising, he walked across the tent and clamped his hand on Harry's shoulder. The heat from his fingers burned Harry's flesh. 'You would give your life and the lives of those you love for your British Empire, and I for the Bedawi who have lived here since Allah threw the first man from the Garden of Eden. There is little difference between the beginning of your Bible and my Koran, but there is a world of difference between our peoples. We are on different sides.'

'We both want to oust the Turk.'

'I want to free my people from the Imperial bonds that bind them. But you?' Shalan looked into Harry's eyes. 'What will you do after your armies have driven out the Turk? Will you leave? Return this land to those who have lived here since the beginning of time?'

'I don't know what High Command has in mind for tomorrow, let alone the end of the war.'

'I can read the future of your army and the future of the desert. I order you to divorce Furja now, before we Bedawi exchange one Imperial overlord for another. British or Turk, the oppression will be the same, foreign soldiers dictating how we live in our own land. When the Turks have left, our war will go on. And when I begin to shoot our new enemies I don't want to shoot my son-in-law.'

'But you would shoot your former son-in-law?'

'If Allah willed it. Because when that time comes, Furja will be settled as a Bedawi wife in the tent of one of her own blood.'

'She is married to me. And she is going to remain married to me,' Harry maintained.

'I ordered you to marry my daughter, now I'm ordering you to divorce her.'

'No! I've been searching for her since the day we took Basra, and no one is going to stop me from finding her.'

'She doesn't want to be found. She has returned to my tent. Under Bedawi law, your marriage is over.'

231

'I sent her to your tent for safekeeping...'

'That's not what she says.'

'Let her tell me that herself.'

'How many times and in how many ways must I say your marriage has served its purpose?'

'Furja would not agree with you.'

'She cannot think for herself. She is ill.'

'All the more reason for me to see her.' Harry turned his head. Two of Shalan's men were closing in behind him. He put his hand on his sword. 'You'll have to kill me to keep me from her, Shalan.'

'Let me speak to him, father.'

Furja stepped through the curtain. It was the first time Harry had seen her dressed in anything other than her red bridal robes. She wore the plain, black garb of the Bedouin women. But the robes were neither voluminous nor shapeless enough to disguise the advanced state of her pregnancy.

Shalan ordered his men to clear the tent. He brushed past Furja without a word and entered his harem, allowing the curtain to fall behind him. Harry stared helplessly, wanting to wrap his arms about Furja and swing her high in the air as he'd done when they'd lived together in Basra, but her pregnancy made him feel awkward and ridiculously shy.

Unfastening her veil, she walked to the corner of the tent furthest from the curtain. Sinking onto a pile of rugs, she beckoned him closer.

'So, Harry, you've been looking for me?' Something of the old mischief glinted in her eyes, but her face was thin and there were lines of

232

strain at the corners of her mouth.

'I was worried about you.' Sitting at her feet, he reached for her hands.

'You left me with Mitkhal. You knew he'd take me to my father.'

'I was afraid you'd get caught in the fighting. That the Turks would capture you.' Images of Basra flooded his mind. The wailing women. The swollen sacks being dragged from the Shaft. The stench of death permeating the cold morning air.

'Were you afraid the Turks would capture my father's daughter, or the wife of a British officer?'

'I don't need reminding you'd be doubly damned in Turkish eyes.'

'I wasn't captured, Harry.'

He tried to smile, but his attention was drawn to her swollen stomach.

'Your son, Harry.' Taking his hand, she pressed it against her.

'Or daughter,' he murmured; awed by the prospect of the new life she carried.

'I'll have no daughters, only sons.'

'How can you expect me to divorce you? Now of all times.'

'My father...'

'I am not interested in your father. Only you.'

'And if I should want a divorce?'

'I'd try to persuade you otherwise.'

'How can I remain married to you when your Great War drives us apart? You have to fight for your Ferenghis. And I have to stay here and worry.'

'Would you worry less if I divorced you?'

'I will always worry about my father and my tribe. Their fate is mine and that of my son.'

'Our son,' he corrected.

'I will worry about you, for our son's sake.'

'I won't divorce you, Furja. Not unless you ask me, and–' he looked into her eyes '–mean it.'

'I cannot stay married...'

Afraid of what she was about to say, he wrapped his arms around her and kissed her, gently, on the mouth.

'I'm carrying your child, Harry. Not an ancient grandmother on the point of death.'

'I'm sorry.' He grinned. 'I've never had a pregnant wife before. I'm not sure how to treat you.'

'Try the same way you treated me before.'

'Then you'll stay married to me?'

'Our marriage no longer makes sense.'

'It does to me.'

'Not to my father.'

'Your father...'

'Is concerned only for me and his grandson,' she interposed.

'You think I'm not?'

'My father and our people have travelled for many years, taking care to avoid the Turks. Sometimes–' her eyes darkened '–we didn't manage it. Now we have to hide from the British as well. And you, Harry, are a British soldier.'

'That could prove an advantage to you and our son. Basra is under our jurisdiction. If you returned there with me, I could install you in a house in the European quarter. You and our child would be miles from the fighting, and the Turks.'

'You promised my father no Ferenghi house, and now you want to go back on your word. Put me among people who would look down on me and my heritage.'

'In God's name, Furja, I made that promise before war broke out. I can't fight, worrying about you and our child every minute of every day we're apart.' He was amazed how easily the phrase had sprung to his lips. 'Our child'. A life he and Furja had created. Were duty bound to love, cherish and protect. He was suddenly afraid. Overwhelmed by the responsibilities of fatherhood.

'Don't you mean Allah's name.'

'Allah! God! What's the difference?'

'A great deal, Harry. You told my father you were a true believer.'

'He supposed...'

'And you lied. Just as you lied about the Ferenghi house you want me to live in.' Anger blazed in her eyes. He reined in his temper. He'd forgotten about Furja's rages.

'I'm not Ferenghi. A milk-faced, useless creature without a brain like cousin John's Maud. I won't allow you to shut me in a safe place only to take me out when you've time to spare,' Furja railed. 'I am Bedawi. Your son will be Bedawi. We'll live as our people have always lived, here, in the desert. It's our home, and neither you nor the Turks will take it from us.' She raised her clenched fists. He caught them.

'I can't bear the thought of you in danger.'

'Like you, sitting in a Turkish command post.'

'I'm a soldier. I have no choice. The minute this show is over, I'm resigning my commission, packing my bags, and...' What then? Back to Dorset? Cool, emerald green fields. Woods with more trees to an acre than grew in this entire damned coun-

235

try. Real trees. With thick, soft leaves, not spikes that cut your hands to shreds if you touched them.

He'd see the grey stonework and oak windows of Clyneswood again. The gardens. Cricket matches on the village green. Tea on the lawn on a warm, windless summer day. The vicar talking over tedious Church matters with his mother. Georgiana stealing his wallet to relieve the boredom, racing ahead of him on the steps of the rockery

'Then what, Harry?' Furja's question shattered the memories he'd retreated into. 'You'll go home? Back to England?'

'Not without you.' He was furious with himself for allowing her to read his mind so easily. 'In the meantime we stay married.'

'Why, Harry?' she questioned, all fight ebbing from her. 'What's the point? You'll have to leave soon. In the next hour or two.'

'Furja, I...'

'You must have learnt many things from the Turks. Things you must tell your army.'

'As soon as I've passed on what I know, I'll...'

'Go wherever they send you and do whatever they ask of you, including killing Bedawi.'

'No!'

'You say that now, in this tent. It will be different when you are with your people.'

Terrified at the prospect of losing her, he reached out.

She shrank from his touch. 'Harry, it's impossible for us.'

'Our child?'

'Our child is of noble lineage, the grandson of Aziz, the great grandson of Shalan. The tribe will 'look after him.'

'He will be half Ferenghi,' Harry flung the hated word at her. 'The son of a British lieutenant, whether you and your tribe like it or not.'

She laid her hand against his cheek. He found her tenderness unbearable after her anger.

'Can't you see how difficult it will be for our son to live among the Bedawi with a Ferenghi for a father? One of the same Ferenghis who are riding roughshod over our people. The Ferenghis who would replace the Turks. I can try to hide him from the British. I couldn't even begin to hide him from the assassin within the tribe unless he and I renounce you.'

He finally understood what she and Shalan had been trying to tell him. His British blood posed a threat to the life of his wife and child. It was as simple and final as that.

'You are saying I have to divorce you for our child's sake.'

'When the Turks have been defeated this war will become a war between your people and mine. You could die. I could die. Our son would have only the tribe. The tribe has the right to demand loyalty to the Bedawi, not the invader.'

Harry rose from the rug. He was stiff, damp, chilled to the bone. His ribs ached from the kicking he'd received when the Turks had picked him up. He turned away from her so she wouldn't see his tears.

'I'll make provision for both of you. I have money. Not only my officer's pay, but a great deal more.' He referred to the gambling winnings he'd banked since he'd been posted to Basra. 'In the meantime there's this.' He tossed a packet of gold onto the rug at her feet. 'I'll give your father letters. The right to draw on my account should anything happen to me before I have time to sort out my affairs.'

'Then you'll divorce me, Harry?'

'You can tell everyone we're divorced.'

Rising, she clung to his back for a moment, burying her face in his shoulder. He gripped her hand.

The curtain opened. Shalan appeared. 'You have yet to say the words, Hasan.'

'I divorce thee.'

'Twice more, while you look at her.'

The tent grew misty. Harry faced Furja. He choked on the words. 'I divorce thee ... I divorce thee.'

The curtain rose and fell. He was alone with only the sound of the rain hammering on the tent to break the silence.


## Chapter Fifteen

*India, Friday December 31st 1914*

'You decided against joining the tiger hunt, Mrs Mason.'

Maud started guiltily, dropping the book she'd been looking at. Miguel D'Arbez leant against the library door, a cigar dangling from his fingertips.

'You assumed you were alone in the house, so

you decided to continue your perusal of my collection of Indian art?'

Maud reddened.

'Please, Mrs Mason, it's refreshing to meet a woman who's not afraid of her sexuality. As your host, it gratifies me to see you making yourself at home.' He opened a cupboard. 'Brandy or gin? If you prefer chilled wine or champagne...'

'Nothing, thank you,' she interrupted, regretting the impulse that had led her into the room.

'There's no need for embarrassment.' He poured two brandies and handed her one. 'I showed you those books last night because I thought they might interest you. We Europeans are, frankly, ridiculous in our attitude to sex. We thrust our young girls into marriage without preparing them for the marital bed. The result is shock, horror, and many unhappy women. The Indians are more practical. By allowing matrons to tutor brides and show them these illustrations they acquaint them with the stimuli needed for successful lovemaking. As a result, Indian girls enjoy happier wedding nights than most British and Portuguese.' He went to the windows and lowered the blinds. 'I hope you don't mind the gloom, Mrs Mason, but sunlight drains the colour from the spines of the books.'

She left her chair. He moved quickly. Before she reached the door, he turned the key.

'I'll scream for the servants.'

'Am I so repulsive to you, Maud?' Gripping her arm with his left hand, he unbuttoned the shoulder fastenings on her lawn dress with his right. It fell to her feet. He brushed his lips over

239

her throat, sinking his teeth into the soft skin below her ear.

She recalled his clinical comments when he'd shown her the pornographic illustrations the night before. He'd frightened her then. He was terrifying her now. But even as she clawed at his hand, the touch of his lips aroused passions that had hovered close to the surface since the night John had first made love to her.

His eyes, dark, mocking, stared down into hers. He pulled something from his pocket. There was a flash of silver and her chemise fell to the floor, its ribbon straps cut through. Before she had time to protest, the blade travelled down the length of her body and she stood before him naked except for her stockings. He pulled a cushion from a chair, tossed it to the floor, and pushed her back until she lay before him. His hands and lips crept over every inch of her body until she could stand the frustration no longer. She tugged at his jacket. He caught her hands.

'I'm going to teach you many things, Maud. First, how to make love slowly. Very slowly.' He ran his fingertips around her left breast, suddenly pinching her nipple with a force that brought tears to her eyes. 'Pleasures should never be hurried. We have the rest of the day. May I suggest we make it a memorable one – for both of us?'


*Basra, Thursday 28th January 1915*


Harry was asleep in the room he rented from Abdul. Despite the icy damp outside, the atmos-

240

phere was close; reeking with the acrid stench of smouldering wood and the cloying perfume of the joss sticks Abdul burned in the girls' chambers. The scents stole into his dreams.

He was in the desert, riding Dorset. It was dark but he carried a burning brand. He was searching for something – he didn't know what. Furja was there. He could hear her calling his name but he couldn't see her. Blades of pain stabbed his lungs, making it difficult to breathe. The Turks were marching towards him, a drummer boy leading the column banging ... banging

He woke, but the banging continued. Someone was hammering on his door. His limbs ached and his eyes stung when he struggled to focus, then he realised the pain in his chest was no nightmare. The room was thick with smoke. Someone had entered while he slept, the brazier had been stoked for the night, and the blinds pulled. How many times had he told Abdul he didn't want the servants in his room whether he was in it or not? The banging started up again, louder, more urgent.

Picking up his mud-stained gumbaz from the floor, he threw back the blanket, pulled on the long shirt, and opened the door.

'Ubbatan, it's your companion. I think he's in trouble.'

'Think, or know?' Harry demanded of Najaf, Abdul's servant.

'Both, Ubbatan. He's in the dice room.'

Harry brushed past.

'Ubbatan, your abba!'

Cursing Arab prudery, Harry turned back and pulled on his outer robe. Barefoot, he padded down the stairs into the narrow passage that led to the private gambling rooms.

'The master isn't here. If there should be trouble, he'll blame me.'

'There won't be trouble,' Harry assured him.

The door to the dice room was ajar, the din deafening. Shouts and curses boiled in an ugly mixture. Harry pushed through the crowd. The dice table lay on its side. Mitkhal stood pinned against the wall, the tip of a gold-handled dagger poised beneath his chin.

'What's the problem?' Harry pitched his voice above the noise.

'We have a tribeless bastard—' the Bakhtairi Sheikh who held the dagger cleared his throat and spat in Mitkhal's face '—who refuses to pay his debts. As I can't have his money, I'll have his miserable hide.'

'How much does he owe?'

'One hundred of the infidels' sovereigns.'

'Najaf, pay the man. Add the debt to my account.'

Najaf beamed. The problem was no longer his. Abdul had left orders the Ubbatan was to be given everything he required. He hadn't specified gambling losses of such magnitude, but he'd said 'everything' and orders were orders. If the Ubbatan couldn't pay the debt, it was his master's sorrow and none of his doing.

'Mitkhal.' Harry jerked his head towards the door.

Slowly, the Bakhtairi Sheikh lowered the dagger. Mitkhal lifted his arm and wiped the spittle from his face in his sleeve. Glaring at the Sheikh, he

242

followed Harry.

'For the second time I owe you my life,' Mitkhal muttered when they reached the passage. 'What can I say?'

'You can promise you won't gamble with money you don't have again.' Harry entered his room. 'There's water in the jug and clean towels next to it.' He picked up his watch and opened it. Ten-thirty. He'd arranged to meet John when his shift finished at midnight. 'You've cost me an hour's sleep.' He threw off his abba and stretched out on the couch.

'I miscounted my losses. When I opened my purse I had less than I thought.'

'One of these days you're going to lose more than you own when I'm not around. And if you gamble with jokers like that one it could cost your life. Have you lost everything?'

'I have my clothes.'

'Your horse?' Harry shook his head when Mitkhal didn't answer. 'What were you thinking?'

'It's Shalan's sister, Gutne. I want to marry her.'

'Does she want to marry you?'

'Yes.'

'When did this happen?'

'When you were visiting the Turks and I was in the desert with Shalan.'

'Does Shalan know?'

'No one knows except Gutne and – Furja.' Mitkhal was wary of speaking the name. Every time his wife was mentioned, Harry's anger flared like a thorn fire. 'I wanted to pay Gutne's bride price. I had some money, but not enough. It would have taken me years to earn what I needed.'

243

'How long will it take you now?'

'You always win.' Mitkhal slopped water from the jug into a tin basin.

'I've had the advantage of a comprehensive education in cheating at an English public school.' Reaching for his cigarettes, Harry shook one out of the packet.

Mitkhal washed in silence. He knew better than to say anything while Harry was in this mood.

'Have you sounded out Shalan? Gutne's hardly a virgin bride. Furja told me the Turks took her when she was 12. After raping her, they...'

'Gutne told me everything,' Mitkhal interrupted.

'What I'm trying to say is Shalan won't set a high bride price. He'll probably take whatever you offer.'

'You're forgetting I'm a tribeless bastard. This is my chance to buy my way into a tribe. To belong. To have sons who can set their sights higher than the Ferenghi gutters of Basra. I wanted that money for my unborn children as well as Gutne. She places no value on herself because the tribe regard her as a whore. I know what that can do to a woman. I watched my mother live with the same shame. If I had gone to Shalan with a bagful of sovereigns – oh, what's the use?' He thrust his face into the water.

Harry left the couch and went to a chest screwed to the floorboards beneath the window. He pulled out a key he kept tied to a cord around his neck and opened it. Removing a heavy linen bag, he tossed it to Mitkhal. 'Three hundred gold sovereigns. Bribe money I've been given to buy the goodwill of the desert tribes. Ibn Shalan's brother-in-law is worth that much baksheesh.'

'Harry, I couldn't...'

'Before you rush headlong up the Karun, go to the barracks. Tell the stable sepoy to saddle Devon and Norfolk. Devon's my wedding present to you. Norfolk I suggest you give to Shalan. There were times when I thought he'd kill me to lay his hands on Dorset, so the gift should please him. If you mate Devon with one of Shalan's stallions you may have the beginnings of a herd of your own.'

'They are your polo ponies.'

'I doubt I'll be playing much polo for a while. Take them, but make sure it is Devon and Norfolk. If I find you've taken Dorset or Somerset I'll stab you myself.'

The silence in the room grew unbearable.

'Harry...'

'Meet me in Ahwaz after your wedding.' Harry slammed the lid on the chest and snapped the lock shut. 'Keep an eye on her for me.' He didn't mention Furja's name; he didn't have to. 'Send a message when the child is born.'

'I will, Harry.'

'Now get out of here.' Harry returned to the couch. 'Quickly, before I change my mind about Devon and Norfolk.'

'I'll be in Ahwaz in one month. Try to stay out of Turkish camps.' Mitkhal thrust the bag of coins into his gumbaz.

'You too,' Harry called after him. 'Be happy.' His voice dropped to a whisper. 'For both of us.'

'Here, Knight. Quick. My eyes are playing tricks.'

'They're not.' David Knight slapped John on the back. 'By God, they're not. It's absolute proof that High Command has taken leave of its senses.'

'Knock it off.' Harry walked into the bungalow John and David shared.

'When did this momentous promotion take place?' John picked up a bottle of brandy from beside his chair.

'This afternoon. You two drink too much.'

'Yes, sir.' Knight snapped to attention. 'He does, sir. Not me, sir. I'm on duty in five minutes, sir.'

'Not a word to anyone about this, Knight.'

'You're right to keep it quiet. The news could start a riot among us common, hardworking officers.'

'It's temporary.' Harry sat on the chair next to John's, but kept his coat on. Despite the stove in the corner, the room was freezing. 'They'll chop me down to size the minute my services are no longer required.'

'If you say so, sir.'

'One more "sir". Knight, and I swear I'll punch you on the nose.'

'Promotion makes him violent.' Knight winked at John. 'You'd better watch him; he might not be safe to drink with. Harry?'

'Yes.'

'Permission to leave.' David ran down the veranda, his laughter echoing above the sound of the rain.

'Brandy?' John offered.

246

'No, thank you.'

'What's the matter, Harry? You've been like a wet blanket since you got back.'

'Nothing.' Unbuttoning his greatcoat, Harry lifted his feet on to a chair. 'Everything – this place – the weather – the war. Take your pick?'

John poured another measure of brandy into his tumbler.

'I meant what I said about you drinking too much.'

'I'm the doctor.'

'That's what concerns me. I might get wounded.'

'I only drink when I've a clear eight hours a-head of me to sleep it off.' John lifted his tumbler and made a wry face as he swallowed a mouthful.

'I could ask you, what's the matter?'

'My cousin's made major and I'm only a captain.' John handed Harry a cigarette. 'Whatever happened to captain, major? Or is it the fashion now to jump two ranks? If it is, could you possibly put a word in for me? If I make lieutenant-colonel I promise to use my influence to negotiate an immediate truce, followed by the evacuation and repatriation of all troops engaged in the Mesopotamian conflict.'

'Some idiot in the propaganda department heard about my little holiday with the Turks, and Cox congratulated me on persuading the Bakhtairi Khans to attack a Turkish column on the Karun when the idea was entirely their own. So, as a reward for things I didn't do, they made me a major. When I told them I didn't deserve or want the promotion, they said as my duties included

247

alliance bargaining with the local Sheiks, a major's uniform would be more impressive than a lieutenant's. "Must show the wogs who's in command, old boy",' Harry aped a staff officer's accent. 'As if any of the Sheiks know or care what bloody rank they're talking to. To them, a Ferenghi's a Ferenghi. An untrustworthy infidel, whether he's a private or general.' Harry reached for the brandy.

'Changed your mind?' John gave him a metal tumbler.

'Every mouthful I drink means one less for you. Half a bottle of brandy is as much as any man should consume in one evening. Medically speaking that is.'

'Thank you, Dr Downe – and speaking of Georgiana...' John unbuttoned his top pocket. 'The mail arrived this morning. I knew I'd be seeing you, so I took the liberty of signing for yours.' He handed Harry three flimsy folded sheets of paper, with "opened by the censor" stamped on the outside.

Harry glanced at the writing.

'Here.' John pushed the oil lamp towards him.

'I'll read them later.' All three letters bore English postmarks. He'd hoped for something from Furja, although he didn't know whether she could write Arabic let alone English. He also knew the likelihood of a letter from her turning up in a military mailbag was negligible, but logic hadn't stopped him wishing for the impossible. 'So, what's new?' he asked.

'There was a riot in the Arab quarter last night.'

'What kind?'

'Obviously not the kind that concerns political officers. A couple of dozen sepoys were admitted with broken heads and bruises. A few buildings were burned down and some locals locked up. Apparently, the Arabs were peeved when they were ordered to hand over their houses to the military authorities.'

'That's understandable.'

'We're here to protect them from the Turks and with the whole countryside from here to Nasiriyeh under three feet of water, billeting's a problem. We've pulled back so many troops from Qurna; Basra's bursting at the seams. It's not as if we're requisitioning houses without paying for them. Abdul told me he's made over a thousand rupees this month from renting houses to the military authorities.'

'Unlike Abdul, some of the locals may not have a whorehouse to retreat to.' Harry made a mental note to check Shalan's house in the morning. He blanched at the thought of hobnailed boots scarring the tiled floors, the garden flattened and muddied by stacks of rifles and boxes of supplies and, worst of all, rows of sepoys' pallets in the bedroom he'd shared with Furja.

'Smythe's overseeing the evacuation of the garrison from Qurna.'

'We fought hard for that ground.'

'We're leaving a skeletal force. The Turks aren't likely to mount a counter attack while the plain is flooded – are they?'

'Not to my knowledge,' Harry replied.

'You should have seen Smythe's platoon. He taught them to punt, Oxford-fashion. They moved the troops down in those flat-bottomed native boats.'

'Bellums.' Harry refilled his tumbler.

'We could hear the sergeant from the hospital veranda. "Begging your pardon, Mr Smythe, sir, we're bloody infantry, not bloody marines." But you must know about the flooding. You sailed down the Karun.'

Harry refilled John's tumbler. 'I did just that, sail down the Karun. From what I saw there is no more Tigris and Euphrates. Just one lake.'

John had seen Harry in many moods. Wild, careless, reckless and, on occasion, downright stupid, but he'd never seen his cousin morose and withdrawn before. 'So, is it true this is the wettest winter Mesopotamia's had in 30 years?' he ventured, making a final attempt at conversation.

'I wasn't here 30 years ago.'

John propped his feet on a table. Oblivious to everything except his own misery, Harry continued to stare bleakly at the curtained veranda windows. When he emptied his tumbler, John handed him the bottle.

'I suppose you heard Shakespear's dead.' Harry replenished their drinks and lifted his tumbler. 'To old soldiers. I never met him, but he must have been quite a man. Admired by the brass, and loved and respected by the Arabs. He must have walked on bloody water. For a Ferenghi to gain Bedouin respect is nothing short of miraculous.'

John heard the bitterness in Harry's voice and said nothing.

'Terrible way to die, alone in the Empty Quarter.'

'I heard he was with Ibn Saud's men,' John said.

'He was. But he didn't understand the Arab way of fighting. Hit and run. Hit and run. He hit and stood his ground. Bloody fool! What a waste of a life.'

'The Viceroy's visiting next week. Inspection of the troops, evaluation of the Expeditionary Force, and last, but by no means least, complete and thorough inspection of the Force's hospitals and field medical service. I volunteered to go upstream tomorrow to get out of it.'

'On the *Comet?*'

'Yes, are you...?'

'You do realise there's going to be a show up there? The natives were restless enough last month. According to the latest intelligence reports, the Jihad is well and truly under way. For Ferenghis that means–' Harry drew his finger across his throat.

'Good God, you don't actually believe intelligence reports, do you?'

'On occasion I even write them. Just this once the reports are right. Ahwaz is no place for a married man with responsibilities. By the way, how is Maud?'

'All right, I suppose.'

'Aren't the mail boats getting through from India? She is still in India?'

'Yes.' John drained his tumbler.

'You're going to regret that in the morning,' Harry warned when John shared the last of the bottle between their tumblers.

'Very possibly, but at this moment the morning is a long way off,'

'And Maud?'

John lurched unsteadily to the corner of the room and opened a travelling desk. He tossed the slim bundle of letters it contained to Harry. 'Read for yourself.'

'Not likely.'

'Go ahead. There's not one personal or private word.' John returned clumsily to his seat. 'In fact, I doubt there's anything personal or private left in my married life.'

'You're drunk.' Guilt stung Harry's conscience; immersed in his own misery, he'd become selfish. Rather than ask for his help, Mitkhal had tried to solve his problems in Abdul's gambling rooms and almost succeeded in getting himself killed. Now John was convinced his marriage was over. Solid, dependable John, who'd always been there to give him a hand out of whatever mess he'd climbed into.

'*Dear John,*' John slurred from memory. '*I am well. I trust you are well. This morning I attended a garden party at the Club with Marjorie Harrap. I've joined the Ladies' Committee, and we're raising funds for the hospital. I must run now to catch the post. Love, Maud.* It reads like a court circular, and that's the most intimate one.'

'It's difficult to put your feelings into words when you're with someone. When you have to write them it can be impossible, especially when you know the censor's going to read every word.'

'If the war finished tomorrow, and it won't – it will be months before I'll be posted near her. What chance does our marriage stand when she doesn't seem to be able to remember me, let alone what we were to one another?'

'You're talking about Maud. You were blissfully happy not that long ago.'

'We were, weren't we?' John asked pathetically.

'You were,' Harry asserted.

'The trouble is I've been too bloody clever for my own good. I told Maud about birth control, insisting we wait before starting a family because I thought there'd be time enough for children when we were settled in England. I even had a mental picture of the house I wanted. Eighteenth-century, rambling, red-brick, with a paddock at the side, and stables at the back. I thought when everything was absolutely perfect – absolutely perfect,' he derided, looking around the shabby room. 'Maud would have been better off with a baby to look after. A baby would have reminded her of me. Given her something to do other than attend garden parties.'

'Babies create problems, not solve them.'

'Furja's pregnant?' John guessed.

'Yes.'

'Congratulations.' John wasn't sure he meant it. Harry and Furja in isolation away from polite English society was one thing. A brown child with the name of Downe quite another.

'She made me divorce her.'

'Why on earth would she do that?'

'The British are riding roughshod over the country and the Bedouin don't like it. A Ferenghi in the family is a liability. Shalan wanted me out, so Furja got rid of me.'

'I'm sorry,' John muttered, unequal to dealing with Harry's problems as well as his own.

'It's probably for the best.' Harry pocketed his letters, took his drink, and walked to the door. He opened it and gazed at the line of oil lamps that threw shadowy pools of light on the verandas of the bungalows. 'She fell in love years ago with a Sherif. Ours was a marriage of convenience, nothing more.'

John called for Dira, his sepoy batman. Five minutes later, the man crept into the room rubbing the sleep from his eyes.

'A fresh bottle of brandy,' John ordered. 'And food for Major Downe and myself.'

'There's only stale bread and a few dates, Sahib. The prices in the market are scandalous. They...'

'Go to Abdul's, you know Abdul's coffee house?'

'Better still, we'll go to Abdul's,' Harry roused himself. 'We've had enough brandy for one night. Coffee and a hot meal is what I prescribe for you, Dr Mason.'

'Go back to bed, Dira.' John picked up his coat.

'We could hire a couple of girls,' Harry suggested. 'Abdul bought some new ones yesterday.'

'I checked them out, along with the old hands,' John stuffed his cigarettes into his pockets. 'There were six cases of gonorrhoea 24 hours ago. They could have all picked up the clap by now. The place is a nightmare.'

'In that case we'll have to find you a nice little virgin; one who has been schooled in the arts of the harem by older, wiser women.'

'Schooled?'

'Don't worry, you won't be disappointed.' Harry's smile didn't reach his eyes as he stepped into the cold, rain-filled night.

# Chapter Sixteen

*Basra, 2 a.m. Friday 29th January 1915*

'They are widows. Fakhri Pasha hung their husbands before you entered Basra and their
husbands' families couldn't support them. Times
are hard. Food is scarce. They haven't been bred
for the work but they are good girls and no one
has touched them since you examined them,
Effendi.' Abdul bowed to John. 'You would
honour me and my house by accepting them with
my compliments.' He pushed two girls from the
line. The shortest, a plump, doe-eyed beauty,
glanced slyly at John and giggled.

'Which one would you like, Harry?' John asked,
embarrassed by the proceedings.

'I think they've done the choosing for us.' Harry
lit the cigarette clamped between his teeth and
spoke to the second girl. 'You know my room?'

'Yes, Effendi.' She preceded him up the stairs.
She was tall, heavier than Furja, not as graceful –
he had to stop thinking about Furja. The
memory of her was eating into him, poisoning his
life. He had to accept he would never see her
again. Never...

'Shall I undress, Effendi?'

He nodded. She averted her eyes when she
began to divest herself of her robes. For once,
Abdul might have spoken the truth. She wasn't

used to the life – not yet. He watched layer upon layer join the mounting pile on the floor. He wondered if Abdul had laid his hands on an illustrated edition of the *Arabian Nights*. The girl wouldn't have looked out of place in a pantomime of *Aladdin*. She stripped down to transparent harem pants and a bolero top that left her breasts uncovered. She hesitated, her cheeks scarlet.

'Those off as well. When you've finished, lie on the bed.'

She did as he asked but he remained in his chair, the end of his cigarette a glowing tip of fairy light that arced through the air as he smoked. He could hear John's girl, still giggling through the partition wall. Stubbing out his cigarette, he left the chair. He heard the girl breathe quickly and tremulously when he removed his own clothes. He didn't ask her name before he heaved himself on top of her.

The whole thing was curiously impersonal. Not unpleasant, but clinical. He needed relief. He used her. When he looked at her afterwards, her eyes were closed, her dark hair fanned out on the pillow – like, yet unlike, Furja. He left the bed.

'I don't please you, Effendi?'

'I need to be alone.' Pulling his gumbaz over his head, he dug into his uniform pockets for change and handed her a few coins. 'They're for you, not Abdul.'

'Thank you. Would you like me to...?'

'Just go.'

Wrapping her robe around herself, she picked up her clothes and ran from the room. He lit another cigarette, listened to John's snores, and wondered if his cousin had been sober enough to appreciate the doe-eyed beauty. Then he remembered the look in John's eyes when he'd talked about Maud and doubted it.

What was it about one woman that could sour all others for a man? Here he was, living in a brothel, and this was the first time he'd done more than look at one of the girls. All he wanted was Furja. Exhausted, pregnant, her magnificent eyes sunk in black shadow – he would have given everything he possessed simply to curl at her feet and watch over her while she slept.

Walking to the window, he flung it wide. A queue of privates from the Dorsets was waiting in the street for their turn in the booths Abdul had set up for the ranks. They were shouting to the sepoys who waited at a door opposite. Being an officer had some advantages, if only in a whorehouse. Closing the window, he turned to the bed. The rumpled sheets stank of cheap perfume and the fishy odour of sex. He had to think of something other than Furja or he'd drive himself mad. Retrieving his letters, he turned up the oil lamp.

Two were from Georgiana: one from his brother. He checked the dates and read them in the order they'd been written.

*London, Monday October 12th 1914*

*Dear Harry,*

*I've been married for two weeks, and as I was the only one in the family to extend congratulations on your nuptials, I expect, no, demand you reciprocate. You are no longer the only black sheep among the Downes. I have been shown the door, cut off with a shilling, or whatever it is that parents do when their* offspring disgrace the family. My husband isn't an Arab, only occasionally blacker than one. He's Welsh, a coal-miner (which explains the colour), and this, in father's eyes, is infinitely worse than being a native, so if you want to try to make amends for your misdeeds now is the time to do it, while I'm the one out of favour. I'm Mrs Gwilym Lewis, and we are, or rather were, blissfully happy.

I met Gwilym at one of Millie Stroud's Fabian evenings. He's a socialist, as every right-thinking individual should be. Tall, handsome, dark, with black curly hair. He's self-educated and left Wales to join the Ambulance Corps. He disagrees with the war, as everyone should, but feels he has to do something to alleviate the suffering, so he volunteered. Last night he left for France and I feel lonelier than I've ever felt before.

Harry, I never knew two people could be so happy together. Why didn't you tell me what marriage was really like in that last ridiculous letter of yours? When this mess is over you must bring Furja to England, and we'll all holiday in Wales. It is going to be over soon, isn't it? So many broken bodies are brought into the hospital every day it's obscene.

I'm used to the old, the chronically sick, the crippled, but not this endless parade of smashed young men. Every morning we watch the new recruits march off to Victoria station. The bands play, people cheer, and all the while wagons are being unloaded at the back door of the hospital. No bands play for the wounded, Harry. They're sneaked in secretly lest the sight deter anyone from volunteering. I spend hours trying to patch together boys who've had half their heads blown away, or their arms and legs hacked off by bayonets. If it all stopped tomorrow, there'd be thousands who'd

258

*find it impossible to rebuild their lives. I hope you man-*
*age to stay where you are. Believe me, you're better off*
*sitting out this war in peace and quiet as far away*
*from the Western Front as possible.*

*I can't tell you how our parents are because we*
*haven't spoken since I drove Gwilym to the house.*
*Father muttered something about the war throwing*
*undesirables in the path of decent young girls and a*
*complete moral decline. Mother cried and the door*
*was closed in our faces.*

*I ate a sandwich in Hyde Park the other day with*
*Michael. He's as miserable as I prophesied he'd be but*
*the fool insists on blaming himself for Lucy's failings.*

*Please give our happiest and best wishes to your*
*wife. Gwilym was thrilled when I told him he has a*
*Bedouin sister-in-law. Perhaps we can take a belated*
*honeymoon in an Arab tent when the world is sane*
*again. You and Furja can stay in our shabby rooms*
*around the corner from the hospital any time. Keep*
*safe and well and don't rush home until a truce has*
*been declared.*

*Your ever-loving sister Georgiana and brother-in-law*
*Gwilym.*

Harry tried to imagine Georgiana in love. He
had a Welsh coal-miner for a brother-in-law. Poor
Michael; he was the only blue-eyed boy left in the
parental fold. Quite a responsibility to shoulder.
Neither he nor Georgiana had been fair to the
lad. Laying his sister's letter aside, he picked up
Michael's.

*Clyneswood, Tuesday 3rd November.*
*Dear Harry,*

*I'm sorry I haven't written for so long. Georgiana*
*told me she'd written to you about my marriage to*

259

*Lucy. I hope you don't mind. I know how much Lucy meant to you, and how upset you were when she broke off your engagement...*

Broke off their engagement! She – furious, Harry continued reading.

*Lucy and I have set up home in London in a mews cottage. We try to spend most weekends at Clyneswood, but Lucy sits on several committees, and is extremely busy organising fund-raising activities for the war effort. We are both well...*

But are you happy, little brother? Harry wondered.

*I would like to join up, but as Lucy says, someone has to stay at home and see the country runs smoothly. Besides, even if I did join up, there's no guarantee I'd be sent to the front. I could end up in a backwater like you. I miss you, Harry. I miss Georgiana too. She's so busy these days, I hardly see her. Lucy sends her regards. I think of you often.*
*Your brother, Michael.*
*P.S. Georgiana is married. Lucy doesn't approve but I rather like him.*

Harry crumpled the letter. Disillusionment and loneliness were etched in every line but it was Michael's own fault. He wasn't a child. He was a man who'd made the mistake of marrying a selfish, manipulating, stupid... No, not stupid – whatever else Lucy was she wasn't stupid. She'd set her sights on becoming mistress of Clyneswood and Michael had been her means to that end. He hadn't stood a chance. Lucy had sunk her claws into him once, and he was more astute than his brother.

He didn't doubt Lucy was enjoying every minute of his and Georgiana's disgrace. She'd never be critical; she'd simply look soulfully sympathetic whenever their names were mentioned. She was probably already presiding behind the ceremonial teapot when social pressures prevented their mother from attending county functions. He visualised her engraved calling cards.

*Mr and Mrs Michael Downe, of London and Clyneswood.*

Could almost hear her whispered confidence. 'Heirs to Colonel and Mrs Downe.' He didn't know whether to hope his brother would live on in blissful ignorance of his wife's calculated scheming, or to pray for an early, and brutal revelation of Lucy's character so he could run as far, and as fast, from her as possible. But perhaps Michael already knew.

*Lucy doesn't approve but I rather like him.*

If he'd been there, he could have – what? He clenched his fists in frustration. How could Uncle John and Aunt Elizabeth have produced reasonable beings like John and Tom and then a creature like Lucy? Seething, he picked up the third letter. It was shorter than the first he'd received from his twin.

*London, Monday November 16th*

*Dear Harry,*

*Gwilym is dead. He was shot trying to retrieve wounded from the battlefield. An officer wrote to me. He couldn't possibly have known Gwilym. The letter was full of platitudes Gwilym would have hated like 'dying for King and Country'. I wish I knew why he had to die. The next post brought a kind letter from a man called Ianto Hopkins who was with him when it happened. Gwilym wasn't alone; I have to be grateful for that. It was a single bullet. Clean, instantaneous. Gwilym didn't suffer.*

Harry flinched. In Qurna, he'd witnessed the clean and instantaneous deaths that were detailed in the final letters home. He'd watched a man drown in his own blood and agony, too far gone to warrant attention from the medic who was trying to save those who still had a chance. In the reality of battle, the dying were counted already dead; there was no time – or morphine – to waste on easing anyone out of life.

Poor, poor Georgie. Poor, poor Gwilym.

*Before Gwilym left, he told me that he believed death brings whatever we expect of it. If we believe in a heaven of pink and grey clouds, and God sitting on a throne, then it will be so. If we believe in nothing ... I can't believe that, Harry – I can't. We'll be together again. I couldn't bear it if it were otherwise...*

*It's mayhem at the hospital. I've been doing double shifts for the past month, but when this is over, I want to go to the front so I can see where Gwilym died. We had so little time together. We had to keep our marriage a secret from everyone except close friends and family in case the hospital authorities sacked me. Even now, in the middle of this foul mess, they won't allow female doctors to marry. God, I want to go out and kill someone, and it's not a Hun I want to shoot.*

*Harry, write to me, please. You're all I have left. Don't die. When this is over I want someone to come back to this insane country and make it right again. Georgiana.*

The ink was blotched. It took a while for Harry to realise the paper was wet. His tears, not Georgiana's, stained the page. Georgiana wouldn't have cried. She'd have sat bolt upright, stony-faced, dry-eyed, while she wrote.

Rising from the chair, he walked to the table, sat down, and picked up his pen.

## Chapter Seventeen

*British camp, Karun River, Nasiriyeh/Ahwaz, Saturday 6th February 1914*

Harry fingered his cards with mittened hands before dipping into the pile of coins on the camp table in front of him. Taking three sovereigns, he dropped them into the pot.

'This is heading too steep for me.' Knight slapped his cards down.

'Not for me.' Geoffrey Brooke picked four sovereigns from his stack and threw them on top of Harry's.

'You don't have to match every bid, Lieutenant Brooke,' John admonished him, in an attempt to save a little of Geoffrey Brooke's money.

'I do know how to play cards, Captain Mason.'

'I wasn't suggesting you didn't.' John picked up the only full bottle of brandy among an array of empties. 'War's getting serious; there's hardly any alcohol left, even medicinal.'

'The Rajputs will be here tomorrow.' Harry matched Brooke's four sovereigns and added an extra one. 'The Indian Army always marches with plenty of liquid reserves.'

'How can you be sure they'll arrive tomorrow?' Geoffrey snapped.

'I saw them today. Less than a day's march from here.'

'You must have a good horse, Major Downe.'

'I do.' Harry ignored Brooke's scepticism. 'Your call?'

'The best man wins.' Geoffrey matched Harry's stake and laid down his cards.

Harry topped Geoffrey's hand. 'Are you sure you can afford to lose this much?'

'Are you insulting me, Major?'

John intervened. 'We've all had enough for one night.' He took the cards and shuffled them together. 'If the Rajputs arrive tomorrow we could find ourselves in a show. Frankly, gentlemen, I doubt we'll be up to it if we don't get some sleep.'

'Goodnight, sir. Sir,' Brooke muttered mutinously, nodding to Harry before following Knight out.

'I wish you'd stop goading that boy, Harry,' John reproached. 'You must have won six months' pay from him in a week.'

'Anyone who plays cards as badly as he does deserves all he gets.'

'It's not his fault you and Reggie Brooke hated one another at school.'

'Don't tell me you feel sorry for the blighter. He's every bit as obnoxious as his ghastly prig of a brother.'

'This isn't school, Harry.' John uncorked the brandy.

'It feels like it. The brass are as pompous and

impervious to common sense as the staff ever were.'

'We didn't live on this knife-edge at school.' John held out the brandy. 'Want me to fill your flask?'

'Can you spare it?'

'No, but I will. Did you see the Rajputs today?'

'They weren't a mirage.' Harry scooped the sovereigns on the table into a leather bag. 'But the force won't be the saviour little boy Brooke's hoping for. There were at least a thousand Arabs marching with them. Sheikh Muhammerah's men. According to Mitkhal, that breed doesn't care for us, any more than they do for Johnny Turk.'

'Then why are they marching with the Rajputs?'

'Bounty. After we've been slaughtered, our rifles and supplies will be lying around waiting to be picked up. The first passer-by will be the Arab rear-guard.'

'Harry...'

'I'm not joking.' Harry fell serious. 'I know the natives. I wish HQ would read the reports I write. If they did, they might stop believing the Arabs hold the same cricket-playing morality as us.'

'You think we're being set up?' John handed him the flask he'd filled.

'Led by the nose like calves to a slaughter-house.'

John sat on his cot. The unrelenting rain, mud, filthy, freezing conditions and uncertainty had pushed everyone in Ahwaz close to breaking point. But Harry had more reason to break than most. He spent his days dressed as a native, scouting the desert with Mitkhal; spent his nights drinking, playing cards, and tormenting Geoffrey Brooke. It wasn't a regime to make for sanity.

'On that cheerful note, I'll take to my bed.' Harry drank from his flask. 'To King and Empire but, much as I love my country, I see the Bedouin with their flocks and tents travelling this land a century from now just as they've done for the last few thousand years, not a line of British troops marching with a Union Jack. Unless we're fighting the Arabs instead of the Turks by then. If that's sedition, so be it.'

'You think we're going to lose this war?' John asked.

'I think that ultimately we're going to leave this muddy, fly-ridden hell hole to the only people mad enough to want it.' Harry kicked off his boots and rolled himself into his blanket.

John continued to sit on the edge of his cot after Harry fell asleep. For the first time he saw the war as more than just an irritation that kept him from Maud and the idyllic English village of his dreams. Harry's predictions brought a sharp consciousness of his own mortality. He pictured the camp overrun. Bodies piled high, his own blood-soaked carcass among them. An icy emptiness, a portent of nothingness, gnawed at his stomach; a few days, perhaps only a few hours from now, he'd cease to exist. He forgot the letters Maud had sent him and remembered their honeymoon.

He imagined her arms outstretched towards him, her glittering dress shimmering with a light that dimmed the lamp. His body ached for her, but even as he returned her smile, the lamp flickered. There was no Maud, only a cold, littered tent that stank of male sweat and cheap brandy. It was bloody cruel. He'd never see her – never make love with her again – and for what?

Pushing his fingers through his hair, he looked around. Somewhere he had a few cigarettes. Did he have writing paper? He had to draft a will, make his father and Tom executors, send it downstream to Basra and pray it reached home. He had to ensure that whatever happened, Maud would be looked after. She was so beautiful, so fragile, and so very helpless.

*British camp, Karun River, Ahwaz,*
*Tuesday 2nd March 1915*

Geoffrey sat astride a canvas stool inside his tent, razor in hand, a canvas bowl of murky water on a stand in front of him. The flap was open but Geoffrey didn't hear the bustle and noise of the force preparing for action. He was remembering Maud. Maud eyeing him across Marjorie Harrap's dinner table, Maud naked apart from her stockings... A shadow blocked out the light.

'Your uniform, Sahib.'

'Leave it on the cot,' he ordered.

'Will that be all, Sahib?'

'No, it damn well won't. This water is filthy. I need clean water to wash in.'

'But, Sahib, that's all we have. The river...'

'I'll have no damned "buts".'

'Sahib.' The sepoy picked up a tinned enamel jug and ran off.

Geoffrey cursed the man and rinsed the lather

from his blade. Bloody sepoys. They never obeyed an order unless you stood over them. He grasped his right wrist with his left hand but failed to stop his fingers shaking. For Christ's sake, he was only going out on patrol. A morning patrol like any other. There were rumours of action but rumours didn't guarantee fighting. And what if there was?

For months, he'd told everyone who'd listen that he wanted to fight. He was a damned coward to funk it. Besides, it would be worth getting shot at to brag to Downe at the card table.

'Brooke, can I come in?' Mason was at his tent flap, brandy bottle in hand.

'Please yourself.' Geoffrey ran his razor over his chin.

'If you've a flask, I'll fill it for you.'

'It's on the bed.'

John ignored Geoffrey's nervousness. 'I try to fill all the officers' flasks before a show. Never know beforehand how long these things will last, and if any of your men are wounded, it's as well you have something to give them. The terrain here is hell for stretcher-bearers. They can't always move as fast as we'd like.'

'I suppose you're staying here with the hospital?'

'Knight drew that straw. I'm going out with the field ambulance.' John found Geoffrey's flask and filled it.

Geoffrey cut himself again, and cursed.

'We all feel the way you're feeling right now, Brooke.'

'What do you know about the way I feel?' Brooke countered. 'All a doctor has to do is hold a fighting man's hand when he's been hit.'

John glanced at Geoffrey. The man hated him, and he couldn't fathom why.

Ashamed of his outburst, Geoffrey retreated into politeness. 'Thank you for the brandy, Captain.'

'Don't mention it.' John laid the flask on the bed and left.

Geoffrey stared at his reflection. If only Mason wasn't so damned reasonable. He'd tried so hard to dislike him...

'Time for patrol, sir.'

Geoffrey wiped the lather from his half-shaved face, rammed on his newly pipe-clayed topee and left his tent, head high, hand on sword. His horse was waiting, restlessly pawing the ground. He only hoped his men couldn't see the trembling coward beneath the immaculate uniform.

The Turks were waiting for them seven miles outside the camp. And not just the Turks. Harry had warned there would be Arab irregulars, but not one man was prepared for the eerie noise of their battle cries or the weight of their numbers.

The Turks began advancing in slow, orderly fashion while the Arab irregulars closed in on their flanks. Geoffrey heard commands being shouted down the lines. The infantry drew back. He was left in front. From somewhere came the order to charge. He drew his sword. His horse needed no spurring. Following the lead of the other mounts, it broke into a gallop. He put his head down in line with his blade. Rifle and gunshots exploded. He heard cracks, saw fire flashes. Men and horses began to scream; their noise drowned in deafening sallies from the Turkish large-bore guns.

The horse on his right wheeled and crashed. He reined in his mount. The faces of the Turkish cavalry, speckled with rain, loomed inexorably closer. He stood in the stirrups and heaved. Blood flecked the foam at his horse's mouth. The horse on his left turned. And, at last, his own.

Riding hard, he glanced over his right shoulder. Sepoys rode behind him. He dug in his spurs, the mist cleared, and in one sickening moment he realised he was on his own. Wherever the rest of the cavalry were, he wasn't with them. Arabs were close on the sepoys' heels. He pulled at his reins again, but his horse refused to obey. A sepoy shouted a warning when hawk-eyed Arabs thundered into view ahead of them.

An Arab stood poised in the stirrups of his galloping horse, holding a rifle with both hands. Dropping his reins, Geoffrey reached for his handgun. Before he unbuttoned his holster, the Arab fired.

Geoffrey's horse crumpled beneath him. Lifting his leg over the saddle, he slid to the ground, landing as his horse crashed screaming beside him. The Arab dismounted and closed in on Geoffrey, rifle cocked. He pulled his kafieh down from his face and ran a slim forefinger along his throat. Geoffrey didn't believe it.

The rest of the troop would appear at any moment. In the meantime, it was up to him to teach the bastards a lesson. Looking into the Arab's eyes, Geoffrey removed one boot, then the other. The native stepped back. Using all his strength, Geoffrey threw his boots into the Arab's face. They hit the native's cheekbones, leaving streaks of mud.

There was a rush of air, a sigh, followed by a thud. He turned to see an Arab holding a sepoy's head. The sepoy's body toppled and crashed into a muddy gulley. A hand closed into his hair. Something hit his neck. He felt warm blood coursing down his shirt. It didn't hurt; there was only a sense of bewilderment. He wasn't going to die. He couldn't die. He'd made so many plans, so many people loved him.

His mother – his sisters – even Reggie... Another blow came. An explosion of crimson burst in his head, obliterating everything, even thoughts of Maud.

*Officers' Mess Regimental Headquarters, India, Friday 5th March 1915*

'It couldn't have been easy for you to leave the Western Front, Reid. With what's going on there, promotion prospects for a bright chap have never been better. But prospects in Mesopotamia are just as good. Look at Harry Downe; he made major last month and now he's acting lieutenant-colonel.'

'I heard.' Charles smiled.

'We need sound chaps out there. That's why we sent for you. Though we got more than we bargained for. Sent for a captain and came up with a major, eh, Reid?' The colonel dipped into his whisky.

'Yes, sir.' Resigned to another half hour of tedium before dinner, Charles signalled to an

271

orderly to refill his glass.

'Tell me.' The colonel peered at him short-sightedly. 'What's it like over there.'

'Bloody.'

'Plenty of action, eh! I know the Western Front is getting most of the press. But this sideshow in Mesopotamia is important. An army fights on its supplies. Oil is vital. Navy couldn't function without it. Not to mention our tanks.'

'We didn't see many of those in France, sir.'

'They're on their way, Reid. Have it on good intelligence. Let's hope the Huns and Johnny Turk don't have the same source. Now where was I? Oh yes, Mesopotamia. We need every man we can get out there.'

'I don't doubt it, sir. But I would have thought you could have found someone suitable here without scouring the Western Front for reinforcements.'

'There wasn't anyone who didn't need six months to get acclimatised, old chap. Every able-bodied man in India is already in the Gulf. Now the rainy season's ending, Townsend's preparing his offensive. Between you and me, I wouldn't be surprised if he didn't stop until he reached Baghdad.' The colonel winked.

'As I understand it, sir, the brief was to safeguard the oil wells and we haven't managed that yet. The pipeline is cut; our position hasn't been consolidated.'

'A detachment went up the Karun last month to sort out the pipeline.' The colonel's lips set in a grim line. 'Heavy losses, number of good chaps gone. You probably knew some of them.'

'I did.'

'They went in a good cause. No better way to die than in harness, eh?'

The platitude was too much for Charles, coming from an officer the colonel's age. 'If you'll excuse me, sir, Johnny Leigh's just come in. I would like to speak to him.'

'Course, old chap. See you again before you go?'

'I sail tomorrow.' Charles barely refrained from adding 'Thank God.' Twenty-four hours in India was enough. There were only geriatrics and subalterns straight from school left. Even the mothers' darlings detailed to the staff were getting thin on the ground. The demands of the war were eating into every reserve of manpower.

'A quick word before you go, Reid. You know that doctor chap, Mason?'

'We're close friends, sir.' Charles braced himself.

'Yes. Um – knew your father. Fine general. Fine chap. Mason's a fine chap too, otherwise I wouldn't say anything. This wife of his – someone has to have a word. Marjorie Harrap tried, didn't get anywhere. What does the girl think she's doing? She's the talk of the regiment. And her husband poor chap, out in Basra.'

'Karun River, sir.' Charles repeated information he'd gleaned from an officer invalided back to HQ.

'Whatever, he can't do anything where he is. Have a word with her, Reid. We've tried offering her a berth home. Basra, even. There are other wives out there but the minx won't go. Bad show. She's affecting the morale of the entire regiment. Can't have our chaps going off to war worrying about who's ... worrying about their wives. Well,

273

come on, then. Drink up. I'll buy you one for the road,' he offered, camouflaging his embarrassment.

'I've arranged to see Mrs Mason after dinner, sir.'

'Glad to see you doing what you can.' The colonel lifted his glass. 'To you. Wish I was going with you. Put in for it. But the damned medics won't let me go. It's this blasted gout.' The colonel pointed to his left leg. Charles suddenly saw through the bluff to the heart of the man. It had probably cost the colonel more to raise the subject of Maud than it had for him to face action in the Boer War.

'I hope you'll soon recover, sir. Thank you for the drink.'

'Next time I see you; you'll probably be General Reid, my boy. Hope you make it. Bad show to let your father outrank you.'

Charles left the colonel to his whisky and gout. The mess was as full as it was going to get. He and Johnny Leigh were the only officers above 20 and below 60 in the room. He glanced at the wall as he made his way to Leigh's chair. No new casualty lists were pinned to the board. Only the one he'd read a dozen times since he'd landed that morning. Neither John's nor Harry's name was on it, but that only meant they'd been alive a week ago when the list had been sent out. The thought of them cooped up on the Karun holding out against a Turkish force that outnumbered theirs five to one was horrific.

'Got your boarding card, Reid?' Leigh asked.

'Yes. You?'

'Sailing tomorrow.' Leigh gave the inane braying laugh that never failed to irritate Charles. 'We're travelling companions, old boy.' He nodded to the colonel. 'The old man been giving you a pep talk about darling Maud?'

'Give over, Leigh.'

'Looks so prim and proper too. And, rumour has it, with natives as well as Portuguese.'

'I said give over!'

'My lips are sealed. Drink?'

Johnny's lips might have been sealed but no one else's were. By the end of dinner, Charles was sick of hearing about Maud. Ostensibly innocent remarks that she'd been seen at this or that ball – soiree – dinner party – Maharajah's picnic – and always with the same man. Charles was beginning to loathe the sound of Miguel D'Arbez's name and he hadn't even met the man. He hadn't been ashore ten minutes before someone mentioned it in the same sentence as Maud Mason. If it had been 50 or even 30 years ago, he probably would have felt obliged to call the man out. As it was, he'd visited Maud twice that afternoon and both times she'd been out.

He'd spoken to Harriet, and that had been difficult with the memory of Emily coming between them. The maid had burst into tears as soon as she saw him; crying first for her dead mistress, then for Maud's behaviour. He'd told Harriet to tell Maud he'd return at nine and he'd expect her to be in. She was.

Perhaps it was the time Charles had spent with Georgiana on his last leave. Georgiana had never been one to bother with her looks. Or perhaps it was the celibate existence he'd led since he'd left Emily; either way, he found Maud mesmerising. When he'd last seen her she'd been an innocent and attractive girl, but the woman who greeted him in a crimson evening gown was no innocent. She exuded glamour and sexual promise.

Her ruby and diamond jewellery dashed any hopes he'd nurtured that the rumours were false. Her tiara alone was worth more than John's yearly allowance and captain's pay combined, and that was without the matching necklace, earrings, rings and four bracelets, two worn above and two below each elbow. He'd seen Emily wearing a few fine pieces, but nothing so outrageously, ostentatiously magnificent.

'Charles, how marvellous to see you.' Maud brushed his cheek with her lips. He reeled at her proximity and perfume. An alluring, addictive scent he wanted to breathe in again – and again. 'If I'd known you were coming I would have kept tonight free. We must dine together tomorrow, but what am I doing allowing you stand in the hall while I chatter? Come in. Let me take your hat. What would you like to drink?'

She led him into the sitting room. The lights were low, the drinks tray complete with two glasses. Preparation for a seduction? He wondered.

'Whisky or brandy? Let me guess. You've dined in the mess, so you want to carry on with brandy?'

He would have preferred brandy but he felt a childish need to assert himself. 'Whisky.'

'Sit down.' She patted the seat beside her on

the sofa. 'Now tell me all about home and France. What are you doing here?'

'Which question would you like me to answer first?' He took the whisky, taking care not to touch her fingers when she handed him the glass. To his astonishment, she filled a brandy glass for herself.

'All of them.' She curled beside him, tucking her feet beneath her.

'Home is home but society is changing. With so many men at the front, women are working. Driving carts, delivering milk, in the munitions factories...'

'How fascinating.' She gazed directly at him until he felt himself drowning in the deep cerulean blue of her eyes – like, yet unlike, Emily's. 'And John's family?'

'All well.' He moved from the sofa to an armchair. 'I saw John's brother, Tom, in France. He's working in a field hospital. John's sister, Lucy, is involved in committee work. Do you know she married Harry's brother, Michael?'

'Yes, I've had a few letters from John's mother. They're here somewhere.' Maud looked around but made no effort to locate them.

'John's father has postponed his retirement until John can take over his practice. All the family were pleased to hear about your marriage. They're longing to meet you.'

'How kind.' If she'd noticed the sarcasm in his voice, she ignored it.

'Have you heard from John?' Charles watched her carefully.

'The mail is dreadful. Sometimes there are no

letters for weeks then I get three or four on the same day. He was working in a hospital in Basra but the last I heard he was going up the Karun. I haven't had anything from him for three weeks. But Harry–' she smiled '–have you heard he's a lieutenant-colonel?'

'It's the talk of the mess.'

'Amazing, isn't it? My father always said Harry would be lucky to hold on to his commission. But look at you. A major.'

'By default; there wasn't anyone else left after the last show.'

'You're being modest.'

'We've covered everyone, Maud, except you.' He finished his whisky and set his glass on a table. 'What are you doing with yourself?'

She looked at him and saw that he knew. God! Didn't anyone in India talk about anyone other than her and Miguel D'Arbez? 'I'm fine, I'm on a lot of committees too; we raise funds...'

'And socialise with the Portuguese and their native friends,' he interrupted.

'Someone's been tittle-tattling.' She refilled his glass.

'Everyone's been tittle-tattling. It started the moment I stepped off the boat.'

'What I do is none of your business.'

'John is one of my closest and oldest friends. I won't stand by and ignore what people are saying about his wife.' He set aside the glass she handed him. 'If you won't think of your reputation, think of John. Of what he'll go through when he finds out, and find out he will, Maud – if he doesn't already know. There's no shortage of people waiting to tell him.'

'When people have nothing to talk about they make things up.'

'Do you really expect me to believe that everyone here is conspiring against you?'

'Oh for heaven's sake.' She finished her brandy and poured another. 'I can't live like a nun until this stupid war ends. John might not be back for years.'

'Other army wives cope with their husband's absences. Your mother...'

'You're a fine one to talk about my mother.'

'She was a damn sight better woman than you.' He left his chair and went to the mantelpiece, where there was a display of framed photographs, including one of Emily. He picked it up. 'I loved her; I would have done anything for her. I begged her to go to England with me, but...'

'She stayed with my father and it cost her her life. It's her I'm thinking about, Charles. Life's too short to be anything but selfish.' She reiterated Miguel's philosophy. 'I've no intention of wasting my best years sitting around waiting for this war to end. I enjoy parties and balls, so why shouldn't I go to them? Miguel's good company, there's a shortage of presentable escorts...'

'There's a shortage of escorts because every able-bodied man is fighting for the survival of the Empire, including your husband. This scandal could kill him, Maud. Have you any idea of the impact bad news from home has on a serving soldier?'

'John would understand. He's not as petty-minded as you and your HQ cronies. He

279

wouldn't mind me enjoying myself.' She tossed back her brandy with a practised flick of the wrist that repelled him.

'He would mind the gossip I've heard about you and Miguel D'Arbez, and the men he passes you on to.'

'Miguel is a friend, he...'

Charles caught her by the shoulders and forced her to face him. 'I won't let you ruin John's life. I'm leaving for Basra tomorrow. We've secured the town; it's safe for civilians. You'll sail with me. They'll find you a room in a bungalow with one of the other wives. If you need to do something, you can work in the hospital. John probably has some leave due. You'll be able to see him, and if you know what's good for you, you'll make him forget anything he might have heard about you and Miguel D'Arbez.'

'Thank you, but no.' She could have been refusing an invitation to afternoon tea. 'I've lived in Basra. There's no society there.'

'It's different now the Expeditionary Force is based there. There are lots of people, your father...'

'If I'm not prepared to go to Basra for John's sake, I'm hardly likely to go there for my father's.'

'The boat leaves at noon. I've bought tickets for you and Harriet.'

'Harriet handed in her notice. She's going to marry a sergeant in the artillery.'

'Good for Harriet.' Charles wondered why the maid hadn't said anything to him earlier, but he wasn't prepared to get side-tracked into a discussion on Harriet. 'I've arranged for you to have my cabin, I'll sleep on deck.'

'I'm not going.'

'You'll board that ship if I have to drag you up the gangplank by your hair. You said life is short. A tour of duty on the Western Front has shown me just how short – and painful. But some pain can be avoided. You're not going to hurt John any more than you already have. Whether he lives for another month or 60 years he's going to be as happy as a whore like you can make him.' He gripped her arm.

'You're hurting me.' She looked into his eyes, hoping to find compassion, but saw only contempt. 'You don't understand. I can't even remember him.'

'You'll remember him when you see him. Start packing and praying he still wants you, because if he doesn't, every decent house will close its doors to you and you could find yourself on the streets.'

She looked from Charles to the posed photograph of John, a frozen smile on his face, his eyes dead, cold. Had she ever really loved him?

'I'll bring a carriage at 10.30. Harriet can come or not, as she wishes. I'll keep the tickets. If you have any ideas of running to D'Arbez with stories of my brutality, forget them. What I said earlier about closed doors encompasses even Portuguese society. They don't like whores who service natives any more than the British. Those jewels you're wearing were obviously designed for Indian royalty.'

'I bought them...'

'Oh, I've no doubt you paid for them, Maud. But not with money. I've heard enough about your exploits to fill the columns of half a dozen

281

yellow press newspapers.'

'You wouldn't dare...'

'I wouldn't do it to the wife of a friend. But an ex-wife who'd run off with another man? Try me. If John needs grounds for divorce, I'll supply him with the names of men who attended dinner parties where the female guests were naked. And picnics where ladies were passed around instead of dessert. Under those circumstances I think he'd consider himself better off without you.'

'You bastard. You couldn't possibly know...'

'D'Arbez teaching you English, Maud?' Charles walked to the door. 'Ten-thirty tomorrow. Be packed and ready.'

## Chapter Eighteen

*The British camp, Ahwaz.*
*Evening of Tuesday 16th March 1915*

'Is that it, Captain Mason?'

John looked up from the casualty list he was updating. 'For now; come back in a couple of hours.'

The sergeant ordered the stretcher-bearers to pick up the last corpse and marched them out. John continued to scrawl notes against names.

*Died from wounds. Died from frostbite. Died from dysentery. Discharged fit for duty.*

He looked down the rows of pallets in the tent. There were two more he didn't expect to last the night. At this rate there'd be no one left for the

Turks to capture when they overran the post. He, along with the other officers, had no idea why the Turks were waiting.

Harry stole into the tent, his eyes glazed with exhaustion, stubble darkening his unwashed face.

'You look as though you need a cot in the officers' hospital tent.' John offered him a canvas chair.

Harry sat down. 'I'll settle for a bath and a meal.'

'While it's quiet?'

'It will remain that way while our gunboat is in the river. The Turks credit it with powers I wish it possessed.'

'They're not planning an offensive?'

'Mitkhal was in their camp four hours ago.' Harry pulled off his kafieh and ran a hand through his hair. 'They're sending half their force to the Euphrates. The next show will be there. If we lose that, it will only be a matter of time before they overrun the Wilyat, including this base. If we win, they'll retreat upstream, leaving the Shatt, the Karun, and the oilfields to us.'

'The locals?' John pressed him.

'The Arab auxiliaries fighting alongside the Turks will desert or switch allegiance to us if they think there's something in it for them.'

'It's reassuring to know there's nothing personal in their slaughter of our troops.'

'The only personal feelings the Arab have is self-preservation for themselves and their families. See to these for me.' Harry dumped a bundle and a packet on the table John was using as a desk. 'Mitkhal took the Dorset lieutenant's tunic off one of Sheikh Ghadban's warriors. It's wrapped around the ID tags we found on the field. The tags were about all the scavengers left.'

'Then it's true, the Arabs are mutilating bodies.'

'It's true.' Harry picked up the packet of papers, 'This, I found next to what was left of Brooke. I thought you'd want to write the letter home. You knew him better than anyone else here.'

'I hoped he'd made it.'

'There's no one left to hope for outside this camp.'

'Drink?' John reached for the bottle that had become his inseparable companion.

'No, thanks, mornings after take on new meaning in the desert.'

'You can't travel out now. You look like death.'

'I have to get through to Basra.'

'In God's name, we're surrounded.'

'The Turks don't kill Arabs. At least, not neutral ones, and Mitkhal and I make credible neutral Arabs.' Harry stretched his arms above his head.

John moved his chair.

'Sorry, I smell like a camel. It's time to organise that bath, supplies, and a couple of fresh horses. Dorset's exhausted. Take care of her for me.'

'Don't you think it's ironic that you're driving yourself harder than your horse?'

'Can't be helped. Night is kind to travellers; they, like the jackals, are grey. Do me another favour when this show is over; and I don't mean this battle, I mean the whole bloody war. Look up Furja and the child if I'm not around. Make sure they're all right. I've left them everything I own but I've a feeling Shalan will be too proud to draw on my account. Check she has what she needs and the child knows about me.'

'Harry, you're going to survive this mess.'

'Just promise.'

John looked at him. 'You know I will.'

John downed half a bottle of brandy before examining the parcels. When he unwrapped the tunic a stream of ID tags fell out. He pushed them aside. The camp clerk could check the names off against the missing in the morning. He pulled the smaller package towards him. A set of tags was wrapped around it, a sheet of paper tucked under the string. It was difficult to read Harry's scrawl; the paper was dirty, the pencil markings faint.

*The personal effects of Sub-Lieutenant Geoffrey Brooke.*

He unfolded a pile of letters from the muddy outer covering. They'd obviously been soaked at some time; now dry, they fell apart in his hands. He removed the thickest wad, hoping to find a name or address. The clerk would have Geoffrey's home address but he wondered if there was someone else, a girl perhaps. A lock of golden hair fell on the table. Tied with a strand of red ribbon, it shimmered in the lamplight, reminding him of Maud and a world where men and women moved in circles where there was no thought or mention of death. Holding the hair, he pieced together the largest sheet of paper.

*My Darling,*

*I'm writing this on my cot in my tent. It's late and the camp is quiet. Knight is on duty, I'm alone, the lamp is lit and I've placed your photograph beneath it. If I close my eyes and hold your lock of hair, I can almost im-*

*agine myself back in the* Star of India. *The steps of the sentries are those of the waiter bringing us champagne, the night air, your breath, the wind, your voice whispering your love. I miss you and those wonderful afternoons we shared so very much. Wherever I go, whatever I do, my darling, my every thought is of you. When this war is over, I'll never let you out of my sight again.*

*We'll find a way to be together no matter what. I've seen your husband, but I remembered what you said and didn't tell him about us. I wanted to. You can't ever go back to him. I can't bear the thought of him or any other man touching you. You're mine now. And always will be.*

*One more push. That's what everyone is saying; one more push and the Gulf will be ours. The minute it's over, please come to Basra. I'll rent a house for us. There'll be gossip, but what will that matter? We'll live quietly and for one another. God, I love you so much it hurts. Goodnight. My love now and for ever, your Geoffrey.*

John laid the lock of hair on the letter and re-folded the paper around it. There was an address on the back. He stared at it, then fumbled through the remaining papers. He shook them. A photograph fell out. A woman smiled up at him from the creased and muddied print. There were beads on her dress. He recognised them. It was the evening gown she'd worn that last night on the *Egra*. The first night they'd spent together. He turned the photograph over. Written in a sloping hand he knew only too well was *To Darling Geoffrey. All my love, Maud.*

## Basra, Saturday April 10th 1915

The political officer laid Harry's report and a map on his desk. At the first rap on the door, he shouted, 'Enter.'

Harry walked in, wearing a colonel's uniform that hung loose on his slender frame.

'Lost weight, Downe?'

'Desert travel, sir.'

'Glad to see you back in one piece, even if there is less of you. Sit down. I presume you've heard the news?'

'That General Nixon's relieved Lieutenant-General Barrett? Yes, sir.'

'Nixon's a very different man to Barrett.' Cox chewed his pen thoughtfully, then changed the subject. 'I've read your reports. The oilfields are surrounded?'

'Completely. Sheikh Muhammerah's lost control, and the tribes are fighting amongst themselves over the spoils of the battlefields. There are more guns in the hands of the natives now than there've ever been. When I left, the Bawi happened to have the most firepower but the situation could have changed since then.'

'You think the Bawi cut the pipeline?'

'I know the Bawi cut the line. And the telegraph wires, sir. They're camped in the fields now, murdering anyone who ventures in.'

'Our force at Ahwaz?' Cox asked.

'Isn't cut off because the river access is, or rather was, clear when I left. But they're surrounded, by hostile tribes as well as the Turks.'

287

'Yet you think this Armenian clerk, without an armed escort, can get the wages in gold through to the oil company.' Cox didn't conceal his scepticism.

'One of our allies is married to the sister of Ibn Shalan. He persuaded Shalan to guarantee the party's safety. Shalan agreed, not because he has any love for us but because he has a hatred of the Turks. I paid Shalan and his tribe to monitor the party's progress.'

'In guns?'

'He gave his word he won't use them against us.'

'You believe him?'

'I believe him,' Harry repeated. 'You did say paying the oil company's native staff was a priority.'

'There's little point in us having an oilfield if we can't pipe out the oil. You don't think we should send reinforcements to Ahwaz?'

Harry set aside personal thoughts of John and the beleaguered troops. 'No, sir, the Turks orchestrated this Bawi rebellion in the hope we'd split our force to deal with it. Qurna is as vulnerable as Ahwaz and no one's suggesting we send reinforcements up river. If my intelligence is correct, the Turks don't know the numbers and strength of our incoming reinforcements from India, and that's one card in our favour.'

'I only wish I knew them. Apart from extra staff officers, HQ either ignores our demands, or divides them by ten.'

'The Turkish force is concentrating outside Basra at Shaiba. And we've more than the Turks to contend with. I've spoken to natives who've seen German spies moving along the Euphrates and the Karun.'

'Wassmuss?' Cox questioned.

'And Meyer. Both have gold and both are playing up to this holy war against the infidel. The Jihad is being preached in every mosque in Mesopotamia and the tribes are responding. They're gathering on the Turkish flanks at Shaiba; but I don't think they'll play an active part until they're sure who is going to win. Then they'll harass the loser and take what pickings they can.'

'I value your opinion, Downe. Tell me, truthfully, is it worth us courting Arab loyalties?'

'It's worth courting them, sir. It would be foolish to rely on them.'

'Even Shalan and your tame Arabs?'

'Our brief is to secure the oilfields, sir.' Harry avoided answering Cox's question. 'I think we should concentrate on Shaiba. If we succeed in driving the Turks back there, they'll be forced to retreat up river from the Basra Wilyat. That route will take them through the Hammar marshes and the Marsh Arabs will finish the job we began.'

'The Marsh Arabs will turn?'

'Not enough to switch allegiance to us, but they'll take every gun, box of supplies, and shred of uniform from the Turks. If the Turks resist, they'll be killed. Not en masse, the Arabs don't go in for that kind of fighting, but they'll harry the stragglers and wipe out any small parties that become detached from the main force.'

'If we win at Shaiba, we secure the Karun Valley and the ground we took on the Tigris last December.' Cox looked at the map. 'The Turks will be forced to retreat to the next point. Which is...'

Harry rammed his finger on the map, 'Amara, sir.'

'The town would be a good front-line buffer to Basra. We'd have the Shatt, the Gulf, and the Karun. It shouldn't be too difficult to keep control of an area that size. We could even reduce our force here and release men for the Western Front.'

'But first we have to win at Shaiba, sir.'

'That's correct, Lieutenant-Colonel Downe. First we have to win at Shaiba.'

*Shaiba, evening of Thursday April 14th 1915*

Darkness had fallen, but it was a darkness punctuated by sunbursts of shellfire and the staccato pinpricks of rifle shot. Harry and Mitkhal stood with their horses alongside the British flank. The guns of the Royal Horse Artillery thundered intermittently on their far left; ahead of them boomed the answering sallies of the Turks.

'No sign of the Turks letting up,' Mitkhal whispered. 'Who told you they were pulling out? An officer who hasn't left Basra since this started?'

'Ibn Muba.'

'Since when do you listen to Marsh Arabs?'

'Since the war moved into the marshes.'

A lieutenant slid through the quagmire towards them. 'Artillery and naval units on the river are due to start a major bombardment in four minutes, sir. Major Harrap's asking if you can be ready to leave by then.'

'We'll be ready.' Harry tugged at his horse's reins.

'You're sure these two can swim?' Mitkhal asked.

'You've never worried about our mounts before.'

'We've never ridden army horses before.'

'These aren't army horses, they're Perry's polo ponies.' Harry shuddered as a gun belched forth from one of the naval units. Too far away to do any damage to the Turks, it merely sounded impressive. He mounted and lay low along the horse's neck. Knowing Mitkhal would follow, he plunged into the floodwater that had burst the banks of the Shatt. His robes billowed, dragging him down when they became saturated with freezing, rank liquid. His horse's hooves slipped, then came a sensation of weightless insecurity when the animal lunged into deeper water and began to swim. The lights of the British forces grew dim. Ahead he could see the glow of the Turkish Army's torches. He heard Mitkhal curse behind him.

An ominous feeling stole through his senses. He remembered Brooke. The stones he and Mitkhal had heaped over his pathetic remains. Would anyone bother to do the same for him?

He shook off the emasculating fear, concentrating on a ridge that rose out of the black waters ahead. Ibn Muba should – would – be waiting on that island.

He had to be positive. Forget everything except the task in hand. Ibn Muba had an insatiable appetite for gold. The Marsh Arab would have made it his business to discover the Turkish losses, their current position and, most important of all, whether rumours of an imminent Turkish withdrawal were true. A quick discussion with Muba and he and Mitkhal would be back

291

behind British lines, relieved of the gold they carried. But what if they weren't? What if they were caught...?

The current dragged him from the mound. His heart thundered erratically for the few minutes it took to guide his horse back on course. Thank God this was the last time he'd have to do this. Planes were on their way from India. Aerial reconnaissance would serve command better than the information he gathered from the natives.

Mitkhal's whisper rose above the sound of the river. 'To the right. A torch flashed.'

Harry watched, counting. One – two – three – darkness. He whistled a snatch of native folksong. The answering whistle was louder, a different tune. The cold and griping fear of death diminished. Ibn Muba was waiting.

*Basra, evening of April 14th 1915*

Charles walked across the parade ground towards the officers' bungalows, stopping outside the one that had been Perry's. He visualised Emily walking through the French windows, her blue silk dress and ash blonde hair gleaming in the moonlight. Her warm smile when she saw him waiting – waiting for what? Death to take him as it had taken her.

A cloud obscured the moon. He shivered from more than cold. Emily was a ghost that chained his emotions and prevented him from living in the present. Wracked by regret and guilt at his failure to persuade her to leave for England with him, he measured the distance between the bungalow and the veranda of the one that had been Harry's.

If only – but there were no 'ifs'. Emily had left her bungalow after he'd gone. Harry had found her when he'd returned from the quay.

If he'd stayed in Basra for John's wedding, he might have heard her cry. Then he could have run out, killed the scorpion, saved her – but not for him. For George Perry. Emily had made her choice. Duty, not love. Or had it been duty? Perhaps she'd fallen in love with India, not him. The tropical beauty of perfumed nights, the heat of sensual, closeted afternoons.

She'd told him she led a miserable, loveless life with her husband but she could have lied. George, like John, had been in Basra and she, like Maud, had been in India – five days' journey from sexual gratification. Like mother like daughter. Had he and John both been played for fools?

Tormented by the thought, he headed for Colonel Hale's bungalow. It hadn't been easy to find Maud accommodation, for the town was ridiculously overcrowded. He'd crawled to every officer he had a nodding acquaintance with, until John's colonel had offered her a room. When he'd accepted the invitation on Maud's behalf, he'd hoped that Basra and the Hales hadn't heard the rumours. After he was waylaid by several fellow officers, he'd realised it was a forlorn hope.

He heard Maud's laughter as he neared the windows. The idea of Maud enjoying herself while John was beleaguered in Ahwaz incensed him. He stopped beneath a lantern that hung from the rafters of a neighbouring bungalow and

293

glanced at his watch. It was just after seven. The Hales wouldn't have finished dinner. If he called now he'd have to drink brandy with the colonel and make polite small talk.

He looked behind the bungalows. The cemetery was less than 20 minutes' walk. He'd asked for directions that morning. The officer had answered his query and moved on. It was bad form to mention death. Fighting, yes – wounds even – but not death. It was too familiar a spectre that stalked everyone.

Maud wasn't expecting him until later, if at all. He'd warned her he might be shipped out to the front immediately. Lifting down the lantern, he continued walking. The lights of the town closed around him like stars crammed into a shrunken heaven. At the top of a slight rise, gates barred his path. He tugged at the bolt and heaved them open. The metal left streaks of rust on his hands. The damned climate! Everything rotted in it.

He gazed at the crumbling grave markers and carved angels that glowed white in the darkness. Lifting his lantern, he read the faded lettering.

*In loving memory of Mary Louise died 12th June 1860 aged one year, three months. Beloved daughter of Major Robert and Mary Sanders.*

*'Suffer the little children to come unto me.'*

*In remembrance of James Brock. Died 14th July 1876 aged seven.*

After a time he saw only the ages. Babies, children, young men and women who had scarcely lived before they'd died.

*Harriet Gould, 19. George Makepeace, 16. Lieutenant William Blair, 20 years 6 months...*

He found the new graves, mounds of earth sur-mounted by temporary wooden crosses. He was stunned by the size of the area they covered. He read the dates scratched into the wood. October 1914, November 1914, December 1914, January 1915, February, March. Already there was a sprinkling of April's. Lieutenant – Private – Ser-geant – Sergeant Major – Colonel – Major – Captain–

No rank was spared and High Command had said this campaign wasn't costly. How many more? How many of those would he know?

He stumbled into a muddy hole. Clutching his lantern, he regained his footing and found what he was looking for. A stone memorial em-blazoned with a cross.

The weather had been kind so far. He brought the lantern closer and read the Gothic lettering.

*Beneath this stone lie the mortal remains of Emily Maud Perry, dutiful wife of Major George Perry. Died July 1914 aged 36 years.*

*'Blessed are those that are undefiled in the way; and walk in the law of the Lord.' Psalm 119*

Had George found out about Emily and him?

*Blessed are those that are undefiled...*

Had Harry lied? Had Emily really died from a scorpion bite?

He picked up a clump of damp earth. It stuck to his fingers.

*'Leave him, Emily. It's not as if you've ever loved him. We can sail on to England together.'*

*'My dear boy, I'm old.'*

*'Barely ten years older than me. What's ten years?'*

*'In four years you'll be a young man of 30, and I'll*

*be 40...'*

He flung the mud to the ground. Emily would never be 40 and he'd never feel what he'd felt for her again. Whether Emily had loved him or not, he'd loved her, and every chance of happiness had gone with her.

Kneeling, he clawed at the sodden earth below her headstone. The air temperature dropped below freezing. The lights went out one by one in the town. As the clumps of sticky earth he tore from her grave piled into a mound, he sank lower into the hollow he'd dug. Suddenly, his fingers hit wood.

The rotten planking gave way beneath his knees. Unable to tear himself away, he spread his legs. Balancing precariously on the earth banks either side of Emily's grave, he tore at the hole in her coffin.

Lifting down the lantern, he saw a shroud, greenish black, decaying at the edges. He ripped up the splintered coffin lid. Emily's hair, still golden, shimmered in the lamplight, curtaining her mould-blackened shoulders. Reaching out, he stole a strand. It came away easily. He wrapped it around his finger. He couldn't avoid looking at her face; her teeth larger, naked in death as they had never been in life, grinned back at him.

Staring at her black, empty eye sockets, he sat back on his heels and wept.

The lantern burned out and dawn broke before he replaced the planks and the earth he'd removed. Finally, he rose from his knees. He took one last look before walking away. He felt as though he'd left his heart and everything he'd lived for in the mud behind him.

## Chapter Nineteen

*Shaiba, 2 a m. Wednesday April 14th 1915*

Harry's spirits were high despite the water that swirled, cold and clammy, to his waist. His arms ached from heaving on his horse's reins, his head swam with undigested information, but one fact shone above all others. The rumours were true. The Turks were pulling out. The first of their large-bore guns was already being hauled up-stream through the Hammar marshes.

We've won! The thought blazed triumphantly. They'd done it. One more push, one more battle, and Amara would be theirs. That's all they needed – the territory as far as Amara…

A bullet whistled overhead. He slid from the saddle, only just managing to keep a grip on the reins. The bullet was followed by another – and another.

'Snipers,' Mitkhal groaned.

'From our own bloody side.' Harry whispered, wary of drawing the attention of Turkish snipers as well as their own. Clinging to his horse's neck, he urged it on.

'Another 20 yards and we'll be out of range of the Turks.'

'I've marked the spot.' Harry fought against the waterlogged weight of his robes. 'I'll shout to the bloody idiots when we reach it.'

The bullets continued to hit the water around them. Harry ducked below the surface. Lungs at bursting point, he rose to the screams of an animal in agony. Bullets were flying from both directions. Mitkhal's horse thrashed beside him; the saddle empty, the reins dangling loose.

'Mitkhal!' he shouted, not caring who heard him. Thrashing wildly, he glimpsed pale cloth floating behind him. He reached out. When his horse refused to go with him, he released the reins and sank beneath the weight of his robes. Another flash rent the sky from the direction of British lines.

'For Christ's sake, stop!' he yelled in English. 'We're on your bloody side.'

The white patch was drifting downstream. He tried to swim but his right hand was numb. Another flash was followed by the crack of a bullet. Voices carried over the water from the bank. A sepoy swam out to him.

'Colonel Downe, there's a rope around my waist. My platoon is holding it. Haul yourself back to the bank.'

'No...'

'I can see your companion, Colonel. With respect, I'm not as tired as you. Go back before you delay me further.'

Harry couldn't argue against logic. Fumbling below the water, he found the rope. Keeping his arm hooked around it, he half swam, half dragged himself towards land. When his feet sank

298

into mud, sepoys waded out to him. He looked back. The sepoy in the water had reached Mitkhal. The men began to haul in the rope. The sepoy was struggling to keep Mitkhal's head above water. Harry dived forward when they reached the shallow. The Arab was spluttering, sweetly, beautifully alive.

'Don't you ever do anything like that to me again.'

Mitkhal gave a wan smile. A medical orderly ran towards them, first aid box banging at his side. Harry and the sepoy lifted Mitkhal and, between them, helped him to the bank.

'Leave him to me, Colonel Downe.' The medical orderly gasped. 'The stretcher-bearers are on their way.'

Harry peeled back Mitkhal's sodden robes. Clots of dark blood on his left shoulder were interspersed with white bone splinters. He'd learnt enough during his wasted year in medical college to recognise a shattered collarbone. He glared at the men milling on the bank.

'What bloody idiot started the shooting?'

The young lieutenant who'd carried Harrap's orders to them earlier hopped from one foot to the other. 'An officer up the line sent down information the Turks were about to attack our flank, sir. He ordered us to fire on anything suspicious.'

'What bloody officer?'

'Don't know, sir.'

Harry closed his left hand around the lieutenant's throat and slammed him to the ground. 'What bloody officer?'

The boy uttered a strangled cry. The sepoy

who'd dragged Mitkhal from the water dared to speak.

'You're holding the wrong man, Colonel Downe.'

Harry released his grip. The lieutenant scrambled upright and backed away. Major Harrap, red-faced, agitated, ran towards them.

'You all right, Downe?'

'No thanks to whoever gave the order to shoot.'

'It came from up the line. Some Johnny who didn't know about your operation.'

'We saw Arab robes, sir,' a sergeant ventured. 'Assumed it was Turkish irregulars.'

'Anyone could make a mistake like that, sir,' the lieutenant squeaked.

'Downe, you've been hit, your hand...'

'Can wait, Harrap,' Harry replied. Someone threw a blanket around him. Until its warmth lay heavy on his shoulders he hadn't realised he was cold. 'I have to find command.'

'Shot of this before you go.' Harrap handed him a flask. 'Lieutenant, escort Colonel Downe and make sure no one else mistakes him for a Turkish irregular.'

Harry found the sepoy who'd rescued Mitkhal and stopped him from throttling the lieutenant sitting on an ammunition box, huddled under a greatcoat. 'Thank you...'

'Chatta Ram, sir.'

'Thank you, Chatta Ram. My companion and I would be dead if it wasn't for you. If there's anything I can ever do for you, look me up.'

'I'll remember your offer, sir.'

'Please do.' Harry glanced back as he walked away. There was something familiar in the set of the sepoy's head.

He looked at his hand. Blood was pouring from the back and he couldn't move his fingers, but it would have to wait. First, he'd go to command, then check on Mitkhal; afterwards, he'd track down a certain officer and discuss the orders that had been sent down the line about an imminent Turkish attack.

*Shaiba, evening of Thursday 15th April 1915*

'Harry, what's this?' Amey held up a bottle. 'One of my sepoys found it in a Turkish trench.'

Harry squinted at the label before taking the bottle into his left hand. 'Give me five minutes and I'll tell you.' He stumbled to the door of the coffee house that housed the officers' mess.

'Damn it, that's German brandy Downe's walking off with, not Turkish piss.' Crabbe made a play for the bottle.

'Could be poisoned,' Harry declared, breaking the seal.

'As we're in this together, we take equal risks.' Crabbe retrieved the bottle. 'Orderly, more glasses.'

Head swimming, Harry staggered to a chair.

Amey grabbed two glasses of the brandy Crabbe was dispensing and sat on the floor alongside Harry. 'Here's to us.' He handed Harry one.

Crabbe climbed onto a table. 'To the King, victory, and the invincible Expeditionary Force.

To us, gentlemen.'

'To us.' Harry and Stephen lifted their glasses but, wary of falling over, remained seated.

'Strange how Crabbe is almost human now. Must be the war,' Stephen slurred.

'It's brought out the best in Crabbe,' Harry agreed. He would have agreed with almost anything at that moment.

'Hasn't brought out the best in Perry.' Stephen looked to the corner where the colonel was sinking his share of the alcoholic spoils.

'I don't want to think about Perry.'

'You're too drunk to think about anything,' Stephen mocked.

'I'm no drunker than you.'

'If you want a neutral opinion, there's not much between it,' a sober voice declared.

Harry tried to focus. 'Charles?'

'If the Turks came back now they'd have a field day.'

'They're too busy retreating through the marches. Seen them myself.'

'Riding pink elephants?' Charles sat alongside them. 'Any brandy for a tired soldier after a long journey?'

'You're on the Western Front,' Harry said.

'I was on the Western Front. The brass said you couldn't win this sideshow without my help.'

'Should never believe the brass. We did all right. Admit it. You just want in on the glory.' Harry waved at the orderly. 'A glass of your finest for Captain...'

'Major.'

'Major Reid.' Harry smiled. 'I outrank you.'

'You must tell me about that some time, and that.' Charles pointed to Harry's hand.

'How is the Western Front?' Amey asked.

'Holding when I left.'

'Have you been home?' Harry sipped his brandy.

'Yes. I saw your parents, Michael, and Georgiana.'

'I'll push off.' Stephen rose unsteadily to his feet.

'Please don't go on my account,' Charles called after him.

'I've an appointment with a lady. And a gentleman never keeps a lady waiting. Especially on victory night when there are dozens of others prepared to take his place.'

Harry turned his bleary eyes to Charles. 'So, you're here.'

'I'm here. But I'm not too sure about you.'

'I've plenty more of this–' Harry held up his glass '–in my quarters. Want to help me drink it?'

'Might be quieter. Sure you can walk?'

'It's not far.' Harry staggered. 'Follow me.'


Charles opened his eyes to a thundering hangover. His head ached before he attempted to lift it, and his mouth tasted the way he'd imagined Ganges delta water would. Harry's uniform was laid out on a chair and there were two empty brandy bottles between his bed and a cot pushed against the wall.

Sitting up slowly, he groped for his trousers. He found them on the floor. Pulling them over his drawers and vest, he opened the door. Two Arabs were sitting on the floor, maps and papers spread around them. It wasn't until the smaller of the two looked up that he realised it was Harry.

'Good afternoon. Sleep well?'

'I don't know.' Charles creased his eyes against the light. 'What did we drink?'

'German brandy and, when that ran out, Turkish.'

'Remind me to never drink it again.'

'There's a bathroom through there. Why don't you put your head in cold water?'

When Charles returned, Harry was alone.

'Coffee?' Harry lifted a pot from a stove in the corner.

'Anything that will make me feel alive.'

Harry poured the coffee into tin mugs. 'Food? I've bread, dates, and disgusting Mesopotamian eggs.'

'Why disgusting?'

'You'll see when you see the chickens. They strut around with their heads held high because they live off flies.'

'Coffee will do.' Charles sat on a stool. 'Did we talk last night?'

'Possibly, my memory's vague.'

'You look disgustingly well.'

'I've had more practice with Turkish brandy.'

'It's good to see you,' Charles blurted sincerely.

'It's good to see you. But it won't be for long. I have to leave for the Hammar Marshes.'

'That's held by the Turks.'

'I'm a political officer, and that's where political officers go.'

'You've left the regiment?'

'I've been seconded to Cox's tribe.'

'What is it that drives you into trouble? No one

304

in their right mind volunteers for that kind of job.'

'How's Georgiana?' Harry changed the subject.

'Bearing up.'

'Really?' Harry looked at Charles.

Charles relented. 'You know Georgiana; she was always stronger than any of us.'

'Did you meet her husband?'

'Yes. Once you got over the shock of his accent, he was likeable enough. Good-looking, I suppose, in a dark, broken-nosed way. He worshipped Georgiana and she adored him. I saw her a week after she received the news. She's hurt but she's a survivor. She has her work, and God knows the war is giving her plenty of it. Georgiana will come through, but I'm not sure about Michael. Lucy's crippling him.'

'He made his bed,' Harry commented.

'Lucy almost caught you and you're more slippery than Michael. The poor lad managed to steal away from her for an afternoon and tried to enlist. There was hell to play when she found out.'

'They wouldn't take him?'

'His leg never healed properly after that fall from the apple tree. You remember?'

'The tree you, John, Tom, and I climbed and he wouldn't. He waited until dark...'

'Climbed it and fell from the top,' Charles finished for him.

'Idiot,' Harry muttered fondly.

'He went to the Press Association and badgered them until they gave him a card on the strength of his English degree. Then he nagged my father into pulling a few strings. He's an official eye-witness on the Western Front.'

'Michael's in the trenches?'

'More often than behind the lines. Lucy doesn't like it and gives him hell whenever he visits his office in London. Which, from what I gather, is as seldom as he can make it.'

'Poor Michael.' Harry reached for the coffee pot. 'How are my parents?'

'Your mother has her committees, and the recruiting drives have given my father and yours new leases of life. Uncle John's not so good. He's aged. I think he was looking forward to John coming home. Speaking of John, I've left Maud in Basra.'

'Is she all right?'

Charles gave him a hard look. 'Why do you ask?'

'Something John said. What made her decide to go to Basra? She hates the place.'

'So I gathered.'

'You forced her,' Harry guessed.

'I thought John might be missing her,' Charles answered evasively.

'You never were a good liar. Paternal interest in Emily's daughter?'

'Nothing like that. Call it a favour to John.'

'John's in Ahwaz. God knows when he'll be back in Basra.'

Charles took the coffee Harry handed him. 'How did Emily die?'

'I wrote to you. She walked out on the veranda at night and trod on a scorpion.'

'She wasn't there when I left at four.'

'Night – early hours of the morning. What's the difference?'

'A great deal if she was trying to see me.'

'There's no way of knowing what was on her

306

mind.' Harry set the pot back on the stove.

'Harry, I loved her. I begged her to come to England with me but she wouldn't leave George. I have to know if she changed her mind.'

'Would it make a difference if she had?'

'I keep wondering if she cared for me as much as I cared for her. If I knew she had, yes, it would make a difference.'

Harry stuffed a map into a saddlebag. How much could he – should he – tell Charles? He'd promised John he wouldn't say a word to anyone about Emily's death but if there was some way of finding out if Furja had loved him, even for a short while... 'I found Emily lying on the ground in front of my bungalow. There's no way of knowing for certain but if you want my opinion, I think she was trying to reach you. I'm sorry, Charles.'

'You're sorry, and we have a war to fight.' Charles turned to the window.

'It won't last for ever.'

'When it's over there'll be time for other things. Georgiana and I talked about it. We agreed after the treaties have been signed nothing will be the same again. Too many people have died. You have no idea what it's like back home. We can never go back to what we were.'


*Hammar Marshes, Tuesday 20th April 1915*

'I didn't think I'd ever feel sorry for the Turks.' Harry watched Ibn Muba turn the duck he was roasting over a dung fire. Another scream tore through the air, piercing, deep-throated, it

307

hovered in the atmosphere, lending menace to the gathering twilight.

'They're only Turks.' Ibn Muba passed Harry a skin of sour milk.

'They were obeying orders.'

'Orders that gave them the right to hang Arabs and boil Arab patriots alive.' Another cry tore through the air. Ibn Muba's opinion didn't make it any easier to bear.

'What in Allah's name are they doing to him?'

'You don't want to know.'

'You're right, I don't.' Harry drank from the skin and corked it. Strange to think he'd retched up sour camel's milk the first time he'd tasted it. Now he drank it without a second thought, proof one could get used to anything – or almost anything, he qualified, remembering Furja's absence from his life.

Ibn Muba lifted the duck from the ashes with the point of his knife. Wrapping his abba around his fingers to protect them, he tore it in half and handed Harry the larger of the two pieces. Harry knew Ibn Muba too well to protest. Another scream rent the air. Ignoring it, Ibn Muba began to chew on his meat.

Harry leant against a rotting palm and prayed for silence. This was the first time since they'd entered the Marsh five nights ago that they'd dared light a fire. The Bani Turuf who lived north of Shaiba had no scruples about slaughtering strangers. Everyone, irrespective of race, language, or costume was suspect and Ibn Muba, who lived in the Kerkha River Marsh, knew few men in the area who'd vouch for him.

Just as Harry had prophesied, the tribes who'd fought with the Turks had scattered when defeat became a certainty. The Bani Lam had returned to their villages; the Bedouin, the desert.

Before he'd left Shaiba, the Bawi were alternating threats with offers of help to British Command. With Shaiba taken, there were troops available to reinforce Ahwaz, and Harry wasn't worried about John and the men in the Karun Valley. With the Turks in disarray, the Bawi's threats were empty ones.

'Your meat's getting cold.' Ibn Muba was offended by Harry's tardiness.

Harry listened; he heard only the lapping of water against reed-choked banks, the cries of night birds, and the scuttle and splashes of water rodents as they foraged between land and water. He bit into his duck; the flesh was black, more smoked than cooked. 'It's good.' He wasn't being polite; after five days of living on dates, it was superb.

'Good? And you've tasted my wife's roast duck.'

'I wasn't so hungry then.'

'Without the Turks our lives will be easier.' Ibn Muba belched and threw a bone into the water. 'With no Turkish tax collectors to bother us we'll eat well, and sleep peacefully for the first time in years.'

Harry remembered the civil administrators and Indian police who were following in the wake of the Expeditionary Force. He said nothing. He only hoped the taxes set by the Indian office would be lower than those set by the Turks.

'You, Hasan, will always be welcome in my village. Your gold will buy guns for my sons and a

309

new boat. We'll shoot more ducks than even we can eat, smoke their flesh, and sell it in Qurna and Basra. I'll be the richest man on the Kerkha, with nothing to do but attend to my wives.'

'I envy you that life, my friend.'

'You have given me much gold, Hasan; surely you were wise enough to keep twice as much for yourself. You could buy two or three wives and set yourself up in my village. Then you would have no need to envy my life.'

'Would that everything were that simple.' Harry wrapped himself in his abba and sat cross-legged, with his rifle nestling in the crook of his arm. 'I'll take first watch.'

Ibn Muba stamped out the fire, and walked to the boat. Curling in the bottom, he settled himself.

Harry stared into the darkness and listened. Watchful, alert, he thought over his conversation with Charles. Now the end of the war was in sight everyone was looking to the future. John had Maud. Whatever their differences, he was sure they'd reconcile and return to England.

Charles would come to terms with Emily's death and find someone else. That left him. He could return to Clyneswood and live there until it was his turn to play the squire. If Georgiana joined him, they could grow into sour, celibate old age together with dreams of Furja and Gwilym to lighten their respective bachelor and spinsterhoods. Forcing all thoughts of Furja from his mind, he walked down to the water. Darkness was lifting, dawn breaking. He'd kept watch the whole night.

The screaming resumed with even more intensity. Gripping his rifle in his left hand, he moved his bandaged right fingers up the barrel, hoping they'd be strong enough to pull the trigger.

'Hasan!' Ibn Muba stirred in the bottom of the boat.

'I hear.' A frenzied splashing travelled towards them.

'It's large but too fast for a water buffalo,' Ibn Muba whispered.

Harry peered into the half-light. Ibn Muba moved to the prow of the boat. He leant over the side and Harry saw the glint of steel when he unsheathed his knife. A man blundered towards them. Naked, barely human, he clutched his head. Fearful moans came from lips shredded to a pulp; blood flowed sluggishly from sockets where the nose, eyes, and ears should have been. Ibn Muba pushed the boat out cautiously, paddling over to where the man stood in the waist-deep water. There was a flash, a cry, then only a red bubble floating on the surface.

'A Turk,' Harry whispered when Ibn Muba paddled back to the bank.

'Whoever he was, he needed to be put out of his misery.'

'I thought Arabs didn't torture their prisoners.'

'We didn't,' Muba replied unsmilingly, 'until the Turks showed us how.'

# Chapter Twenty

*Basra Hospital, Friday April 23rd 1915*

Knight invited Harry into his office. 'Usually, I'd keep an injury like your orderly's in for a month but he's determined to see his wife. I've a feeling if I don't discharge him, he'll climb out of the window.'

'I've secured berths on the *Shaitan*.' Harry took a seat in front of Knight's desk. 'It's going to Ahwaz tomorrow and from there it's a short ride to his tribe's camp.'

'I hope by short, you mean no more than a mile,' Knight warned. 'That shoulder was shattered.'

'I saw it.'

'You can give him the good news, but first I'll take a look at your hand.'

'It's fine.'

'Of course it is.' Knight pinned Harry's hand down by the wrist and began unrolling the bandages. 'Just like your chest and ribs. John told me what an appalling patient you are.'

'How was he when you left?'

'Busy.'

'Bad luck him having to go on to the Kerkha. You'd think the brass would have given him leave now Maud's here.'

'He insisted we toss for Basra, so he couldn't have known about Maud. I won.'

'Lucky heads.'

'How did you know it was heads?' Knight removed the last of the dressings with tweezers.

'Intuition.' Harry had given John a two-headed sovereign on his last birthday.

'I would have been happy to go to the Kerkha. John seemed depressed. I felt he needed the fleshpots of this place more than I did and that was before I discovered Maud was here.' Knight probed gently with his fingers. The bullet had passed through Harry's palm, leaving a hole that was healing, but his fingers were splayed stiff and awkward.

'Try picking this up.' Knight put a pencil on the table. It fell from Harry's grasp.

'It'll get better,' Harry said.

'You shouldn't be on active service until it does. You can't handle a gun with a hand like that.'

'Haven't you heard? Political officers only listen to gossip and dictate notes.'

'I haven't heard that one, but I have heard a lot of other peculiar stories about political officers in general and one political officer in particular.' Knight re-bandaged Harry's hand. 'Now take off your shirt.'

'Come on, Knight,' Harry protested. 'I came here to see Mitkhal.'

'I know about the beating and I'm not asking, I'm ordering.'

'I outrank you.'

'Not in here you don't.'

Harry reluctantly complied. Knight ran his fingers over Harry's ribs, then pulled out his stethoscope. 'Any persistent coughing?'

'Nothing out of the ordinary.'

'I'd like to know what you call ordinary. There's one rib here—' he pressed the right side of Harry's chest, making him wince '—that either hasn't set or has been re-broken. Been in any more fights lately?'

Harry recalled the kicking he'd had from the Turks but said nothing.

'Harry, for God's sake be careful.'

'Considering this is the middle of a war, that's odd advice.'

'It's the end. Everyone knows it, one more battle and...'

'They'll move us to the Western Front.'

'Not you. You'll be put out to grass.' Knight folded his stethoscope away. 'If you want to see Maud, she's helping out in the officers' convalescent ward.'

'I'll do that. Thanks for this.' Harry held up his hand.

'Any time, but don't take it personally if I say I'd rather not see you in here again.'

Harry left the main building, which was reserved for officers. There were two annexes, the left for the ranks, the right for Indians; the overflow was housed in tents in the grounds. He turned right. The orderly directed him to a cubicle. Mitkhal was lying on a cot; his shoulder and arm heavily bandaged, his face ashen against the sheets.

'You're a fine one taking your ease here, while I run myself ragged,' Harry complained.

'I know where I'd rather be. And where I'll be tomorrow.'

'No, you don't.'

'I'm not staying here...'

'I've booked berths on the *Shaitan*. She's leaving Basra for Ahwaz in the morning.' Harry sat on the bed. 'I'm taking what's left of you back to your wife before you do any more damage to yourself.'

'And you?' Mitkhal asked.

'After I've left you with Gutne, I'm going on to Amara.'

'Amara's on the Tigris, not the Karun.'

'General Gorringe's travelling overland.'

'Across country, with the hot weather just beginning? They'll never make it,' Mitkhal predicted.

'They will if I go with them.'

'I'll go with you.'

'The last thing I need is a sick man to take care of.'

'You know nothing about the Kerkha,' Mitkhal snapped.

'Ibn Muba does.'

Mitkhal retreated into sullen silence.

'Don't you want to see Gutne?' Harry asked.

'I don't want to be put out to graze like a lame camel.'

'It will only be for a month or two.'

'During which time you'll take Amara.'

'I hope so indeed, then it'll be my turn to be put out to grass. You're not the only one to be declared unfit.'

'You'll be going back to England?'

Ignoring the question, Harry took a packet of cigarettes from his pocket. Lighting two, he handed one to Mitkhal. 'This war is ending at the

315

right time. You can settle down. Bring up your sons. Live the life you've always wanted.'

'What was it like in the Hammar Marshes?'

'I felt sorry for the Turks.'

'The Marsh Arabs had good reason to take revenge. I wish I could have seen it.'

'You would have heard it first. I never knew men could scream so loud.'

'The Turks deserved whatever they got.' Mitkhal inhaled his cigarette.

'Ibn Muba said much the same thing.'

'So Marsh Arab and Bedouin can agree on some things, after all. Did I tell you about the girls the Turks took from the brothel when I worked there?'

'You never told me you worked in a brothel.' Harry tried not to appear too interested lest Mitkhal clam up. The Arab rarely spoke of his past.

'My mother fell sick when I was a child. She couldn't leave her bed. The woman who kept the brothel she'd worked in liked her, so she paid me to clean the rooms and run errands. When I grew strong enough she gave me a job throwing out the troublemakers. After my mother died, I moved in with her.'

'How old were you?'

'Old enough. I learnt to hate Turks in that house. A captain hired two girls one night. I never found out what they did. What they didn't do was please him. He sent a squad of soldiers the next day to arrest them. We tried to stop them but there were too many and they were Turks. The law was on their side.' Mitkhal drew heavily on his cigarette. 'If there was a trial we never heard about it. That night, we went to the governor's house to plead for them. What we didn't discover until the next day was that while we were pleading, the captain had them boiled alive on the midden in full view of the town. One of them took over an hour to die. She was 12 years old.'

'The Turks have gone for good, Mitkhal.' Harry rose. Mitkhal had closed his eyes, but there was one more subject he wanted to raise. 'Have you heard from Gutne?'

'Her cousin found out I was here; he came to see me.'

'Did he say anything about Furja?' Harry pressed him, knowing Mitkhal would have asked.

'She never leaves Shalan's harem. No one sees her.'

'What will happen to her?'

'Until she has the child, nothing.'

'Afterwards?'

'Shalan told you she will marry a Bedouin.' Mitkhal hated confirming what Harry already knew.

'The child?'

'Will remain with Furja until the age of seven. If it's a boy he'll be placed in Shalan's care; if it's a girl, she will remain with Furja until she marries.'

'Do I have any rights to the child under Bedouin law?'

Mitkhal turned his dark eyes to Harry's. 'You would, Harry, if you were Bedawi.'

'Miss Perry. How delightful to see you. Do you remember me? Grace, Alf Grace?'

'Of course–' Maud plumped out the paper flowers she was arranging before shaking his hand '–but I'm Mrs Mason now.'

'So you married that blighter. What a catastrophe for the rest of us.'

Maud smiled. It was good to see a man with all his limbs intact.

'What are you doing here?'

'Arranging flowers and library books.'

'I mean in Basra.'

'Waiting for my husband. He's in Ahwaz.'

'Is he due back soon?' Grace enquired.

'Apparently not.'

'His loss could be my gain. Would you like to lighten a weary sailor's life by dining with me this evening?'

'Where?' she asked, mindful of Charles's observant eye and her sullied reputation.

'The Basra club. I know a chap there who'd see we fared all right.'

It was tempting. She could leave a note for the Hales so she wouldn't have to face them until morning and she shouldn't feel guilty. The Basra club was a respectable place. John knew Alf Grace as well, so that made him almost a family friend.

'Yes,' she said decisively.

'Terrific. I'll hire a cab. Where shall I meet you?'

'Here, at eight. I promised to bring in some magazines.'

'I'll look forward to it, Mrs Mason.' He kissed her hand. 'Until eight.'

She saw Harry glowering in the doorway.

'Goodbye, Lieutenant Grace.'

Grace turned and saw Harry. He nodded and left.

'Harry, what a wonderful surprise.' Maud kissed

his cheek. 'Colonel Hale mentioned you were in Basra and injured. You must tell me all about it.'

'Some other time, Maud. I'm leaving for the Karun tomorrow. Is there anything you'd like me to give John?'

She blushed. 'What a pity I didn't know. I wrote to him only this morning.'

'I'll get to him before any mailbag. If you'd like to send another letter, give it to Knight and tell him to pass it on to my orderly.'

'Thank you. Harry, you will tell John I miss him, won't you?'

Blue eyes sparkling, golden curls framing a sweet face, blue, silk dress clinging to her figure, emphasising her feminine curves. Maud had never looked lovelier or more alluring. Harry had never felt sorrier for John.


*The Karun Valley, Saturday May 1st 1915*

Harry watched anxiously when Mitkhal slumped in the saddle. The broken-down nags they were riding were all he'd been able to scavenge from the detachment posted from Ahwaz to the oilfield station of Tembi after the battle of Shaiba.

The duty sergeant told him John had taken Dorset on to the Kerkha. He was grateful. If John hadn't taken her, someone else would have and he might never have seen her again.

He hoped their present mounts would last as far as Shalan's camp. Once there, he'd ask Mitkhal if he could borrow Devon. On his present performance, Mitkhal wouldn't be up to travel-

319

ling again for some time.

He damned Shalan for moving up river. He and Mitkhal had been in the saddle for six hours and he doubted Mitkhal could take much more.

'They're to the west.' Mitkhal stared at the empty horizon.

'I can't see anything.' Harry scanned the skyline.

'Can't you hear the camels?'

Harry hauled in his horse. The creature took the opportunity to nuzzle the bare ground. 'It could be a Bawi camp.'

'It's Shalan.' Mitkhal's face twisted in pain. 'I feel it here.' He hit his chest with his good fist. 'I'll be fine now. One or two miles and I'll be home.'

'I'm going with you.'

'You're not welcome in Shalan's tent.'

'I have a right to see my child.'

'You insist on doing this, knowing how much it could hurt not only you, but Furja?'

'I have a right to see my child,' Harry repeated.

'Then you enter the camp as my guest, not the father of Furja's child.' Considering the state he was in, Mitkhal's firmness was impressive. 'And you will make no attempt to enter any tent except mine.'

Shalan's watchmen spotted them before they saw the camp. They alerted Gutne and she walked out to meet them, her dark eyes wide with apprehension at the sight of Mitkhal's massive figure.

'You're hurt.' She glared reproachfully at Harry.

'It's nothing,' Mitkhal protested when Harry slid off his horse and ran to assist Gutne.

'I can see what a small thing this nothing is.'

She and Harry half-lifted, half-pulled Mitkhal from the saddle.

'He insisted on coming. He wanted to see you,' Harry explained.

'And now you've seen me, what?' Gutne railed. 'A husband is no good to his wife dead.'

'A few months' rest and he'll be fine,' Harry reassured.

'Fine for you to take out again, Hasan?'

'There won't be a next time.' Stumbling beneath Mitkhal's weight, Harry ignored the hostile stares of black-robed women and silent men who watched while he dragged his friend into the circle of black tents. No one called out a greeting or lifted a finger to help when Gutne raised the flap on her tent.

'Lay him on the mattress.' Gutne held back the curtain that divided the tent into two. She plumped up a cushion and pushed it beneath Mitkhal's head after Harry had helped him on to a couch in the inner section.

'The war is nearly over, Gutne.' Mitkhal watched every move his wife was making. 'One more battle and the Turks will be finished in this part of the world.'

'Then the Ferenghis will move in.'

'The Ferenghis don't hang innocent people,' Mitkhal reminded her.

'No, they have more subtle ways of dealing with Arabs. And there are fewer of them, which is why I believe the Turks will be back.'

Mitkhal grimaced when Harry propped him up so Gutne could undress him. The bandages on his shoulder were blood-soaked. She carried a bowl to the water jar.

'You'll have to get used to having me around,' Mitkhal murmured, when she returned with water and clean rags.

'You're nothing but trouble.'

'From now on I intend to live a peaceful life. Raise my flocks and my children; make love to my wife every night...'

'A fine sight you're going to be when our son is born.'

A glow spread across Mitkhal's sickly face. Embarrassed at witnessing such an intimate scene, Harry left the tent.

The horses were standing outside, too broken and exhausted to walk another step. He unbuckled the saddles and left them at the tent before coaxing the horses to the camp limits. Devon and Norfolk cantered up the wadi to greet him. He stripped the bridles from the nags and released them before stroking Devon and Norfolk's muzzles. Twilight was gathering. He could smell roasting goat flesh, just as he had done the evening he and Shalan had discussed his marriage to Furja. Was it really only a year ago?

'Hasan?' Shalan was behind him.

'I brought Mitkhal home. I will stay tonight, in his tent. Tomorrow I will ride out.'

Shalan nodded and walked away. Harry called after him.

'Is Furja well?'

'She is well.' Shalan kept his back to him.

'Has my child been born?'

'Yes.'

'Please.' Harry clenched his fingers into

322

Devon's mane. 'May I see them?'

'Not the mother.' Shalan walked on. Soon his tall, stately figure was lost in the darkness.

Harry buried his face in Devon's neck. The sights, the sounds, the smells were overwhelmingly familiar. He could almost believe that if he walked over the rise he would see the red bridal booth. Inside, Furja would be waiting with coffee and food, which they'd ignore. The couch would smell of jasmine like her hair

An hour later, Harry lifted the flap of Mitkhal's tent. The lamps were lit and Gutne was sitting in the outer part.

She held her finger to her lips. 'Mitkhal is asleep.' She offered him a bowl of clean water. 'Food is waiting.'

He washed his hands, dried them on the cloth she gave him, and took the bowl of rice and meat.

'Our food is your food.'

'Thank you.' He sat opposite her. Although he hadn't eaten since leaving Tembi early that morning, he found it difficult to swallow. 'How is Furja?'

'Well, but sad. She wanted a son so much. But you have spoken to Shalan?'

He set the food aside.

'Eat. It is good.'

'It is good, Gutne, but I have no appetite.'

The tent flap opened and an old woman entered with a bundle in her arms. Harry looked at Gutne. She nodded.

Trembling, he rose. The woman handed him the bundle. He took it clumsily, terrified of dropping it. When he looked down there were two babies curled in the blankets. He stood, too petrified to move.

'Twin girls.' Gutne smiled at the expression of pride and awe on his face.

'They are beautiful.'

'Hand them to me. When you sit I will give them back to you.'

Harry sat on a cushion, and rested his back against the saddles Gutne had carried into the tent. He watched her unwrap the two tiny scraps of humanity.

'This is Aza; she is the oldest, and heavier than her sister. When they open their eyes, you will see they are blue, but it is early days and may yet turn dark. And this one–' the second baby opened its eyes and blinked when Gutne placed her in the crook of Harry's left arm '–Furja named Harri. It is not a Bedouin name. I think Furja called her that because it is your Ferenghi name.'

Harry sat with a child cuddled into each arm, looking in disbelief from one to the other. Until that moment, his child had been an abstract idea. Something to worry about whenever he'd thought of Furja. Now he realised: fatherhood was something Shalan had made him renounce before he had known what it meant. If he'd thought of a child at all, he'd thought of a son. A tall, proud, Arab riding Shalan's mares across the desert.

A miniature hand waved in the air. He slid his forefinger into Harri's tiny, perfectly formed fist. The baby grasped it.

'She smiled at me, Gutne.'

Gutne knew about babies and their digestion

324

but said nothing. Harry's happiness would be all too brief without her spoiling it.

Harry laid the sleeping Aza on a cushion next to him, then crouched over her, holding Harri. He gazed at them, fixing their image in his mind. Gutne was right, Harri's eyes were blue, and the soft downy hair on both babies' heads was fair, but their skin was a deep, rich, golden brown, like their mother's.

'Twin girls seemed like an insult to Furja. But she's used to them now.'

'They will stay with her?' Harry remembered his conversation with Mitkhal.

'Until she marries.'

'Is there anyone...?'

'I do not know.'

'I'd rather you told me the truth.'

'There are no plans that I know of. I must see to Mitkhal. If you need my help with the babies, call out.' She walked behind the curtain.

Harry stared at the tiny bundles. His children – his daughters. He glanced around the tent, so alien from Clyneswood, then remembered he was barely tolerated in the camp, and only as Mitkhal's guest. How much of his daughters' childhood would he see? How could he ride away and leave them in the hands of Shalan and whichever Bedouin cut-throat the Sheikh picked as his next son-in-law?

Aza opened her eyes and looked at him. Her eyes were blue like her sister's. Blue, innocent, trusting... He stroked her face tenderly with the back of his finger. Bedouin or not, they were his. He owed them the best he could provide, and that didn't include years of drudgery caring for their grandfather's flocks and marriage at 13 to an old man who was looking for a third or fourth wife to stimulate his waning sexual appetite. Somehow he had to find a way to get them away from Shalan.

Just one more push. When Amara was in British hands, he'd return. If he found someone to nurse the girls, he could take them with him. Back to Basra. And from Basra—

There were so many things to think of, so many decisions to be made. Aza whimpered. He scooped her into his free arm and rocked her alongside Harri. He bent his head to theirs and tenderly kissed them. They were his, and he would make sure Shalan never forgot that fact. Never!

## Chapter Twenty-one

*The Karun Valley, Sunday May 2nd 1915*

The only hint of light in the darkness of Mitkhal's tent was the pale outline of the flap that opened into the night world of scavenging jackals and vigilant sentries. Harry tossed on the couch Gutne had cobbled together, listening to Mitkhal and Gutne's steady breathing on the other side of the curtain. The air was cold but his skin burned as he conjured images of Furja and his daughters.

He held no illusions about his former father-in-law. The Sheikh had sold off his eldest and most beloved daughter to a despised Ferenghi for guns.

When the time came, he would have no qualms about doing the same, or worse, to his granddaughters.

Mitkhal moaned in his sleep and Gutne soothed him. Harry waited until they fell quiet; left the couch, pushed his feet into his sandals, and picked up his abba. Pulling it over his cotton trousers, he stole outside. He nodded to the sentries, who were scarcely perceptible in the gloom, before walking down to the wadi. Devon and Norfolk recognised his tread and trotted up to greet him again.

He shivered when he wrapped his arms around Devon's neck. Summer had arrived, blighting the day with intense heat, but the nights were cool. Norfolk nuzzled his head. He pushed her away. She belonged to Shalan now, and he wanted nothing that was Shalan's.

He was obsessed with gaining control of his daughters' lives. He could be killed tomorrow – next week – next month – and if he wasn't, he couldn't resign his commission while war raged in Europe. Charles had dispelled any illusions he'd had about a swift conclusion to the fighting on the Western Front.

All he could do for his daughters now was leave them letters they might never be able to read and money Shalan would probably leave to rot in the bank before giving it to them. Charles had once accused him of never facing up to any responsibility. He wanted to face up to this one but he simply didn't know how.

A movement caught his eye. Wondering if he were dreaming, he gazed at Furja's disembodied face. She moved and he realised she was robed in black.

'I had to see you one last time.'

He enveloped her in his arms. 'You're cold.' Lifting his abba, he pulled it around both of them. Her face was close to his. 'How have you been?'

'Lonely.'

'I have missed you more than you can know.'

They both started at the sound of a foot scraping on dry sand. Harry turned and saw Norfolk behind them. He pulled Furja down into the shadows.

'Our daughters are as beautiful as their mother.'

'Gutne told me you were kind to them. I wanted a boy.'

'Girls are better.'

'Now you are being kind to me.'

'No, I like girls and I love their mother.' It was the first admission of love he had made in any language. 'Furja...'

'No, Harry, no words. They will not help us. Not now.'

He kissed her. She clung to him, returning his kiss with a passion that seared his skin. If the ground was hard, they did not notice. Nothing existed for either of them outside of the joy they took in one another.

When he woke, it was light. He was frozen, the ground beneath him cold and hard. If it hadn't been for the scent of jasmine lingering on his abba he might have believed that he'd dreamed the entire, beautiful episode.

*The Kerkha River, Thursday 6th May 1915*

Harry's face was crusted with dust and flies, his robes filthy. Even Devon's flanks were caked with dirt, transforming her from grey to piebald. He stood in the stirrups, and searched the horizon for signs of the column he'd been assured was camping close to the bed of the Kerkha. Barren countryside gaped back. He checked his compass. It was times like this he missed Mitkhal. The Arab had a sensory system that could sniff out people over ten miles of desert.

Dismounting, he reached for his water flask. He could survive on soured milk but Devon couldn't. Pulling a circle of cured leather from beneath his stirrup, he cupped it in his hand, poured the last of the water into it, and held it beneath Devon's nose.

'This is it, old girl. You want more; you're going to have to find it.' The horse licked the last of the moisture from the leather and looked at him with thirsty eyes. Replacing the leather, he mounted and set Devon's head north by north east. It was early but the sun burned his scalp through his head cloth. He hoped there'd be time for rest when he caught up with the column. He and Devon could do with a couple of days on full rations of food and sleep.

He promised himself his journey would end when he reached a thorn bush on the horizon. When it didn't, he moved his goal to the next rise. Then it was a rock that turned out to be a dead mule. Not too long dead either; decomposing flesh still clung to its baked hide. An hour later, he hit the Kerkha riverbed. Harry could have howled, for

Devon not himself. The bottom was as dry as sun-bleached bones. He halted. East or west?

'West, Devon.' Digging in his heels, he guided the mare forward. To think he'd complained about the rains. He could have rolled his entire, fly-bitten body in mud at that moment. No one died of heatstroke or thirst in mud.

Devon faltered and he dismounted. Leading her by the reins, he turned a corner and spotted khaki tents pitched besides a shimmering stretch of water. Devon plunged forward and he released her. Sentries moved in, rifles cocked. Shouting his name, rank, and number, he followed his horse. She didn't stop until she was hock-deep in water.

'Do you mind washing in the horses' water? You'd pollute ours.' John was on the bank, soap plastered over his chin, razor in his hand.

'Fine greeting for a weary traveller. The Arabs were kinder.'

'They probably took you for one of their own.'

'That's the idea.'

'The idea is going to get you killed. The sentries would have fired if I hadn't been here to stop them. They thought you were an Arab attack.'

'One man?' Harry raised a sceptical eyebrow.

'They're nervous. Major Anderson was killed by Arabs when he was out on patrol last week.'

'I'm indestructible.' Harry paddled to the sepoy who'd caught Devon. 'Please, see she gets a good rub down and plenty of feed and water for the next couple of days.'

The sepoy nodded as he led her away.

'My tent.' John pointed to one close to the water's edge. 'I'm bunking with Warren Crabbe.'

'Major Warren Crabbe! Crabface?'

'I've never heard him called that. He's all right.'

'You're crazy.'

'I was going to offer to squash in a cot for you.'

Harry tore off his filthy abba and flung it on the bank. 'Do you happen to have a spare pair of shorts and a shirt? These robes and a few squashed dates are the sum total of my present assets.'

He thrust his hands into the water. It was the colour and consistency of lentil soup, but it was cooler than the air. He ducked his head, head cloth, and all.

'You're not wearing your ID discs, Harry,' John remonstrated.

'If I was picked up that would be one clue even Johnny Turk wouldn't miss.'

'And if you get wounded or captured?'

'No one bothers with worthless Arabs. It's too much trouble to kill them.'

'Well, worthless Arab, the bathing tent's waiting. I'll get my orderly to fill a canvas bath for you.'

'Could you possibly get him to wash my robes as well?' Harry asked.

It was midday before Harry cleaned himself up and reported to the CO. Preoccupied by the CO's briefing of an imminent punitive expedition against the local tribes, he headed for John's tent. The sun was high, the air stifling. John was stretched out on his cot, a bottle of brandy and a bowl of water beside him.

'Crabbe's on duty. That's your bed. I see you found my spare shirt and shorts.'

'Yes, thanks.' The thin mattress was luxurious

after a week of riding and sleeping in the desert. Harry pulled out the waistband of the shorts. 'They could be smaller.'

'I order my clothes to fit me, not you.'

'I saw Dorset when I checked on Norfolk. Thank you for taking care of her.'

'I suppose you want her back?'

'Not immediately; I'll be with the column until Amara.'

John tossed a packet of cigarettes to Harry and held out the brandy bottle.

Harry lit a cigarette but shook his head at the brandy. 'I saw Maud in Basra. She's missing you.'

'War's made bachelors of us all.'

'Knight mentioned you'd tossed a coin for the privilege of returning to base. Did you know Maud was in Basra when you used the sovereign I gave you?'

'If I did?'

'She's only in Basra because of you. You know how much she hates this country.'

'Then she should have stayed away.'

'Dear God, if my wife was in Basra and I had a chance of being posted there, I'd put in for a transfer.'

'Your wife's on the Karun, there's a station at Tembi.'

'I'm divorced. I know it's none of my business...'

'That's right.' John lit a fresh cigarette on his stub. 'It's none of your business.'

'We're not the only ones having a hard time. After reading Georgiana's letters I've realised it's easier to fight than stay at home waiting for news that might come in the next hour, next day, or never. We spend 90 per cent of our time bored out of our skulls and the other 10 per cent scared witless, but at least we're not waiting for a bereavement that could shatter our lives.'

'Neither do we go to garden parties and have affairs.'

'No.' Harry was uncertain if he'd heard John correctly. 'Instead we get drunk, and pick up whores in Abdul's.'

John reached for the brandy and drank deeply from the bottle. He was obviously used to drinking that way. It made Harry cringe.

'Is Maud very upset by Brooke's death?' John asked.

'She knew him?'

'She had an affair with him in India. He wanted her to leave me, which is a joke considering I haven't lived with her for months.'

'How do you know?'

'How I know is not important, your reaction is. If you didn't realise I was talking about Brooke, who did you think I was talking about?'

'I wasn't sure.'

'Come off it, Harry. What's Maud been up to?'

Harry had never seen his cousin in this mood before. Drunk and ugly.

'Damn it all, Harry, if it was Furja you'd go after her with a gun.'

'No, I wouldn't.'

'Are you telling me you'd do nothing if you knew she was opening her legs for any man who crooked his finger at her?' John demanded.

'All I know is Charles dragged Maud away from India. I don't know why. I didn't ask him.'

'But you suspected it was because she was sleeping with someone.'

'If it makes you feel better. Yes.'

'And? Come on, Harry, there's more.'

'I saw her flirting with an officer in Basra. It was nothing more than an exchange of words and it wouldn't have happened if you'd been there. Now will you leave me alone,' Harry pleaded. 'I don't know any more, I'm sorry.'

'It's Maud who should be apologising. Who was the officer?'

'I haven't a clue.'

'Who, Harry?'

'I never saw the man before. He was a naval officer. Sub-lieutenant.'

John rolled the empty brandy bottle into a corner and reached for a replacement.

'If you went to Basra and saw Maud, I'm sure you could work something out,' Harry suggested.

'Would you forgive Furja if she had an affair?'

'I wouldn't give a damn what she'd done if she took me back.' Harry recalled the night they'd shared. There wasn't an hour he didn't think of her and their daughters. 'Without her, nothing makes any sense.'

'You're a bigger fool than I thought.' John pulled the cork on the fresh bottle.

'Possibly.' Harry closed his eyes. 'But unlike you, my dreams are based on a living, breathing woman, not the contents of a bottle.'

'That's what makes you a fool.'

*Basra, Tuesday 11th May 1915*

'We're going to use those flat-bottomed native boats, bellums, again. They require hardly any depth of water. Plate them with any old iron lying around...'

'Lying around?' Amey enquired of Smythe.

'Anything solid enough to act as a shield,' Smythe elaborated. 'They hold ten men apiece. The mine sweeping launches will tow them. The *Espiegle, Odin,* and *Clio* will protect the flanks. When we're close to the sandbanks Johnny Turk's dug himself into, we'll break the bellums loose. The sepoys will punt through the reeds. We'll float up quietly and take Johnny Turk by surprise. Imagine it? Sepoys leaping out and...' Peter cut across his throat with his finger. 'Goodbye, Johnny Turk, hello Amara.'

Charles topped up the glasses on the table. 'I can understand why they sent you down from Qurna, Smythe. A lecture from you and every sepoy in the force will believe himself invincible.'

'It worked like a dream at Qurna because the Turks are terrified of our gunboats. It'll be even better at Amara. I've mounted some of our guns on double canoes; between those and the guns on the barges we'll wipe every Turk off the map. Nice town, Amara. Almost European, wide streets, big buildings, plenty of coffee shops.'

'Ladies?' Amey enquired.

Peter didn't reply, preoccupied by thoughts of Angela. Pity his boat hadn't berthed earlier, but the Reverend Butler kept respectable hours and he needed his support too much to risk dis-

335

approval by calling on Angela late at night.

'I understand why you made captain.' Charles raised his glass. 'Gentlemen, I give you a well-earned promotion. Captain Smythe.'

'Captain Smythe.' Grace, Amey, Knight and Bowditch rose and echoed the toast, then sat abruptly. None was sober, but Charles, who'd had a hard time keeping food down since he'd arrived, was the most unsteady. Peter refilled their glasses.

'To General Townshend and his Regatta.'

'Townshend and Smythe's Regatta.'

Amey emptied the bottle. 'Victory.'

Bowditch produced another bottle. 'The King.'

'The King.' The room swayed around Charles.

'Time to pack it in. Can't meet the Turks with a hangover. Wouldn't be fair. Whisky fumes would bowl them over.' Amey dropped his glass.

'It's been a good night celebrating a good man's promotion.' Bowditch tried to slap Peter across the back and missed.

'Good idea, Amey, let's go to bed.' Charles laughed as if he'd told a joke.

'Not room for everyone in my bed, old man,' Amey chortled. 'And Smythe's booked my floor.'

'Can you make it down the stairs, Reid?' Knight slurred.

'Full speed ahead.' Charles left Amey's room, and caught hold of a banister that had the consistency and feel of India rubber. It wasn't only the banister that was wobbling; his legs had developed new joints that sent them sprawling in every direction except the one he wanted to go.

'Captain Reid, sir?'

'Singh?' Charles squinted at the Indian orderly

336

outside his room.

'Can I speak to you, sir?'

'You can, Singh, but I warn you. I'm not at my best.'

'A lady came to see you. She wouldn't give her name, sir, but insisted on waiting. I showed her into your room. I hope I did the right thing.'

'You did, Singh.' Charles pulled his key from his pocket and tried to insert it in the lock. He missed the keyhole and swung back, crashing into the wall.

'The door's open, sir. I thought it unwise to lock the lady in.'

'Good thinking.' Charles lurched into his room. Singh closed the door behind him. A woman sat with her back to him. She was wearing a silver evening dress, her golden hair piled high on her head.

'Emily,' he whispered.

She turned. 'No, Charles, it's only me. Maud.'

The knowledge of Emily's death sliced through Charles's stupor, hitting him anew with a force that had lost none of its pain. He stumbled to the bed. 'Why are you here?'

'You're drunk.'

'Very.'

'I heard most of the force is moving out in the morning.'

'That's restricted military information.'

'Please don't behave like a stuffed shirt, Charles. Colonel Hale told me. He said you're going and you might see John.'

'And if I do?' Charles was finding it difficult to focus and even harder to remain upright. He

337

kicked his feet on to the bed and fell back on the pillows.

'If you see John could you give him this?' She removed an envelope from her handbag and laid it on the table.

'John's moved on to the Kerkha.' He closed his eyes to stop the room spinning.

'How do you know?'

'He wrote to me.'

'I haven't heard from him since I've been here.'

'You know what the mail is.'

'His letters to you get through. I write to him every day. If he wanted to get in touch with me, he would have. Someone's told him about India. Was it you?'

Anger began to clear the alcohol fog from Charles's brain. 'I tried to keep it quiet by dragging you here. I warned you then it would only be a matter of time. Officers feel strongly about brother officers' wives who sleep with men when their husbands are on active duty.'

'But it's all right for wives to sleep with their husband's brother officers, as Christina Dumbarton did with Harry. It's just not done for a wife to make friends outside of military circles.'

'If Miguel D'Arbez had only been your friend I would have left you in India. And you know damn well it wasn't all right for Harry to carry on with Christina. That's why he was posted to Basra.'

'He got off lightly. Christina was packed off to England, divorced, disgraced, and penniless.'

'You think she didn't deserve it? My God!' Charles swung his legs over the end of the bed and sat up. 'You want it all, don't you, Maud? A

338

devoted husband under Turkish fire in the desert and carte blanche to carry on with any man you please.'

'I made one mistake and you want me to pay for that with John's happiness as well as my own. We were happy before this bloody war. Only last August we were here in Basra, and...' She burst into tears. Afraid her sobs would rouse the house, Charles pulled her towards him. She fell onto the bed. He handed her a handkerchief.

Scrunching his handkerchief into a ball, she rubbed her eyes. 'I can't bear it without John. I don't know whether it's because we honeymooned here but I want him so much. I don't know what I'm doing.'

She rested her head against his shoulder. Her skin was smooth and she smelled of magnolias, the same perfume Emily had used. It had been a long time since he'd held a woman. Last August, the *Egra*. He and Emily–

His hands slid to Maud's neck. He turned her face to his and kissed her. She tried to push him away but he persisted, pushing his tongue between her teeth. Aroused by her scent, the silken feel and warmth of her skin, he slipped his hands into her bodice. Reaching for her breasts, he caressed her nipples with his thumbs. She moaned. He thrust her backwards.

'No!' She tried and failed to sit up.

Charles caught at the hem of her dress and lifted it to her waist. She was wearing white silk stockings and short, silk drawers. Forcing her legs apart with his knee, he caressed the inside of her thighs. He whispered a name – Emily's, not hers – but by then his hands had moved upwards and it didn't matter.

Lost in a passion Miguel and his Indian friends had honed to an art form, Maud tugged at the flies on Charles's trousers. Sliding out from under him on to the floor, she kissed his erection through his cotton drawers. She slipped down the shoulder straps on her dress and stepped out of it. Kicking off her shoes, she removed her drawers and climbed back on the bed. Unbuckling Charles's belt, she pulled down his trousers and underpants.

Sitting astride him, she cupped her breasts and thrust them into his mouth. Before Charles could formulate a thought, he was inside her and she was pounding him into the mattress with quick, pulsating movements. He climaxed quickly. She lay panting on top of him.

Overcome by nausea, he pushed her aside and pulled the chamber pot from beneath the bed in time to vomit the last of the whisky in his stomach. Pulling up his drawers and trousers, he staggered to the washstand and splashed his face with cold water. Only then did he turn and look at Maud sprawled on the bed. She had buried her face in the pillow. He thought he heard her sob.

'It's a bit bloody late for maidenly modesty. It was hardly rape. Not in the position you adopted. Damn you for coming here. I could have had what you've just given me from any whore in Abdul's. Christ, I could kill myself and you when I think of what we've done. John's like a brother to me, and we haven't even the pitiful excuse of any feeling between us. Is that all that lovemaking means to you, Maud? An itch that can be satisfied

340

by any man willing to provide a scratching post?'

She lifted her tear-stained face. 'You bastard! Lovemaking was the last thing on my mind when I walked through that door. I came here to persuade you to talk to John. I didn't expect to find you drunk, and...'

'Lonely – aching for the touch of your mother's hand. You knew what you were doing visiting my room alone after midnight. What the hell did you think would happen? In God's name, you could have done something to stop me. Slapped me...'

'You bloody hypocrite. Do you think men have a monopoly on passion? When you get an itch, you go to the Rag. Pick yourself out a Hindu whore or a Bedouin gypsy. Don't look so shocked, Charles. Aren't officers' ladies supposed to know what goes on? Well, this lady knows and envies you. I wish there was a Rag that catered for my needs. Somewhere for me to visit at night instead of going half out of my mind from missing John. He's been gone for nearly ten months, and if I try to relieve myself in the way you take for granted, I leave myself open to gossip. I'm supposed to forget about sex until John comes home, whenever that will be. You're damned right when you say feeling didn't come into it. You used me and I used you. What's the difference between us, Charles?'

He sobered quickly. The aftermath of sex and whisky had left a bitter, unpalatable taste in his mouth. 'If you can't differentiate between acceptable behaviour for a man and a woman...'

'Acceptable behaviour! What do you think women are? Clockwork dolls, who fuck to order? One turn of their husband's key and they open

341

their legs. Two and they close them until they're needed to relieve his lust again. And God help them if they should actually like it, and stray into another man's bed while their husbands are in the Rag. You're worse than a hypocrite, Charles. You're a pompous bastard.'

'For taking what you threw at me, Maud?' His eyes narrowed in contempt.

The room blazed crimson in the heat of her anger. 'For not seeing that I love John. I love him and I used you. Is that what you can't take, Charles? The thought of a woman using you without a shred of feeling for your mind or your pitifully inadequate body. Do you want to punish me for sticking a pin in your masculine pride? How many times have you, John, and Harry visited Abdul's? Ten? Twenty? If I can forgive my husband his whores...'

'Forgive! You forgive John!' Charles's face was white beneath his blond hair.

'I don't know what name you put on what goes on in Abdul's but in my book it's the same mindless fornication we've just indulged in. My only regret is it's necessary. I would rather John had sex with me than a whore, just as I'd rather have sex with him than you. But he's not here – he's–' Tears scalded her eyes. She picked up her dress. 'Don't try easing your conscience by breathing a word of this to John. If you do, I'll cry rape loud enough for the military police to hear. A court martial would put an end to your precious career.'

'You wouldn't dare. There are five officers sleeping upstairs who'll testify I spent the entire evening with them. Even the orderly who showed you in knows you came alone and uninvited in the middle of the night.'

'To deliver this.' She picked up her letter and waved it in front of him. 'To one of my husband's closest friends. But you were drunk. You pounced on me like an animal.' She tore the front of her dress, ripping the bodice wide, exposing her breasts.

'You bitch!' He dived towards her, and she lashed out, tearing the skin from the side of his face with her nails.

'Now you have that to explain as well, Charles. You say one word. It won't matter if it's tomorrow, next month or next year. Those scratches will be remembered and I'll produce the dress. I may even wake the Hales to tell them I was attacked. Colonel Hale is a gentleman. He won't press for names or descriptions when I tell him it will embarrass me to talk about it. But he'll recall the incident if he has to.'

'You've got it all worked out, haven't you? Of all the cold, calculating...'

'If I had it worked out I'd be with John. I love him. I'll do anything to save whatever this damned war has left of our marriage.'

'And if John doesn't want a whore for a wife?'

'That's his decision, not yours.'

He watched her wrap her cape around her torn dress. He remembered Emily. The months of torment he'd suffered knowing he'd never see her again. Tonight, for a few drink-sodden, passionate minutes he'd thought no further than the moment and his own pleasure. He sank his head into his hands. Maud was right: how could he condemn her for giving him that, when he was every bit as guilty as her?

# Chapter Twenty-two

*Basra, Wednesday 12th May 1915*

By 5.30 in the morning Peter had bathed, shaved, and dressed. Restless, conscious of having only a few hours to spend with Angela, he left the house and walked along the waterfront. Abdul's was open. He went in and ordered coffee. The place was empty. He looked at his watch. The hands hovered at a quarter to six. He sipped his coffee slowly. When his cup was empty, he decided to throw all caution to the wind. After all, what could Theo or anyone do to him for turning up on the doorstep at this hour?

He walked through the mission gates as Angela opened her bedroom window. She was wearing one of her grey work frocks but her hair was loose. He watched her pick up a hairbrush, then, unable to contain his excitement a moment longer, he snapped a twig from a fig tree and threw it at her. She looked out and saw him.

Hoisting her skirts to her knees, she climbed out of the window and ran down the path. Scooping her into his arms, he kissed her; a long, satisfying kiss that shocked Theo when he opened the door and saw them locked in one another's arms a few minutes later. Peter smiled and pointed to the insignia on his collar.

'I have my captaincy, Theo. Would you arrange a wedding for my next leave, please?'

*The Kerkha River, Wednesday 12th May 1915*

'Of course there are maps of this area. I made perfectly decent ones myself this time last year.' Harry confronted the staff officer who'd ordered him to scout and map out a route from the Kerkha to the Tigris.

'The General says there are no maps. Never have been,' Cleck-Heaton declared. 'As soon as we've crossed, you ride ahead with the ghulams...'

'Fine, I'll ride ahead with the Arabs,' Harry agreed with uncharacteristic meekness. 'Would you like me to carry a red flag as a marker for the column to follow, or would you prefer a trail of Turkish bodies? I'd try army biscuit, only the birds are very voracious. You know what happened to the trail of bread the woodcutter's children left in Hansel and Gretel. And that happened in a nice, civilised European country.'

'Normal channels will suffice, *Acting* Lieutenant-Colonel Downe. When you have directives for the main force you may send them down the line with your orderlies.'

'Without maps they might not find their way back.'

'The general's orders are explicit.' Cleck-Heaton's face appeared to expand in proportion to his heightened colour. 'You are to scout a

345

route suitable for cavalry, infantry, and artillery carriages.'

'Difficult without maps.' Harry turned his back on Cleck-Heaton and adjusted his kafieh in the mirror nailed to the tent post.

'Ten guineas the staff officer cracks before Harry,' Crabbe whispered to John.

'*Acting* Lieutenant-Colonel Downe...'

'Major Cleck-Heaton?' Harry interrupted.

'I have the distinct feeling you're not treating the general's orders seriously.'

'On the contrary, I am treating them so seriously I am considering whether to make a detour to the stationery stores in Basra to purchase the maps necessary to expedite our removal to Amara.'

'Sir, I find your remarks...'

'Problems, Downe?' The CO approached John's tent.

'GHQ appears to have lost the maps the Frontier Force made of this area, sir.' To Cleck-Heaton's annoyance, there was a note of respect in Harry's voice.

'First I've heard of any maps, Downe. You sure they exist?'

'I'm certain they do, sir.'

'Well if there are any, we don't have them, so we'll have to manage without.'

'This isn't the best time of year to effect a crossing, sir,' Harry advised. 'The river's in flood, the currents lethal. One of the Arabs rode down to Kut Saiyid Ali this morning. The Turks have destroyed the ferry boat and every other craft along this stretch.'

'Then we'll have to rely on our canvas boats.'

'And, the animals, sir.'

'We'll have to swim the horses and mules across.'

'I'll try swimming the river, but I won't risk my own horse on the first crossing.'

'Are you sure you're up to it, Downe? That hand of yours...'

'With your permission, sir, I'll inspect the horses.' Ignoring Cleck-Heaton, Harry saluted the CO and headed for the canvas stables.

Dorset and Devon pawed restlessly in a roped-off stall. Ignoring their whinnies, he walked down the lines, searching for a likely looking mare. This was a decision he would have entrusted to Mitkhal. Every day, he missed the Arab more.

'Ubbatan?' Jabal, one of Muhammerah's ghulams, greeted him.

'Can any of your horses swim, Jabal?'

'All, Ubbatan. But only a fool would try to swim the Kerkha when the snow melts in the Luristan Mountains. The waters can freeze a man who remains in them too long.'

The man confirmed what Harry already knew. He pointed to a mount. 'I'll take the brown mare, Jabal.'

By forcing the mare on a direct course, Harry managed to reach the centre of the river. He signalled with his right hand. Soon afterwards, he heard the yells and shouts of the Punjabis as they drove the mules into the water in the hope they'd follow his mare.

Downstream, a canvas boat loaded with sepoys was fighting a current. He was wondering what they could use as ballast to make a flying bridge

347

when he hit the current that was making the crossing difficult for the sepoys. It carried him back to the centre of the river. He kicked the mare's flanks, but 20 minutes of hard work only carried them further downstream. He glanced behind. The mules were gaining, and his frozen muscles were on the point of seizing.

Braying, the mules panicked when they hit the current and the weakest were swept downstream. Despite his predicament, Harry laughed when he saw the animals trying to climb into the boat. The sepoys, under orders of a furious Cleck-Heaton, were making heroic endeavours to keep them at bay without success. Two mules were tipping the boat with their hooves when a shout from the bank made him look to his own back.

A blow between his shoulder blades sent him reeling. He was caught in a maelstrom of threshing, terrified mules. Striving to keep his head above water, he kept a grip on the reins. The mules kept coming, stampeding over the bodies of those in front; forcing them beneath the surface. Harry glimpsed Jabal mounting a black mare and plunging into the water. It would take the Arab too long to reach him. He had to help himself.

His mare screamed from the blows a dozen hooves were inflicting on her back. He shouted the curses he'd heard Indian muleteers use. The animals backed off for an instant. Sinking his hands into his horse's mane, he half-swam, half-fought every inch of water that lay between him and the opposite bank. A blow to his head from a hoof spattered coloured lights across the horizon. He fixed his sights on a rock. When he reached it, he'd sit on it. Wait for John to come with a brandy flask.

After an eternity of swallowing icy water and dodging mules, his feet sank into something soft. He kicked down – nothing. Holding his breath, he kicked again. His head was below the level of the water, but only just. It was mud. He hauled himself forward. The earth wavered before his eyes, but it was wavering closer.

Ten minutes later, he lay in the shallows, panting on his horse's neck. It wasn't until the sepoys reached him that he realised the mare was dead.

John entered their tent and laid his hand on Harry's forehead.

'I haven't a fever,' Harry snapped.

'Yet. But you have concussion and bruising and your ribs are now as cracked in the back as they are in the front.'

'I like to even things up.'

'It's not funny, Harry. That pasting you received from that damned sergeant damaged your back muscles. Pick up a heavy load and you'll tear the scar tissue wide open.'

'Political officers don't pick up heavy loads. They...'

'Sit around shooting snakes, talking to natives and gambling in bazaars. I've seen what political officers do. I've recommended your removal to base hospital at Basra. You're unfit for duty.'

'I'm a bloody sight fitter than you. There are only two political officers with this force and...'

'With you gone, we'll be down to one.' John made a note in his diary. 'Wilson's a sound man.'

'He won't be if he has to do everything on his own.'

'We've crossed the river. The worst is over.'

'There's a lot of desert between here and Amara and I'm no sicker than anyone else. We all got a soaking today, and a few more ribs were cracked besides mine.'

'If you continue to push yourself I won't be held responsible for your health.'

'No one's asking you to. You will lose that report,' Harry coaxed.

'No.' John opened a packet of cigarettes and Harry filched one.

'It won't do any good. There won't be any transports leaving for Basra until we hit the Tigris.'

'You're right, as usual.' John unlaced his boots.

'You wouldn't be in such a foul mood if you had a drink.'

'I can't. There are too many sick who might need me.' John stripped off his shorts and climbed into his cot.

'Then let's talk about happy things.'

'What are they?' John enquired.

'I have twin daughters.'

John smiled for the first time in days. 'Well done.' He lit Harry's cigarette. 'This should be a cigar.'

'They've blue eyes and fair hair, but their skin is a golden biscuit colour.'

'Babies' eyes are always blue and their hair will probably turn dark.'

'So Gutne said.'

'Did you see Furja?'

'Briefly. This divorce business is foul. I've been trying to think of a way to keep in touch with

Furja and the girls. They're my children and I don't know what to do about them.'

'Surely they'll stay with Furja?'

'Not if she remarries. If this war wasn't in the way, I could find a nurse for them and take them home.'

'To Clyneswood!'

'I don't want them growing up in Shalan's tent.'

'You've always done whatever you've wanted without giving a damn for other people or their opinions. But native children...'

'Half-native,' Harry countered.

'They'd be social outcasts.'

'I've a feeling etiquette and society aren't going to be so important after the war. After the war,' Harry reiterated. 'Now that's a phrase to conjure with. When the killing stops we're all going to have to make decisions. Even you.'

John drew on his cigarette. Harry was right. After the war, he'd have to face Maud. But he didn't have to think about her. Not now. First Amara had to be taken. But when he closed his eyes, images flooded his mind. Maud in bed with Brooke – Maud writing letters; not the brief epistles he'd received, but long, loving letters to Brooke. Brooke! Brooke! Brooke!

He damned the bastard for being dead, when all he wanted to do was kill him.

*Basra, Saturday May 15th 1915*

'It's good of you and Mrs Hale to help our benefit for the Lansing Memorial.' Mrs Van Ess led Maud

351

along the stalls that had been set up in the school hall. 'We need every penny. The Expeditionary Force has been supportive with gifts of drugs and dressings, but the number of patients has soared with the war. Not just the Turkish prisoners the British send us, but the natives. There are so many refugees. And all of them sick and hungry.'

'Every convalescent officer who can walk intends to call in.' Maud smiled at two walking wounded patients from the army hospital who were wrapping parcels for a bran tub.

'They'll be most welcome.' Mrs Van Ess hustled Maud behind a stall garlanded with palm leaves and heaped with sweetmeats in paper cornets. 'Angela, here's Maud.'

'Thanks for coming, Maud, I appreciate the help.'

'If you two will excuse me, I'll check on the other ladies.'

'Apron–' Angela offered Maud a calico overall. 'The sweets are sticky,' she warned, with an admiring glance at Maud's lilac silk dress.

'Thank you.' Maud tied the apron around her waist. 'And congratulations. I saw Peter on the dock when I gave him letters for John. He told me you are getting married on his next leave.'

Angela glowed at the mention of Peter. 'I hoped he'd get his captaincy but I never dreamed it would be so soon.'

'Have you made any wedding preparations?'

'Not really, other than it will be small, and held in the church here. The Reverend Butler has agreed to officiate and Mrs Butler has offered to make a meal for the guests. Given the recent rise in food prices, I felt guilty about accepting.'

'If a bride can't accept gifts graciously, who can? Have you a wedding dress?'

'I'm going to look at silks in the bazaar as soon as Theo can find the time to accompany me.'

'I have a wedding dress and veil. I had it made in India.' Maud eyed Angela's diminutive figure. 'It will be too long for you, but you could have it shortened if you like it.'

'I couldn't possibly...'

'It's new. I never had a chance to wear it.'

'Your mother's death was such a tragedy...'

'Thank you,' Maud interrupted. 'Please, don't feel obliged to take the dress but it's not doing anything but gathering dust in my trunk.'

'I don't know what to say.'

'Don't say anything until you've seen it. Tell me when you're free and I'll bring it to the mission.'

'I'm free tomorrow afternoon, but if you're busy I could see you virtually any evening after seven. I teach all day.'

'Tomorrow afternoon is fine. I'll be glad of something to do,' Maud confided. 'Time is the one thing I have plenty of. I help at the hospital most days, but not Sundays, and even when I'm there I'm restricted to arranging flowers and distributing library books. My lack of training prevents me from doing anything useful.'

'If it's training you're after, Mrs Mason, the Lansing Memorial can offer you that.' Theo picked up a bag of Turkish Delight and tossed a coin to his sister. 'We're short of nurses and willing to train anyone prepared to put in a 12-hour day. Unlike the British, we have no compunction about employing women. We can't afford to be choosy.'

'Theo, that's a dreadful way of putting it,' Angela protested.

Maud considered the idea. Perhaps that's what she needed: 12-hour days that wouldn't leave time to brood about John – or miss the pleasures Miguel had introduced her to. Theo brushed his thick, black hair back from his face, and Maud looked at him. No one could accuse Theo of being handsome. Thin, lanky, his sallow skin was pitted with smallpox scars, and he wore a habitual dour expression. Only his eyes were friendly. Soft, brown, they shone with the compassion that had led him into his profession.

'I'm sorry if I've insulted you, Mrs Mason. We Americans tend to say what we mean without consideration for social niceties. Doctor Picard and I are desperate for nurses. If we weren't, I wouldn't have mentioned the training to a lady like yourself.'

Stung by the 'lady like yourself', she gave him the answer he wanted. 'When can I start?'

'Theo,' Angela broke in, loath to criticise her beloved brother, 'I know you're short-staffed, but it isn't fair to browbeat Maud.'

'The decision is hers. I'll give you a tour of the wards tomorrow, Mrs Mason, so you can make up your own mind. But if you take the post, you won't be soothing the fevered brows of gentlemen heroes. We have no time for flowers or books at the Lansing. There are three wards chock-full of natives. One for men, one for women, and one for children and mothers and babies. We also have four wards packed with Turkish prisoners, and the

British send us more every day. Abandoned by their own forces as soon as they're too weak to walk, most are suffering from combinations of wounds, disease, sores, scars, and maggot infestation. I suggest you use your tour to study the sights and smells. If you survive without fainting, we'll talk business.'

'What time would you like me there?' Maud asked.

'Eight o'clock suit you?'

'You start early in the Lansing.'

'That's when I take my coffee break. I begin work at five.' He tipped his hat and left.

'Theo has no manners,' Angela apologised. 'I'm sure neither he nor Dr Picard intends to be rude, but they're worked to a frazzle. I help out sometimes in the hospital after school, and I'm afraid what Theo said is true. You do need a strong stomach.'

The doors opened and people flooded into the hall. Maud was kept busy for the next two hours serving soldiers and officers. She only caught sight of Theo once. He was talking to Colonel Hale; no doubt begging more supplies for his hospital. The last thing she'd allow herself to do tomorrow was faint.


*Khafajiya, Sunday May 16th 1915*


'Lieutenant-Colonel Downe, is that a white flag on the pole above that hut?' Major Cleck-Heaton glared at Harry with the pent-up fury and frustration that a week of bickering and mutual

355

contempt had brought to a head.

'A white flag is always hung above the house of an alim – religious leader,' Harry informed him.

'They've stopped firing.'

'They have.' Harry surveyed the village of mud and reed houses huddled behind a palisade of palm trunks. 'It's probably a ploy to encourage us to drop our guard.'

'It's more likely they've run out of ammunition. Lieutenant Day, take a platoon and white flag and parley with the enemy.'

'No.' Harry's contradiction rang sharply in the hot, still air. 'Expose yourself, Day, and you and your platoon will be shot to pieces.'

'*Acting* Lieutenant-Colonel Downe, may I remind you that you are not in command? You are a political officer detailed in an advisory capacity only.'

'Go out there, Day, and you'll be killed,' Harry warned.

'If you don't, Day, I'll have you court-martialled for mutiny and cowardice.'

'You're determined to see blood flow, aren't you Cleck-Heaton?' Harry stepped out of the thicket in which they sheltered. Walking slowly, he raised his arms.

'Looks ridiculous in those Arab skirts,' Cleck-Heaton sneered, furious that Harry had managed to outmanoeuvre him. Alex Day unbuckled his revolver and moved back to the Arab ghulams.

'What's Lieutenant-Colonel Downe shouting?' he whispered.

'He's offering "hazz o bakht". Safe conduct.' The Bedouin spat in the dirt to show what he thought of Marsh Arabs. A volley of shots poured from a window. To Alex's horror, Harry fell into a ditch at the side of the palm grove.

A malicious smile curved Cleck-Heaton's mouth. 'We'll show the bastards what we do to natives who kill our officers. Storm the village!' he ordered the Punjabi officers and sepoys behind him. 'Give them the same quarter they gave Lieutenant-Colonel Downe and Major Anderson.'

The Punjabis opened fire. An acrid smell of burning poisoned the air. Alex saw Punjabi officers lighting torches they'd prepared earlier; strips of oil-soaked rags wrapped around bundles of dry reeds. Under cover of their comrades' fire, volunteers ran out and threw the torches on to the huts. Reed thatch flared. Black smoke curled upwards to the blue sky. The sharp crackle of fire and heat of flames filled the atmosphere. Then the screams started. High-pitched cries of panic-stricken terror.

'For Christ's sake, Day, what are you waiting for?' Cleck-Heaton demanded.

Alex marched into the burning village. His platoon followed. Sepoys, led by a burly Sikh sergeant, rammed their rifles through the door and windows of the hut where the firing had started and fired. The door burst open. Half a dozen men stumbled out, their plaited hair flowing behind them. Coughing, eyes streaming, they ran onto the bayonets of the Punjabis.

Unnerved by the sight of raw, bloody death, Alex stood paralysed. Then he remembered Harry. He charged past the sepoys and butchered bodies of the natives to the ditch. It was empty.

He looked at the square in front of the huts. Bewildered by noise and confusion, his platoon stood mutely watching the slaughter.

'Disarm the Arabs,' he shouted. 'Take as many prisoners as you can.' His orders went unheeded. An old man with a grey beard stuck his head out of a window and fired on the platoon. One man fell. With a cry, the others turned their attention and bayonets to the house. Alex continued to shout while his men battered down the door and dragged out the old man. Seconds later, he was one more mutilated body on the blood-spattered ground.

A child cried. Through the smoke, Alex saw Harry on the marsh side of the village. He was carrying a baby and leading a group of women and children towards the reed boats the Arabs used for fishing. Pulling the boats in by their mooring ropes, he began to pack the children into them. The women wailed, clutching at his robes with agitated hands, hampering his movements. Without pausing, he shouted at them in Arabic. Subdued, they fell back into a weeping huddle.

Sepoys began to move in. Harry threw the child he was holding to one of the women and pulled his gun. Less hysterical than those around her, the woman continued to force those who remained on the bank into the boats.

'Day, over here.'

Alex looked from Harry to his platoon. It was easier to follow orders than give them. He ran to Harry's side.

'Give me your sword.'

Alex did as Harry asked.

With a single slice, Harry severed the mooring ropes as the sepoys ran towards them. The woman who had taken charge began shouting. Plunging into the water, she waded out to a boat and climbed in, still shouting and shaking her fist. Alex watched her paddle away. A child crawled onto her lap. It was the child Harry had carried.

'Harry, that little girl – she's European.'

'Arab children are often born with blond hair and blue eyes.' He turned to a non-commissioned officer. 'Sergeant, you wanted to speak to me?'

'Major Cleck-Heaton gave orders that all the women and children were to be taken prisoner, sir.'

'They've escaped.'

'What was that woman shouting?' Alex had to touch Harry before he responded.

'She asked if this–' Harry grimaced at the ruins of the village '–was why I visited them last year. She reminded me I'd eaten their bread and they'd allowed me to travel through their marshes to make my maps.' He handed Alex back his sword. 'She also asked if there was anything in my heart and on my lips beside treachery.'

'But this had to be done,' Alex protested. 'These villagers killed Anderson and our wounded on the battlefields. They fired on you when you tried to talk to them.'

'Wouldn't you fire at armed men who'd surrounded your house?'

'But these are savage, murdering natives. If we treat them with kid gloves, we'd lose their respect, and then God alone knows what they'd do to any patrol or party of wounded they come across.'

Harry surveyed the mess. The fires had flared magnificently but briefly. Sepoys kicked through ashes where huts and well-stocked barns had stood only moments before. A sergeant from the Punjabis was counting bellowing cattle. Broken bodies were heaped everywhere. Cleck-Heaton stood, ankle-deep in blood and gore, shouting orders to a corporal who was organising a stockpile of the villagers' grain.

'You mean they could do worse to us than we've just done to them?' Harry asked.

'We have to do all we can to ensure the safety of our troops in this territory. We have to put an end to the attacks on our scouting parties and our wounded.' Day reiterated the official line as if it was a poem he'd learnt by heart.

'And you're absolutely certain these are the people who attacked Anderson and our wounded?'

'You're the political officer,' Day replied uneasily.

'That's right, I'm the political officer.' Harry thrust his service revolver back into the folds of his robes. 'And at the moment my politically orientated mind tells me we're no better than the bloody Turks. In fact, we're worse. They at least have the excuse of trying to hang on to their own Empire.'

'We have to protect our oilfields,' Day murmured.

'We're a long way from those, Day.' He turned his back on the village and walked towards the horses. 'A long, long way.'

360

# Chapter Twenty-three

*On board the* Comet, *the Tigris River,*
*Thursday 3rd June 1915*

'Amara!'

The cry echoed around the deck. Charles looked past the launches towing the minesweeping hawser, to a cloud of flamingos that hovered above a distant strip of greenery fronting a settlement of whitewashed houses.

'I find it hard to believe the Turks have let go of the town without a fight. And, as we've left the paddle steamers and floating native disasters behind, along with most of our men, I think we're heading straight into an ambush.'

'There's no ambush, Reid; the Turks are on the run,' Leigh crowed.

'They want us to believe they're on the run,' Charles countered. 'It's all been too easy. Finding that gunboat of theirs, the *Marmaris,* abandoned and burning above Ezra's tomb. Didn't you think it peculiar there was nothing worth salvaging on board?'

'What about the mahailas full of troops, and the steamers crammed with stores?' Leigh reminded him.

'The troops were the dog-end of soldiery. Better for the Turks that we feed them from our supplies than they deplete theirs, and I don't call five tons of Turkish army biscuits that aren't fit for mules much of a catch.'

Grace ran up to the rail. 'Message just came through from the aeroplanes. The Turks have run past Amara and they're still retreating.'

Charles lifted his binoculars and scanned the riverbank. 'Muhammad Pasha could have stationed three-quarters of his army under the rooftops, out of sight of our aeroplanes. We walk in and—' He slapped his hand against the rail.

'Why do you find it hard to admit that this bloody war is going our way, Reid?' Amey complained.

'I'm with Reid. It's been too easy. Loading infantry into native boats, pushing up river, capturing everything in sight, no fight, no resistance from Johnny Turk. It doesn't ring true. Johnny Turk's up to something,' Smythe chimed in.

'Stand by to go ashore!'

As the order was repeated along the deck, Charles buttoned his binoculars into their case and checked his sword and revolver.

'Got the jitters, Reid?' Amey asked as the men formed ranks.

Charles looked from the deck to the town with its wide streets and blank-faced, slit-windowed, Arabic buildings that could conceal any number of rifles.

'One general, half a dozen officers, 12 soldiers and 30 naval ratings preparing to storm a town of 10,000 Arabs protected by a Turkish garrison, strength unknown. Damned right I'm nervous, Amey. Why aren't you?'

Charles's uneasiness persisted through the dinner presided over by General Townsend. The food was the best he'd eaten in months: fresh fish, roast duck, and honey-soaked Halva cake, washed down by beer and Chianti provided by the *Comet's* officers. They ate it in the mess of the Constantinople Fire Brigade, a battalion of hand-picked troops who'd surrendered to a naval lieutenant accompanied by ten men and an interpreter.

The bloodless surrender of the brigade was just one example of what had been happening in the town all day. The Governor, flanked by an escort of Turkish officers, had formally handed Amara over to General Townsend the moment he'd disembarked. The *Shaitan* had captured a Turkish gunboat complete with crew of 11 officers and 258 men. Pressing his luck, Lieutenant Mark Singleton had continued upstream and run into 2000 Turks retreating from the Ahwaz front. He'd turned the *Shaitan's* guns on them and the rearguard surrendered, while the remainder hastened their retreat.

A Turkish lighter had been anchored in midstream and utilised as a prison ship. By mid-afternoon, the lighter was groaning and the officer in charge pleaded the retreating Turks be allowed to retreat. And still the Ottomans continued to seek out British officers and hand over their arms.

'Stop frowning, Reid. The curfew will hold. The natives know anyone caught outside before daybreak will be shot.' Amey gave Charles a cigar.

'And if they realise there's no one to shoot them?'

'Soon will be,' Amey assured. 'Nixon and the

363

Norfolks can't be far behind.'

'I hope we'll still be alive when they march in.'

'Gentlemen!' A banging at the top of the table silenced the conversation. 'To us, gentlemen, the victory.'

Leigh slopped brandy into Charles's glass. 'By the time they realise we've pulled a stunt, there'll be so many reinforcements in the town they won't be able to do a thing about it.'

Charles emptied his glass at the toast but he couldn't help wondering how long it would be before the Turks stopped running. And when they did – would they stand and fight?

Charles led a platoon around the deserted streets for two hours, searching the shadows for renegade Arabs, Turkish spies, or anything that would justify his sense of impending doom. Leigh relieved him in the early hours and he returned to his quarters. The air was stifling. Stripping off, he thrust his revolver under his pillow and lay on top of the bed, but sleep eluded him as he remembered Emily – and Maud.

He hated himself and Maud for what had happened but his disgust didn't prevent him from recalling the texture of her hair, the softness of her breasts and thighs, her moans of pleasure...

Ashamed of his erection, he rolled on his stomach and reminded himself he was fantasising about John's wife and Emily's daughter. He'd made love to other women; why couldn't he think about them? Why had the memory of Maud seared into him, obliterating every other woman from his mind? Even Emily.

Charles woke at daybreak to shouting in the street. He dashed out of bed, stopping only to pull on his shorts and grab his revolver.

'What's happening?' he demanded of the sepoy outside his door.

'Arabs are looting the town, sir.'

Lining up his men, he marched them out. For the first time in days, he had a fight he could sink his teeth into. He was almost reluctant to relinquish control to the Norfolks when they arrived in the town an hour later.

That night, there was a full complement of officers in the mess. The speeches were long and euphoric. Afterwards, Charles only remembered Townsend's final words.

'Gentlemen, you've captured Amara, 17 guns, a vital quantity of Turkish arms and ammunition, a gunboat, various smaller craft–' the general paused until the laughter ceased '–and over 2000 prisoners at a cost of only four killed and 21 wounded. I have it on good authority that the Turkish casualties are at least ten times that number. Gentlemen...' The mess stood and raised their glasses to their commander. 'This is war, and it is magnificent.'

Even the stiff drink and the rousing chorus of 'Magnificent victory' failed to dispel Charles's sense that the worst was yet to come.

John tiptoed over the bodies that floored the hospital tent. The men lay shoulder to shoulder, head to toe, but few were wounded. Heat exhaustion, dysentery, sunstroke, and fever had exacted a heavier toll than the few skirmishes they'd fought. The men in the tent were the most acute cases. The shortage of canvas and medical supplies meant only the very sick were privileged to lie in the shade. He'd heard Harry and Smythe talk about Mesopotamian summers, but he hadn't realised that meant temperatures as unrelenting as 160 degrees Fahrenheit. (Their thermometers stopped at 160 degrees). Or plagues of flies so dense they turned the air into a swarming soup of insects.

Balancing on the balls of his feet, he crouched over a sapper. Two rows away, an orderly was sponging the face of a gunner. The patient fought the cloth in a frenzy of delirium, his face and hands white, caked with salt from the river water. John checked the sapper's temperature. If his fever didn't break soon he'd die. He reached for one of the bowls arranged around the edge of the tent, gingerly closing his fingers on its rim until he was sure it was cool enough to touch. He poured a little warm water over the man's face. He wished they had ice and more tents. Late morning was the worst. The advent of midday heat hung like a sword of Damocles and he was invariably at his lowest ebb after another sleepless night.

'Got room for another, sir?' A corporal hovered

at the edge of the tent, supporting a man too weak to stand.

'Space is at a premium but I'll take a look at him.' John rose slowly. Tending patients on the ground played havoc with his leg and back muscles. He reached the man and lifted his eyelid. Too tired to pull out his thermometer, he laid his hand on his forehead. 'He's burning up. Probably heatstroke. Lay him in your tent and...'

'We haven't one, sir. The only shade is beneath that clump of palm trees down by the river, and that's packed.'

'Then we'll have to find room for him here.'

'Where, sir?' The corporal's knees were giving way.

'Orderly,' John shouted to Matthews who was as exhausted as him. He didn't have to explain what he wanted.

'On the end of that row, sir. The burial detail will be along in a few minutes.'

'It's heatstroke. If you want me I'll be in my tent.'

'Sir.' The gunner looked at John with frightened eyes. 'My mate. He's going to make it, isn't he?'

'I hope so, corporal.' John walked out and stared at the river glittering beyond a border of scrubby bushes. If he had the energy, he'd go for a swim although he knew the water would be warm and thick with salt and debris. He walked on.

Two privates were frying eggs on metal plates laid on the sand. For once, the force didn't have to worry about lack of fuel. Less than a minute in the sun was enough to solidify the white and harden the edges of the yolk of an egg. Five minutes seared a slab of meat. He envied the sepoys their hunger.

For the first time since they'd set foot in Iraq the force had sufficient food, thanks to the political officers who travelled around the countryside offering to buy goods from the marsh villagers in exchange for notes drawn on respected firms like Lynch Bros of Ahwaz, and Gray Mackenzie & Co of Basra. Impressed by the names, the natives conjured up supplies the Expeditionary Force hadn't seen since they'd left India. Mashufs – native canoes – loaded with dates, fresh fish, ducks, chickens, eggs, goats, and sheep. Every meal brought a full plate. It was a shame the merciless heat didn't leave more of an appetite.

John stumbled on. Already it was too hot to sleep. Perhaps his idea of working at night and sleeping in the day wasn't such a good one. He ducked into his tent and tripped over a figure stretched out in the narrow space between the cots.

'Damn it, Harry, I could have hurt you.'

'You did.' Harry opened one eye and glared at him.

'When did you get in?'

'Half an hour ago, and I wouldn't ask any more questions. He's in a foul mood,' Crabbe answered from his cot.

'Where did he come from?'

'Amara. He's brought orders that three of our battalions, a cavalry regiment, and a field battery are to proceed there immediately. The rest are to return to Ahwaz. Appears Amara fell easily and they can hold it without a full complement of troops.'

'Who's going where?' John asked.

'Hasn't been decided, but you'll be returning to Basra with the sick. Lucky sod. I wish I had a wife within travelling distance.'

'You haven't a wife,' John reminded Crabbe.

'A girl, then, a woman, anything female. Do you suppose they've organised a Rag in Ahwaz by now?'

John saw a letter on his blanket. Avoiding Harry, he threw himself onto his cot. Stretching out, he unbuttoned his shirt and stripped off. He held the letter to the light as Crabbe began to snore.

'If you don't open it, you'll never know what's in it.'

John looked down; Harry's eyes were still closed. 'I thought you were asleep.'

He rummaged under John's cot for his discarded abba and cigarettes. 'Smythe gave it to me at Amara.' He offered the information although John hadn't asked for it. 'Now, if you'll excuse me I'll finish this smoke, then try to sleep. Even talking requires more energy than I possess.'

John didn't open the envelope until he was sure Harry was asleep. Removing the single sheet of paper, he began to read.

*Dear John,*

*I hope this letter finds you well, my darling, I think of you all the time…*

He couldn't read any more. Brooke was dead so Maud was thinking of him.

But for how long – until the next officer tipped her the wink? She could be taking her clothes off now in a bedroom in Basra. Would she undress as slowly as she'd done during the brief time they'd

369

spent together? Her fingers had always lingered over the pearl buttons on her chemise. She'd never known how close he'd come to tearing the clothes off her. But perhaps adultery was different. There could be constraints on time. Rooms rented by the hour. He – whoever 'he' was – might have to rush because he was on duty in a few hours.

Would he laugh with her when it was over? Slap her lightly on the buttocks and say, 'Thank you, Mrs Mason. Same time next week?' After all, it would be cheaper than the Rag.

He picked up Harry's matches. Holding Maud's letter by the corner, he set it alight, watching the flame lick higher, turning the paper to powder. When only the fragment between his fingers remained, he blew out the fire. There was nothing left. The small square he held was clean. Taking the envelope, he peeled it apart. Paper was at a premium, envelopes luxuries, and he needed an envelope for what he was going to send Maud.

Removing a security box from his pack, he unlocked it with a key threaded alongside his ID discs. Pushing aside the parcel of pearls and gold Harry had given him he lifted out Brooke's letters, and laid them on the envelope. Taking a stub of pencil from his shirt pocket, he scribbled, *The effects of Sub-Lieutenant Geoffrey Brooke killed in action at Ahwaz. John Mason.*

Tying the bundle together, he addressed it to Maud. If the Force was moving out, advance parties would leave tonight. Someone would take it for him. Maud should get it in the next couple of weeks, and if she had any conscience left, he wouldn't be the only miserable one locked into

370

their marriage.

'Be careful with this one. He has a spinal injury...'

'Don't you ever give up, John? There are doctors here who can take over, even from you.' Charles laid a hand on the shoulder of John's dust and fly-spattered shirt. It was difficult to keep the shock from registering on his face. John was still broad, but gaunt and skeletal. Even his face had altered. The cheeks beneath the layer of stubble had sunk, throwing his skull bones into unnerving prominence. Charles had seen many unburied corpses on the Western Front. It required very little imagination to place John among them.

'It's good to see you.' John held out his hand, cutting a swathe through the flies that hovered in dense clouds above the wounded. Overcome by emotion, Charles clasped it. He'd been dreading this reunion with the knowledge of what he and Maud had done on his conscience. Now he was actually with John, it wasn't too difficult. John turned aside to check the pulse of a sapper.

'John, you're incorrigible.'

'I'll be with you as soon as I've handed these men over to whoever's in charge of the hospital.'

'That, Captain Mason, is now. Would you like to book a bed for yourself?'

'Knight, I thought you were in Basra.'

'When the CO asked Base Command to set up a hospital here, they sent the best man they had.' Knight fingered his major's insignia.

371

'Congratulations, Knight. Couldn't have happened to a more modest fellow. How's Hale? Is it as disgustingly hot downstream as it is here?'

'I thought you'd have heard.' Knight shuffled past two orderlies carrying a stretcher. 'Hale died a month back. Heart attack was the cause on the death certificate, but in my opinion it was heat exhaustion due to overwork.'

'He was a good commander. Good man.' The news was too much for John in his present state. He propped himself against the hospital wall.

'Maud told me she'd written to you. Even allowing for the idiosyncrasies of Gulf mail you should have received the letter by now.'

'Her letter was probably thrown in the wrong bag.' John's face was ashen.

'We're not short of doctors, so in the interests of hygiene I suggest you go hose yourself down.'

'I can organise something better than a hose.' Charles led John across the street. 'Harry came in with the advance column in his Arab skirts. He begged a bath and a spare uniform and since then he's been closeted with the POs, which translates as pilfering or political officers depending on your point of view. They hold the reputation of being the best scroungers on the Persian front.'

'Harry didn't need a posting to learn how to scrounge.'

'He taught the others.' Charles ran up a flight of stairs and opened a door. 'Here it is. Home. I'll send my bearer to look for your kit.'

'It's in the same state as this.' John indicated his filthy uniform. 'Kerkha water doesn't remove dirt. It only adds to what's already there.'

'I'll ask my bearer to forage. Here's the bath-room.' Charles showed John a room that held a tinned slipper bath, cane commode, and a table stacked with Turkish towels. 'I had the bath cleaned after Harry used it, the lord knows why. Common sense should have told me you'd be in the same disgusting state. There's water in the jugs. It's not cold but it's clean. Soap's in the dish.'

John picked it up. 'Kay's, wherever did you get it?'

'Harry. I live in fear of what he's going to pull out of his pockets next.'

John tipped the lukewarm water into the bath. Where he'd held the jug, he left black finger marks. When the bath was half full, he threw in the soap and peeled off his clothes.

'You look as though you could do with a drink.' Charles went into the living room. 'Not coming down with anything, are you? Doctors always seem to catch every damn bug going.' The words were out before Charles remembered Hale.

'So it would appear.' John tossed his clothes into a corner.

'I can organise a meal to be brought up here if you're too tired to face the mess tonight.' Charles carried a decanter of whisky and glasses into the bathroom.

'I'd like to eat in the mess. See who else is here.'

'Leigh, Smythe, Amey, Grace, Bowditch – you may remember them from the *Egra*.'

'I remember. Grace was after Maud.' John lowered himself into the water. As Charles had prophesied, it was warm, but after the searing heat of the desert, it flowed soothingly around his

373

raw and aching body.

'Your father-in-law's here too.' Charles handed him a glass.

'Good whisky,' John commented as he sipped.

'Don't you get on with Perry?'

'No.'

Charles couldn't resist asking. 'Anything to do with Emily's death?'

John closed his eyes and ducked his head under the water; he glanced at Charles as he surfaced. 'Perry got blind drunk after Emily's funeral. He was in no state to look after Maud. I felt the best thing I could do was marry her and get her away from him as quickly as possible. He disagreed. I haven't seen him since.'

'If he was drunk, he's probably forgotten the incident.'

'Probably.' John drank half of his whisky, before beginning to soap himself. Charles pulled a chair into the bathroom and sat down.

'Did you see Maud when you were in Basra?'

'She was fine.' Charles tried to sound casual as he topped up their glasses. 'She can't wait to see you. You are going downstream?'

'Haven't received my orders yet.'

'Surely you've put in for leave on compassionate grounds?'

'Didn't think it would be fair.'

'You're too damned fair for words, John. There's no other officer here with a wife within travelling distance.'

'There's Harry.'

'Harry doesn't have a wife, he has a native concubine. If you ask for leave, you'll get it, and

374

they'll probably want you to stay on in base hospital afterwards. I know Basra's packed, but you should get a bungalow.'

'I'll wait and see where they send me.'

'Now you're being ridiculous. When have the brass done anything logical like post a husband to the same town his wife is in?' Charles demanded. 'If you leave the decision to them you'll get posted to the Western Front and Maud will be offered a return ticket to India.'

'You've no idea how heavenly this is.' John bent his knees, lay back in the bath, and stood his glass on his chest. 'A bath, the prospect of clean clothes – good whisky...'

'Was it that rough out there?' Charles followed John's lead on to safer topics of conversation.

'The heat and flies were the worst. The shortage of tents and medicines caused a lot of sickness. But you're the real heroes. Was it really as easy as everyone says to take this town?'

'It was.' Charles tipped more whisky into John's glass.

'Steady, that went in the water.'

Charles picked up the last jug of water and tipped it over John's face. John retaliated by throwing the bar of soap at him. By the time they'd finished play fighting, the floorboards were saturated and they were both laughing. Charles tossed a towel at John and left him to dry himself.

Despite the jocularity, Charles sensed a new reserve. He would have given everything he owned to turn the clock back so he could throw Maud out of his room the night she'd visited.

No woman was worth risking the friendship he

and John had shared since childhood. And no woman was worth the guilt he was feeling now. Not even one as beautiful and sensual as Maud.

## Chapter Twenty-four

*Ibn Shalan's camp, evening,*
*Monday 14th June 1915*

The atmosphere in Shalan's harem constricted Furja like a shroud. She sat in the airless half of the tent that was never opened, and nursed her daughters while her father's wives regaled her with contradictory advice on how to bring up modest girls who would command good bridal prices.

She paid them little attention. Her problems were more immediate. Many seasons would pass before her daughters would be of an age to marry. She wondered if those seasons would see an end to the fighting. Whenever and wherever they travelled, she saw unburied dead. Sun-bleached bundles of skin and bones that had been living, breathing men. Turk. Bedouin, and occasionally skeletons with scalps of light brown or blond hair that sent her heart racing.

Was Harry lying in some corner of the desert now, his sightless eye sockets staring up at the sky? She gripped Aza so hard the baby whimpered. She looked down. There was no denying her daughters' Ferenghi blood; their eyes were still blue, their hair fair. Characteristics that had strangled any love her father might have borne for a granddaughter named Aza.

Harri turned from her breast, yawned, closed her mouth, and slept. Furja looked for the girl who helped her. As usual, she wasn't there when needed.

'Shall I lay the little one down for you?' Dari, her father's youngest wife, asked.

'Thank you.' Furja moved her arm so Dari could take the child from her.

'She is content, this little one. She will have a placid and happy life. But that one–' Dari looked to Aza, who was sucking vigorously, pounding Furja's breast with her small fists '–if she cannot have what she wants she will take it.'

'Her father has a strong will.'

'As does her grandfather.' Fatima, her father's eldest wife, interposed. 'You agreed to forget your unfortunate connection with the infidel invaders.'

'It was my unfortunate connection that gave us guns to defend ourselves.'

'And they–' Fatima pointed to the babies '–along with the deaths of our warriors are the price we continue to pay for those guns.'

Furja fell silent. Fatima continually goaded her, and always within her father's earshot. The argument would never be resolved. The first casualty at the pipeline had been Fatima's favourite brother. His widows and the other widows blamed her for the deaths of their menfolk. If she had not married a Ferenghi, their men would be alive, and she was never allowed to forget that fact.

'When you have finished feeding Aza your father wants to see you.' Shalan's second wife returned from the booth where her father slept. Furja handed Aza, now plump and sleepy, over to Dari. She went to the corner where the bowls and water for washing were stored. Tipping a little water into a bowl, she washed her face, hands, and breasts, refastened her outer robe, and combed her hair. Plaiting it into a single strand, she covered it with her veils. Emptying the water outside, she cleaned the area, determined to give Fatima little cause for complaint, as they had to share the same cramped space.

After checking both her daughters were sleeping alongside Dari, she walked through the curtain of goat hair.

Her father was squatting in front of a low table, smoking and gazing thoughtfully at a rug hanging on the tent wall. It was the last one her mother had woven. He rose to his feet as she entered.

'Walk with me.'

She followed him into the cool evening air. The moon had risen. Huge, golden, it brought memories of the times she and Harry had gazed upon its pitted face from their bedroom in Basra.

'Fatima has reminded me your daughters are of an age when you can think of marrying again.'

'We take up too much room in a crowded harem.'

'Then I will find you a husband. Do you wish to remain with the tribe, or would you like me to look among your mother's people?'

'My happiness depends on the man I marry, not the tribe.'

'Ali Mansur has asked for you again.'

'I refused to marry him two years ago. Nothing

has changed.'

'Two years ago you were a simpering virgin with romantic ideas. Now you're a woman looking for a second husband. You have daughters. Ali Mansur is willing to care for you and your children. It is no easy thing for a man to take the children of another. In your case it will be doubly hard, for your husband will be taking the daughters of a Ferenghi.'

'There is another within the tribe who will give me the position of second wife and take my children.'

'Who?' Shalan stared back at her. Furja saw he already knew.

'Mitkhal.'

'The man is a tribeless bastard. He has no family – no friends except the Ferenghis.'

'You allowed him to marry your sister.'

'He was the only man who ever asked for her. I allowed the marriage for her sake. She is damaged and soiled.'

'Not by her own doing.'

'It is enough she lived through that life,' Shalan said dismissively.

'I have lived with a Ferenghi.'

'A Ferenghi who lived as one of us. You were not exposed to their ways.'

'Only their love.'

'That part of your life is over. Ali or a Sirdieh. Which is it to be?' he demanded.

'Neither.'

'You will take one or the other. You have property sufficient to buy you a position as a second or third wife and redress your daughters' parentage.

In time, the tribe will forget your first husband.'

'I never will. If you do not allow me to marry Mitkhal I will walk out into the desert as my mother did before me,' she threatened.

All he could see were her eyes – dark, enigmatic, the same eyes as her mother. 'I told you when you married the Ferenghi, the marriage was to last no longer than a week. Most women would have left the bridal tent the day after the wedding. You chose to ignore my wishes then, as you do now.'

'I didn't want to marry Harry; you forced me. I didn't want to love him but it happened. We did not want to divorce but you insisted.'

'It was a marriage between a camel and an ass.'

'The camel and the ass were happy. But, as you said, I must look to my future. I will be happiest with Mitkhal.'

'Because he will allow you to sleep on the Ferenghi's mattress?'

'A man may do with his wife as he wishes.'

'Which is why you will marry Ali,' he said forcefully.

'Then you leave me no choice.'

'Take your children with you. It will save me the trouble of killing them.'

'They are your grandchildren.'

'Their throats will be slit one hour after you leave my tent.'

'You would slaughter children of your own blood?'

'Not if you marry Ali. You should be grateful he still wants you. I will have my answer in the morning. Ali, the Sirdieh, or your and your children's deaths.'

Furja looked back at the camp. The lamps glowed, it was time for the evening meal, but she was not hungry. Her father was right. She had no choice, not when she carried Harry's son within her. He deserved the little she could give him – life. What if he was fair like the girls? Would Ali suspect the truth? The punishment for adultery was set, and her father would not hesitate to carry out the sentence. He would see her stoned to death. And her children?

She looked up at the moon. If she married Ali, it would give her time. A few months for Mitkhal to recover, find Harry, and ask him to take his daughters, and hopefully his son. If she succeeded in handing over her children to their father, she'd die content.

*Basra, the evening of Monday 14th June 1915*

'That's the last of your clothes.' Maud laid a calico-sheathed evening dress on the bed.

'Thank you, my dear.' Mrs Hale set down the photograph album she'd been studying. 'You've been such a help. I couldn't have managed without you.'

'You would have, and admirably. You're the strongest person I know. Colonel Hale knew what he was doing when he chose you to be his wife.'

'We did have a wonderful life together. It's only now I'm beginning to realise it's over and I'll never see India again. This will be my last voyage home.' Mrs Hale picked up the album again. 'This is our wedding photograph. We married on

381

Christmas Day in Poona in '90. I'd come out to India to visit my brother after mother died. I met the colonel, captain as he was then, on the ship. To the horror of my chaperone we became engaged before we left the Mediterranean.' She smiled. 'I don't have to explain to you what it was like. Captain Mason told Percy he only met you a month before you married.'

'He did.'

'The war won't last forever. Here–' She pressed a jewel case into Maud's hand. 'Take them, my dear. Take them with my blessing, and when you wear them think of the colonel and me.'

Maud opened the case. 'I couldn't, not your pearls. The colonel only gave them to you last month.'

'He always promised to buy me a pearl necklace for our silver wedding anniversary. Perhaps he sensed he wouldn't live to see it. Take them,' she pleaded. 'It would make an old woman happy to think of you wearing them when you dine in the officers' mess with Captain Mason.' Mrs Hale blotted her eyes with a handkerchief and turned to a pile of underclothes. Folding them between sheets of tissue paper, she stowed them in the drawers of her wardrobe trunk. 'I've no one else to give them to. All our children are buried in India. I hoped that Johnny... He was 16 when he died of cholera. The colonel and I found his death the hardest to bear. The others all died before their fifth birthday. It would have been a lovely family. Four boys and two girls, but it wasn't to be. I'll have my sister's girls to fuss over when I reach Eastbourne. She has five. All married, so my sister

382

will be glad to have me. Her husband died two years ago and since then she's found life lonely, but Beatie always did want others to entertain her.'

'Shouldn't you give the pearls to one of your nieces?'

'They wouldn't appreciate them the way you would. You're an army wife and daughter. You know what it is to lose someone you love to this cruel land. Percy used to say that having you living with us was like having a daughter of our own again; and now he and your dear mother are lying in the same ground. You remind me of myself at your age. Take a little advice from an old woman, my dear. Make the most of the time you have with Captain Mason. Not just because of the war but because life is so very, very precious.'

Maud clasped Mrs Hale in her arms.

'You'll have to excuse a sentimental old woman.' Mrs Hale extricated herself from Maud's arms and picked up her album. Wrapping it in a shawl, she laid it in a drawer of her cabin trunk. 'I might want it on voyage.'

'Would you like me to hang your evening gowns in your wardrobe trunk?'

'No, thank you, dear; they'll not be wanted on voyage. Another piece of advice, dear, about the Lansing. It's such hard work, and now the hot weather is upon us there's so much sickness. They'll wear you to a shadow, particularly as you're moving into the mission. You'll be called out all hours.'

'I need something to keep me busy until John gets here.'

'I don't think the Lansing is right for you,' Mrs

Hale persisted. 'You're not as strong as you think. Still, Captain Mason shouldn't be long now Amara's fallen. Major Chalmers told me when he paid his respects this afternoon that once we've secured the Basra Wilyat we'll consolidate and hold our position. The campaign's almost at an end. I dare say he'll get a posting to Basra, now the colonel's – the hospital's short of doctors. They need a good man in charge. Percy thought a great deal of your husband. As does everyone in command.'

'Do you really think John will be posted here?' Maud questioned.

'I'm sure of it, my dear, all he has to do is ask. There–' Mrs Hale folded the last of her winter underclothes into her cabin trunk. 'I can manage on my own now, dear.' She looked around and Maud sensed she wanted to be alone to say good-bye to the last home she had shared with her beloved Percy.

'I'd like to see you off at the wharf tomorrow.'

'Four o'clock is very early.'

'If I pack my trunks ready for the sepoys to pick up, I can go straight from the wharf to the mission.'

'Well, if you don't mind getting out of bed at the crack of dawn, I'd love to have you there.'

'I'll call you for breakfast.'

'I wish the brigadier wasn't moving in here. I don't like the thought of you living with Americans. They're not like us.'

'Mrs Butler and Angela are very kind.'

'Doctor Wallace isn't, he works you far too hard.'

'It's only temporary. When John returns we'll

find rooms elsewhere.'

Maud kissed Mrs Hale and left for her own room. Her trunks lay bound, sealed and locked, surrounded by hatboxes and valises. Her overnight bag stood empty alongside them. Tomorrow she'd pack her nightdress and toiletries. Then there would be nothing left that was hers. Already the room had the deserted look of quarters waiting for someone else.

She wondered if the brigadier had family with him who would stand photographs on the bedside table as she'd done. How many more rooms would she sleep in before she could live her life the way she'd meant to when she'd married John?

She picked up his last letter. It had been written months ago. She should have followed him out here when the Expeditionary Force had taken Basra. The contempt in Charles's eyes after they'd made love had woken her to the fact that sex wasn't love. She'd only ever cared for John. Miguel and Geoffrey had only been bodies to use when she'd been lonely.

Geoffrey – the principal emotion she'd felt when she'd seen his name gazetted amongst the fallen had been relief he was no longer able to pester her about leaving John.

A knock at the front door sent her racing into the passage. Mrs Hale was trembling in the doorway of her room. Maud knew what she was thinking; many couriers had ridden into Basra late at night carrying lists of the dead.

Mrs Hale recovered her composure first. 'Who is it?'

'Package for Mrs Mason from Captain Mason.

385

I promised the captain I'd deliver it personally.'

Mrs Hale threw back the bolts and opened the door. A travel-stained subaltern held out a small parcel. Mrs Hale took it and handed it to Maud. 'Thank you, Lieutenant.' Maud finally found her voice.

'Don't mention it, Mrs Mason. Good night, ladies.' He was halfway down the veranda before Maud remembered her manners.

'Can I get you anything, Lieutenant?'

'No, thank you, Mrs Mason, I've a bed and a bath waiting in my quarters.'

'How was my husband?'

'As well as could be expected, Mrs Mason.'

'Does that mean he was worn out, Lieutenant?'

'He did say he was glad he was in the medical corps because he was never bored, but I'm sure he'll be in Basra soon. There were a lot of sick in Colonel Dunlop's column. They'll be looking for doctors to travel down river with them.'

'Thank you, Lieutenant.'

'Maud, I'm pleased for you.' Mrs Hale locked and bolted the door. 'Pleasant dreams.'

'You too, Mrs Hale.' Maud returned to her room and examined the package. She tore a fingernail undoing the complicated knots in the string – knots John had tied. Her address written in John's hand was on one side of the package, on the back, his name, rank, and serial number. She peeled off the outer covering. A bundle of papers fell out. Filthy, mud-stained, brittle. Beneath them was a photograph of her. She'd written on it herself, *To darling Geoffrey. All my love, Maud.*

She searched frantically through the papers.

They were all letters she'd written to Geoffrey, except for the top one, which was a letter he'd written to her. There was nothing from John except what was pencilled on the package.

*Effects of Lieutenant Geoffrey Brooke killed in action at Ahwaz. John Mason.*

*The officers' mess, Amara, Monday 14th June 1915*

'To friendship and Clyneswood. Knight, you'll have to take our word it's a beautiful place.'

'I will, Reid,' Knight concurred.

'Way there!' Bowditch charged close with Grace on his back, followed by Smythe with Amey on his.

'Navy versus the cavalry,' Smythe shouted.

'Your jockey's about to fall off.' Harry ducked when Amey crashed into the side buffet.

'The Turks were here.' Crabbe grabbed the salt.

'Crabbe's routing the Turks again,' Harry warned.

'Time to check on my patients.' Knight rose unsteadily.

'I'll come with you.'

'No.' Knight pressed John into his chair. 'You're resting, remember.'

'I remember you and everyone else in this man's army telling me to.'

'Comes to something when a war makes a man forget how to relax.' Charles refilled their glasses from a bottle he'd secreted beneath his chair.

'No danger of that happening to you, Charles.' Harry eyed John, who was edging past happy into aggressive drunk.

'Relaxation is the most important thing after victory.' Charles lifted his glass. 'To relaxation and all sections of the Expeditionary Force. Even political officers.'

'Sit down before I put you down.'

'Acting Lieutenant-Colonel's showing his rank.' Knight watched the race.

'Cavalry's unhorsed.' Charles gazed glassy-eyed at the bundle of arms and legs writhing on the floor that was Amey and Smythe.

'The navy's sunk.' Harry spotted Grace and Bowditch rolling under a table. John filched Charles's bottle and refilled his glass.

'Major Reid.' An orderly hovered before Charles. 'The general's compliments, sir. Would you join him for a drink at the top table?'

'That's what you get for having a general for a father.' Harry had spotted George Perry leaving his seat. He hoped Maud's father would have enough sense to stay away. In John's present mood, it was anyone's guess as to how he'd react if his father-in-law approached him.

Charles straightened his collar. 'Excuse me, gentlemen?'

'And me.' Knight finished his drink. 'See you in the morning, Mason. Not early, you could do with a good night's sleep.'

'Is that a medical opinion?'

'Take it from a superior,' Knight replied.

'Not any longer,' Harry interrupted. 'John was gazetted major this afternoon.'

'In that case, I'll have the hospital ready for your inspection tomorrow afternoon, Major.'

Knight saluted before weaving out of the mess.

Harry took three cigars from his pocket. He handed one to John and laid one next to Charles's glass. 'Have you put in for a transfer to Basra?'

'No.'

'I'm leaving at four in the morning.' Harry struck a match on his boot.

'For the Euphrates?'

'Basra. I hope to wangle a week's leave before I move on.'

'Furja?'

'Shalan doesn't like me visiting, but I'm prepared to risk his wrath. I can't help feeling something's wrong. You haven't forgotten your promise?'

'No.' John lit the cigar.

'Downe, I'm glad to see a former officer of my command doing so well for himself.' Perry sat in the chair Charles had vacated.

'Thank you, Colonel Perry.' Harry forced himself to be polite.

'I had a letter from Maud,' Perry turned to John. 'She said she hadn't heard from you for some time.'

'I sent her a bundle of letters from the Kerkha by courier.'

'Glad to hear it.'

'Most wives are concerned if their husbands are in the front line,' Harry commented.

'Come, come, Downe, when have doctors been in the front line?' Perry sniped.

'When they set up field hospitals. Our casualties at Ahwaz would have been far higher if John and Knight hadn't worked under fire.'

'Really?' Perry picked up the cigar Harry had left for Charles and rolled it between his finger and thumb. 'I must make a point of inspecting these "field hospitals" some time, Mason.'

'You'd be welcome to view the facilities any time.'

'Am I to take that to mean you'd like to see me as a patient?'

'John meant no such thing.' Harry kicked back his chair and faced Perry square on. He hadn't forgotten the beating he'd had at the hands of Sergeant Mullins, or the shadowy figure in the background. Neither had he forgotten the shooting at Shaiba. He'd never tracked down the officer who'd given the order to fire on Mitkhal and himself.

'Are you afraid to let me speak for myself, Harry?' Sweat poured down John's face.

'Shall we have a drink?' Harry grabbed Charles's bottle, praying it wasn't too late to diffuse the scene he sensed brewing.

John swept his forearm across the table. His glass fell, shattering on the tiled floor. 'I'd sooner drink with a Turk.'

'You wouldn't know a bloody Turk if you saw one.'

The mess fell silent when chair legs scraped over tiles. Harry looked up, Charles was walking towards them.

'I demand an apology,' Perry bawled.

'I think the insults stand about equal,' Harry murmured.

'But they won't once you start, will they, Downe? You and this jackass made bloody sure

390

my daughter would turn against me.'

John tried and failed to rise from his seat. Lunging forward, he slid full length on to the glass-spattered floor.

'The man's a nincompoop,' Perry railed. 'He's not fit to be an officer. He's a common drunk. He can't even behave like a gentleman in the mess.'

Harry bent over his friend's inert body. 'Would someone get a doctor?' he called. 'Major Mason is burning with fever.'

Perry was forgotten in the confusion that followed. Charles sent for Knight. Amey and Smythe lifted John out of the broken glass and on to a bench. But when Harry was sponging John's face with ice from a bucket on the table, he caught sight of Perry.

The colonel was trembling, his face livid as he stared with undisguised loathing at John. He downed a brandy someone handed him and Harry noticed a dark patch, too damp for sweat, around his crotch.

The general had said Perry was a good officer and a good man to have under fire. Maybe. But whatever kind of soldier he was when sober, he was clearly insane when drunk.

# Chapter Twenty-five

*Amara, Monday 14th June 1915*

Charles sobered rapidly while he and Harry waited outside the cubicle Knight found for John. Enough of his fellow officers had died here and on the Western Front for him to realise no one was immortal, but for all that, his vision of life after the war included John and Harry. He wasn't sure how he'd cope if they didn't make it. He'd be left with nothing. Emily gone; friends gone...

Knight appeared, pale and serious. 'The fever's bad but I've seen worse. He has some vicious cuts but the glass hit nothing vital. However, he has no reserves. The fool pushes himself the way sepoys push army mules and I've seen them drop dead in harness. He's skin and bone. He needs care, rest...'

'Basra.'

'He wouldn't survive the journey, Harry.'

'It's less than 24 hours. There's a boat leaving at four. If I lay him under a canvas shelter on deck, he'll be no worse off than he is here. In fact, he might be cooler with the river beneath him.'

'Can we see him?' Charles asked.

'He won't recognise you,' Knight warned.

Harry pushed the door open. John lay on a truckle bed, his face and hands bandaged. What little skin could be seen was red and damp. 'I'll be back for him in two hours.'

'I won't take responsibility for moving him,' Knight said.

'Then I will. Let's see if Maud can sort him out.'

Charles followed Harry outside. When he'd arrived in Mesopotamia, he'd had visions of the three of them fighting side by side. Now Harry and John were off to Basra. Was that how their lives were going to be from now on? Snatched glimpses as they travelled in opposite directions; occasional drunken binges in temporary mess halls, then goodbye until next time. 'And by the way, don't get killed if you can help it.'

'You look as though you could do with a night's sleep, Charles.'

'And you.'

'I'll get my kit and horses on board. I'd have slept on a boat locker but I'll have to make other arrangements for John.'

'Do you think he'll make it?' Charles wanted reassurance.

'I intend to host a reunion dinner in Clyneswood when this damned show is over and he'll be there.'

Charles opened the door to his room. His bearer had set out two sleeping pallets beside his bed. They made John's absence all the harder to bear.

'Do you mind if I take both of these?' Harry picked up his saddlebag.

'Help yourself.' Charles glanced at the bag. 'I've never known anyone carry so little kit. That looks too small to hold a change of clothes.'

'It is.' Unbuckling the bag Harry tipped it out. 'A Turkish razor, a Solingen knife, a pack of dried dates and a bag of gold sovereigns dated 1872, part of a hoard we paid to the French. There's nothing here a German officer or wealthy Arab wouldn't carry.'

'John told me you go out without your ID discs.'

'The last thing I need is a couple of tags hanging around my neck to announce I'm a British officer.'

'The Turks shoot Arabs who are friendly to the British. They wouldn't dare shoot a British officer.'

'You fight this war your way, I'll fight it mine.'

'What I'm trying to say is I've just realised how much you and John mean to me.' Charles held up a bottle. 'Last drink for the road.'

'A quick one.' Harry repacked his saddlebag and tossed it, together with his camel skin, on top of the mattresses. 'Did you enjoy your drink with the general?'

'He said we're set to drive the Turks back from the Euphrates.'

'That's hardly news. The brief from the Indian Government at the outset was to secure the Wilyat. That includes the Euphrates. There's little point in us sitting on the Tigris if they can attack any time they want from our left flank.'

'He also told me the security of the Wilyat and oilfields has been designated of secondary importance to territorial acquisitions. Nixon's asked for more troops. Command's set on taking Baghdad.' Charles watched Harry. 'You knew, didn't you?'

Harry took the whisky Charles handed him. 'I heard something of the sort before Shaiba. We hoped the idea would be dropped.'

'"We" being the political officers?'

'Yes.'

'Everything's fallen our way so far, why shouldn't it continue?'

'If we have more troops and supplies we'll probably be in a position to take Baghdad, but there isn't a single sound reason for doing so; what the Command doesn't seem to realise is the closer to Baghdad we get, the closer we will be to the Turkish main supply line and the Berlin-Baghdad railway. The Turks stretched themselves by fighting in Basra. We can take what's left of the Wilyat and hold it comfortably. Beyond it, we could be the ones forced to retreat.'

'You think we've gone far enough?'

'We've secured the oilfields and established British rule in Basra and the surrounding area, so why the emphasis on taking Baghdad? Has the Indian Government a surplus of civil servants looking for new territories to govern? If they have, they'll find Mesopotamia less amenable than Calcutta.'

'I haven't given a thought as to what's going to happen to this place after the war,' Charles said.

'It's all the Arabs think about.' Harry finished his whisky. 'But ours is not to reason why. I didn't learn much in Sandhurst but I did learn that. When you're a general, you can make the decisions. Until then, you obey orders. Even if they come from a halfwit who's never set foot outside HQ except to go to a governor's garden party.'

'Why does Perry hate John so much?' Charles asked.

'Because he married Maud the day Emily died. Perry barricaded himself into his bungalow and got plastered. John couldn't leave Maud with him, and he couldn't take her away without a chaperon, so he married her.'

'John said as much, but after seeing Perry tonight I thought there had to be more.'

Harry picked up his bag. 'Do you know what I'm going to do? I'm going to kick a captain out of bed. I may need help with John on the journey. And a Lieutenant-Colonel, even an acting one, has the right to an aide.'

'And Smythe the right to a wedding?' Charles smiled.

'One of us is entitled to a happy ending. Take care until I get back.'

*Lansing Memorial Hospital, Basra,*
*Tuesday 15th June 1915*

Maud stood a bowl of salt water on a stool beside a Turk's bed. He smiled at her and raised his arm to prove he could move it. While she cut away his dressings, she considered how far she'd progressed since the morning Theo had shown her around the wards. They'd lingered at the bedsides of amputees, men whose wounds were alive with maggots, children whose tiny bodies were covered by pus-filled lesions. She'd steeled herself, survived the tour – and Theo's remarks on women who were afraid to get their hands dirty. Women he termed 'ladies', using the word as an insult.

The morning after the tour, she'd dressed in a grey frock she'd have died rather than wear before the war, and entered the hospital. Theo introduced her to Sister Margaret, a large woman with red hair, and a brusque, no-nonsense Irish approach to life, death, and disease which had been acquired during 30 years of nursing. The sister had shaken her hand, then given her the foulest and filthiest jobs she could find.

She'd worked from before dawn to after dusk, washing out chamber pots that overflowed with excrement and vomit, bathing filthy and verminous bodies and cleansing putrid sores. She bore it all silently because her pride wouldn't allow Theo the gratification of knowing he'd been right about her.

A week after she'd started she'd been tweezing maggots out of a Turkish infantryman's arm when she'd sensed the patient watching her. When she'd finished, he produced a crumpled photograph of a young woman dressed in black with a baby on her lap. She'd asked if the girl was his wife. Neither could understand a word the other uttered but the expression in his eyes when she'd pointed to the baby said everything. He was the first patient she saw as more than a wound.

The next time she'd passed his bed, she'd smiled. The other men saw and produced their own photographs. By means of pointing, trial and error, she learnt their names, and held conversations of a sort. Her smiles won her friends on other wards. A mother in the children's ward gave her a bag of sweets, another, a bunch of flowers. Soon, she found herself an accepted member of the hospital and, for the first time in her life, felt she was doing useful work.

Sister Margaret tempered her hostility and showed her how to do the thousand and one nurses' tasks quickly and efficiently. After three weeks, she was not only washing and cleaning wounds but dressing them. Yesterday, she'd given her first injection. And Doctor Picard was talking about allowing her to assist with operations.

'Nurse?'

Maud looked up from the arm she was bathing. 'Sister.' Sister Margaret might be friendlier, but she was still a force that wouldn't stand being treated lightly.

'An influx of British wounded came in four hours ago from Amara.'

'I heard. I assumed they'd be going to the base hospital.'

'They are, but Captain Smythe is here. Your husband is among them. I'll finish dressing this arm if you'd like to go and see him.'

Maud handed over the cloth, ran to the sink, and washed her hands. Tearing the starched cap from her hair, she raced along the corridor and collided with Peter.

'Is John escorting the wounded or is he ill?' she demanded.

'He has fever. I'm sorry to bring such rotten news. I have a carriage waiting.' Clutching her arm, he led her out into the suffocating heat of the street and lifted her on to the seat. 'He doesn't look too clever.' He flicked the reins. 'Knight says he has no strength. He wanted to keep him in Amara but Harry thought he'd be better off here with you. When I left the doctors were looking at him.'

'He's going to make it, isn't he?'

'He's in the best hands, Maud. Although–' He

smiled. 'I don't know what he's going to say when he comes round and sees you in that uniform. You're the last candidate I expected to join the American nursing corps.'

*Base Hospital, Basra, Tuesday 15th June 1915*

Maud gripped her seat as they drove up to the main entrance of the hospital. Hoping he hadn't been too optimistic, Peter stopped the carriage and helped her down. He and Harry had carried John, more dead than alive, into the hospital. They'd stayed with him until a doctor had arrived but they hadn't needed a doctor to tell them the prognosis wasn't good. Harry had insisted on staying with John, so he'd offered to find Maud, delaying his departure only as long as it had taken him to borrow a carriage from the hospital administrator.

'Is John in the officers' ward?' Maud questioned impatiently when he climbed back on the carriage.

'Yes, but if you give me a moment to take the horses to the stable...'

Maud picked up her skirts and ran, barging into an orderly, almost knocking him over. 'Captain Mason?'

The orderly consulted the list he was holding with irritating slowness. 'We have no Captain Mason.'

'He came in with the casualties from Amara.'

'We have a Major Mason. Major John Mason. Indian Medical Corps.'

'Where is he?' Maud untied her apron and smoothed her ruffled dress.

'In the cubicle at the end of the ward. On the left.'

Maud raced on, only to crash into an officer who was walking down the aisle between the beds. She muttered an apology and tried to pass, but he gripped her hand.

'Maud, it's Harry.'

'Harry, it's good to see you, but I have to go to John.'

'The doctors are with him. Let's sit somewhere quiet.' Pulling her away from the curious stares of the patients, he led her out on the veranda that overlooked the Shatt. The air inside the ward was hot, humid, and heavy; outside it was unbearable, but private.

'How is he?' she begged.

'He has a fever, but all the doctors I've spoken to have said they've seen worse. He also has a few cuts and bruises so he doesn't look very pretty.'

'Cuts and bruises? I don't understand.'

'He passed out in the mess, fell on a whisky glass, and it broke in his face. Maud, you can see him in a minute but I need to talk to you first.' He led her to a cane bench and sat alongside her. 'The worst thing is his lack of strength. The march from Ahwaz to the Kerkha was rough. It's even hotter up country than it is here, and there weren't enough supplies. In fact, there wasn't enough of anything except sick, and you know John. He worked day and night.'

'He's going to die, isn't he?'

'He's weak and he needs a lot of care. But

there's something else. I might be treading on sensitive ground, and you can shout at me if you want, but not John. Something's been worrying him. I'm not sure what,' he lied. 'But I think it's to do with you. If he'd been conscious, I'd never have got him here. He didn't have to go to Amara. Our column divided on the Kerkha and he was offered the chance to return to Ahwaz and from there to Basra. When we reached Amara, Charles and I tried to persuade him to put in for leave but he insisted on volunteering for the Euphrates expedition. He spoke about your letters – said he didn't know you any more. When we met up with Charles and Charles told him you were in Basra, I hoped it might make a difference, but it didn't. If anything, it made John worse.'

'He doesn't want to see me.' It wasn't a question.

'I'm sure he does really, Maud,' Harry said gently. 'But war has a strange effect on people. John's been at the sharp end for months. In Ahwaz, I saw him amputating limbs under fire. Dragging the wounded in himself when the stretcher-bearers were hit. We've all changed, John more than most. I'm sure he needs you. If I didn't believe that, I wouldn't have brought him here. But he needs careful handling. He's not the husband you waved goodbye to in India.'

'I'm not the wife.'

'I don't know what's happened between you, and I don't want to. But I'm as close to John as I am to my brother. You meant everything to him a short time ago. I've been lucky enough to know how that feels and I hoped if I brought him here, you could put whatever's wrong right.'

'Thank you, Harry. It couldn't have been easy for you to say that.'

'I have to make my report. As soon as I'm through, I'll return. Perhaps we can dine together. I know you won't want to leave John, but you have to eat.'

'Thank you, I'd like that.'

He left her on the veranda. Whatever problems lay between John and Maud he'd given them the chance to sort them out. They had one another, and a short time to call their own. He wished he and Furja were as fortunate.

*Mission, Basra, Tuesday 15th June 1915*

Angela was writing on the blackboard with her back to her class when she sensed restlessness.

'Silence!' When the whispering didn't stop, she whirled around to see Peter watching her through the window.

'Class, get out your readers.' Slamming the classroom door behind her, she ran into Peter's arms. Without looking to see if anyone was around, she returned his kiss.

'Do you think Reverend Butler could marry us this evening?'

She wrapped her arms around his chest. 'It'll have to be a late ceremony. The Reverend's visiting the Qurna mission. He won't be back until after ten.'

'I can just about hold out until then.'

She looked into his eyes. 'I'm not sure I can.'

*Base Hospital, Basra, Tuesday 15th June 1915*

Reed blinds closed out the twilight. A fan whirred monotonously overhead, stirring the sluggish air. John lay on his back, his head bandaged, his body covered by a sheet. His skin was pallid, tinged with a greenish hue.

If it hadn't been for the perspiration, Maud could have believed she was holding the hand of a corpse. She hadn't left him since the doctors had allowed her in.

Harry had prepared her for sickness, but not this gaunt, skeletal state. If only – the saddest words in the language. If only she had followed John the moment Basra had fallen. If only she hadn't thrown herself at Geoffrey Brooke; allowed Miguel D'Arbez to seduce her; lost her head with Charles–

John moved. She wrung out a cloth in a bowl of iced water and placed it on his forehead. The small noises of the ward found their way into the cubicle. Men coughing and muttering in delirium. The clink of enamel bowls as orderlies washed ulcerated skin. A doctor had called in earlier to confirm John's fever had broken. He told her John was one of the lucky ones. Leave, rest, feeding up, and he'd be ready to go out and get himself in the same state all over again.

John's eyes flickered open. He stared at Maud, disorientated. This wasn't the glittering, golden Maud of his dreams. This Maud was soberly dressed in grey, her face pale, unsmiling, a frown creasing her forehead.

'Maud?' he croaked. 'Don't go, not this time, please.'

'I'm not going anywhere, darling.' She laid her hand against his cheek. He looked at her again and realised he wasn't dreaming. Then he remembered.

He gave her a look of utter contempt and turned his face to the wall.

*Basra, Tuesday 15th June 1915*

Harry walked along, musing over his superior's generosity. While he hadn't exactly been granted leave, he'd been given permission to visit the Karun and deliver passports to friendly tribes. Blank forms he could fill in, designating the holder an inhabitant of the British occupied territories of Mesopotamia. Forms that could prove useful to Shalan should a British Army patrol stumble across his camp, and, he hoped, prove to the Sheikh that the Turks wouldn't be returning.

Lamps were being lit in streets and houses. The heat was leaving the ground and rising towards the clear, star-shot sky. By the standards of the day, it was cool. He passed a fruit seller and bought a basket of oranges and fresh dates. Entering the hospital from the veranda, he found the ward in semi-darkness, the only light a shaded lamp on the orderly's desk. The orderly pointed to his watch. It took five minutes of rank pulling before the man would allow him into John's cubicle.

John was awake and alone; his eyes fever bright, almost luminous in the gloom.

'Brought you fruit.' Harry dumped the basket on the locker. 'But for God's sake don't eat it until it's been peeled, or you'll get cholera on top of everything else.'

'If I had the strength I'd knock your brains out.'

'Any reason in particular?' Harry found it difficult to keep up the pretence of good spirits in the face of John's wasted body.

'They told me how I got here.'

'We all agreed you'd have a better chance of pulling through if you were in Basra.'

'So you, Charles, and Knight conspired to bring me here.'

'Conspired is strong. Smythe and I carried you on board a river boat and looked after you until we reached here.' He glanced around. 'Where's Maud?'

'I don't know,' John replied in a tone that said he didn't care.

'I don't know what you heard but if there was anything between Maud and Brooke, Brooke's dead. Damn it, I'd forgive Furja anything if she was there waiting for me as Maud was for you today.'

'That's easy for you to say. Furja hasn't been sleeping in another man's bed.'

'The man's dead.'

'One man is dead. God alone knows how many others there were.'

Harry lit two cigarettes and placed one in John's mouth. 'There are a lot of gossipmongers who like nothing better than stirring up trouble.'

'Remember that bundle of letters you found next to Brooke? You wouldn't have given them to me if you'd read them.'

Harry rammed the heel of his hand against his forehead.

'You weren't to know.'

'I should have looked at them.'

'You had no reason to.'

Harry lifted the blinds and peered out at the Shatt. 'Have you spoken to Maud about them?'

'I sent them to her. She knows I did.'

'What can I do?'

'Get me out of here.'

'You wouldn't reach the door.'

'Then keep Maud away from me.'

'I'll tell her to stay away if that's what you want.'

'Wouldn't it be what you'd want if it was your wife?'

'No.'

'Then you're a different man from me.'

'I'm nearly a foot shorter, for a start.'

'Why can I never be angry with you for long?' John's voice was hoarse with the effort it cost him to speak.

'Because I'm charming.'

'I can't cope with her apologies, Harry.'

'I'll tell her. I'll call in tomorrow before I leave. I'll be gone a week so I expect to see you well when I get back. Is there anything else I can do?'

'No.' John closed his eyes.

'Can I tell her that you'll talk to her later?'

John turned on his side. 'Tell her whatever you want, Harry, as long as I don't have to agree with it or see her again.'

# Chapter Twenty-six

*Basra, Tuesday 15th June 1915*

Peter Smythe was waiting for Harry when he left the hospital. His uniform had been cleaned and he couldn't stop smiling.

'When are you bolting on the shackles?' Harry asked.

'Not till 11, when the Reverend returns from Qurna. Maud's helping Angela dress. She sent a message to say she's sorry but she can't make dinner. If you're free, I'd like you to be best man. There isn't anyone else around to do the honours.'

'Put like that, how can I refuse?'

'I was hoping we could dine together. I've been ordered out of the mission until half past ten. Something about bridegrooms getting in the way.'

'Abdul does a nice line in roast chickens, or did the last time I was here.'

'Angela and I had a hard time persuading her brother to hold the ceremony so late.' Peter followed Harry down an alley. 'Theo wanted to postpone it until tomorrow but I told him I couldn't be sure I'd be in Basra tomorrow. Having no official leave makes it impossible to forecast how long I'll be here.'

'A week.'

'Are you sure?' Peter's grin widened.

'I've been given until the 23rd to deliver dispatches to the Karun. As my aide you should come with me, but I dare say I can find pressing duties which necessitate your presence here.'

'I'll never forget you for this, Harry.'

'Afterwards you can remain my aide or return to your unit but I won't be returning to Amara. I've been ordered to the Euphrates.'

'There's likely to be more action on the Euphrates. I'd rather stay with you.'

'Haven't you had enough of fighting?'

'I've hardly seen any action. Amara fell like a ripe plum. And it's not action I'm after, it's promotion. A married man has to look to the future.'

'Dear God, if this is what you're like before you tie the knot, what are you going to be like after?'

An hour later, with a chicken apiece under their belts, Harry and Peter made their way to Harry's room in Abdul's. Harry closed the door and produced a couple of bottles of Chianti.

'Sorry about having to drink in here but, lack of wine aside, you have to admit the meal was better than anything we could have got in the mess.'

'How much longer do we have to wait?' Peter sat on the only chair.

'Bridegroom getting nervous?'

'Guilty.'

'That's why bridegrooms have a best man. To do the worrying for them.' Harry uncorked a bottle and filled a couple of porcelain coffee cups. 'To the bride and groom, Mrs and Mrs Smythe, in–' he opened his pocket watch '–two hours. If you give me the ring, I promise to deliver you almost sober and on time.'

'The ring!'

'You haven't bought one?'

'I gave Angela an engagement ring but I haven't even thought about a wedding ring.'

'We'll walk to the mission via the bazaar. You have her ring size?'

Peter shook his head.

'We'll just have to hazard a guess. Where are you honeymooning?'

'In the mission.'

'In heaven's name, man, no one honeymoons in a mission.'

'There isn't anywhere else,' Peter protested.

Harry produced a key. 'Would you believe that acting lieutenant-colonels are entitled to their own bungalow? I'm comfortable here, but I thought a certain captain might find a use for it.'

'Harry, I'm your slave for life.' Peter reached for the key, but Harry held it back.

'It's yours for a consideration. Call in on John every day until I get back. Get him whatever he wants within reason after taking medical advice.'

'Is that all?'

'For someone on honeymoon, that's more than enough.' Harry handed over the key.

*The Mission, Basra, Tuesday 15th June 1915*

The ceremony passed so swiftly for Angela she didn't feel married when it was over. Maud and Mrs Butler kissed her and offered their congratulations. Harry, Peter, and Theo shook hands. Angela stood for a moment, then looked down at her hand.

'It's beautiful, Angela.' Maud admired the ring Peter had placed on her finger.

'I didn't even know he'd bought a wedding ring until Harry took it from his pocket.' Angela fingered the plain gold band.

'Is it too big?' Peter asked, concerned that she might not be happy with his choice.

'It's beautiful and fits perfectly.' Angela stood on tiptoe and kissed his cheek.

'Photographs,' Doctor Picard called.

Harry offered Maud his arm.

The doctor was an exacting photographer. After an hour spent posing in front of the camera, thoughts turned towards the half-dozen bottles of champagne Harry had provided. Corks popped, toasts were drunk, then, on the stroke of midnight, Harry heard the sound he'd been waiting for.

'The honeymoon chariot. Twenty minutes late.' Harry returned his watch to his pocket. 'Which means the stable sepoy has been using it to ferry customers to Abdul's again. If you find some rice, Maud, we can wave goodbye to the happy couple before everyone falls asleep.'

'Aren't you staying here?' Theo asked Peter.

'Harry found us a bungalow and arranged a week's leave for me. It's amazing the difference a lieutenant-colonel's rank pulling can make to a humble captain.'

'You darling.' Angela hugged Harry.

'Steady, Downe, that's my wife.'

'Then take her from me. If the bride would care to pack we can break up the party.'

After Angela and Maud had disappeared, Harry picked up the last bottle of champagne and carried it over to Peter.

'I've asked an Arab I know to sort things in the bungalow. He'll call every day, but he won't be there until midday tomorrow. I thought you'd appreciate a lie-in after all this.'

Peter turned crimson above his collar.

Harry had difficulty concealing his amusement at Peter's blushes. 'He'll do your shopping, cooking, cleaning and washing. He's discreet and he'll clear off when he's not wanted, which is an advantage when you only have a week to get acquainted with your wife. He also has a pass for the barracks so you don't have to bother about that. I've paid his wages in advance so don't go tipping him or he'll expect double rate next time I want him to work for me.'

'How can I ever repay you?'

'Call it a wedding present. You won't forget about John?'

'I won't.'

Harry held out his hand. 'See you in a week.'

Angela and Peter drove off in a shower of rice and shouted congratulations. When the carriage rounded the corner, Harry waylaid Maud.

'Can I take you home?'

'This is home. I moved in here when Mrs Hale sailed for England.'

Harry glanced around the garden. The Reverend, Mrs Butler, and Doctor Picard were walking back inside. A servant was sweeping the rice from the path. Theo was nowhere to be seen.

411

'I'd like to talk to you, Maud, and I'm leaving in the morning.'

Maud led Harry into Angela's classroom. She left the door open; the light from the hallway would be illumination enough for what she sensed he had to say.

'I spoke to John. I'm sorry; he doesn't want to see you. Not for a while.'

'It's all right, Harry. You don't have to embarrass yourself. I can imagine the message John asked you to deliver.'

'He's sick, Maud. Sick and tired. He'll feel differently when he's recovered.'

She toyed with her wedding ring, pulling it on and off her finger. 'Unfortunately, whatever John told you about me is true. He has every right to shut me out of his life.'

'He's so ill he doesn't know what he wants. He loved you, and whatever you've done, I'm sure he will again. Perhaps in time...'

'Time won't make a difference.' She gripped his hand. 'John gave you a foul job and you've done it tactfully. Will you take a message back? Tell him if he wants a divorce, I won't put any obstacles in his way, and if it will make things easier, I'll return the letters I wrote to Geoffrey Brooke. They should provide evidence enough for any judge.'

'Maud...'

'Please, don't make things worse by offering hope where there is none, Harry. Give him the message and if he'll listen, tell him I love him. I always loved him but didn't discover how much until it was too late. And it is too late, Harry. For both of us.' She pressed something into his hand

and walked away. When he opened his fingers, he was holding her wedding ring.

*Base, Basra, early hours Wednesday 16th June 1915*

'Are you sure this is the bungalow?' Angela asked. 'There's a light burning.'

'It's the right bungalow. Harry's engaged a servant for us.' Peter handed the key to the sepoy who'd driven the landau and asked him to carry Angela's bags inside. He waited until the sepoy returned, then slipped him a couple of coins.

'Right, Mrs Smythe.' He swung Angela into his arms. 'I'm going to carry you over the threshold.'

'Don't be ridiculous.'

'Ssh, you'll disturb the neighbours. Captains aren't supposed to be in bungalows. Harry's relying on us to stay indoors for the week. And, Mrs Smythe, I'll have you know there's nothing ridiculous about tradition. It's unlucky for brides to trip as they enter their new home. Even if it is only home for a week.'

'But it's fine for bridegrooms to trip on their way to the altar.'

'I wish Maud hadn't told you that.' Peter carried her up the veranda steps and through the front door. Kicking the door shut behind him, he kissed her when he lowered her to the floor. A lamp burned on a side table next to a bucket containing an extravagant amount of ice and a bottle of champagne. A note was pinned to the cork.

*You've only a week, so make the most of it.*

He opened the bottle and the cork flew, hitting

413

the ceiling. 'That's a sign of good luck.' He filled
the glasses, and handed her one. 'It's very late.'
He turned aside when he realised the implication
of what he'd said.

'We could take the champagne to the bedroom.'

He picked up the bucket and lamp and carried
them through. A vase containing a single red
flower stood next to the bed.

Angela took the lace from her hair and laid it on
a chair. 'Would you unfasten my dress, please?'

Peter had never felt so ham-fisted when he
eased the rounded buttons from their tiny loops.
After he freed the last one, he averted his eyes
from the chemise of ivory satin and lace he'd
uncovered. 'I'll go into the other room.'

Angela laid a restraining hand on his arm.
'Please stay, we can undress together.'

He turned his back to her and unbuckled his
belt. The rustle of silk resounded in the stillness.
Angela opened her valise, the door closed, and he
realised she'd gone into the bathroom. He rummaged in his kitbag for his nightshirt. Tearing off
all his clothes except his drawers, he managed to
pull it over his head before she returned. When he
went into the bathroom, he heard the creak of
bedsprings as she slid between the sheets.

He washed, cleaned his teeth, and debated
whether to drink more champagne. Until Angela,
he'd never been much of one for the ladies. Now
he wished he'd been more like Harry or Charles.
Neither of them would waste time in the bathroom while their brides waited.

Deciding against the champagne, he returned to
the bedroom. Turning out the lamp, he fumbled

his way to the bed. Folding back the sheets, he sat on the mattress. Angela wrapped her arms around his neck and kissed him. The gesture gave him the courage he needed to lay beside her.

'I've never done anything like this before,' she whispered, snuggling close. 'So if I make a hash of it, you'll give me a second chance to put things right, won't you?'

'I love you, Mrs Smythe.'

'It's just as well you do, Captain Smythe, because I intend to be around to torment you for many, many years to come.'

## Chapter Twenty-seven

A cooling wind from the north blows across the broiling desert and steaming marshlands of Mesopotamia in the third week of June. The Shamal lasts for 40 days and nights. Without it, the summer would be even more unbearable for those forced to swelter through its suffocating hot, humid days and nights. For two months before, the land simmers beneath a relentless sun; in the final weeks the heat is so intense even the flies shrivel and die.

The men in the Expeditionary Force watched the flies depart with envy. If they'd been offered cast-iron proof of an afterlife furnished with cool breezes, running water, ice, and female company, there'd have been a frenzied dash to meet their maker.

A sense of anticipation hung in the searing air. For John, confined to a cot, the anticipation carried the hope of a return to health, if not spirits. For Charles, who'd been given the thankless task of dispensing justice in Amara until a British system could be introduced to replace the Ottoman courts, the advent of cooler weather promised a return to action. Maud waited for the Shamal in the hope it would cut the death rate that had grown alarmingly high in the hospital.

Wounds she fought to keep clean grew green and gangrenous. Theo and Doctor Picard operated day and night, cutting out infection and amputating limbs, and still patients died like the flies around them. She lost weight, sickened by the heat, the sights, the smells, and the waiting. Along with everyone else in Basra, the phrase on her lips was, 'When the Shamal comes.'

Only Peter and Angela dreaded its onset.

Their days had never passed more sweetly or quickly. Peter's imminent departure added poignancy to their honeymoon, making it all the more precious. At night, when they dined with the windows open and the fly-screens drawn, Angela gazed into her husband's eyes by candlelight that flickered low from lack of oxygen, knowing the whole of Basra waited for the wind, except them. For when the Shamal came, Peter would leave, and she could no longer imagine life without him.

*The Karun Valley, Saturday 19th June 1915*

Harry rode through the valley in temperatures of

416

over 130 degrees, and grew increasingly disillusioned with his capability to live like a native. Devon and Dorset, rested after their boat trip, bore the heat better than he did.

The river was low, the waters thick and murky, but both horses drank it and suffered no ill-effects. He travelled by night and rested during the day, although he rarely found shade. The sunlight shimmering over the land played tricks on his scorched eyes. Wizened bushes became Turkish squadrons; clumps of thorn, Arabs; the skin around his eyes reddened and blistered, cracking into sores that wept blood. His mind wavered with tides of heat that blurred his vision and roasted his body. He became preoccupied with finding Furja and wove elaborate, unworkable plots to take her from Shalan.

The second day out from Ahwaz, he fell in with a party of Bakhtairi Khans. They accorded him a traveller's rights; in return, he gave them passports. They asked if he knew a Ferenghi. The question pleased and disturbed him.

Had he become more Arab than British? Thanks to Mitkhal's tuition, Arab ways were now second nature and he felt more comfortable riding in silence with the natives than he did making small talk to stiff-necked officers like Cleck-Heaton.

The more he saw of the desert Arabs the more he admired them. The Bedouin, with their small bags of dates, skins of sour camel milk, and rusted rifles, could outride, outshoot, and outfight the best cavalry officers in any regiment.

He recalled what he had said to Charles in Amara. 'After the war. A reunion at Clyneswood.'

Would he ever live there again? The house in Basra and the tent he'd shared with Furja had been more home to him than Clyneswood ever had. Life with the Bedouin had stripped away the superfluous trappings of civilisation he'd fought against all his life. For the first time he knew exactly what he wanted. Yet he was powerless to do anything about it.

After two days, he parted company from the Khans. The plain stretched unbroken around him. Somewhere out there were his wife and daughters. If Shalan gave him the choice he would never leave them again, even at the cost of deserting the army and the war. Mounting Dorset, he picked up Devon's rein and swam the horses across the river. Mounting a bank, he saw the black dots on the horizon that he'd been searching for.

Kicking his heels into Dorset's flanks, he galloped forward. A mile from the camp, Shalan's men moved in. He slowed his pace and lifted his hands away from his weapons. A dozen warriors rode across his path, forcing him to halt.

'I've come to return Mitkhal's horse.' He pointed to Devon.

'Mitkhal left for Basra five days ago. His wife will take it.' Shalan reined in Devon.

Harry damned the impulse that had led Mitkhal to seek him as he was travelling through the desert, but Mitkhal's absence didn't deter him from attempting to bridge the estrangement between Shalan and himself. 'I've also brought passports.' He opened his saddlebag and pulled out a sheaf of papers. 'All the friends of my government are being given papers.'

Shalan drew his sword and speared one. 'They give us permission to live in our own land.'

'Not permission. They guarantee the holder safe passage through British lines.' Harry thrust a wad towards Shalan. 'I've signed them. All that needs to be done is for the name of the bearer to be written at the top. In English, or Arabic, either will suffice.'

'The last time you entered my village, I warned you were not welcome.' Shalan tore the passports and scattered the fragments. They drifted to the ground and lay curling in the heat. 'Your papers buy you nothing here. Why do you persist in returning when your presence offends me?'

'I came to see Mitkhal.'

'I told you he is not here.'

Harry was conscious that some of Shalan's men had dismounted and were closing in behind him, but weariness made him reckless.

'I would like to see my daughters and Furja.'

'Furja has married a Bedawi. She is no longer your concern, and nor are her daughters.'

'They are my children. I have the right to see them.'

Shalan swung his sword above Harry's head. 'Here, Ferenghis have no rights.'

Ignoring the sword, Harry caught Shalan's arm. 'You cannot take my family and give it to another. You cannot...' A hand gripped his shoulder. He turned and tried to swing a punch, but his fist was gripped in midair. His arms were wrenched and tied behind his back. He was dragged onto Dorset.

He clung with his thighs to the saddle as Dorset

419

galloped alongside the Arabs' horses. The midday sun beat down mercilessly and still they rode. No one spoke, no one rested. At nightfall, they halted beside the river. The Bedouin who'd led Dorset cut the bonds on Harry's wrists. Harry reclaimed his reins. Exhausted, Dorset tried to hobble down to the river, but Harry held her fast.

'Tell Shalan he's not seen the last of me. I'll be back, and next time I will see my children.'

'I think not, Ferenghi. Furja is now my wife. She and her daughters sleep in my harem. Should you ride into Shalan's camp again you will not escape.' Ali Mansur pulled a knife and ran the blade along his thumb, drawing blood. 'Next time we meet, I will take your head to decorate my tent pole. Your little ones will see it every morning when they leave to tend my flocks. Should you place no value on your own miserable carcass, I promise I will give Furja and your daughters a stripe every time I hear your name from today.' Wheeling his horse, he followed his companions back across the plain.

Sensing Harry's lack of concentration, Dorset cantered down to the water. Harry slid off her back and patted her head as she drank. Perhaps it was just as well he had a war to return to. If he didn't, he might go mad.

*Lansing Memorial Hospital,*
*Sunday 20th June 1915*

Maud grabbed the wall when the corridor floor rose in a wave of white tiles; someone lifted her

420

in the air. The head of an Arab orderly came into view. She heard him call for Theo. Then the world turned black.

When she came round, she was lying on a couch in Theo's office. Someone, she hoped it hadn't been Theo, had removed her dress, and covered her with a sheet. He was calling her name and she felt as though he was miles away.

'Mrs Mason, Maud, drink this.' A mixture of water and vinegar was lifted to her lips. Nauseous, unable to swallow, its tepid warmth trickled over her chin. Theo shouted for a kidney dish and held her head while she retched.

'Did you know before you started work here?'

'What?'

'Did you think we were so desperate for nurses we'd take a pregnant woman? Have you any idea of the damage exposure to infections could do to your child?' he reprimanded.

'I'm sorry.' Tears flowed from her eyes.

'If you don't rest you could lose the child. You've lost a little blood as it is.'

She flushed in embarrassment as she realised there was a pad between her legs.

'Perhaps that was your intention. It's obvious the child isn't your husband's. Basra is a small place. Everyone's talking about his refusal to see you.'

'It's none of your business,' she croaked.

'Your health is my business. I've arranged for you to be taken to the mission. There, you will stay in bed, until I give you permission to leave it. Pity, you had the makings of a good nurse.'

'I can be a nurse again.'

'With a child? Can you support yourself?'

'I have a little money and John's salary.'

'I don't think you can rely on that. Men can be finicky about the fatherhood of their wives' children.' He washed his hands. 'Is there any point in asking whose child it is?'

'The child is mine, Dr Wallace.'

'The father's health is a factor to be considered.'

'He was healthy enough when I last saw him.'

'Does he know?'

'That's a peculiar question considering I've only just found out myself.'

'He'll have to support you.'

She couldn't bear the condemnation in his eyes, so she said the one thing she hoped would stir his pity. 'I was raped. Last May. By an officer. Before you ask, I never saw him before, I haven't seen him since, and I never want to see him again.'

'Where did this attack take place?' His tone was sceptical.

'I went to an officers' lodging house the evening before the Amara expedition left. It was a stupid thing to do, but I was hoping to find someone to carry a letter to John. The man... He wasn't living there, only visiting, Colonel Hale found out that much.'

She averted her eyes lest Theo read too much in her expression. The colonel's death meant her version of the facts would never be questioned, but this was the first time she'd told the story she'd threatened Charles with. 'I was hurt. Not badly, just bruises, and my dress was torn. Colonel Hale treated me. I asked him to keep the whole thing quiet because I was ashamed. I didn't want any gossip but most of all I wanted to spare John...'

This time her tears were genuine. A child. She was having a child her husband could and would publicly disown.

'You want this baby?' he asked in a marginally kinder tone.

'Is there an alternative?'

'No legal one.' He went to the door. 'I'll order an ambulance.'

After Theo left, she considered the life within her. A separate entity. A child, and as she'd told Theo, her child. It wouldn't be John's, but then she'd never carry his child, not now.

If she had a girl, the baby might go a little way towards filling the aching void left by her mother. Given the father's colouring, she should be a golden one.

Placing her hands over her stomach, Maud gazed out of the window. Then she realised the palms were stirring alongside the river. The Shamal had arrived.

## Chapter Twenty-eight

*Basra, Wednesday 23rd June 1915*

Harry rode into HQ in the early hours. After seeing Dorset stabled, he walked to Abdul's and spent a fruitless ten minutes searching for Mitkhal before a servant told him that, under the impression he'd been ordered to Qurna, the Arab had left Basra that morning. Cursing, he went to his room, stripped off, and bathed before falling into bed.

When he woke, the sun and temperature were high, although nowhere near as hell-like as the Karun Valley. He breakfasted on dates before donning his uniform and returning to HQ.

The sleepy post of ten months earlier had been transformed into a bustling Army camp that housed thousands. He was shown into his superior's office, gave a brief account of the situation in Karun, omitting all mention of Shalan's hostility, and was ordered to join General Gorringe's expedition to Nasiriyeh. He headed for his bungalow. Farik opened the door, greeting him with a hugely welcoming grin.

'Ubbatan...'

'Have you heard from your master?' Harry questioned.

'You know Sheikh Ibn Shalan, Ubbatan. He never leaves the desert.'

'His daughter?'

'I have heard no news of my master nor my lady.'

'I'm leaving today. Finish what you have to do here. Afterwards, should anyone ask, including your master, you have not seen me since last October.' Harry handed him a couple of gold sovereigns.

Peter emerged, napkin in hand, from the dining room. 'I thought I heard Farik talking to someone. It's marvellous to see you. Join us for lunch. Farik has made the most delicious rice and tinned ham pilaff. There's plenty to spare.' Peter

424

showed him into the dining room.

Angela's initial smile of pleasure clouded when she realised why he'd come. 'You're leaving, and you're taking Peter with you?'

'I have to leave for Qurna today but I can find enough paperwork – genuine paperwork this time, I'm afraid – to keep Peter occupied here until the 26th. I dare not stretch it any longer with the push to Nasiriyeh starting.' He looked at Peter's smiling face and wondered why his friend's happiness cut so deep. Had he become so dog in the manger he couldn't bear to see another man enjoying the pleasures of married life that had been denied him?

'Thank you for giving us a few more days.' Angela left the table to fetch extra cutlery and crockery. 'Peter told me how many strings you had to pull to organise him any time at all.'

'It's my policy to use all the power that comes with this uniform before the brass realise their mistake and take it off me. How's John?' He helped himself to rice.

Peter looked away.

'He's not worse?' Harry rose.

'No, sit down. John's making a good recovery.'

'It's Maud,' Angela interrupted. 'She's ill and going to need some looking after for a while. They're taking care of her at the mission, but she should be with her family.'

'She only has her father and John.' Harry sipped the wine Peter poured for him. 'What's wrong with her?'

'Woman's trouble,' Angela explained. 'Nothing serious, but it will take her a while to recover. I'll

425

take care of her.'

'Are you going to continue teaching?'

'Yes. The Reverend Butler won't be able to find a replacement for me while the war's on and–' she smiled at Peter '–I don't want to leave the mission until it's over.'

'I may be able to get someone to look after Maud.' Harry recalled Emily's maid, Harriet. 'If I can, will you be able to put her up at the mission?'

'If it was someone capable of nursing Maud, we'd find the space. All the staff are working either in the school or the hospital and Theo can't put Maud in the Lansing because of the risk of infection.'

'I'll see what I can do. If you need someone and her father's not around–' he avoided all mention of John '–contact me in Qurna. I've only just enough time to visit John before I leave. Tell Maud I'll call the next time I'm in Basra.'

He said his goodbyes and left, not only because time was short. He'd heard Farik moving in the next room, turning down beds and pulling blinds against the midday heat. It reminded him too much of the house in the Arab quarter – and Furja.

John wasn't quite as gaunt and hollow-eyed as when Harry had last seen him. He was sitting up in bed reading an old copy of the *Westminster Gazette* Peter had scrounged.

'The wanderer returns.'

'Both wanderers.' Harry sat on John's bed. 'I thought you were heading for Hades at one point back there, Major Mason.'

426

'How long are you here?'

'Until this afternoon. I've been attached to Gorringe's force in Qurna.'

'And from there to Nasiriyeh?' John guessed.

'That information is classified.'

'A couple of days in this place will teach you nothing is classified. Someone should invite the staff here so they can hear the outcome of their decisions before they make them. It would save them hours of briefings and meetings.'

'Why should you want to spare them pain?'

'You're quite right. The staff deserve all the agony they get. Good luck, I wish I was going with you.'

'If Nasiriyeh falls as easily as Amara we won't need luck. Do you feel as reasonable as you look?' Harry asked.

'I'm weak, but on the mend. I'll be up in a week or so.'

'Don't push it. I know you. You'll be working here tomorrow.' Harry took out his cigarettes. 'I'm sorry, but I have to talk to you about Maud.'

'You've spoken to her?'

'Before I left for the Karun.' He handed John Maud's wedding ring. 'She asked me to tell you she'll agree to a divorce, and if it will help she'll give you Brooke's letters. She also said she's sorry and she never stopped loving you.'

John dropped the ring onto the bedside table, filched a cigarette, and picked up a box of matches.

'There's something else. Peter and Angela have told me she's ill.'

'Has she tried to do something stupid? Take her

own life?'

'Angela said it was woman's trouble. She asked if there was any family she could contact. I told her there was only Perry and you, but I wondered about Harriet.'

'Charles said he brought her here when he brought Maud but she married a sergeant in the Artillery a couple of days after they arrived.'

'I'll try and track her down.'

'If you succeed, ask her if she'll look after Maud. I'll pay her wages. Maud's still my wife and I won't see her sick and destitute. I'll carry on supporting her until she finds another fool to marry.'

'I didn't doubt you would. I'm sorry things didn't work out.'

'How's Angela?' John asked. 'If she's half as happy as Peter looks, she must be ecstatic.'

'She is ecstatic.' Harry rose. 'Take your time convalescing. I spoke to the doctor. You could go back to India for a spell.'

'I'll think about it.'

'Do more than think. Enjoy a leave for both of us. And for God's sake, take care of yourself.'

After Harry left, John swung his legs to the floor. He stood for a few seconds holding onto the bedhead. Cursing his weakness, he sank back down. Yesterday he hadn't managed to rise. He was getting stronger.

He wished his progress wasn't so damned slow. The doctors were rushed off their feet. They'd been short-staffed to begin with, and their numbers had been further depleted by death and sickness. With another show coming, they needed all the medical men they could get. He lay back and returned to the *Westminster Gazette*. He began a short story by Saki, a writer who never failed to amuse him, but he didn't digest a word he read. His thoughts kept returning to Maud.

Sick and alone in the mission. One way or another, he had to sort out what was left of his marriage.

## Qurna, Sunday 27th June 1915

Negotiating his way past the troops on the quayside, Mitkhal carried Harry's satchel of Arab clothing and empty milk skin on board the *Shushan*. He entered the cabin, found a narrow bench at the stern end, and stowed the kit beneath it. A few minutes later, Harry arrived with Smythe.

'You're fools to travel on this boat.' Mitkhal eyed the guns strapped to the deck on makeshift angle iron frameworks. 'At the first sign of trouble someone will attempt to fire those and blow this vessel to Paradise.'

'Nonsense, she's perfectly sound,' Harry scoffed, kicking a hole in the outside planking of her cabin. 'Grace said she was built for the relief of Khartoum. That only makes her 26. A baby in Expeditionary Force terms.'

'Look what happened to Gordon,' Peter griped, depressed by his separation from Angela.

'Gordon was killed before this little darling was able to get to him.' Grace signalled his presence to the deck officer. 'I hope you gentlemen enjoy the ride. The army likes watching the navy work in this war.'

'The trouble with the navy is that its officers call punting through the marshes work,' Harry shouted back as he walked down the gangplank with Mitkhal. 'You know what to do?' he whispered in Arabic.

'Return to Shalan and spirit Furja, Gutne, and the children to Basra.'

'I know it won't be easy for you to give up your right to live with the tribe.' Harry clasped his friend's hand. 'I wish I was free to go with you.'

'We've been through this, Harry. If Ali Mansur sees you, he'll not only kill you, he'll harm Furja. Trust me. I am better off doing this without you.'

'You have the bank draft?'

Mitkhal patted the fold of his gumbaz over his heart.

'You'll buy them a house somewhere safe?'

'As safe as I can find. I'll leave a message for you at the mission with Mrs Smythe. I've promised you all this a hundred times, Harry, what more can I do?'

'Nothing. Thank you.' Harry embraced Mitkhal, much to the chagrin of Perry and Cleck-Heaton, who were boarding a launch.

'Go; fight your war, Harry.' Mitkhal looked again at the *Shushan*. 'For once, I'm glad I'm not going with you.'

'Tell Furja the minute I can, I'll come for her. We'll go away and I'll never leave her again.'

Mitkhal left, and Peter called to Harry. He waved his hand and shook his head. Ignoring his fellow officers, he stood, staring at the *Odin* and *Espiegle* berthed in front of them. Misunderstanding his wave, Grace and Smythe joined him.

'Beautiful, isn't it?' Grace mopped his brow.

'What?' Smythe asked.

'The scenery, you philistine, we're getting a free Cook's tour.'

'The natives don't shoot at people on a Cook's tour.'

'Ah, but that adds to the excitement. What do you think, Harry?'

'I think this bloody war can't end soon enough for me,' Harry answered.

The engines wheezed, the gangplanks were heaved on board, and the *Odin* and *Espiegle* moved out in front of the flotilla. After a noisy wait, the *Shushan* rode into their wake. Smythe returned to the cabin leaving Harry on deck.

Impenetrable thickets of reeds surrounded them on three sides. To the west lay the open expanse of the Hammar Lake, sprinkled with tiny green islands. On one or two, Harry spotted the peaks of reed huts and the curl of cook-fire smoke. As they chugged up channel, they disturbed herds of water buffaloes. Flocks of ducks and marsh birds screeched and rose in flapping clouds. Once, Harry spied the graceful shape of a mashuf trailing fish traps of date stalks and reeds.

At midday, they left the *Odin* and *Espiegle* at Kubaish. The waterway had narrowed and could no longer accommodate their bows. Half an hour after the gunships disappeared over the horizon, three Turkish launches fired on the flotilla, and Harry had a taste of standing on deck when the guns that had concerned Mitkhal let rip.

431

He closed his eyes as the boat shook from port to stern. Surprised to find the vessel intact when he opened them, he saw the tail end of the launches fleeing across the lake. To add insult to injury, Grace recognised two of them as British-built vessels from Thornycroft's that he'd helped deliver to the Turks before the war.

Joining the others in the cabin, Harry stretched out on a mat. The air was stale and moist. He couldn't move without touching someone. The light that filtered through the portholes turned from harsh white to soft gold. The smell of oil and body odours faded as he stole into an idyll of Furja and flower-strewn courtyards, but before he could savour the images, the flotilla came to a juddering halt.

'Akaika dam,' Grace shouted.

Everyone left the cabin and gazed at the dam that narrowed the only navigable waterway from the Tigris to the Euphrates to a slender canal. Amid much shouting and military salutes, Perry and Cleck-Heaton left their launch in a row boat and, after a cursory inspection, pronounced the barrier a hotchpotch affair that a few charges of gun cotton would demolish.

Harry borrowed Smythe's field glasses and studied the barricade of compacted mud, old canoes, and rotting logs that held the four-foot difference in water level between the Euphrates and Hammar waterway. He'd seen too many rickety Arab concoctions to dismiss them out of hand. Handing back the glasses, he returned to his pallet.

Smythe woke him four hours later for a dinner

of bully beef, dates, and stale bread washed down by warm beer and Chianti. They could hear the curses of the sappers working on the dam, and they were still cursing at midnight. While the men around him snored, Harry tossed on his mat, imagining Mitkhal's journey from Qurna to the Karun.

He fell into a deep sleep as dawn rose and woke to the sound of cheering, almost drowned out by the roaring of water. Smythe was standing over him. 'We've breached it. Come and see.'

A great surge of water poured through the hole the sappers had made in the mud and wood wall.

'Guess what?' Grace shouted. 'We're going to tow the boats upstream.'

Peter stared at the raging torrent. 'Against that?'

Grace flexed his biceps. 'Tug of war. Navy against army, the Hampshires and Pioneers are already lining up.'

'Political officers don't play tug of war.' Harry flicked the cigarette he'd been smoking over the side. 'Only party games like hide and seek and murder.'

'My father taught me that officers and gentlemen never play party games. Only games where skill and strength can win the day.'

'Ah, but we don't play our games with officers and gentlemen, only Turks and Arabs.' Harry grabbed his saddlebag and jumped over the side.

*Basra, Tuesday 28th June 1915*

Maud sat in front of her open bedroom window.

433

Outside, a breeze ruffled the orange trees Mrs Butler had planted during her first spring in Basra. The stray cats Angela fed despite Theo's graphic warnings about rabies played with the morning shadows, chasing the movements of clouds and birds as they flitted across the dry, leprous grass, all the gardener could grow during the hot, dry months.

She opened the jewel case on her lap. Laid out on indented beds of cream velvet were the ruby and diamond necklace, tiara, ring, earrings and bracelets she'd been given, or, as Charles had put it, 'earned' in India.

She picked up one of the earrings and held it to the light. Miguel had assured her the gems were perfect. She had no reason to doubt his word. Even allowing for the vagaries of wartime, the set should bring in enough to keep her and the child for a few years and hopefully, by then, her situation would change. She closed the box and locked it with a tiny key she wore on her watch chain. If anyone could get a good price for the jewellery, Harry would, but it could be months before he returned, and by then her girth would put paid to any claim she had on his friendship.

A knock at the door interrupted her. Angela came in. She glimpsed a figure hovering in the passage.

'Dr Mason is here.' Angela didn't know why Maud and John were estranged, only that they were, and the knowledge made her uncomfortable in John's presence.

Maud braced herself. 'Please, show him in.' She'd written to John the day Theo had told her he was making a good recovery, asking him to call on her before he left Basra. Even as she'd penned the letter, she'd assumed John would disappear back to the war and not bother to contact her again until he could get in touch with his lawyers.

Angela left and Maud heard John's voice. She patted her hair and straightened the front of her dress, grateful he hadn't come a few days earlier when she'd still been in bed. He entered, leaving the door open behind him.

He looked fitter than when she'd last seen him, but he was still a shadow of the man she'd fallen in love with. His cheeks were sallow and he was painfully thin, but his step was firm, and his eyes clear – clear, hard, and unforgiving, she decided, reading reproach in their depth.

'It's good of you to come. Please, sit down.'

Careful to keep six feet of tiled floor between them, he placed a chair in front of hers.

'Aren't you being ridiculously formal?'

'What other way would you like me to be?' He laid his topee and swagger stick on the table.

'I'm sorry. It was a stupid thing to say.'

'You wrote that you had something important to tell me.'

She tried to meet his gaze, but failed. His presence in the intimate surroundings of her bedroom recalled too many memories. She stared down at the grain of the leather on the jewel case. 'There's no easy way to tell you this, John. I'm desperately sorry. The last thing I want to do is hurt you.'

'You should have thought of that before you slept with Brooke.'

435

His bitterness gave her courage. 'I'm going to have a baby in late January or early February.'

He laughed. A short, sardonic outburst that chilled her blood. 'Congratulations.'

'You have every right to hate me.'

'That's generous of you.'

'Please, there are things that need to be said. I'm not going to ask you for anything but I do want you to listen to me for a few minutes.'

'You have them.' He picked up his swagger stick and ran his fingers down its length.

Mustering her courage, she looked him in the eye. 'What I've done is unforgivable. The least I can do is absolve you of responsibility for me. I don't expect you to support me any longer, or recognise me as your wife.'

'New role for you, isn't it? Maud, the martyr. How do you intend to live? I realise this is a charitable institution–' he glanced at the wooden cross that hung on the wall behind her bed '–but I thought even Presbyterians baulked at condoning the fruits of sin.'

'I have enough money to support myself until the baby's born. When it's old enough I intend to work. I don't need your salary. I haven't cashed the army bank drafts for the past three months.' She indicated a package on her bedside table. 'The drafts are all there, and Geoffrey's last letter to me and my letters to him. I don't know much about legal matters but they should provide you with enough evidence to divorce me.' He made no move to take it, so she tossed the parcel onto the bed. 'I wanted to give you that, and apologise for the pain I've caused.'

436

'The father of the child is going to support you?'

'No, I won't be seeing him again.'

'Then another man has stepped in. I take my hat off to him. Most men are too fastidious to take responsibility for another man's bastard.'

'There's no one. I've caused enough misery. I intend to live quietly with my child.'

'Do I know the father?'

She saw torment in his eyes and couldn't add to it. 'No, John, you don't know him.'

'Brooke died months ago,' he cried out.

'It's not Brooke.'

'Dear God, how many men have there been?' His face contorted in anguish. 'No – don't answer that. I don't want to know. Just tell me why. Why climb into Brooke's bed, or any man's, for that matter? I thought we had something special, something – damn it all, I loved you.'

'And I loved you. I didn't mean for it to happen, but you weren't there. I was alone – lonely. I missed you, your warmth ... your loving. One minute you were in bed with me every night and afternoon, the next – nothing. I didn't know when, if ever, I'd see you again. It's not an excuse, only an explanation.' Drained, she leant back in her chair.

He rose and picked up the package.

'Take care of yourself. You deserve someone better than me. After the war I hope you find her.'

He looked at her. A step would have brought him to her side. He lifted his hand as though he were going to touch her. Instead, he turned his back. He walked through the door and closed it behind him. She followed the echo of his footsteps as he headed down the passage and into the front hall.

John waved to Angela as he climbed into Harry's Landau. The sepoy whipped the horses and drove down the street. The interview had been easier than he'd expected. Maud had been most accommodating. He was free. He owed her nothing, financially or emotionally. She had given him everything he'd intended to demand.

He pulled his topee down so it covered his face. He had gained what he wanted, so why were tears pouring down his cheeks?

## Chapter Twenty-nine

*Nasiriyeh, Tuesday June 29th 1915*

'You going out?' Smythe asked when Harry stripped off his shirt and reached for his gumbaz.

'We've no maps and the natives don't trust us. If I can persuade them a battle's brewing and suggest they vacate their date groves and homes until after the show, I might save a few lives and make a few friends. We could do with some.'

'Do you need help?'

'I've been ordered to take a platoon to cover my back.' Harry pushed a knife into the sash he'd tied at his waist.

'May as well make it mine.'

'I've no idea what we're up against. It might get rough,' Harry warned.

'Anything's better than manhandling supplies, heaving boats up the dam, and waiting for another meal of liquid bully beef from a blown tin. I swear the last consignment I saw were round.' Smythe picked up his topee.

'Reconnaissance missions are not strolls in the country. Your men will need eyes in the back of their heads.'

'Like Qurna and Amara?'

Harry tied his kafieh on his head. 'There, we knew where the enemy was, give or take a few hundred yards, and they wore uniforms. Outside of this boat the enemy could be anyone, Arab, Turk...'

'Do you want me or not?' Smythe broke in.

Harry reported to his superior while Peter mustered his platoon. When Harry returned, he delivered his orders.

'Stay at least 50 yards behind me, out of sight, and don't come unless I whistle.' He pushed two fingers into his mouth and let out a shrill, piercing shriek.

'Got it, sir,' the sergeant answered in a broad West-Country accent.

Smythe followed Harry's progress along the towpath towards a low mud wall that cut across country about a mile upstream from the dam. After ten minutes, he gave the signal for the platoon to move out. When Harry reached the wall, he stepped over it. Keeping close to the palm thickets, he ran from grove to grove, only pausing when he could take cover.

He was alert to any sign, any movement, that

might indicate a Turkish presence. The under-growth rustled with the scurrying of wildfowl and water snakes. Once he saw an Arab crouching beneath a palm a couple of hundred yards ahead, but when the man saw him, he fled as though he'd seen a ghost. A ghost, Harry reflected grimly, or a man about to become one.

After an hour and a half of nerve-wracking scouting, Harry checked his position. A noise on the opposite bank alerted him. He saw a clean-shaven Turkish private and a moustached officer emerge from a grove. The officer spotted him.

Harry pulled out his revolver and fired four shots in quick succession. The officer fell. Blood poured from the private's arm. Terrified he'd alerted a regiment, Harry dived into the undergrowth and slithered back along the route he'd travelled.

Motioning Peter's platoon to silence, he waved them into cover. They lay on their stomachs, waiting. Flies and mosquitoes crawled over their sweating bodies. Harry with his flowing robes was better off than the men in their shorts, but his abba and gumbaz offered little protection against the spiny leaves that could pierce any number of layers of cloth. After an hour, he signalled to Peter to follow him. Leaving the men, they crawled to the spot where he'd fired on the Turks. Their bodies lay on the towpath, stripped naked, their throats slit from ear to ear.

Harry knew he need look no further for signs of life. The Arabs were watching. The Turks had no doubt been forward scouts like himself. If others had been within earshot, the Arabs wouldn't have risked finishing what he'd begun.

Sickened by the bloodied corpses, Peter retched. The sound drew a shot, probably from a looted Turkish gun, Harry reflected. He saw Peter writhe. A second shot flew overhead. He threw himself on top of Peter.

'It's my leg,' Peter panted from between clenched teeth. Rolling on his side, Harry tore the kafieh from his head, and swabbed at the blood. A bullet had entered Peter's calf below the knee and exited above his ankle. He wrapped the kafieh around the wound, tying it in place with his agal.

'We're going to have to make a run for it,' he muttered when a third bullet slammed into a palm above their heads.

'That's a laugh.'

'Afraid not, here goes.' Grabbing Peter's collar, Harry dragged him towards the river. Before Peter had time to protest, he found himself immersed in water. 'For God's sake, I'm wounded. Now you're drowning me.'

'Quiet!' Harry reached for a log.

Peter's leg burned; he wondered what infections the river water carried.

'They'll run out of bullets soon,' Harry predicted optimistically, paddling close to the bank. Hooking his elbows over the log, he rammed his fingers into his mouth and whistled. The sergeant crawled out of the grove. Harry waved. The sergeant stole towards them, stiffened, and keeled over, landing face down in the water. Keeping his head low, Harry swam towards him. The hilt of a knife protruded from the sergeant's back.

'Can you cling to this log?' Harry asked Peter.

441

'I think so, but what are you going to do? You can't stay here...'

'Go.' Gripping a clump of reeds, Harry pushed the log with his feet. It shot forward, carried downstream by the current. The sergeant's rifle lay close to where he'd fallen. Harry tried to swim to the spot but his robes hampered his movements. Diving under water, he pulled off his abba and untied his sash. Retrieving his knife, he clenched it between his teeth. Wearing only his cotton trousers, he surfaced and made a grab for the rifle.

If any Arabs were watching, they didn't show their faces. Standing waist deep in water, he fired a volley in the hope he was within earshot of the flotilla and someone would send a rescue party.

Every time Peter tried to put any weight on the log, it rolled, ducking his head below water. His right leg was numb, and it wasn't easy to swim or tread water without it. Eventually, he found it easiest to hold on to the end of the log and drift behind it. Conscious he was a target for any sharpshooter on the towpath, all he could think about was getting back to the flotilla to summon assistance for Harry. Debris flowed past. The roots of plants that had broken away from the bank, rotting husks of palm and vegetables and, once, a naked, water-blown body.

The log moved out into mid-stream and he found himself in the middle of a shoal of fish. Turning his head, he saw his right leg trailing puffs of blood. To his horror, he realised the fish were feeding off him. Thrashing his arms, he kicked in an effort to dispel them, not caring who heard his noise. A shot whistled above his head. Then he heard the most wonderful sound in the world.

'Hold your fire. No Turk has that colour hair.'

'Colonel Perry?' Peter peered cautiously over the log.

'Smythe, what in God's name are you doing?'

'Trying to get downstream, sir,' he muttered as two privates from the Hampshires waded into the water and dragged him onto the bank.

'You've succeeded, captain.' Perry looked at his injured leg. 'We'd best get you to the hospital ship. Volunteers to escort Captain Smythe to the flotilla, Sergeant. At the double.'

'Lieutenant-Colonel Downe is still upstream, sir. My sergeant was killed.'

'Turks?' Perry interrupted.

'Don't think so, sir. There was a knife in his back.'

'Damned murdering natives.'

'Lieutenant-Colonel Downe and the rest of our party...'

'Don't worry, we'll get to them. Privates.' He dismissed Smythe's escort. 'Rest of you, follow me.'

The privates rolled out a canvas stretcher and lifted Peter onto it. One of them picked a couple of sucking fish from his leg and tossed them into the river.

'Ready to go, sir?'

'Anywhere as long as it's not back into the water.'

'Effendi. Psst. Effendi?'

Harry glanced cautiously above the bank. A leathery brown face framed by reeds stared back

443

at him. He shifted his knife from between his teeth into his hand.

'You want to speak with me?' he asked in Arabic. The man had seen him first; if he'd intended to kill him, he could have done so already.

'The Turks have gone. Your men are dead. I'm sorry.'

'Why should you be sorry Ferenghi are dead?'

'Because you English will win this war and then you'll punish those who opposed you, and reward those who assisted you in whatever modest way was open to them.' The man smiled, revealing gaps in his brown teeth. 'I can show you where your comrades lie.'

'Is it far?' Harry questioned warily.

'A very little way.'

'How do I know the men of your village aren't waiting there to kill me?'

'My village is just above the dam, Effendi. It was the home of my fathers. I would like it to remain my home. If I help you, perhaps you will spare it.'

'I'll not spare it if your people have taken anything from the dead Ferenghis. Or if there are Turks within your walls.'

'There are no Turks within our walls, or Turk lovers.' The man avoided any mention of Ferenghi goods. 'If I show you where your soldiers lie, will you spare it?'

'I will consider the matter.'

'I would like one of your pieces of paper.'

Harry smiled. The certificates of immunity, subject to good behaviour, the political officers had been dispensing to friendly villages were apparently more highly prized than he'd realised. 'If you help me I will do better than that. When we have driven the Turks back I will give you our flag to fly from the house of your alim.'

'And the paper?'

'That as well.'

'Then all the men in my village will help you. I swear it on the lives of my sons.'

Harry took the Arab's hand and climbed out on to the riverbank. Careful to keep the rifle above water, he emptied the sergeant's ammunition pouch and reloaded the gun with as much show as he could muster. He'd seen Arabs swear all manner of things on everything that was sacred only to break the oath minutes later if it had been made to an infidel.

Cocking the rifle, he held it in his left hand, and followed the man. There was no point in caution. The verdure was so thick a platoon could have hidden a foot from his path.

The corporal and privates lay in a clearing next to the towpath. They'd been stripped of clothes and weapons. All had been shot through the head except the corporal; he'd survived the Turkish ambush only to have his throat slit by the Arabs.

'Men of your tribe?' Harry asked.

'No, Effendi, I swear it.'

'If I find our weapons or uniforms in your village I will burn it and slaughter every man in it old enough to bear arms.'

'You would be right to do so, Effendi,' the man cringed.

'I need tools. Something to dig,' Harry ordered, 'and blankets to cover the bodies.'

'If you clothe the dead in blankets, Effendi, the living will dig them up to steal the cloth. If you bury them as they came into this world, they will rest in Allah's grace for all eternity.'

'Blankets.' Harry pointed the barrel of the rifle at the man's chest.

'I will get what I can, Effendi.' Terrified more by the look on Harry's face than the gun, he scuttled into the bushes.

Closing the corporal's eyes, Harry looked at the privates. They were all men he'd known by sight.

'Downe.' Perry walked into the clearing. 'What the devil's gone on here?'

'Arabs finishing what the Turks began. I sent a native to fetch spades and blankets.'

'Bloody wogs,' Perry cursed. 'I'd like to kill a dozen of the bastards for every one of our wounded they've slaughtered and our dead they've dug up.'

'As long as you don't include the man I sent to fetch tools and blankets. I promised him and his village immunity.'

'Are you mad, Downe?'

'If we don't cultivate the friendly natives, we'll never survive this war.' He straightened the stiffening limbs of the corporal.

'The only good wog is a dead wog.'

'We need their food, their knowledge of the terrain, and the intelligence they can supply of Turkish troop movements.'

'Effendi?' The native tapped Harry's arm.

'Where the devil did he spring from?' Perry asked. 'I set pickets...'

'He's the reason we have to make friends and

446

trust those who offer us their services, Colonel
Perry. Still want to kill him?' Harry asked.

Peter dreamed he was falling over a cliff –
falling... He landed with a bump that bruised his
back and brought his right leg viciously to life.
He opened his eyes. The private at the front of
the stretcher lay in a tangle of canvas on the
towpath, the back of his head shot away. The
private behind him pressed him into the dirt.

'Bloody, murdering Turks.' Using Peter's
shoulder as a rest for his rifle, he fired to the
landward side of the path. 'You alive, sir?'

'Think so,' Peter muttered between clenched
teeth.

'We're going to have to take cover, sir.' Rolling
on his back, he grabbed Peter by his sleeve and
dragged him into the reeds. They fell into a wet
gully. A grinning face looked down on them.
Peter watched the smiling Turk force the barrel of
his rifle into the private's mouth.

An explosion shattered the private's skull, spattering the greenery with gobs of crimson. Peter
flailed, not knowing or caring which way he was
crawling as long as it was away from the Turk. He
had no thoughts of bravery, no coherent thoughts
of any kind. Only an image of the private's head
as it had burst outward.

He dragged himself forward using any part of
his body that could gain a purchase on the soggy
ground. He was conscious of his own pathetic
whimpering and the Turk's laughter as he
followed him. Footsteps squelched in the mud
behind him. He dived deeper into the reeds. He

447

hit water but continued rolling into the swamp. Drowning wasn't so bad. At least your head remained intact when you drowned.

*Akaika dam,*
*the early hours of Wednesday 30th June 1915*

Harry paced the perimeter of the camp, squinting into the darkness, listening for a footfall on the towpath or coming through the reeds. The tug of war teams were hauling up the *Shushan,* the last vessel in the flotilla to remain below the dam. At first light, the Navy would press on and begin clearing the Euphrates of Turkish mines. He had orders to go with them and interrogate any native who might have knowledge of the location of the mines but he didn't want to leave the Akaika without discovering Peter's fate.

If he'd seen him shot to pieces like the rest of the patrol, he'd have buried him, mourned, and walked away with even more murderous feelings towards the Turks than those he already harboured. A search had uncovered drag marks that ended with the stripped corpse of an identity tagged Turk. A Turk with his throat cut. He'd been left wondering if the Turk had made the drag marks, or Peter. And if Peter had been there – if he still lived.

'Last patrol in.' Crabbe handed him a mug of tea. 'No sign of him.'

'Thanks for checking.'

'We old Gulf hands have to stick together.'

Harry offered a cigarette to Crabbe. 'I never

thought I'd say this, but you're all right. This time last year you drove me mad.'

'Soldiering in peacetime drives everyone mad.' Crabbe shied away from emotion. 'Spit, polish, and parading to no useful end.'

'Are you saying you like this bloody war?'

'Not the killing.' Crabbe squatted beside a fire and flicked his ash into it. 'A man would have to be an idiot to like that, but the spirit of the thing, men pulling together. Where I come from, the law was self first and hang the rest. I wanted more, but I never wanted to make officer. I was happier when I was with them.' He nodded towards the campfire of the non-commissioned officers. 'It's not easy to behave like a gentleman when you've been brought up a scrubber.'

'My family's been telling me that I don't know how to behave like a gentleman since the day I was born.'

'When you want to, you fit in. You know what to drink, the right jokes, the right way to hold your knife and fork.'

'Here, the most important things an officer should know is how to spot a Turk and shoot straight. I'd rather have you at my back than half the officers here.'

'Do you want to send another patrol into that reed bed?'

'I'd like to lead one in there. If I don't make another effort to find Smythe I won't be able to sleep nights.'

'He knew the score when he went out with you.' Crabbe didn't try to dissuade Harry from going out again. 'I'll ask for volunteers. Leave at dawn?'

Harry spent the rest of the night wandering from campfire to campfire, drinking one cup of lukewarm tea after another with the men and smoking hand-rolled cigarettes. The camp was breaking up: tents were being flattened; boxes of supplies handed upstream to the boats. Men stuffed mosquito nets and crumpled, well-read, precious letters and magazines into their kit bags. When dawn broke, it was a relief all round. No one wanted to linger at Akaika, and with the *Shushan* above the dam, they didn't need to. Harry threw the dregs from his last cup over a fire and straightened his back.

'Effendi?'

He didn't turn around. 'You must give me a lesson in infiltrating enemy lines, Akim. If you've come for your flag, you'll have to wait until we've searched your village.'

Akim stepped out. 'We've found one of your men, Effendi, a man with hair like fire.'

'Where is he?'

'In my village, Effendi. My neighbour found him in the marsh but he is crazy. He screams and hits things that are not there.'

Harry grabbed the first man in sergeant's uniform he saw. 'I need eight men for a patrol and a stretcher.'

'Jump to it, Sergeant Mills.' Crabbe barked from behind them.

Harry and Crabbe heard Peter's screams before they saw the roofs of Akim's village.

'As I said, Effendi, a demon has entered his

450

head.' Kicking aside bleating goats and scavenging children, Akim cleared a path. 'Perhaps two,' he qualified as Peter's voice dropped from a high-pitched screech to a guttural whine. 'They are fighting for possession of his soul.'

Harry ducked into Akim's hut, blinking to stop his eyes streaming in the smoky interior. Peter lay on a reed mat, thrashing wildly, his eyes rolling. Harry pulled aside a poultice of leaves that covered his leg. The skin was raw, but there was no infection. Peter sat up and lashed out, hitting him to the floor. Harry shouted for Crabbe. The major entered, took one look at Peter, and slammed him soundly on the jaw.

'Sorry, Smythe,' he apologised when Peter fell back, unconscious.

Harry laid his hand on Peter's head. 'He's hot, but not feverishly so, and his leg wound looks clean enough.'

'I've seen men like this in Africa after they were cut off from the rest of the troops. God alone knows what happened out there. Perhaps he saw the Turks kill the privates. From what you said, there wasn't much left of them. He might come around in a day or so.'

'If he doesn't?'

'He will. The only question is to what. I've seen men who've gone through much the same experience lead suicide charges into enemy lines. I've also seen them cowering in trenches refusing to move even with an officer's gun in their back. Either way, they died with a bullet in their guts. I'll call the stretcher-bearers.'

'You will search my village and give us your flag

to fly over the hut of our alim?'

'So you can alternate it with the Turkish wasm?' Harry had spotted the flag half hidden in the rafters.

'It's there to keep the water from the roof, Effendi.'

'With our flotilla on the Euphrates you'll need more than that to keep your heads dry, Akim. But for this–' he looked at Peter '–you'll get your wasm.'

## Chapter Thirty

*Basra, Thursday 8th July 1915*

'Major Mason, I'm not happy.' Colonel Allan, Hale's replacement as commander of the Indian Medical Service, handed John his orders. 'You've just recovered from fever and you're heading into an area where it's endemic. I've seen Gorringe's dispatches. A quarter of his men are sick. The natives are stabbing our men in the back while the Turks attack from the front. There are no pack animals on his boats and won't be until reinforcements reach him. That means every case of supplies has to be manhandled into any area away from the river, and by the officers as well as the men because the natives refuse to co-operate. The temperature's 110 and the mosquitoes and flies even more vicious than the Tigris variety.'

'All of which makes me think I could be more

use on the Euphrates than here, sir.'

'GHQ welcomed your request because no other medical officer has volunteered for that swamp hole. A steamer leaves for Suq-ash-Shuyukh tonight. Cox took the town two days ago and they're using it as a base to mount our operations on Nasiriyeh. As you insist on going, I suppose I'd better wish you luck.'

'Thank you, sir.'

'Don't thank me, Major. If it had been my decision, you'd be sailing for India. This war is Scutari all over again, with the sick nursing the sick and no Florence Nightingale to take charge. If you won't think of your own health, think of the service. I need all the doctors I can get. Too many are falling by the wayside.'

'I'll try not to fall again, sir.'

'My compliments to your wife. I understand she's in Basra. One more reason I can't understand your request. Perhaps I should talk to her.'

'Please, don't,' John said. 'Goodbye, sir.'

John had hated applying for a transfer to the Euphrates behind the colonel's back, but Allan had recommended him for a three-month leave. He couldn't face India, with or without Maud. And he couldn't stay in Basra. Too many officers were congratulating him on managing to get stationed in the same town as his wife and people were beginning to notice he never visited the mission. Particularly since he'd been moved to the convalescent ward and allowed to leave the hospital for short periods during the day.

He'd visited the mess and Basra Club and, ignoring the advice of his doctors who had a greater regard for his liver than he did, drank. For the last three nights, his fellow patients had helped him out of the club into a cab and into his bed. This morning he'd swung his feet to the floor, clenched his aching head, and realised he had a problem. But that didn't stop him from reaching for his brandy.

He promised himself it would be different on the Euphrates. He'd have work to keep him occupied. With nothing to do and Maud a short walk away, it was only natural he'd turned to drink.

He glanced at his watch when he left the building. He had four hours to kill before boarding the steamboat. He might as well spend it in the cool of the mess. He whistled for a cab. He'd find someone to talk to, read the *Basra Times,* catch up on the latest gossip, refill his flask. And have a drink. Just one – for the road.

*Atabiya Canal, the Euphrates*
*Monday 12th July 1915*

Harry sat with his back to a trench wall and sketched a rough plan in his notebook. He closed his eyes, visualising the Turkish position he'd viewed from the back of a mule he'd borrowed from Akim. Opening his eyes, he squinted at his draft. It resembled one of the impossible battle positions the military history tutors used to pin on the board at Sandhurst. He could almost hear the tutor.

'Gentlemen, if you'd care to pinpoint the weak points in the enemy's troop deployment.'

Only there were no bloody weak points. He pulled his head cloth over his temples, trying to concentrate. The Turks were flanked by marsh, fronted by an open plain broken by a canal... He drew the dotted outline of canoes in the centre of canal. An hour ago, he'd watched a party of Turkish infantry load three native mahailas with stones and sink them, presumably in the hope they'd foul the keels of any hostile craft. He sketched in a few clumps of camel thorn in the no man's land that stretched between their own and the Turkish trenches and took his time outlining the only vegetation: a clump of 16 date palms that shaded a stretch of the river.

At length, he studied the finished map. It wasn't comprehensive enough to use as the base for an attack but it would have to do. The generals were set on trying to take the Turkish mounds that night by bellum, just as they'd done at Qurna. He and the other field officers had tried to tell the staff that in Qurna they'd had accurate maps that had been refined by air surveillance. They'd known the depth of the water, the position of the Turkish posts, the sites of the Turkish machine guns, the strength of their forces – here, all they had was his pathetic sketch.

Smythe sat on a sandbag alongside him. Harry closed his notebook. Peter was no longer the happy-go-lucky officer who'd volunteered to accompany him on patrol at Akaika. He'd come out of his hysteria in an acute nervous state. He jumped if someone rattled a tobacco tin. The sound of flying bullets sent him screaming. An animal or man crying out in pain brought tears to his eyes. His unease, like most undesirable emotions, proved infectious, and officers and men were giving him the cold shoulder.

Living on the edge, as they all were in these trenches, it was hard to sympathise with what Cleck-Heaton termed a 'damned malingering coward'. The Force doctor was no help. All he dispensed were Beechams pills to calm Peter's 'nerves' along with 'pep talks' designed to drive him back into a military frame of mind.

'We're going in tonight?' Peter's hand shook as he drew on a cigarette.

'So I've heard.'

'Command's assigned me to the 24th Punjabis. They know I led one of the bellum attacks at Qurna.'

'Your leg hasn't healed. I'll put in a word.'

'Don't. I know what everyone's saying about me. I have to go in. If I funk this, I'll be finished. I may as well shoot myself, before the Turks get to me.'

'You're sick. Any fool can see that.'

'It's not just what they're saying, Harry.' Peter's hand trembled so much he dropped his cigarette.

Harry took another from his packet, lit it, and pushed it into Peter's mouth.

'I have to do it to prove I still can cut it. That I'm not the coward everyone believes I am.'

'A coward wouldn't have followed me at Akaika.'

'A coward came back.'

Peter rose from the sandbag. Harry watched him walk away. Twice Peter stumbled and fell. Damn the staff. He'd warned it would be suicide to attack the Turks when they knew so little about their defences. And they were sending out sick men. Including one in the throes of a nervous breakdown.

*The Euphrates front, night of 12th July 1915*

Four hundred men waited in the bellums drawn up alongside the *Shushan*. In the next bellum, Harry could hear Peter's breath coming in quick gasps. He wished there was time to reassure him, but orders to advance were already being whispered down the lines of boats.

They hit problems at once. Every few minutes, Harry or his lieutenant had to step into the shallows to push their bellum out of the reed banks. All sense of perspective was lost in the darkness. Boats bumped into one another and men cursed, the noise carrying over the water.

Harry was sure that he saw the cap of a Turkish soldier on a mud bank ahead. Whispering an order to beach the bellum, he palmed his handgun and stole out of the boat. Waving his men forward, he led an attack on a ragged stump of palm. Feeling foolish, he motioned the men back. A shell exploded above them. A private stood in a boat to their right, his tunic and hair ablaze. A group on their left were hit by machine gun fire.

'The bastards are behind that ridge.' Peter splashed, knee deep, through the shallows. Harry guided his bellum around the mound to support Peter's attack. Shells landed in the mud around them; mercifully few exploding on impact. A massive roar rent the air. The smell of burning hair and flesh permeated the night; screams echoed through the fusillade. The Turks fired from un-broken lines ahead and to the left and right. They'd paddled into the centre of the Turkish defences.

Harry stood upright in his bellum and urged the men to retreat. The entire area was a mad-house of gun flashes and machine gun fire. Peter rose on the crest of the ridge, his figure thrown into silhouette by the fire raging behind him. Two of his men had turned the Turkish gun they'd taken and were firing on the Turkish lines. Peter laughed and drew his sword.

Harry turned to see Turks clutching at his bel-lum. He fired. One fell into the water. His men hammered at the hands that sought to delay them with rifle butts. His sergeant screamed when a bayonet skewered his stomach.

Harry fired at the shadows closing in on them. Water rose over his boots. His bellum was sink-ing. Shouting for his men to follow, he leapt out and ran until the ground disappeared from be-neath his feet. Kicking upwards, he swam.

Pausing for breath, he glanced back. The attack had become a massacre. From the opposite bank the retreat sounded. He grabbed a boat, heaved out the dead men inside it, and climbed in. A private from the Punjabis joined him.

'Haul in all the men you can reach.' Harry reloaded his gun. When he looked up, Peter was still laughing and running through the water brandishing his bloody sabre.

Peter didn't stop laughing when he halted in front of a Turk who held up his hands in surrender. He was still laughing when he severed the man's windpipe.

*The Karun desert*

Mitkhal knew he was being watched. Whenever he left his tent, men found the need to clean their guns, polish their swords, smoke their tobacco, and always within sight of him.

Exhausted by pregnancy, Gutne had become slow and less observant. Concerned by her lack of strength, Mitkhal bought a black slave girl, Bantu, from Shalan to carry the water and tend to his goats. Gutne gave up her household chores but she continued to make daily visits to Furja. Incarcerated with her daughters in the tent of Ali Mansur, Furja never appeared, not even to watch over Ali's flocks.

The summer grew hotter, the thorn withered, and Mitkhal bided his time. Waiting and watching as others watched him, careful not to say an untoward word or make a rash gesture. Not even when he was alone with Gutne. He'd promised Harry he would get the women away, but he was beginning to feel he'd taken on an impossible task.

Questioning Gutne, he discovered Furja was never alone. Ali Mansur's mother and sisters shared her harem, her meals, and were at her side even when she washed and fed her daughters. She left them only when Ali summoned her to his bed. Gutne also volunteered the information that Furja was unhappy. Not that she complained, but she never laughed as she used to and there was a sad look in her eyes.

He'd lifted his eyebrows at the revelation and said it couldn't be helped. For once, Gutne had shrugged off the torpor she'd fallen into and told him he'd grown heartless.

At the height of the hot season, the men became restless. There was talk of raiding villages. He was questioned about the movements of the Turks and the British. He answered as best as he could, hoping that, soon, news would reach Shalan of a fight, a skirmish, anything that offered the possibility of loot. If the men left the camp he would have to go with them, but a lame horse could force his return.

The drought had brought the tribe close to the river and British boats sailed the Karun. He'd an authorisation from Harry tucked into his shirt and a bag of sovereigns. If he could get Furja, Gutne, and the twins on board a British vessel they'd be safe. All he'd have to do was reach Basra, purchase an anonymous house, and get word to Harry.

He continued to attend the coffee circle and evening meal, to smile at his neighbours and speak of goats, horses, and the war everyone knew was drawing to an end. He looked after Gutne, escorted her to Ali's tent and back, waited and prayed. The chance would present itself eventually. When it did, he'd take it.

*Amara, Thursday 15th July 1915*

'Everyone's sick,' Amey complained to Charles when they entered the mess. 'There I was talking to Meakin – he even nodded his head as though he agreed with what I'd said, then keeled over.

Dead as a doorpost. Knight said he'd probably been walking around with fever for days. He's the fifth to go like that this week.'

Charles mopped his face. 'The temperature hasn't dropped a degree from this afternoon.'

'It has. When it gets cooler you just forget how hot it was earlier.' Amey sat in a chair and called to the orderly. 'Mine's a whisky and soda, and make it a large soda. What's your poison, Reid?'

'Same.' Charles continued to mop his face.

'Give Major Reid the same and put it on my chit.'

'You lucky people look as if you've been here for hours.' Knight joined them.

'We've only just got here,' Amey said. 'Whisky?'

'Please.' Knight sat next to Charles.

'Make that three whisky and large sodas,' Amey shouted to the orderly who was mixing the drinks.

'Heard Mason's been sent to the Euphrates.' Knight took out his cigarette case.

'I expected him to be sent to India,' Charles said sourly.

'Relief doctor told me he volunteered. Beats me why, with his wife in Basra.'

Charles didn't answer. The whisky came and he downed half a glass in one gulp.

'Steady.' Knight put a hand on his arm. 'I should not have to warn an old hand like you about the effect of too much cold drink on a warm stomach.'

'I don't feel so good,' Charles mumbled. 'Those bloody Persians know how to spin out evidence. I couldn't make head nor tail of what was going on today.'

Knight put a hand to Charles's forehead.

461

'You're burning up,' he announced in a resigned voice. 'It's bed for you, old man.'

'You're not getting me into that blasted hospital.'

'That blasted hospital is very well run. However, seeing as it's you, I'll leave you in your quarters tonight, but if you're still running a temperature in the morning I'll have to admit you. Can you make it upstairs?'

Charles staggered to the door like a drunk trying to prove his sobriety. Amey and Knight followed him up the stairs. Charles's bearer, Chatta Ram, was standing in the doorway of his room, the uniform Charles had worn to the courthouse slung over his arm.

'Ram, I feel...' Charles slumped; Ram swung him into his arms and carried him to his bed.

'Fever?' Amey asked Knight.

'Heatstroke,' Chatta Ram diagnosed when he unfastened Charles's belt. Unbuttoning his fly, he pulled down his trousers. 'If one of you gentlemen would be kind enough to turn back the cover I'll get him into bed.'

Amey waited until the bearer lifted Charles off the bed, then did as Ram asked. When the bearer had covered Charles, Knight walked to the bed and pulled back Charles's eyelids. The whites had turned pink.

'You're right,' he said grudgingly, peeved by the sepoy's temerity in diagnosing Charles's illness. 'Do you know what to do?'

'Sponge with cold water, plenty of liquids, rest.'

'That's about it. I'll call back after dinner.'

'Odd chap, that bearer of Charles's,' Knight said

462

to Amey when they returned to the mess.

'Charles swears by him. The man saved Harry's life at Shaiba, then latched on to Charles when he reached here.'

'There's something not quite right about him.'

'Like what?' Amey asked.

'If I knew I'd tell you,' Knight answered irritably, noticing their drinks had been cleared away. 'Same again?'

Charles raved most of the night. He drifted through a nightmare world of bombed-out trenches, cold rain, and freezing mud that he recognised as the Western Front. Everywhere were images of death – grinning skulls surmounted by metal helmets; shreds of flesh clinging to barbed wire; craters filled with corpses – and everywhere he walked, serene, smiling, Maud glided alongside him. First in a shimmering evening gown, then naked, she enticed him onto a chaise longue fashioned from corpses.

He wanted her so much he couldn't help himself. He kissed her, then saw the skull-like features of John behind them. He tried to move away, but she hooked her legs over his thighs, pinning him fast. Her mouth closed over his, sucking the breath from his body.

Exhausted, he fell back. Her limbs caressed his, tormenting, teasing. He tried to resist when she made love to him, never once losing sight of John's sad, reproachful eyes while Maud coaxed and stroked him to a climax. He shouted, begged her to stop...

'Charles! Wake up, Charles!'

When he opened his eyes, tears of relief flooded onto the pillow. Ram was wiping his face with a cool flannel. He was in his room at the Amara barracks. Daylight was shining through the window. 'I must get to the courthouse.'

Chatta Ram pressed him down. 'You're not going anywhere, Sahib. You are ill.'

Charles sank back, recalling his nightmare. 'Did I say anything in my sleep?'

'You said many things, Sahib, but I do not hear your private words.' Chatta Ram picked up Charles's hairbrush from the table and brushed his hair away from his face.

Charles nodded, grateful for Chatta Ram's tact and ashamed of the sickness that had made him lose control.

'I will wash you, Sahib.'

It wasn't until Chatta Ram went into the bathroom that Charles realised. When Ram had woken him, he'd called him Charles.

## Chapter Thirty-one

*The* Shushan, *Saturday 17th July 1915*

'This is getting to be monotonous,' John complained when he walked into the cabin on board the *Shushan*.

'What?' Harry asked.

'One or the other of us laid up.'

Harry tried to sit up without straining his left

shoulder. 'I've a clean bullet hole. Given the odds of the last show, that doesn't give me much to complain about.'

'I saw the report, 150 dead. What went wrong?'

'Everything. I had a bad feeling from the start.'

'I suggest the next time you have a bad feeling you keep your head and shoulder down.'

'Like you? What the hell are you doing here?'

'Working, there's a shortage of doctors.'

'A severe case of fever rates three months' convalescence.'

'Not when there's a war on.'

'You might be able to lie to everyone else, but not me. Leave is one thing I do know about. Still–' Harry relented '–it's good to see your ugly face. Drink in the mess tonight?'

'I'm relieving the duty doctor in half an hour.' It wasn't just work. John had woken on the river launch in Qurna to be told that he'd shown his travel orders to his companions in the mess in Basra before he began drinking. If he hadn't, he wouldn't have made it out of the town, let alone to the Euphrates.

'Any news of reinforcements?' Harry asked.

'A thousand today and a thousand more on their way.'

Harry pushed the flat of his feet onto the deck and levered himself up.

'Novel way of getting up.'

'I'd like to see you do as well with half a hand and a shoulder like a colander. I'm going to vet the reinforcements. If we're going to take this bloody town they'd better be good.'

John followed Harry on deck. The West Kents

were offloading their gear onto the bank.

'Good men?' John asked.

'They'll do.' Harry noted their raw, sunburned skin. 'They could have done with a couple more weeks to get acclimatised.'

'Time seems to be in shorter supply than anything else.'

'How's Maud?' Harry ventured.

'I saw her. I'll divorce her as soon as this show is over.'

'Is that what you want?'

'She's pregnant.'

'Brooke?'

'No, I checked with Theo Wallace; the dates are wrong. I asked, but she wouldn't tell me who the father was.' John pulled his topee over his eyes so Harry couldn't read his expression. 'Actually, I couldn't give a damn.'

Harry laid his hand on his cousin's shoulder. He knew exactly how much John's damn was worth. He'd been hurting the same way ever since Shalan had told him Furja was married. They stood in silence for a few minutes watching the men, guns, and supplies offload down the gangplanks.

'Last town,' Harry said. 'Then we can go home.'

'To start again on the Western Front?'

'Can't be any worse than this place.'

'Nowhere can be worse than this place,' John echoed.

*The battle of Nasiriyeh, Saturday 24th July 1915*

Peter had been in a trench for 36 hours. He was

sick of the latrine stench, booming guns, crashing shells, and, above all, the sense of fear that hung in the air, crippling initiative and tainting the atmosphere with foreboding.

Since the last attack, he'd been riding high. He'd killed and remained alive. That proved he wasn't a coward. But could he do it again? A shot landed short of the trench, causing a landslide of earth over the sandbagged wall.

'Christ, that was close.' His sergeant shivered.

Peter jumped to his feet. He had to do something before his nerve broke. 'Reconnaissance!' He yelled above the shellfire. 'Supporting rifles!' When the men were in position, he pulled out his field glasses and stepped up on to the sandbags. Sticking his head cautiously over the top, he scanned the terrain. The *Shushan* was pushing upstream towards the Turkish trenches, the guns strapped to her deck blazing shot into enemy lines. To the left, the artillery was shelling the Turkish flank. Ahead he could see rifle pits in the Turkish trenches and, behind them, a mound topped by a machine gun. A shot exploded on the wall behind him. He threw himself to the ground. When he lifted his head, he saw his sergeant covered with a layer of sandy earth. Clean earth. No blood. Lower down the trench, a tangle of broken limbs moved beneath a shattered sandbag. He shouted for stretcher-bearers. Another shot fell. A stretcher-bearer slid to the ground, clutching his leg.

'Snipers, sir. They're in no man's land,' a corporal yelled. 'Do you want me to take a party up top to see if we can winkle the bastards out?'

Peter spat dirt from his mouth. 'Not you,

corporal, me. Volunteers!'

Peter had his volunteers, 20 of them. Nerves stretched by the fusillade, like him they preferred to risk action than being hit like a sitting duck in the trench.

Peter surveyed the terrain again. In another five minutes, the *Shushan* would be alongside the Turkish flank. Once it fired down the trench, there'd be panic in the line. Aiming to time his attack to coincide with the next blast, he unbuttoned his handgun.

'One – two – three.'

He blew his whistle and mounted the sandbags. His men followed. The shots kept coming but they were intermittent, desultory. The Turks were running in a thick khaki line, more concerned with evading the *Shushan's* guns than the attack only a few had spotted heading for their front line.

Throwing himself over a barrier of thorns, Peter dived in front of a Turkish trench. He peered into it and found himself staring at a petrified private. Firing at point blank range, he blew the man's face away. His sergeant and two privates dropped beside him.

The sergeant pulled a pin from a grenade and lobbed it further up the trench. 'Do you want to drop into the trench?' he asked above the screams.

'We're doing well enough where we are.' Peter crawled forward. He could see no movement in the trench, only bodies. The skin over his stomach was being torn to shreds by camel thorn, but he didn't give a damn. He'd discovered the secret of war. Terrifying the enemy more than yourself.

468

While he was on the attack, he was invincible. He believed it. And he had to keep on believing it if he wanted to survive.

On board the *Shushan*, Harry put plugs of cotton wool into his ears but they offered little protection against the deck-splitting cannonade that threatened to tear the vessel apart every time the guns were fired. The sight of the *Shushan* and its sister ship, the *Medjidieh*, had terrified the Turks. They'd run down the trenches, away from the river, even before Captain Nunn ordered the guns to fire. Through the smoke of shot and shellfire, Harry could make out the wharves of Nasiriyeh.

A subaltern ran along the deck. 'Captain Nunn's compliments, sir, there are white flags on the roof-tops in Nasiriyeh. Could they be flags of truce?'

Harry peered through the smoke. The lieutenant was right. There was a profusion of white flags, just as there was a profusion of bullets flying from the Turkish barracks on the bank.

'I don't see any signs of a truce, lieutenant. Do you?'

'No, sir.' The lieutenant scuttled back. Harry pulled his gun from his holster with his injured right hand. It lay heavy in his palm. He'd been practising. He could fire it if he had to. The way Nunn was pushing ahead, they weren't an advance guard; they were on their own.

John's hands were shaking. He hadn't had a drink in three days and for two of those the battle had pounded around him. A non-stop torrent of wounded poured through the field hospital he'd set up in a second line trench. There were more Turks than British, but the injuries were as horrific on both sides.

Men screamed in agony from the stretchers laid out in rows in the dugout. There wasn't enough morphine to ease their pain. In fact, there wasn't enough of anything except wounded. Taking a deep breath, he gripped the operating table to stop himself trembling and looked down at the body in front of him. The boy was from the West Kents. Eighteen years, with splintered stumps for legs.

'Bone saw, sir?' Mathews offered the instrument.

John lifted his hands and they began to shake again. 'Chloroform.'

Mathews clamped a mask over the boy's mouth. Turning his back, John reached into his pocket for the flask he still carried. Tipping it into his mouth, he waited for the brandy to take effect.

'Hold him down.' He picked up the saw. The stumps had to be neatened. Discolouration that might mean infection sawn off. Blood vessels tied and cauterised. He'd clean up this body and turn to the next. It was no different from any other job. All he had to do was concentrate on one task at a time.

*Nasiriyeh, morning of Sunday 25th July 1915*

An hour into the occupation, Harry began to wonder what they were doing in the town. The inhabitants from the mayor down had received the British contingent with the same absent-minded courtesy and lack of warmth as the population of Amara in

470

June. He was left with the uneasy feeling that if the Ottomans stopped running and marched back down the main street they'd be accorded the cheers that had been denied the conquerors.

Allocated to light duties courtesy of his wound, he'd been given two clerks and the task of liaising between the townspeople and the Force. Hedged in by a crowd protesting their houses were too small to lodge soldiers, he was being simultaneously regaled by tales of lost property and relatives killed in the fighting. He dropped all pretence of listening to study the street. A patrol was stopping and searching every able-bodied man.

One alim, more persistent than the others, grabbed the hem of Harry's tunic and pulled him into an alley. Harry signalled to a clerk to alert the patrol. They followed. The crowd thinned, and by the time they reached the massive double doors of a mosque, the alim was the only native left.

A strange buzzing emanated from the building. The alim heaved the door open. Harry stared.

He'd railed often enough against the lack of facilities for their own wounded, but in almost a year of fighting, he had seen nothing to equal this. Men lay three and four deep, covered in vomit and excrement.

The living and barely living had been heaped indiscriminately among the dead. The stench was horrendous. A forest of hands rose towards the doorway and a cry went up, growing louder and harsher until it echoed against the domed ceiling.

'This is my mosque, Effendi. I am only one man. I have no one to help.'

'There must be young, healthy men among

those who use this mosque?' Harry insisted.

'None know what to do, Effendi.'

Harry's temper snapped. 'Fetch a dozen strong men here. Now!' He grabbed the old man by the neck of his gumbaz. 'Or I will kill every elder of this mosque.'

'I will try to find someone, Effendi.' The Arab backed away.

'Go to the wharf and round up as many able-bodied Turkish prisoners as you can control,' Harry ordered the lieutenant in charge of the patrol. 'Bring them here and order them to carry out the dead. Whatever you do, don't go in there yourself, or send any of our men in. Get the prisoners to heap the corpses in the far corner against that wall. You–' he pointed to a private '–go to the *Shushan* and ask for petrol. Tell them it's for burning corpses. These bodies have to be cremated here, or we'll risk carrying God knows what infection into the town.'

Harry moved the rest of the patrol down the street. The alim remained conspicuous by his absence, but the lieutenant returned with 15 Turkish prisoners.

'Get these prisoners working, Lieutenant. If any of them show the slightest sign of trouble, shoot them.'

'Sir?' The lieutenant was an Eton 'wet bob'. From sixth form to Mesopotamia in two months.

'Shoot them,' Harry repeated. 'You can shoot Turkish prisoners for disobeying orders, Lieutenant. It's allowed. You'll create problems if you don't. If they can get one over on you, you'll be lying at the bottom of that cremation pile with the corpses.'

'Where will you be if I need you, sir?' the lieutenant asked when Harry turned his back.

'The quay. I have to find a doctor. This place needs more than I can give it.'

'Damn it all, I've not nursed our wounded to sink them into that shit.' John indicated the steel deck of a launch covered in dried manure. 'The least you can do is clean it. Horses and mules have stood on it for over a week.'

'We've been ordered to evacuate the wounded to Qurna immediately.' The staff officer emphasised 'immediately'. 'There's no time for niceties.'

'Niceties be damned. There's no way I'll authorise you to put wounded on that deck. They're going to reach Qurna alive if I have to kill you and every other red-collared moron to do it.'

'That sounds suspiciously like a threat, Mason.' Perry stood beside the staff officer.

'Damn it all, some of these men have abdomen and stomach wounds. If they come into contact with that filth they won't survive to see Qurna.'

'But they will survive lying in this sun while you argue?' Perry turned on his heel. 'Lieutenant?'

A subaltern snapped to attention. 'Sir.'

'Begin the evacuation of the wounded.'

'Take one step, Lieutenant, and I'll report you.'

'Major Mason is not in command, Lieutenant.'

The stretcher-bearers picked up their loads and moved onto the gangplank. John swung his arm wide. Harry stepped in front of him.

'Hit Perry and he'll have you court martialled.'

'I couldn't give a damn,' John cried out of sheer

frustration. 'Look at those decks. They can't even be swabbed down now the men are lying on them. There are no mattresses, not enough containers for drinking water. If the orderlies redress those wounds, they'll have to use river water. Stinking water choked with corpses...'

'Over-emotional again,' Perry sneered. 'I'll say what I said before. You're not fit to be a man, Mason, much less an officer.'

John dodged past Harry and swung a punch.

The lieutenant stood open-mouthed, staring at the senior officer sprawled amongst the filth on the wharf.

'Report this, Perry, and I'll have you up for engineering the deaths of the wounded by neglect,' Harry warned.

'I obey orders.' Perry's face was purple with rage. 'Which is more than can be said for either of you.' He brushed rotten fruit from his uniform. 'You've not heard...'

Harry dragged John away. Leading him around the corner of a warehouse, he pulled out his brandy flask and handed it to his cousin. 'Do you want to spend the next 20 years in a military prison for striking a senior officer?'

'Someone has to do something. Those men won't last a day in those conditions.' John tipped the flask into his mouth.

'Then write a full report. I'll see it gets to the right man.'

'A report will be too late for those poor bastards.'

'It might do something for the next lot. If there's any justice, one day Perry and the staff will be on

474

those boats.'

'How in hell are the staff going to get wounded?' John asked.

'A shell might find its way to HQ.'

'If it does, it will be lobbed there by our own side. The Turks find our staff officers too useful to kill them.' John handed back the flask. Harry pushed it into his pocket. He could tell by the weight it was empty.

By nightfall, as many of the 104 British bodies as could be found had been buried. All 429 wounded who could be moved had been loaded on to ships and sent downstream, and by sunset even John was too tired to protest at the conditions they were being shipped in.

Over 1000 Turkish troops had been captured and the Turkish dead and wounded had been estimated at over 2000. Four Turkish casualties for every British. The Basra Wilyat had been secured.

## Chapter Thirty-two

*Qurna, the evening of Wednesday 18th August 1915*

Peter breathed in a lungful of air. It didn't have higher moisture than oxygen content and his clothes were damp and sticky with sweat, not humidity. The men striding purposefully along the quayside looked fitter and stronger than those he'd left in Nasiriyeh. Without him noticing, somewhere en route between the Euphrates and the Tigris the atmosphere had grown lighter, less laden with flies and mosquitoes.

'Mason's pissed again,' Leigh shouted to no one in particular.

'Keep your voice down,' Crabbe hissed. 'Cleck-Heaton's in the stern.'

'Everyone knows about Mason's drinking,' Leigh brayed. 'Fool can't hold it.'

'And you can?' Crabbe snarled when Leigh tried to rise from the corner of the deck where he and John had drunk themselves into a stupor during the voyage.

'I'll give you a hand.' Smythe joined Crabbe when he struggled to lift John upright.

'Are you sober?'

'Not as a judge, but A1 compared to these two.' Peter kept serious drinking for the late evenings. During the day, he found it comparatively easy to hide behind the mask of bravado that had sustained him during the battle at Nasiriyeh.

'Let's get him on the quayside. If anyone asks, he's succumbed to another bout of fever.'

'What about my fever?' Leigh giggled.

John's bearer, Dira, found a carriage. He helped Peter lift John in and they managed to get Leigh into the opposite corner. It was a short drive to the house Peter recalled being requisitioned for the use of senior officers after the first battle of Qurna. A sepoy was on the veranda.

'Billeting officer said I was to expect six officers. He said nothing about a lady. These quarters are for officers only. No ladies,' he complained to

476

Crabbe, who was the senior officer present.

Leigh grinned lecherously. 'That's what we need. Ladies.'

'You wouldn't know what to do with one.'

'Would and all, Crabbe, I've a son,' Leigh retorted with a smirk.

'I don't see any ladies.' Crabbe relinquished John to Dira.

'That's because I'm inside the house, Major Crabbe.'

Angela walked out of one of the rooms. She was wearing a smart blue travelling outfit that seemed vaguely familiar. If Peter had had a better memory, he might have recognised it as Maud's.

'Seems you're fixed up, old boy,' Leigh leered.

Crabbe pushed Leigh towards the orderly. 'Show Lieutenant Leigh to his quarters.' The orderly left, still muttering about ladies. 'It's nice to see you, Mrs Smythe.'

'And you, Major Crabbe.'

Dira returned after laying John on his bed. Picking up Peter's kit, he carried it past Angela into the bedroom behind her. Crabbe looked from Angela to Peter. 'Smythe, say hello to your wife.'

Peter followed Angela into the room. He waited until Dira dropped his kit, then closed the door. 'What the hell are you doing here?'

'I thought you'd be pleased to see me.' Angela was as taken aback by his anger as she was by his appearance. He looked thinner, older, and harder than she remembered.

Stung by the reproach, he forced a smile. 'I am. I just didn't expect you.' He looked around. There was a single camp bed, a case he presumed

477

was Angela's, and a table and chair.

'Harry wrote.' She omitted to mention that she'd written to Harry first asking why Peter's letters had changed since he'd been wounded. 'He said you'd be passing through Qurna on your way to Amara. He gave me the date and this address.'

'Harry's too damned romantic. I've only a few hours...'

'Two days.'

'I'm leaving first light tomorrow.'

'All troop movements up the Tigris have been delayed for 48 hours.'

'Why?'

'Does the army need a reason for doing anything?'

Peter sat on the chair. His head ached from the sun. He was tired and filthy. It wasn't that he didn't want to see Angela; he simply didn't want to see her, here, with Leigh and the others waiting outside the door. He'd separated his life into compartments, professional and private, and he didn't want her straying out of the one she belonged in.

'I'm sorry. I'll go.' She pinned on her hat and picked up her case.

He blocked the door. Taking the case from her, he pulled her head down onto his chest. 'I smell like a camel. I haven't had a bath in months. I'm worn out...'

'I can put up with your smell if you can.'

'The orderly doesn't like ladies.' He kissed the top of her head with cracked lips.

'And your fellow officers are smirking.'

'They're jealous.' He pulled her close. He had forgotten what it felt like to hold her.

She smelled sour wine on his breath, his clothes, impregnated with dirt and sweat. His hands went to the buttons on her bodice. He undid them quickly, tugging at them when they wouldn't give way.

She'd imagined their reunion a thousand times during the past few weeks. It hadn't been like this. She'd envisaged Peter telling her about the fighting, touching her tenderly, taking time to get to know her again after so many weeks apart.

He opened her dress and tried to push it over her shoulders. Turning her back, she took it off. Shy and a little afraid of the rough stranger he'd become, she went to the bed and untied her petticoats. He was on top of her before she finished. His stubble scraped her face. He didn't bother to remove his clothes. His filthy drawers chafed the skin she had so carefully washed and perfumed. Closing her eyes, she steeled herself to take his brutal thrusting.

She'd seen the dark scar at his temple, noticed the limp when he put weight on his right leg, and realised there were other scars that couldn't be seen, every bit as real as the visible ones. She was angry with herself for being insensitive. Peter had a right to her understanding, and it was her duty as his wife to give it to him.

Images of war flashed through Peter's mind when he used his wife. Blackened mounds of dead in dugouts; the faces of the soldiers he'd blown away; rotting, month-old corpses dug up and discarded by Arabs searching for loot—

He gripped Angela's arms and tried to obliterate the memories by losing himself in her body.

Not once did he look at her face, or consider her feelings.

When he'd done, he rose, kicked the chamber pot out from beneath the bed, and relieved himself.

He'd long since acquired the trench habit of urinating indiscriminatingly. It never entered his head to consider Angela's feelings. Buttoning his fly, he glanced at the washstand with its basin and jug of water. He was too filthy for that.

'I'm going to find a bathroom.' He picked up his kit. 'When I've finished we'll eat, but it might be difficult to turn up anything decent. I can hardly take you into the mess.'

She managed to hold her tears in check until he'd left the room.

When Peter emerged, clean and shaved, from the makeshift bathroom in the cellar, he ran into Crabbe and Grace, who'd arrived from Amara. They were setting off for the mess in company with a fragile-looking Leigh, and John, who was dressed in a uniform as immaculate as only Dira could make it. But his starched collar and pressed trousers couldn't conceal his trembling hands and bloodshot eyes.

'Smythe, you rogue, join us?' Grace invited.

'He can't. He has a wife in tow,' Leigh crowed, still tipsy.

'Do any of you fellows know where I can take Angela to eat?'

'Why don't you send Dira out to forage?' John suggested. 'He has a nose for a good cook shop and I've a couple of bottles of wine in my bag you

480

can have.'

Peter nodded. If he'd wanted a romantic dinner with Angela, it would have been a good idea, but he was strangely reluctant to spend the evening with her. He envied the others the noise and company of the mess. 'Join us?' he pleaded. 'Angela's bound to have news of Maud.'

'I'll have a drink with you later,' John promised.

'Tell you what, old boy.' Leigh slapped Peter's back. 'We'll all have a drink with you later. How's that?'

'You weren't invited.' Peter went in search of Dira.

Feeling slightly ridiculous, Angela sat opposite Peter on a camp chair while Dira poured John's wine, and served hors d'oeuvres of rice, eggs, and nuts. After he'd piled their plates high, he disappeared down the street to fetch the main course. Peter wolfed down the food while Angela stared at her plate.

'What have you been living on?'

'Blown tins of bully beef and rancid butter, and there wasn't enough of those.'

'So that's why you all look half-starved.' She pushed her plate away.

'Can't you eat any more?'

'I'm not hungry.'

He finished what was left on his plate and pulled hers towards him. She refilled their glasses. It'd have been easier to make conversation with a stranger. Then, she could've talked about the mission and her husband fighting on the Euphrates.

'Will you stay long in Amara?' she asked.

481

'Doubt it. The force has moved out to Kumait and Ali Gharbi to set up front buffers to consolidate our position. We'll probably be sent there as a relief column.'

'I can't see that the troops up river need relieving more than you. You all look dreadful. Particularly John Mason.'

'That's what John looks like these days. He drinks too much,' Peter revealed.

Dira walked through the door, carrying a smoking pot. 'Roast chicken and rice, Sahib.' The bearer laid the dish in the centre of the table.

'Thank you, Dira,' Angela smiled. 'You've done us proud.'

'For dessert, Mem Sahib, I have found light pastries stuffed with apricots and custard. They will go well with Major Mason's brandy.' Dira served the chicken and left.

Angela struggled with the food, but a lump in her throat prevented her from swallowing. Every time she looked up, Peter seemed to be too preoccupied with eating to talk. It was a relief when John and the others returned as Dira was serving coffee. They joined her and Peter, but she sensed from the strained politeness that her presence was inhibiting the men. Making her excuses, she rose from the table.

'Would you be kind enough to spare me a few minutes, Mrs Smythe?' John asked. He caught Dira's eye. 'Take Mrs Smythe's and my coffee onto the veranda. You don't mind, do you, Peter? I'd like to catch up on the Basra news.'

'Be my guest.' Peter reached for the brandy Dira had brought with the coffee.

John and Angela went outside. Half a dozen camp chairs were grouped around a travelling table next to a plot that should have been a flowerbed. Dira brought them a pot of coffee, a large, fruit-filled pastry, and brandy.

Angela picked up the coffee pot. 'Milk and sugar?'

'No, thank you. After campaigning, I'm not used to life's refinements.'

Angela poured out the coffee and cut two slices from the cake. 'I know I shouldn't have come. But I've been worried about Peter. His letters have been strange. I'd to see him to find out what was wrong.'

'Have you found out?' He pulled out his cigarette case.

'No.' She shook her head as he offered her one. 'But he's changed.'

'War does things to men. I don't think anyone can understand what's it's like until they've been through it.'

'Then tell me what it's like. I need to understand what's made Peter this way.'

John lit a cigarette and hunched over his coffee. 'Peter went missing for a while after he was wounded. The men with him were all killed.' John recounted the bare facts, but his colourless account only served to accentuate the horror for Angela. 'I'm not sure how he survived the massacre because he's never talked about it. When Harry found him in a native village, he was in shock. Later – he wasn't himself for a while, then–' John picked up the brandy Dira had poured for him and drank it. 'There are two options open to a man in war. He can either become a killer or be killed. Those of us who've become killers have lost something of ourselves in the process.'

'Are you saying Peter's become a killer?' Angela was obviously horrified by the thought.

'He's better at it than most. But, if I may be immodest, we all are, or we wouldn't be here.'

'Has he killed many men?'

'Oh yes.' John took out his brandy flask and refilled his glass.

'What about you?' she asked tentatively. 'Have you killed anyone?'

'Not intentionally, but probably more than most. Being a doctor's a different kind of nightmare. I stand around, scalpel in hand, while shells fly, deciding which one of half a dozen severely wounded men is the most likely candidate to benefit from surgery.'

'You choose who's to live and who's to die?'

'Constantly.' He tossed back the brandy.

'But the others, Harry – Major Crabbe – none of them are like Peter.'

'We all have our own way of dealing with war. Some–' he refilled his glass '–turn to drink, like Leigh and myself. Others, like Harry, treat it as all a huge joke; a few, like Peter, build shells around themselves and pretend to be tougher than they are. But none of us is the same man we were at the beginning of this mess. I'm sorry. I'm probably not making much sense. As you see, I've had more of this–' he picked up his glass '–than is good for me.'

'At least you've talked to me. It's more than Peter did.'

'Don't be too hard on him, Angela; this war

can't go on for ever. Sooner or later it will end, and then we can all get back to normal.'

She sipped her coffee and wondered if Peter would ever become 'normal' again. Then she looked at John slumped in his chair, and debated whether to mention Maud. Maud never spoke of John, or the baby Theo had told her in confidence was the result of rape. He'd checked Colonel Hale's records. Colonel Hale had noted the treatment he'd given Maud after an attack by an unknown man.

It was tragic. John and Maud were such nice people; she was fond of them both. And she couldn't help wondering why John wouldn't even try to come to terms with what had happened.

'How's Maud?' John asked, making her start guiltily.

'Keeping well. She did a little teaching in the school, but not any longer.'

'Has she told you we're divorcing?'

'Yes. I'm sorry. You seemed so happy...'

'We were, now we're not,' he interrupted. 'I'm glad Maud has a friend like you to turn to.' He heard the sound of laughter and wished Peter would whisk Angela away.

'I hate to see you both so unhappy,' she ventured.

'Surely Maud isn't unhappy. She must have lots of friends calling on her.'

'No one calls on her. She spends most of her time rolling bandages for the hospital, or sewing for the baby.' She wondered if she was doing the right thing in telling John as much. 'But I don't think she's lonely. There's always someone to talk to at the mission. People are always calling in for something. Maud's become good at dealing with their requests for help.'

The picture Angela painted was very different from the existence John had imagined Maud leading. He decided the father of her child had to be in Amara or Nasiriyeh.

'She must spend a lot of time writing letters.'

'She wrote to Mrs Harrap in India the other day.'

'Is her maid, Harriet, taking care of her?'

'Harriet calls on Maud several times a week, but she hasn't moved into the mission. She's living in rooms with several other non-commissioned officers' wives.'

'But she'll look after Maud and the baby?'

'After the baby's born. Yes, she says she will.' Angela had sensed friction between the maid and the mistress, but saw no point in mentioning it to John.

'Maud's written to no one besides Mrs Harrap?'

'No one I know of.' Angela was unnerved by the intense expression on John's face.

'It is possible Maud could have sent letters without your knowledge?'

'I don't think so. I write to Peter every day and as, a result, pick up and forward all the mission's mail from the post office.'

Peter joined them. He spoke briefly to John, then escorted Angela to their room.

John sat alone on the veranda for a long time afterwards. He didn't reach for the brandy bottle again. Instead he reflected on his own and Maud's loneliness. Could he accept Maud's child;

forgive her for betraying him with a permanent reminder of her infidelity living under his roof?

He conjured an image of the English village he had dreamed of. The home he'd wanted for Maud, himself and their children. The image seemed tarnished, spoilt. Like the apples that had grown on a diseased tree. They looked fine until you bit into them and tasted the brown, rotting cores.

Peter undressed and climbed into bed as soon he and Angela reached their room. Closing his eyes, he turned his back on Angela and relaxed within minutes into sleep. Disturbed by the day's events, Angela lingered over her nightly task of brushing out and plaiting her hair. An hour later, she undressed and slipped on her nightgown. Holding up the bedclothes, she slid into the narrow bed and lay beside her husband.

Sleep did not come easily. Peter tossed and turned, lashing out with hands and feet, pounding, kicking, forcing her to cling to a few inches on the edge of the cot until her fingers ached from the strain. She heard Major Crabbe and Johnny Leigh shout goodnight to John before walking across the courtyard. The quiet shuffle of Dira's feet when he collected their glasses.

Peter shifted; she rolled into the hollow behind his back and laid her hand around his waist. His breathing slowed to a deep, regular rhythm. Gradually her thoughts grew less coherent, her limbs heavier until she too slept.

Angela woke to shouting, confusion, and pain. Her throat was constricted, preventing her from breathing. She opened her eyes. Peter was kneeling on her, screaming. His voice vicious, alien...

'I'll kill you, you Turkish bastard. I'll kill you...'

She tried to cry out but the sound died in her mouth. She struggled desperately, attempted to prise his hands from her neck; dug her nails in with all the strength she possessed. But his grip was too fast, too strong.

'Thought you could sneak up on me. You bloody murdering Turk...'

Her heart pounded as she fought for her life. His shouting grew louder. Her fingers sank into the soft skin at his neck. He relaxed his hold for an instant. Tearing herself away, clutching her neck, she ran from the bed to the grey outline of the door. Peter followed and reached it the same time as her. He pressed his hand on one of the panels. Holding it shut.

Panic-stricken, she hammered wildly with her fists and cried out for help.

Picking her up by the shoulders, Peter hurled her aside. She slammed across the room into the stone wall.

'You can't hide from me you, murdering bastard.' He lumbered away from the door, fumbling towards in her in the darkness.

'Angela!' She recognised John's voice, then the sound of the door handle scraping up and down. 'Angela,' he repeated urgently.

She couldn't move her jaw to call back to him. Peter was still blundering in the darkness, cursing and swearing.

The door shuddered on its hinges when something heavy slammed against it from the outside.

John's voice was joined by others. She cowered in the corner furthest from Peter's shadow.

'If anyone's behind the door, stand back.' A pistol shot blasted. The door shattered inwards in a welter of splintering wood. Torch and candle light flooded the room. John and Major Crabbe burst in, Alf Grace behind them. Disorientated, blinking, Peter stared at them. He looked at Angela. At the blood on his hands. Sobbing, he sank to his knees.

Leaving Peter with Crabbe, John carried Angela to his room. Laying her on his bed, he explored her battered face with lightly probing fingers. 'You're going to have two beautiful black eyes,' he diagnosed calmly. 'If I hurt you, scream.'

She waited for the pain to intensify; when it didn't she breathed a sigh of relief.

'As you probably guessed, that means your nose isn't broken.' John pulled his bag closer to the bed and removed a bottle of surgical spirit. 'I'm going to clean up these cuts. There's not a lot I can do for the bruising. Can you talk?'

She winced when she tried to move her jaw. He touched her face below her ears. 'I'm sorry, I know that hurt. Your jaw is dislocated. I'll push it back in a moment. It's not going to be as bad as it sounds.' He held her face firmly in his hands then moved quickly.

She screamed.

'All over.'

She saw tears in his eyes. 'You're too sensitive to be a doctor,' she croaked.

'Only where ladies are concerned. It's not fair to

489

ask you this after what I've just done, but can you open your mouth so I can check your throat?'

She did as he asked.

'That's fine.' After bathing her face, he tied a bandage from the jaw to the top of her head. 'That's just a precaution; you can take it off in the morning. There.' He fastened the knot. 'Are you hurt anywhere else?' he questioned delicately.

'No,' she whispered. Footsteps sounded outside the door.

'I don't want to see Peter. Please.' She clutched at John's hands. 'Please...'

'Mason, it's Crabbe, can I come in?'

John looked to Angela; she nodded.

'Yes. Will you ask Dira to bring a shot of brandy, please?'

'I'm holding one.'

He opened the door. Crabbe was on the threshold. 'How are you feeling, Mrs Smythe?' he asked, clearly embarrassed at the sight of her lying on the bed.

'She's going to be fine.' John took the glass from him.

'I left Smythe with Grace. He needs something to calm him.'

'Give him a couple of these.' Placing the brandy on the bedside table, John dug into his bag and produced a bottle of pills. Shaking out four, he handed two to Crabbe, and kept two back. 'I'll be along in a minute.'

'Don't leave me,' Angela pleaded. 'Please, I don't want to be alone.'

'I won't leave until you're asleep,' John said.

'Please.' Clutching at his arm, she pulled herself upright. 'Please...'

'Take these.' He gave her the pills and the brandy.

'You'll stay with me until morning,' she begged.

'I can't do that. Think of your reputation.'

'Please...' She flung herself into his arms and Crabbe rescued the brandy and pills.

'Mrs Smythe, Major Mason and I can't sleep in your room, but we can move our beds outside your door. Will that be all right?'

'We won't leave the veranda,' John promised. 'Now will you take these?' He pressed the pills into her hand. She put them into her mouth and washed them down with the brandy.

'I'll find Dira, and see about moving the beds,' Crabbe closed the door.

'You promise not to leave the veranda?'

'You can talk to us through the door.' John helped her back onto the pillows. 'But I warn you, Major Crabbe snores. I know because I shared a tent with him in the desert. Now, try to relax. You've had a blow to your head, and the only way to heal those bruises is by taking plenty of rest.'

Her eyelids drooped as the drug he'd given her took effect. 'Whatever you've given me is strong,' she murmured.

He walked onto the veranda. Dira had carried out two cots and was fastening mosquito nets over them. Crabbe was smoking.

'Is she going to be all right?' Crabbe asked.

'There's no permanent damage. Cuts, bruising, shock, and a dislocated jaw.'

'I didn't realise Smythe was so close to the edge.'

'None of us did. Did he take the pills?'

'Yes.'

'I'll look in on him. With luck, he should sleep until morning. By himself. After this, no one should sleep in the same area as him.'

'That could be difficult when we go upstream. Can't you get the man sent to India? He's certifiable.'

'You'd have to be dribbling at the mouth to pass that selection board. Poor Smythe.'

'Poor us having to live with him.' Crabbe turned back the blanket on his cot.

## Chapter Thirty-three

*Basra, Friday, 20th August 1915*

Maud left her bed at the first scream but Theo was at Angela's door before her. He opened the door and turned up the lamp.

'Another nightmare?' he enquired, his voice thick with sleep.

Trembling, Angela swallowed her tears and sat up in bed. 'I'm sorry.'

'I'd rather you told me the truth of what happened in Qurna instead of endless apologies and that absurd story about falling against a carriage wheel.'

'I...' Angela shook uncontrollably.

Maud gathered her into her arms.

'Please, stay with me, just for tonight,' she begged.

'Of course,' Maud murmured.

'I'll get you a sedative.' Theo looked at Maud and jerked his head towards the door.

'I'll get my slippers and dressing gown,' Maud said tactfully.

'Leave the door open,' Angela pleaded.

Theo did as Angela asked before following Maud to her room. 'Do you know what happened to her?' he demanded, when she lifted her dressing gown from a hook on the back of the door.

'She told me the same story she told you.'

'If I find out that Smythe...'

'Until Angela tells us any different, we have to believe her.'

'You don't mind staying with her?'

'Not at all.'

'I could get the servants to carry your bed into her room.'

'It's not worth waking them at this time of night. If Angela wants me to stay with her again, they can do it tomorrow,' Maud suggested.

'You were here when Angela returned. Were there any signs that she'd been attacked?'

'If you mean raped, Dr Wallace,' Maud answered bluntly, 'I saw no evidence of it.'

'Why do strangers find it so easy to talk to me about their problems, and not my own sister?' He left and returned a few moments later with a couple of pills. 'I hope you both get some sleep.'

Maud took them, her slippers and gown, and returned to Angela's room.

'I'm being a nuisance. Theo is furious...'

'Not angry,' Maud reassured her, 'but worried. He doesn't believe the carriage story.'

Angela swallowed the pills. 'Theo thinks Peter attacked me?'

'Did he?'

'Promise you won't tell Theo?'

'I won't,' Maud agreed solemnly.

'He did, but not in the way Theo thinks. Peter was having a nightmare. John said he wasn't even awake. The next morning, Peter was dreadfully upset. He couldn't bear to face me and I couldn't bear to sit in the same room as him. That's why I asked John to arrange passage back here.' She gazed at Maud with frightened eyes. 'You have a wonderful husband.'

'Had a wonderful husband.' Maud turned down the lamp.

'Lock the door.'

'I'm here...'

'Please, lock it,' Angela implored hysterically.

Maud turned the key before slipping between the sheets.

'I wish I'd never gone to Qurna. I should have realised from Peter's letters he didn't want me.'

'Of course he wants you.'

'John said after the war the men will return to normal but I don't think any of them will be able to. It's not just the beating... It's what happened before. Peter was always so gentle and...'

'He forced himself on you?'

'Not exactly, but he was rough.' Angela searched for words that would explain what had happened in Qurna. 'It was as if I didn't exist. As if I was just something for him to use.'

'Like a girl in the Rag.'

'Rag?'

494

'Brothel,' Maud clarified. 'Command set them up wherever the regiment goes. They're a military institution. All the officers use them. John, Harry...'

'Peter?' Angela was shocked by the idea of her husband and men she knew consorting with loose women.

'If he didn't, he'd be the only officer in the regiment who abstained. Remember your wedding night. Was he as nervous as you?'

'Almost.'

'But I bet he knew what to do and he'd done it before.'

'And John?' Angela ventured.

'Was an expert,' Maud said flatly.

'Everyone says it's different for men. That they need the private side of married life more than us.' Angela sought Maud's hand under cover of the blankets. 'It's obvious John still loves you.'

'He'll never admit it.'

'Perhaps you could have this baby adopted.' Embarrassed by Maud's silence, Angela continued, 'Theo told me you were raped but only because he wanted me to understand your situation. There's been such awful gossip.'

'I can imagine.'

'It's odd to be talking to you like this. Peter and I never discussed anything intimate.'

'Did you try?'

'Yes, but Peter became so uncomfortable every time I tried to mention it, I gave up. Americans are different to Europeans. My mother explained about sex and love when I was 12.'

'My mother only talked about love in the poetic

sense. Everything else came from John and, unlike Peter, he liked to talk about sex – and put his ideas into practice. It was dreadful when he left. I didn't know what to do with myself. If there had been a Rag for officers' wives I'd have been first in the queue.'

'Maud!'

'Haven't you missed Peter that way?' Maud asked.

'It sounds dreadful to admit it.'

'Why?'

'Because no respectable woman ever talks about sex. Mrs Butler leaves the room if anyone as much as hints a mare is in foal.'

'You could talk to Theo. He is a doctor.'

'I couldn't possibly talk about the private side of married life with my brother.'

Maud slipped her hand around Angela's waist. 'I had a friend in India, Louisa. We used to talk about it. Even comfort one another sometimes.'

'Comfort?' Angela echoed, in confusion.

'Help one another.' Maud conveniently forgot to mention that Louisa had been living with her husband and brother-in-law. Or that Louisa's brother-in-law, Miguel, had generally made a threesome with the two of them and occasionally expanded their 'sessions' to include one or more of his male friends.

'Isn't it sinful?' Angela gasped when Maud moved her hand lower, lifted both their nightdresses, and slid her hand between Angela's legs.

'Making love to another man would be sinful.' Maud moved her fingers lightly, expertly. 'How can it be wrong for two women to take pleasure

496

this way?' Moving closer, she kissed Angela on the lips. Her free hand moved to Angela's breast. Moments later, she was surprised at the response she'd evoked.

But then, as Miguel had frequently said, sex was a primal urge. And what could possibly be wrong in satisfying a basic, God-given need?

*The Karun Valley*

Furja tossed on her mattress in Ali's harem, dreading her husband's return. It wasn't that Ali physically mistreated her. She had no scars to show her father when he visited. Ali was outwardly solicitous at all times, the embodiment of the perfect Bedouin husband. But there were a hundred ways of killing a wife's spirit without lifting a hand against her. And, during the six months of their marriage, Ali – and his mother – had discovered every one.

She frequently wondered why Ali had asked for her. At first she'd felt like a trophy he'd brought back from a battlefield and didn't know what to do with. When she announced her pregnancy six weeks after their wedding, all he could talk about was his coming son. Using her health as an excuse, he'd insisted she stop weaving carpets and spend her days resting within the confines of the harem.

Imprisoned, she began to dream of sky. Brilliant, daytime summer sky, washed blue and gold. Deep purple, velvety desert night sky, lit by a huge, golden moon. Every time the tent flap opened, she started, hoping to catch a glimpse of the outside world. She rarely did. Instead, she wasted her days in the gloomy heat of the tent, listening to Ali's mother and sisters berate her in terms too subtly phrased for her to raise objections. She'd never thought making love to a man could be so difficult. Before marrying Ali, she'd assumed that if she closed her eyes it would be no different to lying with Harry.

But everything was different. The feel of Ali's skin beneath her fingers, the texture of his hair, his smell, the thoughtlessness that made no concessions to her mood or pregnancy and, above all, the lack of empathy between them. She and Harry had communicated in every way, not just words. Ali merely used her to satisfy himself, and when he'd done with her; there was only emptiness, lightened by thoughts of the coming baby and memories of Harry.

Her mother-in-law talked incessantly about the baby, and how she would take charge of him as soon as he was born. Her sisters-in-law delighted in combing through her jewellery and wardrobe until she was forced to hand over most of her possessions. The sovereigns Harry had presented her on their marriage and the gold and pearls he had given her on the day of their divorce she'd smuggled out to Gutne in her daughters' clothes.

Her Aunt Gutne was her saviour. She visited every day and brought fresh fruit Mitkhal bought from the traders who plied the Karun River. There was enough left for her, even after Ali's sisters had taken their share. But, more important than the presents of food, was the support Gutne gave her. She'd lived as a slave in a Turkish harem, and while her condition in Ali's harem was not exactly slavery, there were similarities.

As soon as the girls were weaned, Gutne kept them in her tent overnight. Given the advanced state of Gutne's pregnancy, Furja protested, but she pointed out she had a slave to share the responsibility if the girls woke and, unlike Furja, a quiet tent and all the time she needed to catch up on her sleep during the day. Gutne's kindness deprived her in-laws of the opportunity to complain about their sleep being interrupted by the whining of the Ferenghi brats – their usual description of the twins.

She feared for the future of her children because they were dependant on Ali's goodwill. Every day the girls grew fairer, and she worried about her son, and what Ali's reaction would be if the baby should look remotely like Harry in feature or colouring. She pressed her hands over her swollen abdomen. Only four more months–

A footstep in the outer tent put her instantly on the alert. She pretended to be asleep, hoping Ali would leave her alone. She heard him stumble and wondered if he'd been smoking weed. The curtain moved. She kept her eyes tightly closed when he sat on the ground beside her. Then she choked, opening her eyes wide as a hand clamped over her mouth.

Mitkhal, wearing Ali's abba and head cloth, was beside her. He released his hold. Her mother-in-law moaned in her sleep. Mitkhal put his finger to his lips and pulled her through the curtain into Ali's sleeping alcove. Bound hand and foot, Ali lay unconscious on his mattress. Taking her hand, he led her outside. Keeping low, they crept to the wadi where the horses were tethered. Crouching between the animals, she breathed in deeply. Despite the smell of horseflesh, the desert air was strong and sweet, making her head swim.

'Stay low, the watchmen are over there.' Mitkhal pointed to their left.

'Gutne and the children?'

'Are in a fruit seller's dhow on the river. I took them there when most of the men were eating in your father's tent.'

'Mitkhal, you won't be able to return. You and Gutne will be outcasts...'

'We know.'

'Harry won't want me...'

'Harry will take you back however you come to him. Without you, he's like a boat without a rudder. That's enough talk. If we're to escape your father we must be in Ahwaz by morning.'

'Not Basra?'

'Your father will expect us to go downstream. He'll have every boat heading that way stopped and searched. When Shalan has stopped looking for you, we'll go to Basra, not before.'


*Basra, Monday 30th August 1915*


'What a wonderful surprise.' Maud kissed Harry's cheek. She was beautiful even with her thickening waistline and the shadows beneath her eyes. But the sparkle of the Maud he remembered from pre-war Basra days had gone, as had her fashionable clothes. She was dressed in a sober grey dress that could have been Angela's. 'Where have you sprung from?'

'Nasiriyeh.'

'Poor Harry. You look dreadful. I prescribe rest and good food.'

'For me and every other man in the Force?'

'I can't invite every other man in the force, but I can invite you. Have breakfast with me.'

'Actually, I've come to see Angela.' He followed her into the dining room where the maid had laid out bread, butter, cold meats, cheese, and fruit.

'She has her breakfast in bed. Do sit down.' She set out a place setting for him.

'Is Angela ill?'

'She has been but she's making a good recovery.'

'Nothing serious I hope.'

'No.' Maud dismissed the subject and he assumed Angela, like Maud, was pregnant. He picked out some dates from the fruit bowl and laid them on his plate.

'It's good to have company. Theo and Doctor Picard get up horribly early to go to the hospital. The Reverend and Mrs Butler are visiting one of the villages today. There's only Angela and me here and as she's not well enough to work we planned to spend the day gossiping and knitting.'

'That doesn't sound like a day's activities for the Maud I remember.'

'I don't think the Maud you remember exists any more. Oh Harry, I'm so glad you're here.' She stared at him for a moment. 'I need to ask you a favour.'

'Ask away.'

'Mother always used to say it was better to ask men for favours after a good meal. I think I'll take her advice.'

In between mouthfuls, Harry talked about Peter, Grace, her father, Crabbe: in short, everyone except John. When he finished, he pushed his plate aside, allowed her to pour him another cup of coffee and pulled out his cigarettes.

'Do you mind if I smoke?'

'I don't mind, but I won't join you. I can't smoke any more. Not since...' She glanced down at her stomach.

'Now is the time to ask me what you will.' He shook out a match. 'I haven't eaten like that since before the war.'

'I have some jewellery I want to sell. Rubies and diamonds set in gold. Could you see to it for me?'

'I'm no expert when it comes to jewellery, and the market in luxury goods has slumped. You'll get a better price for them after the war.'

'I can't wait. I need the money to keep myself and the baby until I can work again.'

'Surely John's salary...'

'I told John I can manage without his money.'

'Aren't you being naïve?'

'I prefer to think of it as fair. Why should John support me?' Taking a deep breath, she met his steady gaze. 'I assume John's told you about my situation. He used to tell you everything.'

'He mentioned the child wasn't his.'

'It isn't.'

'The father?'

'Isn't in a position to help.'

'If you know where he is you should contact him,' Harry advised.

'The fault and the child are mine,' Maud said briefly. 'Will you sell the jewellery for me?'

'I'll try, but what are you going to do after it's born? Basra's not the best place to bring up a child. Haven't you any relatives back home?'

'England isn't home. I've never been there. I have an aunt in London. I don't even know her address. But please, don't concern yourself. The problem is mine. After the baby's born, I'll think of something. Theo said I had the makings of a good nurse, and nurses will always be in demand out here.'

'But the wages won't support you and a child. Besides, what would you do with it when you're working? And there's the risk of carrying disease.'

'I haven't made any firm decisions. I can't seem to think further than the birth. Afterwards, there'll be time enough to make plans.'

'You could contact your father.'

'I don't know where he is.'

'Amara, last I heard. But a letter with his name, rank, and number should get through.'

'If I'm desperate, I'll remember that.'

'John will help you–' he began.

'That's why I offered him a divorce, Harry. I want to release him from his obligations to me.' She rose from the table. 'I'll see if Angela's dressed.'

Angela was darning a pile of men's socks when Maud showed Harry into the mission sitting room. Her hair was loose, hanging around her

503

face, and although it was nearly three weeks since she'd visited Peter, the damage he'd inflicted was still evident. Time had lightened the bruises from black to blue and yellow, but her jaw was still stiff and painful and Harry couldn't help noticing she was very nervous. A clatter of dishes from the kitchen was enough to startle her and when he stood in the doorway and exclaimed, 'Good God, what happened to you?' she almost burst into tears.

'Angela fell against a carriage wheel in Qurna when she visited Peter. Now, if you'll excuse me, I'll leave you two to gossip while I get those things for you, Harry.'

'Maud told me you'd been ill.' Harry sat on a chair opposite Angela. 'I had no idea it was an accident. Does Peter know?'

'He was there. I'd rather not talk about it.'

'You are on the road to recovery?' His voice was full of concern.

'Fit as a fiddle, and, as you see, using my bruises as an excuse to laze around. When did you get in?'

'Early this morning.'

'And you came straight here, how kind. Are you going to be in Basra long, because if you are, you must dine with us? Theo and the Reverend Butler would love to see you.'

'I won't know how long I'll be here until I get my orders. I had an ulterior motive in coming here. Have you any messages for me?'

'No,' she replied in surprise. 'I saw Peter in Qurna. Major Mason, Major Crabbe, and Lieutenant Grace were with him, but they didn't give me any messages. Should they have?'

'I told my Arab orderly to contact you. I hoped you wouldn't mind, but I didn't want to risk any communication going astray at HQ.'

'Of course I don't mind, but I'm sorry, Harry, there's been nothing.'

'Would you know if anything had come while you were in Qurna?'

'Of course. Maud hasn't left the mission in weeks.'

Harry sat back while she continued to plan the dinner party they'd hold in his honour. After a few minutes, he ceased to hear a word she said. His mind raced across the miles that separated Basra from the Karun. Had Shalan discovered what Mitkhal intended to do and killed him and Furja?

Harry remained in Basra for two weeks. He haunted the mailroom, visited the mission daily, and plagued the life out of Abdul to the point of accusing him of withholding his mail. He received letters from Michael, who, to escape Lucy, was living and working almost exclusively on the Western Front as a journalist; Georgiana, who'd plunged headlong into her work in an attempt to come to terms with her grief; even his father sent him a congratulatory note on his acting lieutenant-colonelcy. Postcards arrived from Charles's father and John's parents but he barely glanced at them. He couldn't summon any interest in what was happening in England. Only the Karun.

According to the dispatches he devoured, apart from the eternal scrapping of the Bawi the valley was quiet. The victories at Nasiriyeh, Amara, and

Shaiba had driven the Turks and Germans further up the Tigris. What disturbed him was there was no mention of Sheikh Aziz Ibn Shalan or his tribe. It was almost as though they'd been wiped from the face of the desert.

In between reading intelligence reports, he dealt with the mountain of paperwork that found its way to his desk. Being deskbound added to his depression. Days merged, followed by nights spent gambling in Abdul's. Maud's jewellery had been as impossible to dispose of as he'd predicted. The set was valuable but not to Arab taste, and there wasn't a European in Basra who wanted them. He tried them all before telling Maud it would take time to sell the rubies. Meanwhile he kept the set in Abdul's safe, using it as an occasional gambling stake in the hope that the stones would whet a Sheikh's appetite. They didn't, and as he was a careful gambler, they were always returned to the safe when the tables closed at dawn.

Basra teemed with rumours. Two distinct and warring factions emerged in the Expeditionary Force. The one that held sway in the mess supported HQ at Simla, the Indian Office, and General Nixon. They believed they were in Mesopotamia to annex it to the Indian Empire. But no one could answer Harry when he asked what they intended to do with the place once the British ruled. Apart from the oil wells and a few date palms there wasn't much worth taking, but that didn't deter Nixon's supporters from advocating an advance on Baghdad.

The political officers countered the arguments by pointing out an advance on Baghdad'd mean doubling their existing supply lines, and they did not have enough troops to hold Nasiriyeh, Basra, Amara, and Ahwaz, let alone start a new campaign. The natives were unpredictable and capable of carrying out cold-blooded murder, especially on wounded, solitary soldiers and small patrols. Even as he joined in the arguments, Harry knew it was a futile exercise. Decisions about Mesopotamia's and his future were being made elsewhere.

All he could do was wait for an edict that would determine where he spent the next few years, if he was lucky enough to live that long. And for a smuggled message to make its way out of the Karun Valley. For him, waiting was by far and away the worst bloody thing about the whole damned war.

## Chapter Thirty-four

*Aziziyeh, Friday 12th November 1915*

*Dear Angela,*
*I think of you all the time. I am desperately sorry for what happened at Qurna. I will never be able to forgive myself. I realise you probably don't want to write or see me again but I want you to know that I love you. I'll always love you…*
Peter stared at the crumpled piece of yellowed paper, all he'd been able to forage, and read what he'd written. Then he remembered how Angela had looked the morning after he'd beaten her. He

picked up the sheet of precious paper, tore it in half, and continued to tear it into tiny shreds. Reaching for a cigarette, he lit it with shaking hands. The small pile of paper was a testimony to his inadequacy. He wanted to write to her. He wanted to see her. But even if he could get to Basra, he knew he wouldn't be able to face her. The best solution was for him to be killed in action. That way she'd receive the maximum widow's pension, and he'd be out of his misery.

Wallowing in self-pity, he imagined the telegram arriving at the mission, pictured Theo, his face grave, serious as he handed Angela the yellow envelope. Her fingers trembling as she tore the paper open. Were there still envelopes in Basra?

'Boat's in.' Amey ducked into the tent. 'It's packed with reinforcements.'

'Then the rumours are right; there's going to be a show,' Peter muttered.

Amey plunged his hands into a bowl of water and splashed the dust from his face. 'Want to go to the dock to see if anyone we know has turned up?'

'No.'

'Snap out of it. You're not the first chap to hit his wife, and it's not as if you meant it.'

'Got a drink?' Peter cut Amey short.

'If its brandy you want, you know where to get it.' Amey jerked his thumb at the wall of the tent. 'That's if Mason's left any.'

'He's not...'

'As a lord. Knight's working his shift again. I don't know how much longer we can cover for him. I saw Perry giving him a hard look at dinner last night.'

'Once the show gets under way he'll pull himself together.'

'I'm not so sure.' After voicing that cheerful thought, Amey left.

Peter threw his cigarette through the tent flap. Pushing his topee on his head, he stepped outside. The air was barely warm. The flies had returned but they wouldn't last long. Another few weeks and the freezing rains would begin. The officers who'd kept their tunics and trousers had already stowed away their summer kit. The men weren't so fortunate. Their winter kit hadn't arrived.

He entered the tent John shared with Knight. John was stretched out, clutching an empty brandy bottle. Peter retrieved the bottle and stacked it with the others. There were no full bottles anywhere to be seen. Amey was right; John's problem was past covering. If he didn't curb it, someone in command would notice, and being drunk on duty meant a court martial.

'Smythe, where the hell are you? Come and see what the boat's dragged in.'

Peter stepped outside. Amey was with Charles, Charles's bearer lagging behind with Charles's kit.

'Good God, man, you're yellow. Your liver must be in one hell of a state. Are HQ so desperate they're emptying the fever wards now?' Knight called from the hospital tent.

'Orders were every available man to Aziziyeh,' Charles panted, exhausted by the short walk from the wharf. 'I was available.'

'And sick. If you find a cot you can bunk with Mason and me.'

'John's here.' An enormous smile lit Charles's

509

sallow face. 'Harry?'

'Nasiriyeh, last we heard,' Peter answered.

'Even I know he's in Basra.'

'Then we may see him yet. Put Major Reid's kit in my tent,' Knight ordered John's bearer.

Charles nodded in reply to Ram's questioning look. He glanced into the tent and saw John stretched out and the empty brandy bottles in the back corner.

'Whatever he was like the last time you saw him, he's ten times worse.' Knight lifted a camp chair and a couple of stools out of the hospital tent and set them outside his own. He pushed the chair in Charles's direction. 'My biggest worry is someone in command will catch on. There are only so many bouts of fever a man can have in one week.'

'Why don't you stop him?'

'Taking it off him when he's like this is no problem.' Knight slipped his hand beneath John and produced a flask Peter had missed. 'But, sooner or later, he'll sober up enough to go on duty and then he'll raid the medical supplies. I've tried. Believe me, I've tried to stop him but it would be easier to prevent him from breathing.'

'How long has he been as bad as this?' Charles frowned.

'Since he returned from Basra.' Amey offered his cigarettes around. 'He's left his wife, as much as anyone can leave a wife in wartime.'

'That's Mason's business,' Knight growled.

'He wouldn't mind Charles knowing. He was quick enough to tell the rest of us.'

'He was probably hoping to kill the gossip with an overdose of honesty,' Charles commented.

510

An awkward silence was punctuated by Ram's appearance with a cot. Knight cleared a space while Charles studied the men around him. Peter looked as though he'd hit despair and slid downwards. Knight was irritable and exhausted. John was out cold. Only Amey was his usual ebullient self. That left him, weak, sick, with barely enough strength to cope with living in a camp.

He hoped the Turks were running true to form. If they weren't and stood their ground, there could be a battle which none of them was strong enough to withstand.

*Basra, Wednesday 10th November 1915*

Harry faced his superior across his desk. 'Aziziyeh for Baghdad?'

'You have it, Downe.' Cox gave him a hard look. 'I heard you and Cleck-Heaton had a spat in the mess.'

'The idiot said we could take Baghdad without extra divisions. When I pointed out that we'd be stretching our supply lines to breaking point by travelling that far upstream, he suggested we could reinforce the front line on the Tigris with troops from Nasiriyeh who were only sitting on their backsides.'

'At which point you hit him.'

'He deserved it.'

'I don't doubt it, but you only succeeded in getting yourself noticed. Need I remind you your lieutenant-colonelcy is only an acting one, Downe?'

511

'I was happier as a subaltern.'

'What's the problem?' Cox probed. 'You've been at the nub of every argument in the mess for the last two weeks, Harry.'

He knew what Cox meant. Too many officers were cracking up after the long, hot summer. His colonel was wondering if he was joining their ranks.

'I'm angry with the idiots who want to take Baghdad. Even if we get it, what are we going to do with it? It's hardly within commuting distance of Westminster.'

'What we do with it is not for the likes of you or me to determine. Our business is to implement policy, not question it.'

'And the extra troops we need, if we're going to Baghdad?'

'We're getting two divisions from France.'

'Soon enough for them to join us at Aziziyeh?'

'They haven't left France yet.'

'Is there anything coming from Aden?'

'I've heard that rumour too. As far as I know, it's just a rumour.' The colonel produced a bottle of whisky and two glasses. He filled one and passed it to Harry. 'We're only a sideshow to the main event. The best we can hope to accomplish is a good headline for the London papers. That way the civilians have a victory, albeit a second-class one, to gloat over. Apart from propaganda, there's precious few of those coming from the Western Front.'

'It's that bad?'

'There and Gallipoli. We're finished on the peninsula.' Cox drank his whisky and topped up their glasses. 'Intelligence estimates the Turks have 7000 men and 19 guns deployed on the upper Tigris and 2700 men based in Baghdad. There's something else but I'd be obliged if you'd keep it to yourself.'

Harry nodded.

'A friend in the Indian Office sent a message to me by courier last week. The War Office estimates there will be 60,000 Turks in Mesopotamia by January.'

'Christ!'

'Pray he's wrong, Harry.' The colonel drained his glass.

Harry picked up his orders and buttoned them into his top pocket.

'Good luck, Downe.'

'If your friend is even close to the truth, sir, we're all going to need that.'

Harry left the barracks and hailed a carriage. He hoped even at this late hour to find Mitkhal waiting but there was no news. He checked his credit with Abdul. The Arab was holding 1700 sovereigns of his gambling gains. He took 1500 in gold and the jewellery Maud had given him to sell. He gave Abdul a copy of his will for safekeeping after adding a codicil leaving Maud her jewellery. Everything else went to Furja and his daughters, with Mitkhal, John, and Charles acting as executors. He hoped one of them would survive him.

He packed his kit, left it by the door, and walked to the bank where he placed the gold and jewellery in his safety deposit box – a box to which Mitkhal held a key. There were over 6000 sovereigns in it.

He'd been lucky at the gambling tables. He checked his account. He hadn't touched his allowance or salary for almost two years. He exchanged the balance for a credit note before going to the mission.

He found Maud sewing a baby's dress, her figure swollen, her face and ankles puffy. Dropping her sewing, she held out her hands.

'We must be winning this war if a lieutenant-colonel can afford to take an afternoon off. I'll get tea.' She set her hands on the arms of the chair, intending to lever herself up.

'I can't stay, Maud. I've received my orders. The boat leaves in two hours. I came to give you this.' He handed her an envelope. 'Abdul sold your jewellery.'

'He did!' She laughed out of sheer relief. Buying the brushed cotton for the baby dresses had taken her down to her last ten pounds. 'I can't thank you enough, Harry.'

'Thank Abdul. He probably sold it for less than it's worth but the bank draft should keep you for a while.'

She leant across and kissed him. 'If there's anything I can do for you, just say the word.'

'There is actually. Do you remember my servant?'

'The Arab?'

'I've been expecting him for months. I told him to leave a message here for me. Should he turn up, you will give him anything he needs.'

'Of course. Aren't you going to say goodbye to Angela and Theo?'

'Say it for me. How is Angela?'

'Her bruises are healing.'

'Is she likely to have any messages for Peter?'

'I don't think so,' Maud replied guardedly.

'Then I must go. This war isn't going to wait.'

'There's going to be another battle, isn't there?' she asked.

'Possibly. But Johnny Turk's always run from us before. No reason to suppose he's going to change his form now.'

She looked at him. The face that only a year before had been unlined and carefree was thin, creased and worn, and there were premature strands of grey in his fair hair. 'Look after yourself, Harry. A lot of people care about you. More than you realise.'

'You should know by now I'm indestructible.' He kissed her cheek. 'Goodbye, Maud.'


## Chapter Thirty-five

*The Tigris above Aziziyeh,*
*Sunday 21st November 1915*

Charles crossed the ground when the church parade broke up and clasped Harry's arm. 'I was hoping you'd turn up.'

'Can't have a show without me.' Harry looked Charles over. 'If we were in Clyneswood in the spring we could lose you in the daffodil wood.'

'Everyone's here.' Charles led the way to the tents. 'John, Knight, Smythe, Amey, Crabbe...'

515

'I saw most of them on parade except John.'

'He and Knight are on duty.'

'Duty's preferable to standing around listening to bloody sermons. Whose bright idea was it to lecture the men on tithes before a show?'

'Padre Powell. "Take the minds of the men off what's to come, eh what?" I'm bunking with John and Knight, but Amey and Smythe have room for you.'

'I'm going out with the advance guard.' Harry reached for his pocket watch and opened it. 'In two hours, but I have to change somewhere.' Harry picked up his kitbag. 'Lead me to your tent. That way I can dump my spare gear on your bearer.'

'He's back with the Mahrattas. Got commissioned yesterday.'

'You trained him well.'

'Not really, he started out that way.' Charles opened the tent flap. 'I can't offer you a drink. We don't keep any.'

'John?' Harry asked.

'You know.' Worn out by the church parade, Charles sat on his cot.

'I've seen it coming for a long time, but as he's not here, here's to those who can handle it.' Harry produced a flask.

Charles unscrewed the cap and drank. 'That's damned good brandy.'

'I filled it in Basra.'

Remembering his liver, Charles screwed the flask shut and handed it back. 'You always hear ten times more than anyone else, what's the score?'

Harry stripped off his tunic, shirt, and ID discs,

and piled them on Charles's kitbag. 'God help us if we don't take Baghdad tomorrow. All the evacuation plans are to take the wounded forward. Townsend's estimated our casualties at 2400, which even the staff believe to be on the low side. The "hospital ships", if you can call the rust buckets that, only have facilities to carry 1500. If the Turks don't run, we could find ourselves retreating downstream, but Amara has a lot to offer. You can stand me drinks and dinner in the mess. Either there or Baghdad.'

*Battle of Ctesiphon, Monday 22nd November 1915*

'There is the tomb of Salman the Pure, Effendi. It's bad luck for the Infidel to fight in the shadow of one so venerated by the faithful.' Ahmed made an indirect reference to the disturbances in one of the Indian regiments who'd refused to fight on their holy ground.

'It's worse luck for the faithful to fight beside one of the great monuments of Western civilisation.' Harry indicated the Roman arch that dominated the settlement of Ctesiphon. Ahmed fell silent, leaving Harry to reflect on the madness that had driven so many Empires to self-destruct in this filthy land.

The Bedouin had been travelling the desert and the Marsh Arabs laying their fish traps when Alexander the Great had died from fever contracted in the Mesopotamian swamps. The Romans pushed aside the tribes and marked the desert with magnificent edifices, which the

Bedouin had used for centuries to shade their livestock. And now the British had chosen to fight here. He hoped it wouldn't prove to be his empire's as well as Alexander's Armageddon.

The moment the first rays of dawn touched the horizon, whistles echoed down the lines. Men crawled from hastily scraped dugouts and began to advance across the plain that separated them from the Turkish front line, 5000 yards away. Harry waited until the British and Turkish Arab irregulars and camelry closed in on the flanks, before kicking the camel beneath him.

He and Ahmed moved forward. At that instant, the British artillery guns boomed into life behind them. Shells streaked into the enemy's trenches.

Harry spurred his camel on until it ran alongside the advancing Dorsets. A spurt of rifle fire brought down men in the front line. He drew his revolver, and headed for the mass of Turkish Arab irregulars; waving the men behind him into an inferno that had none of the impersonal qualities he'd experienced standing on the decks of the river launches.

By 11 o'clock, Harry was bloodied and exhausted. He gazed across the plain littered with the broken bodies of men and horses and saw the Dorsets had taken the arch of Ctesiphon.

The Turkish artillery chose that moment to crash into action. His camel bolted. He clutched at the reins, but he was too late. Slithering sideways, he landed on the body of John's orderly, Singh.

None of the Dorsets had eaten in over 24 hours

but, hungry, thirsty, and exhausted, they followed their officers into the Turkish forward trenches and turned the guns so they faced the Turkish second line. Only then did the CO hand down the order for a respite. Peter drank from his water bottle before climbing a pile of Turkish dead to peer over the parapet. He reloaded his revolver blindly while he scanned the Turkish second line guns. The line wasn't their last. There was another, and, in the distance, he could make out a fourth.

'We did it.' Charles slumped at his feet. He was breathless, his sword dangling from one hand, his revolver loosely cradled in the other.

'Are you wounded?' Peter asked in concern.

'Pooped, it's a long run across that plain.'

Peter pulled out his binoculars. A whistle blew and men surged forward. 'Christ, what bloody idiot did that?'

An answering whistle resounded from the Turkish trenches and a line moved forward to meet their own.

Peter vaulted over the edge of the trench. Charles tried to follow, but stumbled and fell back. He looked at his revolver. The barrel was empty. He pulled out his ammunition pouch and reloaded it. He didn't have the energy to go and fight the war; he'd just have to sit and wait until it came to him.

'Stretcher-bearers!' John screamed. Around him was a Dante's Inferno of dead and dying. They continued to flood in an endless stream, crawling in on hands and knees, helped by those who were still able to stand. A few were even carried in by bearers, but he was finding it impossible to summon any to carry them out. He was being buried under an avalanche of groaning men. He continued to scream for orderlies, for bandages, for instruments, for stretcher-bearers. None appeared.

A man lay on a trestle in front of him, blood pouring from a neck wound. He plunged in his hand. Holding the severed artery together, he fought instinctively for the man's life, yet he didn't cease screaming for stretcher-bearers. The tables had to be cleared. If they weren't, there'd be yet more dead on his conscience.

'Sir, where can I put these?' A sepoy stood at the front of a stretcher buckling beneath the weight of three men.

John thrust his hand deeper into the neck of the man whose artery lay exposed. 'I want bearers to evacuate the wounded, not bring them in. We can't take any more.'

'All transports to the river are full, sir. The launches won't take any wounded, not while the battle's still going on.'

'Someone has to do something,' John ranted, as if he could bully the world back to sanity.

'All wounded to be evacuated to the forward lines and Baghdad.'

John looked behind the stretcher-bearers and saw the red collar of a staff officer. 'All wounded to be taken forward to Baghdad,' Cleck-Heaton reiterated parrotlike.

'We've taken Baghdad?' Knight could only be recognised by his bloodied apron.

'We will by the time these get there.'

and lit a fire, but most of the men were too weak to crawl to it. He hadn't seen a water carrier or cook all day but those who were conscious didn't complain. Some cried out in agony, but there wasn't one word of reproach.

He turned his camel and picked his way back to the field, wanting to protest for them. He longed to smash his fist into someone. To shout, to scream at an injustice that forced wounded men who'd fought to the limit of their strength to lie on wet ground to wait for treatment that, if it came at all, would probably come too late.

Charles slowly blinked his way to consciousness and excruciating agony. The pain was so intense it was impossible to determine its source. Pressure was being exerted on his body from a dozen points. He jerked and hit the unyielding surface beneath him. He had difficulty breathing; his head was free, but an enormous weight pressed on his chest. The smell of sweat, blood, and something sickly sweet and putrid cloyed around him. He heard the harsh, guttural sound of an Indian muleteer and realised he was travelling in one of the wooden supply carts.

He recalled the trench – Peter – the sound of the whistle blowing. He'd tried to follow but he'd fallen back, drawn his gun, and waited. Beyond that, nothing. Someone whimpered above him. He didn't know how much longer his lungs could stand the pressure. It was raining. He felt cold, wet drops on his cheeks.

Overhead he caught glimpses of blackness slashed occasionally by a short-lived streak of shellfire. A cutting wind chafed his head, freezing it, in raw contrast to the crushing warmth that blanketed his body. The jolting ceased. Moans became screams when the bodies above him were lifted from the cart.

The weight was taken from him. He breathed in, shuddering, when damp, icy air hit his lungs. His teeth chattered. He was so cold and it was so black that afterwards he couldn't be sure whether he had remained conscious or not. He heard Matthews, but the voice was distant, remote...

'The doctors can't cope. Sort out those who aren't too badly wounded and take them to the steamers.'

He couldn't have dreamed the voice, or the order. He had to be awake. Footsteps squelched in mud. Fingers prodded his battered body. He opened his mouth, intending to tell whoever it was to leave him alone, but he was simply incapable of making the effort.

Crabbe hadn't slept in 24 hours, but he showed no sign of fatigue as he supervised the loading of the wounded onto the steamers and launches that could be spared. He checked each cart as it arrived. If there were less than six men crammed on the wooden boards, he sent the sepoys back to pick up those with broken limbs or spines, who had flung themselves out of the unsprung transports rather than endure the agony of the trip.

All around men milled in half-illuminated chaos, bewildered, shocked, most too exhausted to think about what they were doing. A steamer loaded above the water line with over 400 wounded had been tardy in leaving and he was trying to cram 200 more on to its packed decks. He saw bullet wounds that had been hastily dressed by half-trained hands. Men with string tied around bleeding limbs to act as tourniquets. Men half dead from cold, thirst, hunger, and weariness.

Angered by the incompetence of it all, he shouted at a stretcher-bearer, demanding he return a cart of wounded, who hadn't received any medical attention, to the field hospital.

'It's no use screaming at the men. Try the brass.' Harry stood next to him.

'It's bloody disgraceful. Look at that man.' Crabbe pointed to an English officer from the Mahrattas who was bleeding from a head wound. 'If he's seen a doctor I'm a monkey's arse!' he exclaimed, reverting to sergeants' language.

'We have four field hospitals; each equipped to deal with a hundred casualties. At the last count, there were 4500. Have you seen Charles or Peter?'

'No.' Crabbe capitulated and waved the cart with the untended wounded on. 'But I know there are only nine officers left in the Dorsets.'

'One in the Mabrattas, two in the 104th Rifles, and four in the Gurkhas and Punjabis.' Grace stepped out of a small boat on to the bank.

'Have you seen Charles, Peter, or Amey?' Harry asked.

'No, only a stupid staff officer who's keeping a tally of the casualties. Anyone would think he was talking about cricket scores.' Grace produced a flask and offered it to Crabbe and Harry. 'One hundred and thirty British officers have gone down.'

'That's a third of our strength.'

'All the Indian regiments are below half strength. Men as well as officers.'

'What was it like on the launches?' Harry drank deeply before returning the flask to Grace.

'Better than here,' Grace answered cryptically.

Harry stubbed out his cigarette. 'I'm going to look for Charles.'

'I could do with some help here,' Crabbe said tersely.

'So could the men still lying on the field.' Harry led his camel away.

Harry joined the stretcher-bearers and uninjured officers who were scouring the plain in search of anyone alive. He met Perry, who grudgingly told him he'd seen Peter in the forward trenches, but he found no one who'd seen Charles. At dawn, he carried two more bodies to the pile of dead awaiting burial. Lying to the side of the mound was a smaller heap of officers. He recognised Alex Day and, below him, the blood-soaked face of Stephen Amey.

He rested his head against his camel's neck and looked to the new light dawning grey and cold in the sky. He felt none of the elation he had experienced at Sahil; only a miserable sense of waste, and loss.

If this was war, the generals could keep it.

'This boat is full.'

'The doctors say this officer has to go downstream, Sahib.' Chatta Ram bowed and scraped, as only the sepoys knew how.

526

'I couldn't give a hang what the doctors say.' Cleck-Heaton pushed his lamp in Ram's face. 'I've seen you skulking round the camp. Took me a while to work out why you look familiar; you're the spitting image of your father. Your skin's lighter, but then you'd get that from your whore mother.'

Ram stared Cleck-Heaton in the eye. 'I have to get this man on board.' He dropped his subservience along with his Indian accent. 'If you'd allow me to pass, sir.'

'Not until I've seen who's so hellfire important.' Cleck-Heaton pulled the blanket from the figure Ram held in his arms. 'I might have guessed,' he jeered, still smarting from the punch John had given him. 'Downe and Mason's chum. Well, your bloody half-brother can wait for treatment like everyone else, Ram. That is your name isn't it? Or is it Reid like your mother, you wog bastard?'

Charles tried to focus on Cleck-Heaton. Half-brother? The man was mad.

'Major Reid is badly wounded. Please, let me pass so I can take him on board.'

'I said this ship is full, you, half-breed bastard. If I had my way, you Anglos wouldn't be allowed into the Army as sweepers, much less given commissions. Ought to be shot, the lot of you. Fucking mongrel misfits. Now move on before I have you arrested.'

'Cleck-Heaton!' Perry walked towards them, a thunderous look darkening his face.

'Sir.' Cleck-Heaton snapped to attention, deferring to Perry's rank. Taking advantage of the interruption, Ram ran up the gangplank, but not before Charles overheard Perry admonishing

Cleck-Heaton.

'How dare you! Reid's father was a general. The rank alone entitles him to our loyalty, not to mention regimental honour as a past officer. No one has mentioned the subject for over 20 years and you bring up it up here, of all places. Shouting it out for the ranks and wogs to hear. Christ, man, have you no sense of propriety?'

Charles looked into Ram's face. It was long and thin, like his own. His father's was round. He'd never seen a photograph of his mother. He'd asked Harry's mother if he could have one once. He'd been 14, on his way back to school after the summer recess. He'd packed his picture of his father and he'd wanted one of his mother, like the other boys, but his aunt had told him it would upset his father. He'd never asked her about his mother again.

He'd learnt at an early age not to talk about the dead. But the lack of photographs hadn't erased an image he'd carried for years. Of a beautiful, fair, young woman walking into his nursery in India. A woman with an oval face and bright blue eyes who'd smelled of roses and wept when she'd held him close.

Chatta Ram prised the packed bodies roughly apart. It was still raining, but he knew Charles would be better off on deck than below. Here he'd breathe fresh air, and river water was within reach. He ran his fingers over Charles's leg. The wound was clean – for the moment. The bullet had passed through, but Charles hadn't recovered from the fever. He had no strength left to fight infection…

'Are you my half-brother?'

'Major Cleck-Heaton mistook me for someone else.'

Charles was sick, but not sick enough to believe the lie. 'Is our mother still alive?'

'Yes, she's alive.'

The engines started. The sepoy laid his hand on Charles's forehead but he jerked free. The movement brought pain. He laid his head on the bare deck and listened to the groans of the wounded shut in below. Regimental honour! How could his father have allowed him to take a commission in India without giving him a single word of explanation or warning?

## Chapter Thirty-six

*Ctesiphon, 4 a.m. 24th November 1915*

'Downe!' Perry called into the trench where Harry was sheltering from the hurricane force wind that was driving clouds of dust over the plain and into the crevices where the troops had taken refuge. Harry pulled his kafieh higher and crawled towards the command officers.

'Reconnaissance,' Perry barked. 'We need to find out what the Turks are up to.'

Harrap looked at Harry's slight figure swathed in Arab robes with something akin to pity. 'We won't withstand another attack like the last.' He pitched his voice below the wind. 'This line has had six attacks in the last six hours.'

'I've been with General Hoghton,' Harry said. 'He only just managed to hold on to his line. He's almost out of ammunition.'

'We all have our problems,' Perry refused to look further than his own command. 'There's no time to lose. We need that information.'

'I know this is hard on you, Downe,' Harrap sympathised.

'If I see anything further than my nose up there, I'll try to live long enough to let you know.' Harry crawled back to Peter. Belting his robe, he put his foot on a sandbag.

'Go over the top and you're a dead man, Harry,' Peter warned.

'Refuse and I'll give Perry an excuse to shoot me in the back.' Thrusting his knife into his belt, he took his gun in his left hand and vaulted out of the trench.

Harry could see only a few inches ahead as he wriggled over the plain. Once or twice, when the dust cleared for an instant, he thought he glimpsed the flicker of Turkish torches but he couldn't be sure.

He inched forward; taking cover behind the bodies littering the field. One groaned. He drew the knife from his belt, clamping it between his teeth. A knife was silent, and he couldn't afford to alert the Turks.

His eyes stung from dust and peering too hard for things that weren't there. Just as he was becoming accustomed to the spasms of fear that trickled down his spine, the Turkish guns crashed into life again. He pressed his face into the dirt and clamped his hands over his head. The guns continued to boom, shattering his eardrums, but reason stole through his fear. They were too far away to be of any immediate danger. Lifting his head, he saw the faint but definite glimmer of lights dancing in the swirling dust.

Digging in his fingers and toes, Harry pulled himself on. He hit the coarse cloth of a sandbag. Gripping his cocked gun, he lifted his head and peered down over the edge of a parapet, half-expecting to see a Turk looking up at him. Sticks wrapped with oily rags burned raggedly in improvised holders on the wall. An ammunition box lay ripped apart on the floor; bodies were piled in a corner. Crouching low, he ran back towards the home trench.

He lost his footing when he hit the British line and fell into a dugout. A man jumped on him and he cursed his Arab robes as he belted out his name, rank, and number. The private stepped back and Harry looked at the ragbag of insignia around him. Regimental pride had disappeared on the casualty transports. The survivors had been lumped together: signallers, Mahrattas, Dorsets... The veteran British troops looked exhausted, the Indians incredibly young. Most of the experienced sepoys had been sent to the Western Front.

'We winning, sir?' a corporal from the Dorsets ventured.

'No one's winning against this damned dust.'

He tried to sound cheerful. 'Where's Colonel Perry?'

'Ahead, sir. A messenger's just come from HQ. Johnny Turk's shelling the road our wounded are taking to the river.'

'They're shelling our hospital ships too, sir,' a private added. 'Damn their eyes.'

'We're still going to push through to Baghdad aren't we, sir?'

Harry recognised the plea behind the question. There were so many dead, so many wounded, so many missing – he felt the same way about Charles and Amey. All this suffering had to have some purpose. If it didn't, if it was for nothing, there was no point in struggling to carry on. They may as well shoot themselves.

'Yes, corporal, we'll reach Baghdad. It may take us longer than we anticipated, but we'll get there. I promise you that.'


*Ctesiphon, 25th November 1915*

'Order to retreat, sir.'

Peter stared at the messenger as though he were insane. 'We can hold the line. Damn it, we can...'

Crabbe laid his hand on Peter's shoulder. 'Word has come from HQ. The Turks have reinforcements and are regrouping. We can't keep this up. It's costing too much.'

Peter looked across at the Roman arch. He'd taken it. Him and the regiment, and now they were going to hand it back to Johnny Turk. Why had they bothered to fight?

'Take half the men,' Crabbe ordered. He shouted down for every second man to fall out and follow Captain Smythe.

Peter looked back. The armoured cars of the

cavalry had moved in on their flanks, ready to cover the retreat. He remembered Charles and Amey. Why, damn it – why?

He slammed his fist into a sandbag. A private from the Mahrattas was staring at him. From down the trench he heard a scrap of doggerel being sung to the tune of 'Keep the Home Fires Burning'.

*'Some calls it Ctesiphon. Some calls it Cestiphon. But I call it Pisstupon.'*

If the Tommies had anything to do with it, they'd be back.

## Umm-ut-Tubul, 30th November 1915

A shudder tore the *Firefly* from stem to stern as a shell shattered her bridge. Bowditch flung himself onto the deck, banging his head against Harry's. They both skidded against the cabin wall.

'Good shots, these Turks.' Harry shot Bowditch a grin.

'You're insane. We're done for. We're...'

'Going for a swim?'

Some of the ratings had already thrown life rafts overboard and were jumping after them. Through the smoke and fire, Harry saw the prow of the *Sumana* turn towards them. On their right, smoke rose raggedly from the deck of the *Comet*.

'We can't abandon her,' Bowditch protested when the signal blew. 'We need every craft. We won't stand a chance without them.'

'We won't stand a chance if we stay with them.' Reaching for his rifle, Harry took an ineffectual pot shot in the direction of the Turks on the bank.

'Doctor!' A blackened rating appeared from below deck, his hair seared to a grey frizzle, his uniform pocked with scorch marks.

'We need a doctor, *sir*,' Bowditch reprimanded.

Harry looked for Knight. He'd seen him ten minutes ago, but there had been so many wounded, even before the Turks had started firing, that Knight could be on any one of the half-dozen barges packed with wounded the *Firefly* was towing. He grabbed the rating's arm. 'You'd best get off while you can.'

'Not while me mate's below deck, sir. The steam pipe broke above him when we were hit. It cracked clean in half. He's in agony. Proper agony, sir.'

'I'll see to him. You find the doctor, send him here, then get yourself off,' Harry shouted above the crackle of flames.

'Harry, she's going to blow any minute.'

Harry shook off Grace's restraining hand. 'See you on board the *Sumana*.' He swung down the ladder. A tide of men surged towards him and he clung to the side of the narrow passageway. After they passed, the hold fell quiet enough for him to hear screaming ahead. It was high-pitched, continuous, the screech of machinery when the oil runs dry.

He kicked open the door of the engine room. A man lay curled on the floor, his face and upper arms skinned raw, his clothes clouding with vapour where the boiling steam had burst over him. Two men crouched beside him.

'You two, on deck, now. Didn't you hear the signal to abandon ship?'

534

'But our mate...'

'That's an order.'

The men hesitated.

'A direct order,' Harry barked.

The men looked back as they left. There was a crack, and the whine ceased. Harry saw a tooth embedded in one of the man's bloody lips.

He crouched besides what was left of the seaman. 'You need those teeth to chew army biscuits,' he said gently. 'Don't think you're going to get cake soaked in milk just because you're wounded.'

If the man heard him, he gave no sign. The terrible whining percolated through his throat once more. Harry rested his hand on the man's left leg, the only part of him that was whole. Sliding around to the back of the seaman's head, he removed his revolver.

'Downe.' Knight joined him. Pulling out a syringe, he filled it with morphine. 'Soon have you right as rain, old man.' He slid the needle into the raw flesh on the man's forearm. When he finished, he wiped the needle and tossed the syringe into his bag. A few moments later, the seaman fell mercifully silent. Knight glanced at Harry's gun. 'I hope you're around if I'm ever in that state.' He climbed the ladder. 'You would have been right to use it if I hadn't arrived. My way is kinder but just as sure.'

'Then you...'

'Eased him out of his misery. He's not the first, and with what's going on there's no hope he'll be the last. Drink.' He thrust a flask at Harry when they reached the deck. Harry took a long pull and handed it back. He was angry with himself

535

for not being more sympathetic towards John. He'd thought nothing could be worse than facing the aftermath of a battlefield.

He'd been wrong.

*Basra, 30th November 1915*

'There's a man to see, Mrs Smythe, ma'am.' The native girl who worked in the mission kitchen hovered in the doorway of Maud's bedroom.

'An officer?' Maud immediately thought of Peter – and John.

'No, ma'am.' The girl had difficulty in getting her tongue around the 'ma'am' Mrs Butler insisted on. 'A Bedouin. He says he knows Lieutenant-Colonel Downe. I said Mrs Smythe was at the hospital, so he said he'd see you.'

'That's very good of him,' Maud said caustically, recalling Harry's insubordinate orderly. 'Show him into the vestibule.'

The girl bobbed a curtsy. Maud left her chair. Massaging her aching back, she walked into the hall.

'Mrs Mason.' Mitkhal looked coolly at her.

'I remember you from the barracks.' She didn't mention Furja's house. 'Harry's not in trouble, is he?'

'He's with the force upriver,' Mitkhai answered in careful English, 'and the reports are not good. That is why I would like to get there as soon as I can. He may need me.'

'I thought he never went anywhere without you.'

'He had to this time.' A few curt words from

536

Maud had been more than enough for Mitkhal. 'I must see Mrs Smythe.'

'She won't be back for hours. She's working at the hospital. If you've heard what's going on up-river, you must have heard about the conveys of wounded.'

'I have. Thank you, Mrs Mason.' He turned on his heel.

'Wait,' Maud walked slowly after him. 'Is there anything I can do?' she asked shamefaced, recalling how much Harry had done for her.

'Nothing, thank you, Mrs Mason,' Mitkhal replied politely. 'Good day to you.'

Maud returned to her sewing, but she was no longer pleased with the string of daisies she had embroidered on the hem of the baby dress she'd made. Angela, always Angela – why did people never turn to her for help?


*Umm-ut-Tubul, 30th November 1915*

'If we hadn't rested at Aziziyeh we wouldn't be in this mess.' Grace held out his hand as Harry climbed, wet and shivering, onto the deck of the *Sumana*. Harry accepted Grace's help and crawled against the boards close to the wall of the cabin.

Grace watched Harry settle before dropping his hand in a sharp downward movement to signal the gunners. The guns exploded, and Harry clamped his hands over his ears. Unlike the ships' officers, he'd never become accustomed to the shattering noise.

'We stayed at Aziziyeh for two days because the

537

infantry couldn't walk another step,' Harry reminded Grace, as soon as he could hear himself speak. 'You should try marching and carrying your own kit. It's not like cruising down the Tigris.'

'There goes the *Comet*.' Grace hadn't heard a word Harry had said.

Harry watched smoke rise from the sinking vessel. 'Aren't you going to shell the *Firefly?*'

'Some poor bastard's holed up in the engine room. We're hoping the Turks will be kind to him.'

Harry almost said the man was dead. Then he recalled what Knight had done. It looked as though the whole fleet was burning. Barges, launches, the *Comet, Shaitan,* and now the *Firefly* left for the Turks. He ducked when the *Sumana* edged closer to the wreckage of the *Comet*. Bullets flew from the bank. A seaman fell alongside him. Harry grabbed the dead man's rifle and ammunition pouch. Taking careful aim, he returned the fire.

Ratings and officers were heading out to the *Comet* on rafts to help the survivors. Harry shivered from cold and his soaking in the Tigris. His eyes stung from smoke. The skin rubbed from his fingers as he repeatedly pulled the trigger of the rifle, but he was luckier than the poor sods who lay wounded and helpless on the hospital barges that trailed upstream in the wake of the crewless *Firefly* and *Comet*.

The *Sumana* pulled downstream and Harry looked back. The hospital barges weren't the only ones to be abandoned. Supply barges drifted alongside them, and he guessed the brass had left the goods in the hope the Turks would use them to care for the injured. He prayed that the faith of whoever had given the order to leave them would be justified.

*Lansing Memorial Hospital, Basra*

'I'm sorry for keeping you waiting ... Mitkhal, isn't it?' Angela stepped out of a ward, jumped over the head of a patient, and squashed against the wall to make room for a stretcher to pass.

The wards had overflowed into the corridors and the stench was overwhelming. Mitkhal glanced at the man lying on the floor. He was filthy, his hair and beard alive with lice. He returned Mitkhal's stare contemptuously and spat on the hem of his robe.

'As you can see, we're impossibly busy, but I'll collapse if I don't get a cup of tea. Will you join me in the kitchen?' Angela sidestepped gracefully around the patients. Mitkhal felt oversized and clumsy when he followed her into a small, dark room. 'Would you like tea?' Folding a towel around the handle of a kettle on the stove, she lifted two cups down from the cupboard.

'Thank you.' He was amazed by her familiarity. No English lady had ever offered him tea when he'd lived at the barracks. Angela spooned three ladles of tealeaves into a battered metal pot. 'I've been trying to get in here since I started at six this morning. I could do with something to eat too.' She opened the cupboards. 'There are only dry biscuits, but you're welcome to one.'

'No, thank you, tea will be fine.'

'How is Harry? I don't mean to be rude, but I'll have to go as soon as I've drunk this. The convoys haven't stopped for the past two days. The military hospitals are bursting with British and Indian casualties. They can't cope with the Turks as well, so they're sending them here. I've suspended my classes to help until the crisis is over. You don't ... you...?' She stared wide-eyed at Mitkhal.

'I haven't heard anything about Captain Smythe. I hoped you'd be able to give me some news.'

He realised there was no way that he could ask her to look after Furja and Gutne. What little spare time she'd have in the next few weeks, Maud would commandeer.

'I haven't heard from Harry or anyone in weeks.' She stirred the tea and handed him a cup. 'But that's not to say none of them are here. If they'd arrived with one of the convoys they'd have gone straight to the mission.'

'Angela, where the dickens are you?' Theo stuck his head around the door.

'Theo, this is Mitkhal. He's Lieutenant-Colonel Downe's orderly.'

'He's not...'

'Mitkhal was hoping we'd have news of Harry.'

'Can't help you, I'm afraid.' Theo gave Mitkhal a sympathetic glance. 'We haven't seen any of the officers since they went upstream. Angela, another convoy has come in and we haven't finished dressing the wounds on the last.' He turned to Mitkhal. 'Could you give us a hand?'

'I'd like to, but I have to go.'

'I'll see you out. I need some fresh air.'

'Goodbye, Mitkhal, I hope to see you again

very soon, when I'm not so busy. You must come and have tea with us in the mission.' Angela held out her hand. Mitkhal shook it. 'If you should need anything and you think we can help, Mrs Mason is at the mission.'

'Thank you, Mrs Smythe.'

'For what?' she asked.

'The tea.' He followed Theo through the door.

'You meant what you said to my sister? You haven't heard from my brother-in-law,' Theo asked as soon as they were out of Angela's earshot.

'I haven't, but if I can find someone to take care of my wife I'm going upstream.'

'We could find a bed for her at the mission.'

'I'm hoping to place her with relatives,' Mitkhal lied diplomatically. He held out his hand. 'But thank you for the offer, Dr Wallace.'

'You'll let me know if you hear anything?' Theo shook his hand.

'I'll try to send a message to you.'

'Dr Wallace!' an orderly cried hysterically.

'I have to go.'

*Basra*

Mitkhal plunged into the network of lanes that led down to the river. If he asked, Abdul would take care of Furja and Gutne, but both were near their time and Abdul's hospitality would be well meaning, not comfortable. Also, Abdul's house was a public one. Arab ghulam, gambling Bedouin, British soldier, Jewish merchant, Turkish spy were in and out at all hours. It wouldn't take Shalan long to find the women if they were living there – or the Turks.

He saw the Turkish threat to Furja as a real one. The political officers, including Harry, scoffed at the rumours that the Turks had put prices on their heads, but he'd heard how large those sums were. Accurate figures had reached even Shalan's corner of the Karun. The former wife and children of Harry Downe would prove invaluable hostages to anyone interested in collecting the bounty on Harry. Furja and the children could be kidnapped, Gutne hurt, or taken with them and, if Abdul was busy, their absence might not be noticed for hours.

He felt as though he were being torn between the love he bore for his wife and coming child, the promise he'd made to Harry to care for Furja, and the ties transcending friendship that bound him to Harry.

If only he didn't have this overwhelming feeling of foreboding that Harry was in danger...

He carried on walking back to the dhow he'd berthed in the shadow of a British launch, and while he walked, he mulled over his problems. But he was still careful to take a circuitous route and check every few yards to make sure he wasn't being followed. It was times like this he cursed his height. One of Shalan's tribesmen had only to catch a glimpse of him for him to be recognised.

He was in a narrow, nondescript alleyway when he saw a British officer. There was nothing here to draw an officer, unless...

He dived into a lane that ran between two high-walled houses. One of the walls curved slightly. Set into the curve was an ironwood door banded with closely worked metalwork that was more than merely decorative. He knocked; when there was no reply, he tried the handle. The door was locked. He knocked louder. The door opened and he ducked below the lintel, only to have his hands roughly bundled behind his back. He tried to push past his assailants but the breath was elbowed out of his body and he was slammed against the garden wall.

'Zabba, I need to see Zabba,' he stammered breathlessly.

'Of course you do,' an old woman wheezed. An enormously fat body veiled in unrelieved black waddled towards him.

'Zabba, don't you know me?'

She paused, frowned, and finally beamed, showing twin rows of pink, toothless gums. 'Little Mitkhal, by all of Allah's graces– Let him go, you brutes.' She tapped the men who held him with her fan. Mitkhal was released and he stepped forward, rubbing his wrists. He nodded to the two massive black slaves who'd held him, to show he bore no malice.

'Come.' Zabba tapped her fingers on his chest. 'You will take coffee with me. I have ten years of your life to catch up on.'

Mitkhal put his arm around the old woman and kissed her rouged cheek. 'You look as young and beautiful as ever.'

'What do you want from me this time, Mitkhal?'

'A favour.' He looked across the garden into the reception room, where two British officers were sharing a bottle of whisky. The location couldn't be more perfect. Close to the river for ease of movement, especially at night. The house was quieter, more discreet than Abdul's, well-guarded, and, knowing Zabba, only patronised by those rich enough to afford its expensive favours; principally wealthy merchants and British officers with private means. The kind of people who would avoid trouble at all costs.

Furja and Gutne would be safer here with Zabba than in the barracks or the mission.

'A very big favour, Zabba.' He hugged her as they walked across the garden and up the stairs to her room.

## Chapter Thirty-seven

*Basra, Sunday December 5th 1915*

'In God's name, this is unforgivable!' Colonel Allan gazed in horror at the launch berthed in front of him.

'We did what we could,' Lieutenant Ashford, the Eton 'wet bob' of Nasiriyeh, and lately of Ctesiphon, apologised.

'These men haven't been washed, fed, had their wounds dressed or their bandages changed in...' The doctor's rage abated when the lieutenant turned deathly white.

'Thirteen days, sir,' Ashford whispered. 'We did what we could without rations or medicines, and we had to fight every inch of the way. Past Turks, past Arabs...' He swayed and crashed to the deck.

544

Allan ran on board. The launch was awash with excrement and vomit. Men lay inches deep in their own filth and, for all his 15 years in the Indian Medical Service, he gagged at the sight of limbs putrefying in an advanced state of gangrene. He bellowed for stretcher-bearers and he picked up the lieutenant. Despite the cold, the boy's body burned through his thick winter uniform. Someone carried him away. He turned to the injured man lying closest to him and lifted the bandage on his leg. A spiral of maggots fell into the mess on deck.

'Is it bad, sir?' the private from the Dorsets asked. The face was that of a child but the eyes were those of an old man.

'No, private.' Allan fought to keep a grip on his emotions. 'Once we've moved you out of these disgraceful conditions we'll soon have you right.' He ordered the stretcher-bearers to take the boy to one of the ambulances on the quayside and moved on, examining each man in turn, concentrating on the individual, trying not to look into the blind, staring eyes of those who hadn't lived to see port.

He switched off his emotions, adopted clinical mode, and began estimating men's strength, deciding who would survive surgery, and who would not.

Those with the best chance, he sent to the hospital. The dead he ordered piled against the cabin wall. He commanded his men to hose a portion of the deck for the third category: men who still lived, but probably weren't going to make it. He gave them a shot of morphine, a smile, and told them they'd have to wait a while longer. If any

545

survived, they'd be carried off the ship last.

Like all military doctors in Mesopotamia, he'd learnt to make unpleasant decisions swiftly and put the consequences out of his mind – during working hours.

The pile of dead mounted as he progressed along the deck. A stench of decay and gangrene emanated from the hold and he steeled himself, knowing he'd have to go down there as soon as the decks were cleared. He came across an Indian sergeant crouching over the body of a major from the Dorsets. The Indian watched mutely as he made a cursory examination. High fever, maggots in a gaping leg wound... He hesitated. The major hadn't regained consciousness during the examination – a bad sign. He'd lost a great deal of blood...

'Over there,' he shouted to the bearers, pointing to the stern.

'I'll carry him to the ambulance, sir.' Chatta Ram lifted Charles from the deck before the orderlies could reach them.

'He's not strong enough to withstand the journey, Sergeant.' Allan pulled out his syringe and filled it with morphine. When he looked up, he saw the sergeant marching erect in his soiled uniform down the gangplank. He turned his back. Perhaps the Indian was right. After all, who was he to play God with men's lives?

'Reckon it must have been hell upstream, sir.' A corporal from the Hampshires tugged a handkerchief over his nose.

'It must have been, Corporal.' Allan watched the first ambulance move off. The Indian followed behind it with a straggle of walking wounded. It wasn't until the man turned a corner that he realised that the back of his tunic was blood-stained. He'd been wounded himself.

*Kut, Monday 6th December 1915*

John Mason stood in front of the building that had been requisitioned as a hospital. Armoured cars were thundering their cumbersome, noisy way out of Kut, cavalry following in their wake. John recognised Gerard Leachman riding amongst them, the last political officer with the force besides Harry.

Knight joined him. 'Leachman's the only man I've ever met who gets on with everyone.'

'Harry does pretty well,' John countered.

'Harry isn't astute enough to avoid idiots like Cleck-Heaton.'

The cavalry halted at the newly dug trenches on the outskirts of the town and saluted the watching men.

'We'll be back.' The cry resounded around the cold, dreary streets.

Harry walked out of HQ with Crabbe. 'I'll be back too.' He helped himself to one of Knight's cigarettes. 'And sooner than you think, so don't go drinking all the whisky and smoking all the cigarettes that arrived in the last delivery.'

John looked at Harry's Arab robes; saw the two gulhams waiting.

'Do you want any cigarettes now? I've a few packs I can spare.'

'I'll make this my last. It wouldn't be wise to take British cigarettes where I'm going.'

547

Crabbe shook his head. 'There has to be a better way of collecting intelligence.'

'If you come up with any ideas, let me know.' Harry gripped John by the shoulders. 'Don't go hitting any more staff officers. Wait for me to do it for you. Everyone knows the POs are mad, so they let us get away with murder.'

'We can handle Cleck-Heaton's charges,' Crabbe said. 'And we'll be fine. Living in the lap of luxury while you rough it out there.'

Harry thought of the Turks closing in on Kut and said nothing.

'Reinforcements will come before it gets too bloody.' Crabbe read Harry's thoughts.

Harry studied the curve of the river, empty except for the *Sumana* and a few native mahailas Townsend had retained to use as ferries. The briefing he'd attended had been short and to the point. The Force had 39 guns, ammunition, which hadn't been counted or collected, and 10,000 men, 7500 bayonet carriers and 1500 sabre carriers, every last one exhausted. The most favourable estimate of the Turks bearing down on them was 20,000. And they wouldn't be exhausted, or short of supplies.

The staff had crowed over the recent arrival of winter uniforms and supplies, including whisky and cigarettes for the officers' mess, as though the goods would turn the tide in their favour. Harry knew better. It was all very well for the staff to chant that one British sapper was worth ten Turks. Maybe it had even been true in the early stages of the war when they'd faced the tail end of the Turkish army, but it wasn't true of Khalil

548

Pasha or Nur-ud-Din's men. If the reinforcements Crabbe had spoken about were coming, he would like to know from where. There weren't any seasoned troops left in India and the Western Front needed every man it could get.

Meanwhile, he had to ride up river, count the Turks, and return with a figure that would be more acceptable to the brass – if he lived. He trod his cigarette under foot.

'I've left a parcel on your bed; look after it for me,' he said to John.

'Of course.'

'Take care, the lot of you.' Checking his milk skin and date bag were strapped to his saddle, he climbed on and kicked the beast. 'Kush, you stupid brute. Kush.'

The camel swayed to its feet. The Arabs spurred their mounts. Soon, the three of them were no more than distant silhouettes on the road. One more group of Bedouin searching for loot on the abandoned battlefields.

John had seen Harry ride off before, but this was different. Defeat was staring them in the face. The Turks were out there. Well-fed, strong, fit; ready to take on the world. The question was no longer who was going to win. Only how soon.

Harry walked his camel along the line where the sepoys were digging trenches. He passed the liquorice factory and the troops ferrying grain from the factory storehouses. After crossing the centre of the town, he rounded the curve of the river and rode out into the open countryside on the left bank. Dusk fell as he and his ghulams reached the town limits.

The temperature plummeted. Pulling his abba close, Harry hit his camel. Whipping up speed, he trotted blindly into the darkness, the ghulams keeping their own camels a few lengths behind his. Images of John, Peter, Knight, Crabbe, and the others in the beleaguered town intruded. How long would it take 20,000 Turkish troops to overrun the exhausted garrison at Kut and move on?

Would Nur-ud-Din halt at Amara or march until he had retaken all the ground the Ottoman Empire had lost, including Basra and the Karun Valley?

Ctesiphon had added a new dimension to his concept of dying. The end of his existence and onset of nothingness rarely worried him except during the early hours when he couldn't sleep. What terrified him was death as he had seen it on the battlefields – brutal and degrading. The bestial cries that had come out of no-man's-land from men who had nothing left to beg for except a swift end; men with their genitals or faces shot away. Men who lived for hours, sometimes days, drowning in their own blood and the freezing mud; screaming until they could scream no more.

The thought of ending that way haunted him. As a professional soldier, he should have been prepared to die from the day he enlisted. But he hadn't even considered death when he'd sailed to India with John and Charles, only the good times his own and Charles's father had reminisced about in the smoking room at Clyneswood.

The afternoon polo matches, drinking bouts in the mess; dinner parties with ladies; at which point the general had always looked solemn, as befitted a man who had lost his wife to fever at an early age. Balls, parties, rides in the countryside at dawn and sunset – no mention of a bloody, miserable death in the mud of Mesopotamia.

Soldiers were paid to fight. The risk was early death. He could hardly blame the army for his own lack of foresight in not realising the obvious. But he wondered if John or Charles had considered the implications when they'd taken their commissions. From the time they'd been old enough to join their fathers for brandy after dinner they'd heard stories about 'poor old Carruthers, who'd bought it in Poona in '84'. But the poor old Carrutherses of this world had died in their beds of fever, or heroism in a tribal skirmish. There'd never been a hint of anything like this mass slaughter.

Aside from his prayer for a swift death, there was the question of loyalty to the Arabs who'd placed their trust in the British Empire: Arabs who'd never have done so without his persuasion.

Nur-ud-Din would not be merciful towards natives who'd aided the British, so where did that leave Muhammerah, and the other Arabs who'd acted as ghulams and scouts – and Shalan – and Furja?

He harried his camel on. He'd promised so many Arabs that the Turks had been ousted permanently; men who'd supported him on that understanding. Now the best he could hope for was that they – and Furja – would survive.

If she did, would she find happiness with her new husband? The thought twisted in his gut like

551

a knife. Perhaps that was why Mitkhal had left no messages for him. Mitkhal was happy with Gutne, and Furja was happy with Ali.

His daughters would grow up calling another man father. They'd never know anything about him, never need him...

A shot rang out, slicing through his thoughts. It hit his camel squarely in the centre of the forehead. The beast crumpled. He was pitched onto the riverbank. Stunned, he heard the tramp of marching feet. The ghulams took off. He didn't blame them. If he'd been in their position, he'd have done the same.

'This is the Ferenghi known as Hasan Mahmoud.' Ibn Muba stood beside a Turkish major. The Marsh Arab lifted his lantern higher so Harry could see his triumph. 'This is for my village and all the villages on the Kerkha, Hasan.'

The sergeant fastened the first chain around Harry's wrists.

*Kut*

John lay on his cot, too exhausted to undress – or drink – although he'd taken care to fill the flask that nestled in his uniform pocket during his 24-hour stint at the hospital.

'Major Mason, open the door.'

He forced his eyelids apart. It was dark. He wasn't sure whether he'd slept or not.

'Major Mason!' Another door opened. John heard Peter's voice raised in annoyance.

'What the hell–? Begging your pardon, sir.'

552

Light flooded into his room and he saw Peter in his long, woollen underwear standing to attention in the corridor.

'Major Mason.' Perry entered and stood before him. Making an effort, he forced himself upright.

Perry held a sheet of paper. 'Major Mason, you have been charged with striking a superior, refusing to carry out orders, and...' Perry paused, his face was impassive, but John saw a jubilant gleam in his eyes. 'The murder of Lieutenant Stephen Amey at field ambulance four during the battle of Ctesiphon.'

The light from the corridor wasn't sufficient to illuminate the paper. John realised Perry had taken the trouble to memorise the charges so he could study him while he reeled them off.

'That's preposterous!' Peter exclaimed. 'There's no way John would kill anyone, much less Amey.'

'Court martial to take place tomorrow at 15.00 hours, Major Mason.' Perry didn't turn his attention away from John. 'Until then, you will be held under open arrest so you can continue working in the hospital. The shortage of medical personnel has forced command to take this step. You will have the freedom of your room and the hospital. Do you understand the charges, Major Mason?'

'Yes, sir.' He'd been expecting it, but it had been a long time coming. Now it had actually happened, the only emotion he felt was relief the waiting was over.

'Sergeant Greening will remain with you at all times. Should you attempt to deviate from the route between this room and the hospital he has orders to shoot you.'

An angry murmuring buzzed in the corridor.

'You may appoint an officer to defend you, Major Mason. Should you have difficulty finding one, the court will appoint one for you.'

'He'll have no difficulty.' Crabbe pushed past Perry and joined John in his room.

'I'm sorry, sir. I didn't want to do it; no one did,' Sergeant Greening explained. 'The colonel had to order me to stand guard. I wouldn't be here if he hadn't.'

John gave the sergeant a remote smile. 'I'm glad he chose you. You'll need a chair to sit outside. Unless...' John looked at the bed he'd vacated.

'Outside the room will be fine, sir.' Taking a chair, the sergeant left.

'That bloody man. Cleck-Heaton may have filed the charges, but we all know who put him up to it. Perry's not going to get away with this. I'll defend you...'

'Thank you, Crabbe, it's very good of you,' John gave a remote smile. 'But I'm afraid the facts speak for themselves.'

'For Christ's sake you can't blame yourself. You're a doctor, not God. You can't save everyone.'

'Not everyone, just Amey.' John lay on the bed. Peter joined Crabbe inside the room and shut the door in the face of the officers crowding the corridor.

'We have to get to work on your defence.' Crabbe pulled a pencil and notebook from his pocket. 'Light that lamp, Smythe.' He placed the candle he was holding on John's locker. 'We'll start by making a list of all the people who were at the field hospital when you had that brush with Cleck-Heaton.'

'There's no need. I killed Amey. I lost my temper and released my hold on a severed artery that could have been sewn back together. That makes me guilty.' John reached for the flask in his jacket.

'Damn it, you can't just take this. Perry's thrown the book at you. Don't you understand, you fucking idiot? They're intent on shooting you.'

'I hope they do.' John turned his face to the wall.


*Turkish HQ, The Tigris Valley above Kut-el-Amara, Thursday December 9th 1915*

Harry expected the Turks to shoot him where he'd fallen. During the night that followed, he wished they had. After chaining him, they stripped and searched him, ramming their fingers into every orifice of his petrified body. When they finished, they bundled him, naked, across the saddle of a horse, before leading it at a gallop for two freezing, numbing hours. Then, they dumped him in front of a campfire.

He lay there shivering for what seemed like an eternity before he dared lift his head. Hundreds of well-aligned rows of canvas tents faded into the darkness along with neat stacks of rifles, ammunition, and cook fires. He remembered the exhausted men and low supply dumps he'd left in Kut. If this was Nur-ud-Din's army, it was better organised and supplied than any Turkish force they'd come up against before.

A group of officers wandered over. Tin mugs

and cigarettes in hand, they prodded his shivering body with their boots while they continued to talk among themselves. One man stepped forward; kicking Harry on to his back, he questioned him in rough, heavily accented Arabic.

'What is the strength of General Townsend's force? How has he deployed the defences at Kut? What information have you been sent to gather?'

Harry considered brazening it out. Ibn Muba wasn't in sight. His colouring was wrong for an Arab, but there was always his pigeon German – then he glimpsed a blond head shining in the firelight and remembered the Berlin–Baghdad railway.

'I am Hasan Mahmoud. I was a horse trader in Basra but I lost everything in the war. I am trying to get to my brother in–' He thought quickly; Ahwaz would never do. He was too far from the Karun valley. 'Baghdad,' he gabbled hastily. God help him if by some miracle the Turks believed him and sent him there.

'Nice try, Lieutenant-Colonel Downe. Your Arabic is excellent, but the ruse won't work this time. Even without Ibn Muba's assistance I would have known you.' The language was English. A Turkish officer squatted on his heels and peered into Harry's face. He was holding a poster. 'I compliment your command of a difficult tongue. My Arabic is nowhere near as good and I have had many more years to study it than you.'

The officer was handsome. Taller and slimmer than the short, squat, thickset Turks around him, he had a pencil fine moustache and a full head of dark hair. 'I was hoping you'd return the compliment and commend me on my English. I studied in your country. At Cambridge. May I introduce myself? I am Murad Pasha but we will not stand on ceremony. You may call me Murad. Would you like a cigarette?' He took one from a gold case and offered it to Harry. Harry looked at it, but his hands were still chained behind his back.

'How stupid of me, Lieutenant-Colonel Downe, or may I call you Harry? You cannot smoke because your hands are bound.' He shouted an order.

Harry's hands were pulled painfully higher and the chains removed. He massaged the circulation back into his wrists. Someone threw him a blanket. He grabbed it, and draped it over his shoulders, more anxious to cover himself than shelter behind its warmth. Murad Pasha gave him the cigarette. It was already lit, and he watched the Turk warily from beneath half-closed eyelids as he drew the smoke into his lungs.

'Your commanding officer made a mistake when he sent you to us, Lieutenant-Colonel Downe. Surely you didn't expect to fool us again with this ridiculous charade of Arab robes? I see from your expression you are surprised we know so much about you. But you are famous.' Murad pushed the poster he was holding under Harry's nose. It was caricature of his features, resembling a cartoon drawing from *Punch*.

'Poor Colonel Bilgi in the Karun Valley was relegated to the ranks for believing you. A fate worse than death for one such as him. He was not a popular commander, however, and I feel he deserved the punishment after giving you our summer campaign plans. But please, do not insult our intelligence any longer. We're both professionals. I will not lie. If you answer my questions, I promise you an easy death. Should you refuse to co-operate, I promise you will long for such a death. We have men here who are expert at prolonging a man's life when he is no longer recognisable as a man.'

He thrust pencil and paper at Harry. 'Sketch Townsend's displacements in Kut. Tell me how many able-bodied men he has left. As you see–' he indicated the camp around him '–you have lost the war. The Germans are winning on the Western Front.' He looked to where the German stood warming his backside on the campfire. 'And we will win on this front. Help me plan a swift death for your comrades, Harry, and I will order an easy death for you. It is more than a man out of uniform deserves.'

The offer hung tantalizingly sweet in the cold night air.

Harry had no illusion of rescue, or escape. He was going to die; the only question was how. He finished his cigarette, threw the stub into the fire and repeated, 'I am Hasan Mahmoud. I am a poor horse trader from Basra...'

'Perhaps it was foolish of me to expect otherwise, Lieutenant-Colonel Downe.' There was grudging respect in Murad's voice. 'Forgive me for taking leave of you, but I am squeamish about these matters. We will talk again tomorrow, when I hope to find you in a more compliant frame of mind.'

Murad and the German walked away. A sergeant

took Murad's place; a mountain of a man with the inane grin of a backward child. Behind him stood an emaciated lieutenant. The sergeant pulled the blanket from Harry and tossed it aside. Heaving Harry's hands behind his back, he chained him again and kicked him on to his side. The lieutenant lit a cigarette with a sulphur match that flared with a beautiful green-blue flame. He handed it to the sergeant who puffed on it before applying its end to Harry's right nipple.

Harry screamed as excruciating pain shot through his chest. His body arced until his feet hit his hands. The sergeant removed the cigarette and puffed on it again.

The chains chafed Harry's ankles when his knees were yanked apart and the glowing end pressed to his testicles.

Harry screamed and cursed – in Arabic. He was Hasan Mahmoud. If he forgot that for an instant, he would cause the death of every man in Kut. He had to forget John, forget Kut, forget everything except Hasan Mahmoud ... Hasan Mahmoud...

The cigarette was removed but not the pain. The lieutenant lit another. The sergeant puffed on his again.

Harry screamed as the flesh smouldered below his right eye. He began to gabble in Arabic, telling them about the Bedouin. The women who waited for their men in the harems of the black tents.

It didn't take long for him to discover that Hasan Mahmoud was a drivelling coward. He would tell them everything he knew, but Hasan Mahmoud was an Arab with nothing of importance to tell. And he was Hasan Mahmoud.

# Chapter Thirty-eight

*Kut, Saturday December 12th 1915*

'Sir, will I be able to – I mean will I...?'

Knight took pity on the middle-aged rifleman. 'Your wife won't notice any difference, corporal.' He could sense every man listening intently, including Greening, who stood armed and at attention at the door.

'But, sir, I've only one left.' The corporal was bright red but Knight knew his embarrassment stemmed from talking to a MO, not from the audience of fellow soldiers. There was no room for modesty in the barracks.

'One's all you need.' Knight suppressed a smile.

'Then why do we have two?'

'Back-up in case of accidents.'

'But what if she notices? What if she says something?'

'Tell her what I've just told you.' Knight pulled the blanket over the rifleman's legs. 'The wound's healing well. You'll be fine and, if you want to, you can father any number of children, providing your wife is willing.'

'Reckon she won't be too keen, seeing as how we've nine already. But thank you for putting my mind at rest, sir.'

Knight moved down the ward, followed by whispers of 'told you so', and 'your missus better look out when you get home; you'll be at her day and night just to prove a point'.

John was checking a drainage tube in a sergeant's chest. The man would have died if John hadn't operated, implementing procedures they'd read about in the *Lancet*. He damned the staff and their ludicrous order that he could only work under supervision. Crabbe had fought to get the charges dismissed; but three delays due to Turkish bombardments hadn't helped; neither had John's reluctance to speak in his own defence. When the hearing had finally been held, they'd all been so exhausted nothing made any sense.

Least of all the staff's decision to postpone the verdict.

John finished checking his patient and left the ward. The hospital had been set up in a merchant's house. Four light, airy reception rooms had been turned into wards but only one had access to the gloomy kitchen. Glazed tiles offset the dreariness. Tints of gold and silver glittered among jewelled shades of emerald and sapphire brushed into curiously beguiling, abstract patterns. While admiring them, John noticed a teapot on a cupboard. It was still warm. He poured himself a cup. Leaning against the stove, he siphoned off its warmth and cleared his mind of everything except the tile pattern. A shell crashed behind the building. Matthews' voice rose above the blast.

'Bleeding hell that were close.'

John didn't flinch. Sipping the lukewarm tea, he began to count the tiles.

'Any news?' Knight joined him.

'About what?' John enquired absently.

'Your court martial. I thought they'd have sent for you this morning.'

'They haven't as yet.' John resumed counting the tiles. There was another crash.

'Bloody Turkish artillery.' Knight tossed the contents of the teapot into the slop pail. Opening the stove, he raked the wood and set the kettle to boil. 'Would you believe I actually found myself wishing Townsend had given in to Nur-ud-Din's demands for surrender three days ago? If he had, you'd have had to take your chances with the Turks along with the rest of us, and Cleck-Heaton's charges would be forgotten. We wouldn't be sitting in this blasted bombardment...' Another shell cut him short.

'The brass would have had me shot before they surrendered.'

'You can't be sure of that. But I'm damned sure if they find you guilty they'll shoot you now.'

'If a shell doesn't get me first. I appreciate your concern, Knight, but my fate doesn't seem that important in the scheme of things.'

'Been drinking again?'

John pulled the flask from his pocket, and shook it. 'I haven't filled it in days.'

'Major Mason?'

'What is it, Sergeant Greening?' Expecting the worst, Knight's hand shook as he opened the door. They couldn't shoot John – they couldn't–

'Colonel Crabbe's here to see Major Mason.' Crabbe walked in, carrying a bundle under his arm.

Knight looked at Crabbe's face. 'They've sent for John?'

Crabbe shook his head. He handed John the parcel. 'One of the ghulams brought it in ten minutes ago. I think the beggar was on his way downstream when the Turks got wind he was one of ours, so he hightailed it back here. The damned coward said he ran when Johnny Turk fired the first shot. It killed Harry. If we believe the bastard we can console ourselves with the thought that Harry died quickly.'

John unfurled the robe. Streaks of dried blood stiffened the surface. He lifted it to his face and held it against his cheek. Turning his back on Crabbe, he took a few steps. When he crashed into the tiled wall, the first blinding tears fell from his eyes.

*The Turkish camp besieging Kut,*
*Saturday December 12th 1915*

The tent shielded Hasan from the wind and rain if not the cold. When dawn broke on the first morning, men had come to the campfire with mess tins. One had looked at him and vomited. After that, they carried him into the tent.

Since then, time had lost all meaning. Hasan welcomed Murad's visits because the Turk would lay a blanket over his body and wouldn't allow anyone to hurt him when he was present. The rough wool chafed his burns, but the pain was worth it, because he was no longer naked. Hasan trusted Murad; he did not burn or torture him.

He only asked questions – questions in an alien tongue.

Whenever he tried to tell him he didn't understand, Murad would leave, the blanket would be removed, and the pain would begin again. He lay chained hand and foot, unable even to crawl. Every time Murad left, the sergeant and lieutenant returned, and fear relaxed his bladder and bowels. The Turks didn't have to touch him to provoke the response. He lay in his own excrement and stank. He could see it in the lieutenant's disgust when he drew near. A few times the pain was so great he lost consciousness. Then buckets of freezing water were thrown over him.

He'd been thirsty enough to lick the drops from the filthy canvas floor, too far gone to care what he was drinking, as long as it was wet. Then the blanket would fall over him again and Murad would return with his civilised voice and gentle ways.

He offered to tell Murad everything he knew, but every time he spoke, he made Murad angry. He did not know why. He told the Turk about the desert and the marshes. The mashufs he'd seen filled with fish and dates. He no longer felt hunger – the only sensations that penetrated the fog in his mind were pain and thirst – but it pleased him to think of shining dates and fish cooking over a dung fire. Murad didn't want to hear about food. Sometimes other men came. One was fair, with blond hair, but he never spoke. Only stood and watched.

For the second time his hands were unchained but he was too weak to move them. The sergeant wrapped the soiled blanket around him and lifted him on a chair. It was wrong.

Murad was asking questions and the lieutenant and sergeant were there. He tried to tell them the sergeant and lieutenant should go away, but they didn't listen.

Too weak to sit, he fell from the chair. The sergeant kicked him; one of his ribs cracked, but the pain wasn't as agonising as the ones from the burns. The sergeant threw aside the blanket and lifted him back on to the chair. His legs were spread-eagled and tied. They were going to emasculate him. Why else would they expose him? He lowered his chin in an effort to conceal his fear.

The sergeant tied his left hand to his leg; his right he pressed down on the scarred surface of a table. Murad questioned him and the lieutenant produced a knife. The sergeant's grip tightened. He watched the Turk straighten his fingers. His hand...

He tried to pull it away but the sergeant's grip was strong.

The knife was long-bladed, sharp – like a butcher's knife. Where had he seen a butcher's knife? Of course – in the market in Basra. Without warning, the lieutenant brought the blade down on his little finger. He stared at his knuckle and nail, severed and lying on the table.

Blood pumped from the stump and pain shot up his arm. The chair rocked when he threw himself back with a strength born of agony.

Questions rained swifter than he could answer. He tried to reply. But his words were drowned in his screams.

The knife came down again and embedded itself in the table. There was now only a bleeding root where his little finger had been. Through his cries he could hear Murad's voice, soft, insistent.

The lieutenant prised the knife from the table. Murad asked another question. Then it was his index finger, lying in three neat blood-stained pieces next to the remains of his little finger. He sat sobbing in his own filth. He would do anything they wanted to put an end to it. Anything...

Murad called him Harry.

'My daughter's name is Harri.' He offered them the life of his child.

Murad's face loomed close to his. The knife came down again – his voice was swallowed in yet another whine. His forefinger joined his index and little fingers.

Another question; another flash. Another question; another flash. He no longer had the strength to moan. He whimpered, offered to say whatever they wanted to hear until there was only his palm left. Murad fell silent. A man walked into the tent and shouted. The sergeant left, returning a few moments later with an iron bar that glowed red hot at its tip.

Murad caught his shoulders and shouted yet more questions that he failed to understand.

The chair he was tied to was knocked on the floor. He lay on his back. Every part of him was pain. They didn't need to hurt him any more. He would do whatever they wanted. Why wouldn't they listen?

The iron glowed closer. The lieutenant knelt beside him and caught his head in his hands. The sergeant moved the tip of the bar slowly, inexorably towards him.

Murad asked one last question before the hot iron plunged into his right eye. The last thing he saw before he drowned in agony was a blond head.


*Kut, Wednesday December 15th 1915*

Leigh sidled over to Peter's cot. 'Do you know which regimental mess received a year's supply of drink before we dug in?'

'Yes.'

'Come on, old man, tell Uncle Leigh all.'

'So you can beg hospitality. Not bloody likely. The fewer people who know, the greater the share.'

'Come on... I say, you look peaky.' Leigh greeted Grace, who had stayed on in Kut with the crew of the *Sumana*. 'Not bad news about Bowditch? He was doing all right last I heard.'

'I've come from the hospital. Harry's dead and they've passed the death sentence on Mason. Came to get him while I was there. He's to face a firing squad in an hour. Crabbe and the senior MO are with the staff now but it doesn't look good.'

'Where have they taken him?' Peter left his bed and fastened his collar.

'The basement of the supplies depot. It's no good trying to see him. I went there to pay my respects. No one's allowed to approach the building without a pass.'

'We'll see about that.'

Leigh grabbed Peter's coat. 'You want to give them an excuse to shoot you too?'

'We could go to the mess,' Grace suggested. 'Crabbe will have to pass it when he leaves HQ.'

'It's not Crabbe I want to see.'

'If you want to see John, Crabbe's the only one who can help you. They can't do anything until he gets there. As John's defender, he has to witness the execution.'

Peter had seen a court martial and execution before the war. But the blighter had deserved death. John didn't. And to take a doctor from the hospital and shoot him when there were more sick and wounded men in their camp than healthy seemed the ultimate obscenity of war.

John sat on a wooden bench in a damp, windowless cellar. A candle burned on a table Greening had scrounged. He heard sentries pacing the stone passage outside. It had been cold in the hospital, but not like this. The temperature had to be below freezing.

He held out his hands and studied them. All the training, all the knowledge he'd acquired at the cost of countless hours of study, had come to nothing. He would have been better employed joining Harry in every drunken escapade. That way, at least he'd have pleasurable memories to look back on. As it was, all he could recall was tedious hours locked away with books, and professors who could make the most interesting topics boring. What brief interludes of enjoyment there'd been had always come courtesy of Harry.

This time had been given him so he could

prepare for his own death, not mourn Harry; but he deserved death. He'd made a shambles of his life. His wife wasn't even carrying his child, but perhaps Maud had never really been his, not in the sense he'd wanted.

He'd searched for an ideal, a soulmate he could lavish love on and exact love in return. He'd tried to explain how he felt about marriage once to Harry and his cousin had laughed, telling him he'd been reading too much Byron and Shakespeare. Harry had been right. Women were not ethereal creatures to be put on pedestals and adored. They had feet of clay, like Maud. Why was it that whatever he thought about, he always returned to Harry?

Harry, Charles, and him. Charles had disappeared, probably drowned in the mud at Ctesiphon. John pictured his friend's tall, slim body sinking inch by inch until he was covered with oozing black slime. Harry – the pain of losing Harry was almost too great to bear. He had so many memories of Harry.

Harry creeping into the school dormitory late at night, his shirt stuffed with pastries he'd wheedled from the girls in the cake shop. How old had they been? Ten? Twelve? Women had succumbed to Harry's charms even when he'd been a child.

Harry setting out for school from Clyneswood with a pig's bladder full of his father's whisky stuffed into the case of the violin he never played. Harry leaving school to the cheers of the masters and the sobbing of the boys.

Harry thrown out of medical college, surviving

569

the rigours of Sandhurst, smiling through it all, even the magnificent engagement party his parents had arranged for him and Lucy. And Harry had still been smiling a week later when he'd met him and Charles in London.

'You don't mind, do you, John, but I've decided to break it off with your sister. It's for the best. She's much too good for me.'

He'd been so charming about the whole episode everyone had forgiven him, except Lucy. Charming, headstrong Harry sitting on the edge of the sofa in his quarters in Basra saying, 'She's my wife, actually. And we get on.' Harry picking Furja up and whirling her in the air. Harry in love. Really in love and not giving a toss for anyone's opinion except his own. How he'd envied Harry that one quality. The ability to ignore the rest of the world and live his life his way.

The bolts grated. He rose to his feet, his limbs stiff with cold. Perry entered, as correctly attired as ever. Siege conditions hadn't affected his bearer's ability to cope with his laundry.

'I've brought you paper, ink and a pen, Mason. You may write to your family. Delivery will depend on the censor. In order to mitigate the distress your disgrace would cause your relatives, they'll receive a telegram detailing your death from fever. The staff decided against "fallen in battle". That means your widow will only be entitled to the lower rate of pension, but considering the circumstances I think you'll agree it's generous of the army to consider your relatives at all.'

'Can I write more than one letter?'

'Command will look sympathetically on any

570

letter to your immediate family. I've been asked to enquire if you have any last requests.'

'Only time to write to my parents, my wife and brother, Tom. He's my executor.' John sensed Perry might be swayed by the necessity of leaving Maud adequately provided for. 'There's one more thing. Harry Downe left a parcel with me. Mainly letters to be forwarded to his family and a few personal things.'

'Such as?'

'His pocket watch, photographs.' Hatred burned for the first time in months as John was forced to itemise what remained of Harry's life.

'As they belong to Lieutenant-Colonel Downe they won't be confiscated. What do you want me to do with them?'

'Give them to Smythe.' John glared at Perry. 'Will my effects be confiscated?'

'Confiscated and scrutinised by the censor. They may or may not be forwarded to your family at the senior duty officer's discretion.'

'Your discretion, Perry?' John dropped the veneer of politeness. 'I give you my word as an officer that there's no mention in my papers of Emily or the way she died. The only people who knew the details were Harry Downe, you, and me. Now Harry's dead and I'm about to be shot, I think you can consider your sordid secret safe.'

Perry left, slamming the door behind him. John picked up the paper and pen Perry had set down beside the candle. He suppressed an irrational desire to communicate with Harry or Charles. If the church was right, he would be doing that soon enough.

*Dear Maud*
*I haven't long to live.*

His handwriting looked suspiciously firm for a man at death's door. He toyed with the idea of mentioning fever but decided against embellishing his last letter with lies. Besides, it wasn't as though Maud would care. She'd hardly be a conventional widow.

*I hope you get this. I trust you won't waste time grieving for me. I'm not in pain and now Charles and Harry have gone there doesn't seem a great deal left to live for. Write to my brother, Tom, care of my father. He has the authority to administer my estate and will arrange payment of the annuity I set up for you. If it will help, you may name the child after me.*

He hoped she'd understand the significance of the last sentence. He dare not be more explicit because of the censor.

*Thank you for the happy times. There were some.*
*John Mason.*

He looked at the paper that was left. Only two more sheets. He'd have to be brief.

*Dear Mother, Father, Tom and Lucy.*

*If you are reading this, I will be dead. Please don't grieve on my account. Thank you for all the love and happiness you have given me over the years...*

Memories flooded back, of picnics in the woods at Clyneswood and Stouthall. His mother supervising a train of small children and nannies while his father gaily led the way through mud and mire.

Holidays from school. His father taking him to the library and suggesting books he might read. His father giving him his first official glass of brandy, not knowing Harry had upstaged him years earlier. His first cigar, his first...

'John?' Crabbe stood in the doorway. They'd opened the door and he hadn't even heard it being unlocked. 'The verdict stands. But the sentence has been postponed.'

'Why?' John felt cheated. All this preparation for a delay. He wanted it over with.

'Knight and the senior MO argued without you the number of deaths will soar. They pointed out you're the most experienced surgeon and they couldn't cope with the existing casualties with one less doctor, let alone treat any more. You're to be escorted to the hospital every day by Sergeant Greening and he'll remain with you at all times. When you're not working, you'll be kept here, under guard.'

'For how long?'

'Until the casualties stop rolling in or the Turks break through. Whichever comes first. They've issued orders that you're to be shot as soon as it's expedient.' Crabbe moved closer. 'If you want to make a run for it I'd be glad to help.'

'Leave the wounded to take my chances on getting through the Turkish lines?' John smiled. 'Thank you. I appreciate the offer and all you've done for me, but, no.' He looked at his unfinished letter. 'I suppose I'd better get on with this.'

'If it's your last letter home, that would be wise. A couple of ghulams are going through the lines tonight and if I know Perry, he'll put your letters in their bag. Given their chances, it might be as well if you make copies and leave them with me. If I get out of this I promise to deliver them.'

'Thank you. If you get me more paper I'll do that.'

'For Christ's sake, stop thanking me...'

'You did all you could, Crabbe. You couldn't have won. Perry has it in for me. It's nothing to do with you. It's personal.'

'We all know he was angry with you for marrying his daughter on the day his wife died.'

John smiled wryly at the way gossip had woven a story out of so little known fact.

Crabbe retreated. 'I'll leave you to finish your letters. Is there anything you want?'

'More paper if you can scrounge it. I'd like to write to Charles's father and Harry's family.'

Crabbe hesitated. 'I can't help thinking none of this would have happened if Harry had been around. He'd have found some way to get the charges against you dismissed.'

'How? By murdering Cleck-Heaton or Perry?'

'Knowing Harry, both if he had to.'

'Then it's just as well he's not around or we'd both be facing a firing squad.'

Harry, Charles, and him. Three, two, one. Soon there'd be none. Just like the nursery rhyme.

Crabbe noticed the mould on the wall. It was just as well they were going to shoot John soon. No one could survive a Mesopotamian winter sleeping in these conditions.

'Will there be a little time at the end?' John touched the amulet Furja had given him, which he kept in his breast pocket next to Harry's box of pearls and gold. 'I have some things...'

'Keep them. When it happens I'll be there.'

'Just in case you're not, send the contents of my

pockets to Harry's Arab wife. Mitkhal will know where to reach her. And tell her "thank you, but it didn't work for a Ferenghi". She'll understand. I can't write. I don't think she can read English.'

'I'll see you later.' Turning his head so John wouldn't see his face, Crabbe banged on the door. When it opened, he walked away.

'Major Mason, sir.' Sergeant Greening hovered in the doorway. 'I'm right sorry about the verdict. We – all the non-coms, that is – think it's wrong.'

'Thank you, Sergeant Greening, but for your own sake you shouldn't be talking this way. Not even to me.'

'I don't care,' he answered defiantly. 'When the verdict was announced they asked if I'd like to stand down but I hoped you wouldn't mind if I stayed.'

'You volunteered for this duty?' John asked.

'To stay with you, yes, sir.'

'That's uncommonly kind of you, Sergeant.'

'My wife thinks highly of you. That's Harriet, sir. She was Mrs Perry's maid.'

'Major Reid told me she'd married a sergeant. I'm very pleased for you. Harriet deserved a good man. Congratulations, I hope you both have a long and happy life together when this is over.'

'It's good of you to say so.' The sergeant fumbled in his pocket. 'I got this for you, sir. It will keep the cold at bay.' He pulled a small bottle of brandy from his pocket. John was touched. Brandy prices were sky-high amongst the troops. He dreaded to think what Greening had traded for it.

'Thank you, Sergeant, but I daren't take it in

case I'm searched. Would you keep it for me, please?'

'I'd be honoured, sir. There's still hope, isn't there? I mean, Major Crabbe can do something to stop it, can't he?'

'Afraid not.' John found himself comforting the man who'd been ordered to shoot him. 'We'll have a drink together later, after I've got these letters out of the way.'

'Yes, sir.'

Greening shut the door. John picked up the pen. It was strange; for the first time in months, he actually didn't want a drink.

## Chapter Thirty-nine

*The Mission, Basra, Friday December 24th 1915*

Maud straightened the crepe paper crackers she'd made, rearranged the bowls of salted almonds, and checked the carafe of red wine was 'breathing' on the sideboard. Since typhoid fever had broken out among the Turkish POWs in the Lansing, the Reverend and Mrs Butler had joined Doctor Picard, Theo, and Angela in working long hours at the hospital. But that morning they'd all been determined to return in time to join her for Christmas Eve supper before attending the midnight service.

She studied her handiwork. The table looked attractive and the chicken broth smelled appetising. She hoped the roast beef would live up to the cook's promise. It was difficult to buy good-quality beef in Basra.

'Ma'am Mason, there's a gentleman to see you, an officer gentleman.'

'Show him into the sitting room, Aiyesha.' She checked her reflection in the oval mirror set in the sideboard and wondered what the officer wanted. Christmas greetings from her father, perhaps? So little news had come from upstream the past month. She went to the door. The officer was standing with his back to her in front of the fire.

'Merry Christmas–' she discreetly checked his uniform '–Colonel...'

'Allan, Edward Allan, Mrs Mason. I knew your husband in India.'

'Thank you for calling, Colonel Allan, but my husband is with General Townsend.' Suddenly she knew exactly why he had called.

Faint, she sank down on the nearest chair.

'Is there anyone besides the maid in the house with you, Mrs Mason?'

'No, the Reverend and Mrs Butler and the rest of the staff are in the Lansing.' The words tumbled out. If she kept talking, he wouldn't be able to tell her. And until someone actually said the words, John still lived. 'Typhus has broken out among the Turks. The regular staff are nursing those in quarantine, so of course extra people...' A sharp pain shot through her stomach. She clenched the arm of the chair and cried out as a gush of water spurted from between her legs. Her face flamed when she saw the puddle spreading over the rug.

'If I'd known you were pregnant and alone in

577

the house, I wouldn't have come.'

A second pain gripped Maud. She clutched her swollen stomach.

'Are these the first pains?' he asked.

'My back has been aching all day. But it's been aching a great deal lately.' She moaned when another pain came. He opened the door and called to the maid.

'We have to get Mrs Mason to bed. Quickly! Can you walk, Mrs Mason?'

Maud rose unsteadily from the chair, only to fall back at the onset of another pain. Colonel Allan scooped her into his arms and carried her into the passage. The maid ran ahead to Maud's room, flinging the door wide.

'We'll need plenty of hot water, old sheets, newspapers, some strong cord or twine, and a pair of scissors. Are there any other servants in the house?'

'The cook, sir.'

'Tell him to get the things and bring them here. I need you to help me.'

'The baby isn't due for another two months,' Maud protested.

'Are you sure of your dates?'

'Quite sure.'

'You would be, I suppose, with leave being the way it is. Oh well, it can't be helped. It looks as though this one's in a hurry to get here.'

'It will be all right?'

'No reason why not.' He looked around as he lowered her into a cane chair.

'I'm sorry, I've soaked your uniform,' Maud apologised, mortified that any man should see her like this.

'After some of the things that have been spilt on it recently, amniotic fluid is a welcome change.'

'You're a doctor.' She gripped the arms of the chair when another pain took hold.

'I am.' He stripped the bed back to the mattress and threw the covers into the passage. Taking off his jacket, he hung it on the back of the door. Turning up the oil lamp, he asked, 'Where did the water in the jug come from?'

'The mission well. It's clean.'

Filling the bowl on the washstand, he scrubbed his hands. 'Have you anything waterproof I can cover the bed with. A rubber sheet, tarpaulin?'

'Angela – Mrs Smythe – put a parcel in my wardrobe last month. She said...' Her voice tailed in pain. He opened the wardrobe. A brown paper parcel prevented the hems of her dresses from hanging straight. He lifted it out and tore it open. The first thing that fell out was a rubber sheet. He carried it to the bed.

'Close the door and the curtains,' he ordered Aiyesha when she returned. Pulling a sheet from the parcel, he spread it over the rubber. 'I'm going to lift you onto the bed, Mrs Mason. Then we're going to undress you.'

He laid Maud on the bed. She gagged at the smell of rubber. He lifted the chamber pot from beneath the bed and held it until she finished retching, then, with the help of Aiyesha, he undressed her. He removed everything, but by the time he'd finished, the pains were so strong Maud no longer cared. Aiyesha sponged her legs while he washed his hands again. He helped

Aiyesha pull a fresh nightgown over Maud's head, keeping the hem above her waist.

'I'm going to insert my fingers into you. I'll try not to hurt you but I need to know how much longer we have before the baby puts in an appearance.'

Maud gripped the bedhead and stared at the ceiling.

'I thought so.' He removed his hands and washed them again. 'It's going to be over very soon. That's it, lie back. It's quite warm in this room, but a baby likes it warmer. Stoke up the fire, Aiyesha.'

He took charge, issuing commands as if the Arab girl was one of his orderlies. His voice was soft, his manner gentle.

The cook knocked on the door, bringing the things he'd asked for. The pains ebbed and flowed with increasing frequency. Maud felt as though she were being torn in two but the colonel was there, holding her hand, smoothing her hair away from her face – reminding her of John. She wondered if the manner was the result of medical training, then remembered what Marjorie Harrap had said when she'd become engaged.

"You can have no idea how gentle your fiancé was. He brought my son out with considerably less pain and embarrassment than Major Harrap inflicted putting him in."

She closed her eyes, imagining it was John caring for her. The colonel told her about Cambridgeshire in spring, Cambridgeshire in summer, in autumn; by the time he reached winter, the pains were horrendous and she was screaming.

'Push, Mrs Mason. Bear down, push... Aiyesha, hold her shoulders. Push, Mrs Mason.' His voice grew insistent. A flood of water and blood gushed as something tore inside her. 'Wait!' he commanded, and she stopped pushing. 'When the next pain comes, another push.' She did as he asked. He lifted his hands. A baby was in them. A wriggling, screaming baby with a down of fair hair covering his head.

'Congratulations, Mrs Mason. You have a son. He's small, but all there, very much alive, and judging by his colouring, he takes after his mother.' He wrapped the slippery, squalling bundle in a towel, checked his mouth for debris, and laid him on Maud's nightdress.

She cradled the baby in her arms. Still screaming, he opened his eyes. They were blue. Blue and fierce.

'He's so furious, so alive,' she murmured, totally unprepared for the feelings he engendered.

'We'll have one more push when you're ready.' He dealt with the afterbirth and cut the cord. While Aiyesha washed and dressed her in a clean nightdress, he took the baby and bathed him in warm water, talking softly until gradually the baby quietened, only to start up again when he wrapped him in a towel and laid him on a chair. 'You're going to have to watch that one.' He lifted Maud in his arms so Aiyesha could remake the bed with clean sheets and blankets. 'He likes attention.'

'I'll try to give it to him.'

The colonel laid Maud in the bed, picked up the child, and handed him to her. Aiyesha carried out the rubber sheets and bundles of newspapers.

After the maid left, the colonel pulled a chair close to the bed. 'John didn't suffer. He died of fever. The report said the end was painless.'

'When?'

'Two weeks ago, at Kut.' He went to his jacket and extracted some papers. 'These are his last letters. Some of them are addressed to his family but I thought you'd be the best person to send them on.'

Tears streamed down her cheeks and fell on the baby's towel. John was dead. She'd never see him again, never be able to convince him that, despite everything she'd done, she'd loved him. Really loved him.

'John wouldn't have wanted you to cry, Mrs Mason. He'd have wanted you to think of yourself and his son.' He pushed his index finger into the minute palm of the baby's hand. 'Are you going to name him after his father?'

Choking back her tears, she shook her head mutely. 'He may grow to look more like John. Fair babies often turn into dark children.'

'He looks just like his father now.'

He glanced at her. Her eyes were closed. Perhaps he'd imagined the bitterness in her voice. A door banged, and someone ran down the passage. He smiled as he shrugged his arms into the sleeves of his tunic. He hadn't wanted to deliver the news of Mason's death but he'd felt obligated. And it hadn't turned out too badly. After the all the deaths, a birth had been just what he'd needed.

582

Angela carried a tin of homemade biscuits and cake through the packed aisles of beds in the officers' convalescent ward. After the Lansing, she'd believed herself immune to the sight of wounds and suffering, but there were so many men here she'd seen in the barracks, officers Peter had introduced her to.

Nearly all had limbs missing. Trunks ended in flat beds where legs should have been. Shoulders had been carefully bandaged to conceal the stumps of arms. Arms finished in dressed wedges that left no room for hands.

Her brother and Colonel Allan had told her about the boats that had taken almost two weeks to journey downstream from Ctesiphon and Kut. How the men on board hadn't had their injuries cleaned or tended in all that time. How gangrene had set into almost every wound, giving the surgeons no option other than to amputate. But their descriptions hadn't prepared her for the reality of the shattered bodies. She forced herself to walk on, smiling, greeting those officers she knew.

'Mrs Smythe.' An orderly stopped her. 'Major Reid is in the end cubicle. Colonel Allan told him you were coming. He is expecting you.'

Charles was sitting up in bed. He was pale, but intact. Angela sat on the chair the orderly placed for her. She'd been closer to John and Harry. John had been kind and gentle and Harry was Harry, but Charles Reid, with his immaculate uniform and correct military bearing, had intimidated her.

Unintentionally or not, on the few occasions they'd met he'd made her feel like the gauche colonial most of the English officers believed her to be. 'It's good of you to visit, Mrs Smythe.'

'I brought some Christmas cake and biscuits.' She laid them on his locker. 'I wasn't sure what else to bring. If you need anything, I'd be only too happy to get it.'

'Thank you. But Colonel Allan has been very kind since I sent my bearer upstream. He brings me everything I need.'

'I would have thought you'd need a bearer now more than ever.'

'They're short of men in Amara.' A cold silence had fallen between Chatta Ram and himself after Cleck-Heaton's revelations. He'd written to his father demanding the truth. In the meantime, the bearer had been a reminder of ties he'd have died rather than own.

'Maud sends her regards. We didn't find out you were here until Colonel Allan told us on Christmas Day, and by then she'd had her baby. The colonel and Theo won't allow her near this place because of the risk of carrying infection to her child.'

'In that case, Mrs Smythe, you'd best make this visit a brief one.'

She wondered if he'd meant to sound sarcastic. 'Please, don't concern yourself about me, Major; I've given up teaching to work in the Lansing. I'm immune to infection.'

'It's good of you to spare the time to come here. Colonel Allan told me the Lansing is packed.'

'We're very grateful to Colonel Allan. I dread to

think what would have happened to Maud if he hadn't called on Christmas Eve.'

'She might not have gone into premature labour,' Charles commented uncharitably.

'The colonel didn't know she was pregnant. And it was the colonel who told us you'd survived. We all thought...'

'I'd died alongside John and Harry.'

'Harry is posted missing.'

'Missing presumed dead. A staff officer from HQ called in. He told me Harry was sent behind Turkish lines to estimate the strength of their forces. A ghulam who went out with him returned with his robe. It was covered in blood. Apparently, Harry was killed by the first shot.'

'Maud is devastated.'

'I bet she is,' he lashed out viciously.

Angela pitied Charles because he had lost his two closest friends. She could understand his bitterness; she'd wanted to hit out at the world when her parents had died. But understanding didn't make it any easier to talk to him. 'As soon as Maud is able, she'll call and see you,' she ventured, believing that as Maud had seen more of Charles than her, she had to be closer to him.

'I'll be out of here before Maud is able to leave her bed.'

'Then perhaps you'll stay with us at the mission. You can share my brother's room. He practically lives at the hospital now, so he won't disturb you.'

'Thank you, but accommodation isn't a problem in Basra any more. And, as soon as I'm fit, I'll be returning upstream. Someone has to bail the force out of Kut.'

'You didn't happen to see anything of Peter while you were upstream?'

He felt a pang of remorse. She'd visited him in a ward full of mutilated men. She'd brought him food and he'd been infernally rude. He recalled Peter as he'd last seen him, going over the top, fighting long after any normal man would have given up.

'Yes, I saw Peter.' He smiled and his face muscles ached. How long had it been since he'd smiled? 'Peter's company held the Roman Arch at Ctesiphon for over 24 hours, and the whole time they were dug in, they were under tremendous pressure.'

'You mean they were under fire.'

'Yes, but don't worry; the last I saw of Peter he was fit and healthy. His name's not on any of the casualty lists. I checked.'

'So have I. But I haven't heard anything. Maud received John's last letters, but there was no mention of Peter in them.'

'John wrote to Maud?' He was surprised.

'He said he knew he was dying, but he wasn't in pain and she wasn't to grieve for him. He told her to name the child after him if it would bring her any comfort. But John was always kind, thinking of others, never himself.'

'That's John.' Charles turned away from her. His leg was throbbing painfully. Would Harry and John have taken their commissions if it hadn't been for his determination to follow in his father's footsteps? He could almost hear Harry's voice raised in drunken glee. 'Just like school. All for one and one for all.'

586

'We're going to miss them dreadfully.' Angela was having difficulty keeping her emotions in check. 'I can't believe I won't see them again. It must be much, much harder for you. Peter told me the three of you grew up together.'

Silence fell between them again, but this time it was a silence devoid of strain.

'Will you be writing to Harry's family?' she asked eventually.

'Yes.'

'Please tell them how much he meant to us at the mission and to Peter. I've written to John's parents, brother, and sister, but Maud didn't have Harry's family's address.'

'I can give you the address of Harry's parents and his twin sister.'

'I didn't know he had a twin. Is she like him?'

'Georgiana? Good lord no. Nothing like. That's not to say she didn't get on with Harry; she adored him. She's a doctor. Works in a general hospital in London. The news will hit her hard. She lost her husband early in the war. He was the ambulance brigade on the Western Front.'

'I'm lucky to still have Peter.'

'And he'll come back.' Opening the drawer on his locker, he pulled out a clean handkerchief and handed it to her. She wiped her eyes.

'Thank you, Major Reid.'

'Could you bring yourself to call me Charles? There's hardly anyone left in Basra who does. And don't worry, we'll go up there and get Peter and the others out before the Turks get them.' He smiled again; she saw life returning to his eyes. 'Although God help the Turks if they do capture him. Would you believe he's a tiger under pressure?'

She remembered the night in Amara. 'I would, Major Reid.'

'Mrs Smythe, how nice to see you.' Edward Allan walked into the cubicle.

'Thank you, Colonel Allan.' She held up Charles's handkerchief when she left her chair. 'I'll return this clean.'

'I'll look forward to your next visit.' Charles was surprised to find he meant it. It had been good to talk about Harry and John with someone who'd known them.

'I'll write those letters; perhaps you could find the addresses for me by next time, Charles. Goodbye, Colonel Allan.'

'Quite a lady,' Allan commented after she left. 'She puts in 14-hour days at the Lansing, helps Mrs Butler run the mission, and finds time to visit you. Smythe is a lucky man.'

'Have you met Peter?'

'No. Right sort, is he?'

Charles recalled Harry's introduction to Basra. 'You're bunking with a chap called Peter Smythe; he's definitely one of the right sort.'

'Yes, he's one of the right sort.'

'Glad to hear it. Right, old man, let's take a look at this leg of yours.'

# Chapter Forty

*Turkish camp outside Kut*

Hasan fought consciousness. Consciousness brought agony and humiliation. But pain forced him to the surface. Someone was lifting him from the ground.

'Lieutenant-Colonel Downe.'

'I am Hasan Mahmoud...'

'There is no time to lose.' It was Arabic, but strangely accented.

Shooting pains prevented Hasan from opening his eyes. His whole body burned, his skin was raw. He mumbled, 'Let me die.'

'Take him.'

He was handed to another pair of hands. A robe was wrapped around him. He felt its warmth and increased pain where it touched his burns. He tried to open his eye. He saw only a faint blur of blond hair in front of him.

'I am Meyer. You saved a woman and children in the Kerkha, Lieutenant-Colonel Downe. Thank you for my family's life.'

The words meant nothing.

'You'll carry him to the British?'

'I promise to do so, Effendi.' Hasan knew the voice. He struggled to remember.

'Meyer, what are you doing?' The language was Turkish, the voice Murad's. He couldn't understand it, but the man who had given him up could.

'If he had any information to give, it would be useless now. The British are dug in.'

'We have orders to kill him.'

'Murad, you're a decent fellow. We'll gain nothing from killing him.'

'But we could lose a great deal by sending him back. The British will mark us down as barbarians. Have you any idea what they'll do to our POWs after seeing that?'

'Go.'

The man who was carrying him walked forward. Hasan heard blows. Men were fighting. A cold wind brushed over his face. Then Murad spoke in Arabic.

'Take him to the outskirts of the camp and kill him. As mercifully as you can.' There was the clink of coins. 'You do not have to tell Herr Meyer.'

'I won't, Effendi.' That voice again.

He was thrown roughly over a horse. Head one side, feet the other. Artillery and gunfire crashed in the distance. Furja would never know what had happened to him, but then she had Ali Mansur.

His pain grew more intense at each footfall. He whispered they'd gone far enough, but the horse kept moving. He longed for death so his pain would end. But it didn't come.

*Outside the Turkish camp, the Tigris.*

'Harry! Harry!'

'I am Hasan Mahmoud. I am a...' Water was on

590

his lips. Freezing, like the air.

'Drink.'

He did not want to make the effort.

'Drink, Hasan. Furja needs you.'

'I have no wife. Ali Mansur...'

'Ali Mansur has no wife. Furja is waiting for you. Drink.'

He forced himself to open his jaws and swallow.

## The Tigris Valley, below Kut

Once he was clear of the Turkish lines, Mitkhal exchanged his horses for dhow passage for himself and Harry to Basra. He'd chosen their mounts from among the best in the Turkish stable. They were worth more than the cost of the passage, but he felt he'd struck a fair bargain. The dhow was owned by a Sheikh who was harrying the retreating British cavalry so it would remain unmolested by Arabs. The Turks and the British were too busy killing each other to concern themselves with native boats. He had hopes of a safe journey.

He lay Harry under a canvas shelter at the stern and waited for the sun to rise. For two days, he had sat on the fringes of the Turkish camp offering his services as a scout, using information about British troop movements within Kut as an incentive to the sergeant responsible for recruiting Arab irregulars. Unfortunately, his information was based on the same observations the Turks could make any time they trained their field glasses on the British lines. But his patience and perseverance won through.

The sergeant gave him odd jobs. Nothing requiring intelligence or capabilities beyond brute strength, but gradually the sergeant and, more important still, the German had come to trust him. He'd dug graves, covered latrines, and cultivated the German, speaking in his best Turkish, intertwined with a few German phrases Harry had taught him. And while he'd worked, he'd heard bestial screams from a tent closed to everyone except the sergeant, Turkish officers, and the German.

He heard the name Hasan Mahmoud repeated in the screams, and when his suspicions hardened, he'd not known whether to wish life or death for Harry.

When the sun rose high enough to shed light under the canvas, he sank a skin into the river, tore a strip of cotton from his gumbaz, and peeled back Harry's blanket. He sat rocking on his heels, tears blurring his vision, not knowing where to start.

Every inch of Harry's skin bore burn marks and bruising. In many places, including his chest and genitals, the skin had been torn away and raw flesh dripped gobs of dark blood onto the boards of the boat. In other areas, scabs had formed, some oozing yellow and green pus. The stump, all that remained of Harry's right hand, had failed to heal but the blood that flowed from it was as yet untainted. The right side of Harry's face was swollen, an encrusted burn running from nose to temple covering his right eye socket.

The boatman took one look at the human wreckage and pronounced Harry dead. Mitkhal offered him gold if he would stop at Amara and find a doctor. That night they berthed. The boatman disappeared, and returned with a native physician who demanded payment before administering opium. The doctor waited until the narcotic took effect before covering Harry's wounds with herbs, spices, and scraps of paper containing the words of the prophet. By the time he finished binding Harry with linen, nothing could be seen of his body except the tip of his nose, his mouth, and his left eye.

Mitkhal bought enough opium to see Harry through the remainder of the journey and the boatman weighed anchor.

Mitkhal neither ate nor slept for the next 48 hours. Crouching over Harry, he forced drops of water and opium between his cracked lips. He stroked Harry's throat gently until he swallowed, nurturing the flicker of pulse in his wrist, willing him to live. The whole time Harry raved, repeating the name Hasan, and the cover the political office had manufactured for him, until Mitkhal thought he would go mad.

Mitkhal dosed Harry heavily with opium an hour before they berthed in Basra. They reached the quay at midnight. Mitkhal paid the boatman a bonus and warned the man on threat of death to hold his tongue if anyone asked questions about his passengers.

Under cover of darkness, he rolled Harry in a blanket and carried him off the dhow. Ignoring the carriages, he walked into the side streets, changing direction and halting several times. After half an hour, he crept to Zabba's door. He knocked and gave the correct signal. The doorman opened the portal and stared at the bundle slung over his shoulder.

'Quickly,' Mitkhal hissed. He skirted the shadows in the courtyard. Ducking away from the brightly lit windows and sound of music and laughter, he headed for Zabba's private quarters. A lamp burned in the living room. Setting Harry on a divan, he called for Gutne. His voice fell into ominous silence. He called again, opening doors that led to the bedrooms. They were empty. Fear beating a tattoo at his heels, he ran into the courtyard and Zabba. She held her finger to her lips and led him back to her quarters.

'Where are my wife and Furja?'

'Safe, your friend's lady has sense. It was not easy to keep little ones cooped up in my rooms and your wife gave birth to your son.'

'A son? Is he – are they–?'

'Mother and son are well. When your friend's lady discovered the house next door was empty, she gave me enough gold to buy it for her. Before she moved in with your wife and the children, she had the street entrance bricked up. You can enter only through the back courtyard to this house.'

'Thank you, if there is anything more to pay...'

'There is nothing more to pay,' Zabba interrupted sharply. 'You've always been quick to pay your debts, Mitkhal; let others pay theirs. I've not forgotten your mother, or all the things you did for me over the years. I'll see no one disturbs you, or tells anyone that you, your family and friends are here.'

He unwound the blanket and laid his hand over Harry's left hand. It was warm. He could feel the

594

pulse beating in the wrist. Zabba turned up the lamp.

'Is this a disguise, or is he hurt?'

'He was tortured by the Turks.'

'I'll send for a doctor. Don't worry. He has no love for the Turks, or the British.'

'It would be safer for him to come here than Furja's house,' Mitkhal agreed.

'Leave your friend with me while you go to your wife. I'll send for you when the doctor arrives.'

Mitkhal hesitated.

'Go to the back courtyard and you'll see the new door. Knock twice and the servant Furja sent for will open it.'

Mitkhal checked on Harry one last time before going through the house to the back courtyard. As Zabba had said, there was only one door set in the wall. The cement round it gleamed new and white. He knocked and Farik called out. He answered with his name, and Farik pulled back the bolts.

He found himself in a larger courtyard than the one he'd left. Farik pointed to a door set into the centre of the wall opposite. Light shone through glazed windows, illuminating a high-ceilinged living room, simply furnished with low tables, cushions, and brightly coloured rugs on the walls and floor.

Bantu opened the door. She ran to Gutne's room and Mitkhal followed. His wife was lying in bed, a small bundle under the bedclothes next to her. She looked up and smiled. The noise of the door opening woke Furja's little girls. He could hear her trying to quieten them in the next room when he wrapped his arms around Gutne.

'My son?'

'Is soon going to be the same size as his father if his appetite is anything to go by.' Gutne looked into his eyes. 'Did you find Harry?'

'He is with Zabba. She sent for a doctor.'

'What happened to him?' Furja was in the doorway, her face pale in the lamplight.

'He was tortured by the Turks.'

'What did they do to him?' Furja's voice was unnaturally quiet.

'It would be better if you sat down.' Taking Furja by the arm, Mitkhal guided her to a low nursing chair in the living room.

'I must go to him.'

'Not until I tell you what to expect.' He forced her into the chair and crouched at her feet. 'He doesn't even look like the man we knew. That's not all. He doesn't know who he is. When he speaks, he only repeats the name Hasan Mahmoud.'

Furja rose from the chair. 'Take me to him.' She saw him hesitate. 'Don't worry, Mitkhal. I won't cry when I see him.' Squaring her shoulders, she walked dry-eyed through the door.

*Expeditionary Force, mailroom, HQ Basra*

'Here's another one for Lieutenant-Colonel Downe.' The corporal pushed a crumpled letter to one side of the sorting table.

'Return it to sender. His family will have heard the news by now.'

'There's no address on the outside, sergeant.'

'Then use your initiative, boy. Open it. If there's

an address inside, send it back.'

The corporal opened the letter and read the address inside. He copied it onto a plain brown government envelope. *Georgiana Downe...* He admired the handwriting. Firm, with feminine flourishes. He would like to meet Georgiana Downe. But then a toff like her wouldn't want to meet a non-com like him. Feeling like a Peeping Tom, he scanned the first few lines.

*My dearest Harry*

That was better than the *Hello Flip* his sister began her letters with.

*I have been following the fortunes of the Expeditionary Force in the newspaper. I'm sorry for being so dense when I wrote to you earlier about sitting out the war in peace and quiet. I had no idea things were so bad in Mesopotamia. Papa and Uncle Reid were in town yesterday and I had lunch with them.*

*Now Gwilym's dead, Papa's decided to forgive me and I haven't the heart to tell him to go to hell. God knows he deserves it, but Gwilym wouldn't have wanted me to turn my back on my family. They're both worried about you and John and Charles. They spend hours poring over the casualty lists. They say they didn't know war would mean this slaughter. That when they were in the Indian army – but I don't want to write about when they were in the Indian army.*

*I don't believe their tales of glorious battle. I think they read them in Boys' Own books, and now they've reached senility they believe they actually lived them. Damn them, and every old man who thought this war would be a lark. We're paying for their stupid notions of chivalry with the lives of the men we can least afford to lose.*

*Of course, I patted them on the head and told them you'd come through all right but I'm worried about you, Harry. So many boys have been killed out there. There's a nurse on one of my wards, Clarissa Amey, her brother Stephen is in Mesopotamia, and she's in the most appalling state about him. Apparently, they haven't heard from him in months. If you see him, please tell him to get in touch with his parents.*

*I know you, Harry; you're always up to your neck in scrapes, please, please, for my sake be careful for the next couple of months. After that, I won't need to worry. Michael and Tom will be joining you and they've promised to take care of you for me. No one's supposed to know where their force is going, but Uncle Reid had a word with someone at the War Office on Tom's behalf. Tom has been trying to get a transfer to the Indian Medical Service for months. He's concerned about John as his letters have been a bit strange. I hope John's all right; give him my special love the next time you see him.*

*Michael's on the same boat as Tom. He plagued his editor until he agreed to transfer him to Basra. I think they did it to get him out of their hair. I believe he volunteered just to get away from Lucy. He's never actually told me but I'm certain there's something seriously wrong with their marriage. After Michael heard about Ctesiphon, he wouldn't rest until he received his ticket. I wish the army would take women doctors; if they did, I'd leave on the next boat. Please, Harry, take care of yourself until the reinforcements get there. I'm going to need you when this world returns to sanity. That's if it ever does.*

*Your loving sister, Georgiana.*

'What are you doing, corporal?'

'Nothing, sergeant.'

'This nothing wouldn't include reading other people's mail, would it?'

'No, sergeant.'

The sergeant moved on, and the corporal pushed Georgiana's letter into the envelope. He wrote *Return to sender. Unable to deliver* on the envelope and wished he could write more. She sounded a nice lady. But then... A glow warmed him at the thought of the news he'd be able to carry back to the barracks. Reinforcements were on their way. He'd had it official-like.

## Chapter Forty-one

*Furja's house, Basra*

Furja sat on a chair in her bedroom and waited. Just as she'd waited through the long hours of every day and night since Mitkhal had carried Harry into the house. The cramps in her stomach were increasing in intensity and frequency. Soon, the son she'd waited so long for would be born, and his father would remain comatose; a bandaged log unable to recognise his own child. Around her, the house was silent.

The high walls closed out the noise of Zabba's house and the street. Her daughters were sleeping in their room, with Bantu lying alongside them. Mitkhal and Gutne had retired unusually early because she'd quarrelled with Mitkhal.

He'd been angry with her for sitting up day and night alongside Hasan, telling her that if she insisted on carrying on in that fashion, she'd be no use to anyone, least of all her husband, coming son, and daughters.

But she could not help herself. She could not bring herself to turn Hasan's care over to another, not even Mitkhal.

Hasan moaned and she grasped his left hand, the only part of him she could caress without fear of causing him pain. The only part the Turks had not crushed, beaten, or burned. She gazed at his left eye, willing him to open it, but he settled back into his deep, unnatural sleep.

Even if he'd opened his eye, she doubted he'd have recognised her. Early that morning, when she'd applied fresh layers of salve to the patches of skinless flesh that covered most of his body, he'd opened it, but his gaze was focused inward, into a world she could only guess at.

She'd stopped thinking of him as Harry. The mere whisper of the name was enough to send him into frenzy. When the doctor witnessed the response, he'd taken Mitkhal to one side and warned him Hasan's mind was seriously damaged. That no one could live through the torments he'd endured and escape with his personality intact.

That day she told Mitkhal she intended to bury Lieutenant-Colonel Harry Downe. It wouldn't be difficult. Mitkhal had heard in Abdul's the British army believed Harry was dead. He'd remain so.

When – she was careful to say 'when' – he recovered, he would become the man he believed himself to be, Hasan Mahmoud. They'd keep

600

him within the house and away from the British soldiers. If he never saw them again there was no reason to suppose he'd recall his other identity.

Mitkhal had replied she was welcome to try to persuade Harry to adopt a new identity, if he ever came around. The 'if' had chilled her. It hurt to know that even Mitkhal was giving up hope.

From that moment, she'd thought of nothing except the transformation of Harry into Hasan. She could see from the way Mitkhal behaved with Gutne and his baby that he didn't want to return to the war.

Both he and Hasan had done more than enough for the Ferenghis. The British could continue to fight the Turk without the assistance of either her husband or Mitkhal. The time for them to fight would be when the war was over. Then, the Bedouin would have to unite in dispelling the victors from their land. Until then, she intended to do all she could to ensure that they lived their lives in peace and quiet.

Another pain came and she cried out. 'Hasan? Wake up, I need you. And your son needs you.' She pressed his hand over the contracting muscles in her stomach. Why wouldn't he wake? Did he still believe himself to be in the Turkish camp, or was he reluctant to face up to the wreckage of his body? She placed her mouth close to his ear. 'Hasan, it's Furja. I need you. Now please, Hasan. Wake up!'

He moved slightly, moaning as pressure was applied to his sores.

Pouring water into a bowl, she forced it between his lips. 'Don't give up. Not while we

601

still have one another.' She flicked her fingers in the water and dabbed them on his face. 'Hasan!'

Another pain came. Soon it would be time to call Mitkhal. He would fetch Zabba. The old woman had brought Gutne's son into the world with the minimum of fuss; she would do the same for her.

Poor Mitkhal. She had thrust the responsibility for the entire household onto his broad shoulders. It was Mitkhal who lifted Hasan for her when it was time to change dressings. It was Mitkhal who propped her husband up when she forced water and broth into his mouth. Mitkhal who'd carried her sobbing, terrified daughters away from the bandaged figure after she'd forced them to kiss Hasan in the hope they would wake him.

It was Mitkhal she turned to when she'd wanted to discuss cutting the amount of opium the doctor was feeding Hasan, and it was Mitkhal who gave her the courage to halve the dosage without the doctor's consent. And it would be Mitkhal who made the arrangements for this baby, unless – she pushed her hair away from her face.

The room was hot. Farik had stoked the stove high earlier that evening; he'd said frost was coming. Restless, she left the chair and walked to the window. Ice had formed on the windowpane.

Another pain came, sharper, more urgent. There was no time left. She returned to the bed.

'You are worse than the most stubborn camel, Hasan. I need you! And the children need you. You cannot leave me to face this world alone.' Another pain came, too sharp and unexpected for her to stifle. She heard movement in the next room. Mitkhal was coming. 'Hasan! Wake up!'

His eyelid flickered.

She'd been a fool. It wasn't gentleness he needed. She slapped his hand, hard. 'Our son is coming. Wake up, you lazy brute. Do not let me face this by myself.'

Mitkhal knocked at the door. 'Furja?'

'Come in, Mitkhal.'

He entered. She was breathing heavily as she stood next to the bed. Her eyes were bright with tears, but there was a smile on her face.

'Here is Mitkhal, Hasan. He will fetch someone who'll help bring our son into this world. Will you stay with me and hold my hand while he is born?'

He struggled to sit up and fell back onto the pillows. 'I'm very weak, Furja.'

'It doesn't matter, Hasan. I don't want you to do anything. Simply be here, with me.'

He smiled at her, a crooked smile that shifted the bandage over his right eye. Blinded by tears, Mitkhal ran out of the house to fetch Zabba.

## Chapter Forty-two

*Furja's house, Basra*

It was warm and peaceful in the living room. Mitkhal and Gutne were asleep. Their baby had been restless and keeping them awake at night, so when he finally slept Mitkhal and Gutne had gone to bed too. Bantu had fed the twins in the kitchen and was now singing them to sleep in the bedroom opposite Furja's. Hasan was sitting, propped up in a chair, Furja half-lying, half-sitting on a pile of cushions at his feet, feeding a fair-haired baby.

'That must hurt,' Hasan murmured, watching the child suck vigorously at her breast.

'No.' She smiled. 'It doesn't.' She shifted slightly. The baby was growing tired; a few more minutes and he would be asleep. 'Are you sure you're strong enough to sit up this long?'

'I'm sure. If you can put up with this ugly face of mine.'

'You're only saying that to play on my sympathy. Your face is that of a desert brigand. I find it most attractive.'

'Then I should be grateful to the Turks for re-modelling my features.'

'No. Hasan, you should be grateful to Allah the ever-merciful and Mitkhal for bringing you back to me,' she snapped, stemming his self-pity.

The baby stopped sucking. His lips hung slackly around her nipple, his mouth full of milk. She pulled him gently away from her. His head lolled slightly to one side, sleepy and satisfied. She held him out to her husband. 'You can look after Shalan while I wash.'

'I don't know what to do with babies,' he said, terrified at the thought of holding the precious bundle.

She curved his right arm with its bandaged stump, and laid the baby in it, leaving his left hand free to caress the child. 'You don't need two hands to care for a child.'

He watched her walk into the bedroom and fill a basin with water. 'I wish I could remember more.'

'You remember the important things. Me, the twins, Mitkhal, Gutne – my father's anger with you.' Opening her robe, she washed her heavily veined, swollen breasts.

'My parents, my tribe...'

'Mitkhal told you. You are tribeless bastards. An upbringing in the gutters of Basra is best forgotten.'

'The Turks didn't think so. They wanted me to tell them something.'

'They wanted you to tell them the positions of the British troops in Kut.'

'Because I rode out from there?'

'That's what Mitkhal said.'

'Then may all the Ferenghis writhe in the torments of hell for eternity.'

'That I agree with.' She dried herself and took the sleeping baby from his arms, settling the child in the wooden crib Farik had bought in the market. Catching hold of her husband's hand, she led him to their bed.

'The doctor said...'

'The doctor knows nothing about me, Hasan, or you. I've had enough of being a mother; I want to be a wife again.'

He could scarcely breathe. The bandages on his chest were tight, the room airless. He was frightened of what the Turks had done to his body, but most of all, of disappointing her. He could scarcely move, let alone make love to a woman. The slightest touch was sheer torment. He had a sudden flash of memory when he lay on the bed. Clear

605

blue sky, hooves thundering over the desert, a grey horse. 'I would like to return to the desert, Furja,' he said, as she slid alongside him.

'We will one day, Hasan. When Ali Mansur marries again and we can buy off his anger, my father may forgive us.'

'I hope he does.' He looked at the sleeping baby. 'I would like him to grow up a Bedouin. In your father's tribe.'

'So would I, Hasan.' She leant over and kissed him very gently on the mouth.

He gazed at her and felt the stirrings of a love he hadn't forgotten. 'How long will it take Ali Mansur to marry another?'

'As long as it will take the Ferenghis to fight this war and leave our land.'

'That could take years.'

She kissed him again, longer this time and with more passion. 'Are you complaining?'

'No, my love.' He stroked her hair with his left hand when she unfastened his robe.

She was careful to keep the weight of her body away from his. Only her lips and her fingers moved lightly across his damaged flesh.

'No, my love, I'm not complaining,' he whispered.

The publishers hope that this book has given you enjoyable reading. Large Print Books are especially designed to be as easy to see and hold as possible. If you wish a complete list of our books please ask at your local library or write directly to:

**Magna Large Print Books**
Magna House, Long Preston,
Skipton, North Yorkshire.
BD23 4ND

This Large Print Book for the partially sighted, who cannot read normal print, is published under the auspices of

**THE ULVERSCROFT FOUNDATION**